THE ULTIMATE WEAPON. . . ?

"Last night, the wing of a prison hospital in western China was destroyed. There'd be nothing to it, but for two apparently unrelated things. First, there was supposed to be an old caucasian prisoner there, and, second, not a vestige of an explosive was found. Nothing. And our witness insists that it didn't blow up. The report is that it—*melted*."

Their eyes locked together. Hard face looked at hard face. "All right," Tarp said with a brittle smile. "I know the answer, but I'll ask the right question: What melted it?"

"Arthur Beecham's particle beam, of course," Penhurst replied.

Tarp was silent for a very long time. Penhurst let the silence go on and on until it was broken by a deep, muffled vibration, as if the edge of a great sheet of metal had been struck. "What on earth is that?" he asked.

"The sunset gun." Tarp's voice was a growl. "They shoot off a little cannon every evening at the girl's camp across the river. On the Canadian side. A little bit of empire in the night."

Penhurst smiled into the darkness. "A sunset gun, good heavens! A vestige, to be sure. The last little bang of British might."

"Unless your old friend Arthur's weapon really exists, you mean. If it does, it'll be the empire's sunset gun for sure. . . ."

GEORGE BARTRAM

THE SUNSET GUN

PINNACLE BOOKS NEW YORK

This is a work of fiction. All the characters and events portrayed in this book are fictional, and any resemblance to real people or incidents is purely coincidental.

THE SUNSET GUN

An original Pinnacle Books edition, published for the first time anywhere.

First printing, April 1983

ISBN: 0-523-41867-1

Printed in the United States of America

PINNACLE BOOKS, INC.
1430 Broadway
New York, N.Y. 10018

THE SUNSET GUN

chapter one

He woke.

The fluorescent light fell like a reflection from snow on the concrete wall. It cast gray shadows on the coarse blanket and on his sallow skin. He had crooked his head into his right arm for warmth and now, waking, he could see the fine mass of wrinkles where the skin folded in upon itself in the bend of his elbow. *Old man's skin*. Like the pouchy, folded skin of an old lizard.

He could hear the guards chanting their morning exercises in the courtyard. He no longer was aware that they were chanting in Chinese—slapping their hands and leaping and bellowing slogans of political righteousness against the December cold. It was all mere chatter to him now—all of it quite understandable, quite negligible, like the merely human thinking that went on at the surface of his mind, now in Chinese, now in English: *I am cold. It is morning. My bladder is full.* Under that gabble, which was no more important to him than the wind, was real language: *numbers*.

Exponents.

Equations.

As cool as the light; as hard as the concrete wall.

As he did every morning, he sat up and rested on the side of the bunk until the blood stopped churning behind his eyes and his breath no longer tasted sour. As always, he stared at the beautifully blank wall opposite the bunk and let his real language of numbers build its castle there, rank upon rank of linked equations—beautiful equalities, elegant solutions. The imaginary castle of mathematics was the thing that had kept him alive and sane all these years, this miracle of mathematics and science, which grew now before his mind's eye like a magic castle in a fairy tale. It reached out in turrets and crenellations, climbed in towers toward the ceiling, came forward toward him over the cell floor in courtyards and keeps, a living construction.

And then. . . .

He leaned forward. His eyes narrowed, as if to see in the everyday world what his brain had created in that more than real one.

There was a new tower!

And not merely a tower, but a whole structure of new equations, the foundation of a whole new wing. It needed only a little attention to be built up completely, to be made new and solid, to be finished. . . . He gasped. *To be finished!*

He leaned back, his frail weight on his hands. *To finish it*. He knew at once that it could be finished now. After so many years. Because of some leap that his brain had made while the rest of him—this old lizard—had slept. And all in a night! The structure had been created as if by magic. And now he could finish it all, working consciously, awake; indeed, his brain was already working at it. He needed no pencil or paper. He had been computing inside his head for thirty years.

To finish it!

He heard the guard coming and he stood up. His

body shivered in anticipation of the winter air outside. His mind was working, however, in a place where there was neither heat nor cold.

In glory, he thought. The hymns of his childhood came back to him. School, cold mornings, chapel, and the headmaster leading them in hymns. *Glory*. He felt a boy's exultation, believing that he knew how the holy men must have felt when they looked up on the face of the godhead.

I have seen the glory.

And the power!

Tarp woke—and waking, grinned. May sunlight, dappled into gold-green splashes by the trees, poured down the log walls and across the rough board floor. The odor of pines tinged the air, in which the crispness of the Maine night still lingered. Despite that touch of cold, Tarp thrust the red wool blankets from him with a kick and a surge of his body that brought him to a sitting position on the end of the bed, where he sat and stretched like a great, pleased animal. He was still grinning with the sheer pleasure of the morning as he quickly pulled his right foot back to stretch the thigh muscles, then the left, and then he stood up into a pool of sunshine.

He was naked, and he stayed naked as he washed, then filled a kettle with water and put it on the propane stove. He shoveled instant coffee into a big cup the color of a Greek olive. From a battered tin box, he took a thick loaf of bread, which he crooked in his left arm so that he could saw off thick slices as if he were cutting an enemy's throat. When the smell of toast was strong on the morning air, there was a thump at the cabin door, and he grinned again and crossed to it.

"Right on time," he growled.

An animal waited at the very edge of the log porch. It was ready to spring away—or to do battle. It was a badger, fiercest and biggest of the ground animals.

Tarp tossed it a piece of toast. It waited. He put a hand forward toward the toast and the badger snarled.

"You're my kind of beast, my friend," Tarp said cheerfully. The badger snarled again. "*That's* what I call a relationship."

When Tarp withdrew into the kitchen, the badger ate the toast and then lumbered forward to perch in the doorway and watch him with bright, suspicious eyes.

"Haven't forgotten me, at any rate," Tarp said. He pulled a faded blue shirt over his head. "Think I'd gone forever, hey? Think the baddies got me this time?" The badger made no answer. Tarp had long since concluded that the badger paid no attention to his words. Tarp ascribed that indifference to wisdom on the badger's part, and such wisdom made it easier for him to talk to animals than to humans.

He zipped up the front of a very old pair of blue jeans and then, barefoot, crossed to a board in the cabin wall, pressed it, and reached into the dark opening for the holstered pistol that had waited there all winter.

He moved about the cabin, unpacking two canvas duffel bags, putting the sparse furniture into an order that matched a blueprint in his mind. Whenever he turned toward the door, the badger retreated; when he moved away, it returned to watch him. It ate three more pieces of toast and cleaned up the remains of a tin of sardines.

Now Tarp stood by the window that looked down over the little lake where the seaplane had dropped him the evening before. A stranger looking in that window might have been disturbed, even frightened, for Tarp's face looked angry. He was only thinking, however; like the badger, he had evolved a mask to keep potential enemies at bay. Terrible as he looked, he was simply thinking of what he would do that day: repair the dock, get out the old canvas-and-wood canoe, rig the cane rod that had been his grandfather's. But he looked as if he were plotting a murder, at the least.

A bell-like electronic note sounded behind him.

"Bogeys," he muttered to the badger. Now his face was truly ugly.

There was a computer terminal concealed in the upper half of a cupboard. The touching of seven keys brought a schematic map of his hundred-acre tract to the screen in white on bright blue; in the lower right-hand corner, three red dots flashed to mark the three sensors that had been triggered. Tarp fingered more buttons; the map disappeared and numbers began to flicker down the screen.

"One bogey, but with three legs." Tarp raised his eyebrows. "What d'you make of that, badger? What walks on three legs in the morning?" He called the map to the screen again, and the display showed that a fourth sensor had been triggered.

"Coming up from the river. Came over from the Canadian side, maybe." He turned from the console and threaded the pistol holster on his belt, snugging it tight against his back just by his right kidney. The small gun was not one that most men might have chosen, but he felt secure with it—a Colt Woodsman in the short-barreled version, thirty years old and mottled with use, a small weapon made to carry in a pack or in a holster like this for emergencies.

"Scram, badger."

He threw a crust beyond the doorway. It was a signal. The badger scrambled from the porch, plucked the crust from the pine needles, and vanished; as he was doing so, Tarp was pushing his feet into mocassins and raising a trap from the floor; and then he, too, was gone, and the cabin was as silent and empty as it had been all winter.

Tarp made his way to a little gully that deepened as it ran down to the river. His feet moved silently over the granite, barely disturbing the shallow water in the tiny pools. Silence was his protection: he knew where the intruder was, and he trusted his own eyes and ears.

Fifty yards from the river he climbed the rocky bank and moved through new clusters of bright green fern; he stopped, sniffed, listened, and curved back toward the river again. Once he smiled thinly at the trail that his intruder had left.

From the shelter of two pines that grew above the high-water mark, he looked down at the boulder-strewn water. At its edge, a twenty-two-foot aluminum canoe had been beached, its square stern weighted heavily with a powerful motor. Two men lolled on the rocks, smoking—two blank-faced loggers from the Canadian side of the river.

Four minutes later, he eased the pistol from its holster and pointed it at the back of the tweed hat that covered his intruder's head.

"Don't move."

"Wouldn't think of it, old boy. You've taken your sweet time about finding me, I must say."

Tarp stepped to the man's left side, keeping a safe distance from him. "Hamish Penhurst, as I live and breathe."

"A piece of him, at any rate. May I move my head now?"

"Only your head."

The old head twisted to reveal a slow, rather merry grin. "You've never learned proper trust of your fellowmen," the old voice said mockingly. The face was a very aristocratic one, and so was the voice, both of them restrained and witty and most at home in London club rooms and government offices. "How are you, Tarp?"

Tarp studied him. He did not look pleased. He looked like the badger, ready to bite. "Come up to the cabin," he said. "Walk ahead of me."

He did not holster the pistol until they were on the porch.

Tarp looked the old man over. Hamish Penhurst wore, besides the tweed hat, a British rain jacket of dark, tarred cotton, a sweater so heavy it looked like brown armor, and tweed trousers that were of impeccable cut, although baggy now with wear.

"Dressing the part?" Tarp murmured.

"Just what I had on when I decided to visit you, my boy."

"Very impulsive."

"Oh, very."

Hamish Penhurst carried a walking stick. Tarp gestured toward it. "The third leg. Sword or gun?"

"Shotgun. And a survival knife, actually. Handy in the American woods, I thought."

Tarp brought two chairs from the cabin and set them on the porch. One was an ash frame laced with leather like a snowshoe; the other was a ladder-back made a hundred years before in his barn by a Maine farmer. Tarp set out the loaf of bread and a pot of English marmalade whose excellence surprised Penhurst, and he made coffee for them both. Penhurst watched him, watched a loon on the small lake, watched the badger poke its nose out from a patch of low greenery.

"By God, that's a badger!"

"Yes."

"Damned dangerous."

"So they say."

"Didn't think they were found over here."

"Imported."

"Pet?"

"I don't keep pets."

"Very good thing, too. Damned dangerous, making a pet of a wild creature."

"You might keep that in mind, Hamish."

Penhurst raised his thin eyebrows. "Symbolism! And so early in the morning, too. My, my, this marmalade is excellent! I only wish I could persuade my wife that we could afford it."

Tarp stared at his guest, who was quite unperturbed

by the attention. "Retirement suits you, Hamish," he said judiciously.

Penhurst grunted. His mouth was full.

"Didn't I read that the latest media sensation makes you out to be a Russian mole, Hamish?"

Penhurst swallowed, nodded, dipped his knife into the marmalade again. "Oh, dear, yes. It made all the papers, *and* the television. 'Former Head of MI-5 Called Soviet Spy,' and so forth. Went on for days. It was all the work of one fellow who's trying to drum up interest in a forthcoming book—Viktor Balkan."

"I thought Balkan was supposed to be a KGB flack."

"Oh, no, no—that was cold-war talk! No, he's simply a sensationalist, and I was 'it.' Made me out the fourth man in Burgess-McLean, and all that. Sold lots of papers. Kept one tabloid from going under until it got hold of a good royal-pregnancy rumor."

"*Were* you a Russian mole, Hamish?"

"Now, would I tell you if I were?"

"You might give something away. Men often let the truth slip in odd ways—you taught me that."

"You don't credit me with much cleverness, I must say. If I were a mole, Tarp, surely I'd be a most talented one. After all, one doesn't rise to the top of MI-5 with dunce's brains for flotation gear, you know."

"Sometimes I wonder."

Hamish Penhurst rubbed his long fingers together to free them of crumbs, and then he took out an enormous pocket handkerchief, which he then used as a napkin. Showing far more deference to Tarp than might have been expected, given the difference in their ages, he said rather humbly, "You mustn't really judge us by the sort of idiots who are put in charge of American intelligence, my boy. I told you that many years ago when I tried to recruit you. We make our mistakes, but we admire merit. Your people put merit into a pigeonhole and then appoint your top men from something called 'the business community.' It could be worse only if they appointed from the clergy."

Tarp knew that Penhurst was appealing to his pride—his still-wounded pride. He had to resist responding gratefully to this attack on the people who had ended his own career. Brusquely, he said, "All right, what are you doing here, Hamish?"

"I came on business, of course."

"Of course. Please don't smoke."

Penhurst stopped in the act of taking out a cigarette case. "I'm not to smoke?" he said piteously. "Not at all?"

"It's poisonous."

"I shall perish."

"Better you than me."

Penhurst sighed and put the case away. "I heard you'd got odd, but this not smoking is positively lunatic! They say you're a vegetarian, too."

"I got curious to see what I could live without."

"Oh, it's like that, is it!" Penhurst slapped his hands down on his knees and stared out at the lake. His thin face was all pink and white, as if the colors had been chosen by a portrait painter who wanted to paint only the good part of being old. When he spoke next, his voice seemed to come from very far away, so that Tarp had the eerie sense that he was listening to a far-distant telephone call. "Do you know who Arthur Beecham was?"

Tarp concentrated. The name would doubtless show in an instant on his computer if he touched the right buttons, but he hated leaving everything to the machine. "It's in my head someplace—awfully vague—let's see: defector. That's all I've got—defector. A very long time ago."

"Nineteen forty-nine. Not so very long ago, if you're my age. And the label 'defector' was an American one, because we British didn't think that he defected at all."

Tarp was genuinely interested, and he leaned forward. He was always tantalized by these crumbs of fact that lodged in crevices of the memory. "I'm getting something more—*science*—a physicist. Right?"

"Very good. Anything more?"

"Atom bomb?"

Penhurst made a face. "Oh, everybody was supposed to be working on the bomb in forty-nine. *Not* good, Tarp! Arthur Beecham was one of a pair of positively brilliant young scientists who were working in a field called particle physics when everybody else was trying to make bigger and louder bangs. In fact, it was Arthur who first proposed that a coherent beam of atomic particles could be used as a weapon."

" 'Arthur'? A personal friend?"

Penhurst nodded vaguely. "He was a year or two ahead of me at school. I used to see him at Hutcherson's dinners before the war—sorry, Hutcherson was our house master. Not relevant, anyway. But Arthur Beecham was one of those odd-looking, dotty young men who have no social life and who are no good at games and who turn out some years after school to be geniuses." It was Penhurst's turn now to lean forward, so that their heads were close together, as if they were two old cronies muttering about remembered glories.

"I didn't see much of Arthur during the war—old-boy dinners weren't very high on the list, you know—and then one day he came to see me at MI-5. I was third in line by then, and I suppose it was well known that I had the PM's ear—we had a family connection through my mother's side, so that some of her people even used the name 'Churchill' with a hyphen—that isn't vey relevant either, is it? Oh dear—where was I? Ah, to be sure, Arthur came to see me. It was nineteen forty-five, and he was just as dotty as a duck, but he'd made a reputation for brilliance by then and so I had the sense to listen to him—and he told me about his particle beam. Or, rather, about the theory of the particle beam. It wasn't practical yet, he said." Penhurst held up a finger. "Keep that 'yet' in mind." The finger fell. "He said he must get through red tape and reach the PM, and it was vitally important, and the Americans mustn't be allowed to get ahead of us, and so on. Well, I didn't suppose that Winston would cut me socially if I sent Arthur to see him, and as a consequence of the meeting I made an appointment for him. And what do you think happened?"

Tarp simply shook his head.

"The PM called me in specially and said I was to say nothing to anyone, least of all the Americans, about Beecham's work. He made me swear I wouldn't mention the thing at all! Well! Winston was devious, of course. I suppose he was jealous because the Americans had the bomb, and all of that. Well, it was easy enough to do as he asked, as nobody seemed to care much about Arthur, what with the war nearly over. I did snoop about a bit myself and find that Arthur'd been given a research facility way out on Dartmoor, specially budgeted by the PM."

Tarp glanced shrewdly at the fine old face. "You said he was one of a pair. What happened to the other one?"

"Jimmie Malloway. Jimmie was killed in a car crash in forty-eight."

" 'Jimmie'? Another personal friend?"

"One of my sisters had some notion of marrying him. Barely an acquaintance."

Tarp went into the cabin for the kettle and made more coffee and then said slowly, for he was thinking now, "And what happened to Arthur Beecham?"

"He's supposed to have been killed."

"How?"

"Mountain climbing in Nepal. Nineteen forty-nine. A body was produced—also the testimony of a couple of *sherpas*. But some of us were always skeptical."

"But it wasn't a defection?"

"It was as far as the Americans were concerned."

"Odd place to defect if you were going to Moscow."

"The thought was it was more likely Peking."

"Oh, yes, Peking was definitely the place to go in nineteen-forty-nine."

"Well, Arthur was known to be dotty. *We* believed that he'd been kidnapped, however."

"Ah, the sinister East. Sold into white slavery?"

"I'm quite serious. Kidnapped for his genius, of course."

"By the prescient followers of Mao, who, ten years later, would still be trying to make steel in their backyards but who somehow knew all about particle beams. Could it have been the insidious Doctor Fu-Manchu, do you think?"

"If you're going to make fun, I shall certainly leave."

"Good."

"Oh, do be serious! Arthur was a noted physicist; he could have been grabbed by anybody back in those days. Could have been taken by some free-lancer and sold to the nearest buyer."

"Ah, what days those must have been, Hamish! Parachuting into the Forbidden City one day, free-lancing physicists the next . . ."

Penhurst frowned. "I am really here on *serious* business."

"Well, I try to be serious sometimes, too. But, Hamish, I was *in* China in those days. Nobody I knew cared about physics. We were all concerned with staying alive. You make it sound like Gilbert and Sullivan." He raised an eyebrow. "*The Pirates of Peking*."

"*Do* try to find a middle ground between schoolboy levity and your usual dreary solemnity, there's a good fellow. I've come all the way across the ocean in the clothes on my back—I happened to be fishing at Broadlands, Tarp, at *Broadlands* when this news came—and I left all that to come here. It's serious business."

"When what news came?"

Penhurst looked at him, his face suddenly hard. Seeing that hardness, which was normally so handsomely masked, one could understand how he had climbed to the top of an intelligence service—even how he might be a Soviet spy. "Last night, the wing of a prison hospital in western China was destroyed."

Tarp waited. "And?"

"There'd be nothing to it, but for two apparently unrelated things. First, there was supposed to be an old caucasian prisoner there; and, second, not a vestige of an explosive was found after the hospital wing was destroyed. Nothing. And our witness insists that it didn't blow up. The report is that it—*melted*."

Their eyes were locked together. Hard face looked at hard face. "All right," Tarp said with a brittle smile, "I know the answer but I'll ask the right question: what melted it?"

"Arthur Beecham's particle beam, of course."

They had spent the rest of that day alternating periods of discussion with long, thoughtful silences. Penhurst had gone for a very long walk, during which he had smoked as many cigarettes as possible; Tarp had twice consulted his computer and had spent almost two hours with it the second time. After still more conversation, they walked down to the river and sent Penhurst's boatmen home with instructions to return the next morning. Now, as the sun went down behind the mountain at their backs they sat again on the log porch, glasses of malt Scotch in their hands and the bottle between them.

"What do you think, then?" Penhurst said.

"I think it's science fiction, but it's possible. That's the trouble—everybody agrees the thing is possible, but nobody thinks it's practical."

"Arthur said it wasn't practical *yet* back in forty-six. That's a good long time in which to make something practical."

"But not a proton-beam weapon, Hamish! It takes an enormous amount of power—enormous! Half a dozen jet engines set up to drive generators, at the very least.

Plus capacitors, the auto-resonant generator—a huge layout. And you've said yourself, there's not a hint of such a layout in China—no satellite photos, no spy reports, nothing. It's as if you wanted me to believe that somebody had put up a duplicate of London Bridge without leaving any tracks." He held up his hand as Penhurst tried to speak. "But—*but*—worst of all, who in hell would destroy a prison hospital as a demonstration of such a weapon? Now, tell me that. I can't wait to hear what you'll say. Do you think your old friend Arthur is now so nuts that he melts down hospitals to prove the wonders of science?"

"It's a puzzle, I know."

"It's not a puzzle; it's a mess."

"Well—there are a few unresolved bits, I know—."

"Unresolved bits!" Tarp's agitation brought him to his feet. The excitement was proof that he was interested. "Bits! It's an entire, ungodly, unresolved disaster!"

Tarp bounded down the porch steps. The lake and the cabin, the sun setting behind them, were already deep in the shadow of the mountain, but the utterly still water reflected a sky that was still steel-blue. Tarp's voice came harshly from the gloom. "Why me, Penhurst? Because it's China?"

"That was the idea, my boy."

"I said I'd never go back."

"What you said was—I was there, remember—'I will never go back to goddam China even if goddam Uncle Sam has his left ball in a goddam Chinese vise.' " Penhurst cleared his throat as if to clear it of the quoted vulgarity. "Arthur Beecham's particle beam has no relation, I believe, to either a Chinese vise or American balls."

It was almost black in the clearing around the cabin now. Penhurst had to squint to make out the restless figure below him. The loon sang its crazy song from the lake, wild and mocking, as if, like the badger, it was wise and knew what fools men are.

Tarp was silent for a very long time.

"And you want me because I'm an outcast, isn't that it? You're retired and I'm an outcast, and they've pulled us both back because there's nothing lost if we fail. Is that it?"

Penhurst said nothing. He let the silence go on and on until it was broken by a deep, muffled vibration, as if the edge of a great sheet of metal had been struck. "What on earth is that?"

"The sunset gun." Tarp's voice was a growl. "They shoot off a little cannon every evening at the girl's camp across the river. On the Canadian side. A little bit of empire in the night."

Hamish Penhurst smiled into the darkness. "A sunset gun, good heavens! A vestige, to be sure. The last little bang of British might."

He heard Tarp's foot grate on the earth as it turned toward the cabin. "Unless your old friend Arthur's weapon really exists, you mean. If it does, it'll be the empire's sunset gun for fair."

chapter two

In early 1977, a recently retired major general of United States Air Force intelligence caused a furor by announcing that the Soviet Union had scored a major breakthrough in the development of a proton-beam weapon. He believed that this work had been done at Semipalatinsk, where satellites had detected large amounts of the hydrogen gases associated with the supercooling that was thought necessary to such a system.

The idea was denied by the Carter White House. Neither the Office of Science and Technology Policy nor the USAF Scientific Advisory Commission was persuaded by the evidence that was eventually published in *Aviation Week*, despite that journal's past record of knowing some things better than the government did. The United States' own Project Seesaw, set up to examine the feasibility of a beam weapon, had been abandoned only a few years before.

It was the major general's view that the Soviets might have their particle beam operational as an antimissile system by 1980. However, that year came and went without the appearance of any such system.

Such systems, as Tarp had learned, were thought to be far from development, and all theories about them postulated layouts of great size. No responsible scientific thought believed that China could develop such a weapon.

"Sheer technological jingoism," Penhurst insisted. "The U.S. and the Soviets think they have monopolies on hard science. They forget the advances that the rest of us have made." He sounded almost grumpy. "It was an Englishman, after all, who invented the thing."

"In theory."

"Well, of course in theory. But you must rid yourself of the notion that every scientific breakthrough takes billions and billions of dollars and enormous physical plants."

"But—China?"

"*With* Arthur Beecham!"

"Isn't that more jingoism, Hamish? Benighted Orientals taught by white genius?"

"I don't mean that. I mean that Arthur could have done splendid things all by himself."

Tarp stared at him. They were inside the cabin, talking by the light of a single lamp, around which three moths circled as if seeking a hidden door. "My God, Hamish, you don't mean to say you think he did such a thing alone!"

Penhurst, for the first time, looked unsure. "I don't know what to think. That's why I want you to go to China and look around." He stared at the mildewed sleeping bag that Tarp was unrolling on the board floor. "See here, you don't really mean for me to sleep down there, do you?"

"I certainly do."

"Any proper host would put his guest in the bed."

"Any proper guest would wait for an invitation."

"I'm not a proper guest. I'm a man on an important mission."

"Good night, Hamish."

"But, see here. . . . Oh, dammit. Good night."

In the morning, Tarp was up before the first jays screamed in the clearing. Penhurst, despite his objections, slept soundly. Tarp stepped over the old man's slender body, pulled on his clothes, and then slipped outdoors and breathed deeply of the cool morning air. The badger came, snarled, got a crust of bread.

Tarp caught three fat brook trout and then visited the riverbank and was back at the cabin before the sun was fully above the mountain. Penhurst had mastered the propane stove by then and had coffee waiting, and now he was standing in front of the computer console, studying its dead gray screen.

"Good morning, my boy."

"Trout for breakfast."

"And some of that capital marmalade, I hope! Tell me, does this machine tie you into anybody else?"

"No."

"Nothing—no research service, no rental time—nothing?"

"Nothing."

Penhurst grunted. "I want to keep all this ultrasecret, you know."

"Let's eat."

He fried the trout to a crackled gold and laid them on big Ironstone plates with thick slabs of bread. Both men were silent as they ate; Tarp stared at the computer screen, which was brilliant now with an orange surveillance grid.

"There," he whispered when a light glowed. "Somebody out in the river."

"My canoe, I daresay."

"Maybe."

Tarp pressed a button. The river seemed to pour into the room, the sound of its water amplified several times.

A volume adjustment separated the sound of the heavy outboard motor from the slurping chatter of the river.

"They're a bit early." Penhurst sounded quite casual, but then he frowned at Tarp. "Did you have that audio receiver set up when I came over yesterday?"

"Set it up this morning." Tarp held up a finger as the sound of the motor changed. Penhurst did not understand the meaning of the altered sound, but Tarp could see clearly what was happening: the big freight canoe was slipping sideways into a huge eddy behind the boulder that lay thirty yards out from his detector, and the motor was beginning to race as it chewed into the aerated water at the boundary. Tarp frowned now, too, and then he gave a grim little smile as a human voice could be heard shouting something. The engine changed tone again, became throatier, and then it bellowed like an animal in pain.

"Running it at the bank," he muttered.

There was a hollow, metallic bang and a confused mixture of voices, and the motor was shut down. Two men spoke confusedly. Three more metallic booms sounded as the canoe was pulled up on the rocks.

"Amateurs," Tarp said with clear disgust.

Penhurst's eyebrows rose. "Do you think—."

Tarp held up his finger again. The voice on the speaker was jumbled by the sound of the river. Tarp fiddled with dials but the sounds could not be separated. After twenty seconds, a light glowed on the surveillance grid. Tarp looked at Penhurst. "Two of them. One's come up the bank and is about twenty yards in—probably under a big old pine that's down there. It's a good cover. You care to try out that walking stick of yours, Hamish?"

"Oh, certainly. Had it for years, never had occasion before." Penhurst balanced the walking stick in a hand. "Dickie Mainwaring gave me this stick. He was number two in the Home Office, you know. I was at Oriel with his brother."

"Of course you were." Tarp's grin could be disarming. He began checking the little Colt.

Minutes later, they were moving along the faint path that led down to the river. Penhurst looked quite cheerful, as if the possibility of action had energized him, bringing that bright, young color to his cheeks and lighting his intelligent eyes. Tarp looked sly and wary and dangerous.

"I shall simply keep chattering away in my usual engaging fashion, then," Penhurst whispered. "You deal with the chap under the tree."

"How many shots does that stick hold?"

"Two. Not to worry."

Tarp touched the old man's shoulder as a signal and glided away. He was thinking how fit Penhurst looked. *No fat. Years younger than his real age*. He lingered briefly over a vision of Penhurst and the physicist Beecham when they were young. *Young. Were old men really different when they were young?* Then he was concentrating on the patterns of light on the forest floor, on hints of movement and changes in bird song and breeze, on his own silent, secret passage over the moss.

He could hear Penhurst's voice from the path. He was talking exactly as if he still had a companion and not a care on earth. "And there were three of us out there with all those Yugoslavs, and our task, you see, was to get this fellow Djadlik killed because he was one of Tito's *partizans* and HM's government were still backing Mikhailovitch just then. Well, we'd made this arrangement with the Nazis that they'd mine a very ancient stone tower and blow it when I gave the signal—meaning, when poor old Djadlik went in to make it secure—and there we were, three foreigners and all these rather fierce-looking Yugoslavs. . . ."

The man crouching under the drooping branches of the long-needled pine was about twenty-eight or thirty, quite tall and just beginning to put on fat. *Former jock*,

Tarp thought. The man had a rather flamboyant mustache, as if he had some hope of doing commercials for deodorants or cigarettes; he was waiting in a form of wrestler's crouch as if he meant to spring out and do battle with Penhurst. *An actor*, Tarp thought contemptuously. *Tarzan in designer jeans*. Penhurst went jabbering on as if nothing mattered in the world but his Yugoslav story. The man under the tree could see him through the branches now, and he must have been able to see, too, that Penhurst was alone—or at least that Penhurst's supposed companion was not visible, because he had to look past pine needles and branches and roots, so he could not be sure of anything.

Tarp glanced aside at Penhurst's profile, twenty yards away and moving toward the river, and then he concentrated on the man under the tree. The man was leaning forward on one hand like a sprinter getting ready to come out of the blocks. He had an Ingram SM-11 in his other hand. His bent left leg had begun to quiver with tension.

Then Penhurst's shotgun boomed. As if it had been the starter's gun he had been waiting for, the man under the tree tried to burst from his concealment up the mossy slope in front of him, but as he moved Tarp fired once at his left foot and the powerful surge degenerated into an awkward and painful collapse into the bank in front of him. The man bellowed with pain. He tried to roll on his back and extract his own gun, but Tarp had already moved and was crouching behind the trunk of the huge old pine tree.

"Drop it," he said quietly.

The man's eyes slewed toward him. Tarp knew the idea that was in that stubborn head, and he fired again and dirt and needles flew an inch from the man's right ear.

"Don't do it," Tarp murmured. "Put your weapon down and lock your fingers behind your head."

The man did as he was told. Tarp came from behind the tree. "Get on your feet," he said.

"You shot me!"

"Yeah, I'm a real bad person. Get on your feet."

"I'm shot!"

"Yeah, that's why you're bleeding. Come on, get up and turn around."

He picked up the Ingram. At the edge of the trail, he stopped. Penhurst was standing at the riverbank, silhouetted against the sky beyond.

"Hamish?"

"Doing capitally, my boy! Come ahead."

The big man groaned as he limped forward. His shoe made a sucking noise because of the blood in it.

"My, my, he's quite a large one, isn't he!" Penhurst glanced back once and then returned his attention to the rock shore down below, where another, smaller man was kneeling on the round stones with his hands locked behind his neck. Another SM-11 lay about ten feet from him. "He had just decided to light a cigarette," Penhurst said. He was quite delighted with himself.

"Down you go," Tarp said. He nudged the big man, who balked. "Do it, or I'll push you down face first. Now *go*!" The man scrambled down the bank, whimpering. At the bottom, he sat heavily on a rock and said to his kneeling colleague, "The bastard shot me. Without warning!"

Tarp went down after him. While Penhurst covered from the bank, he went through both men's pockets and spread the findings on a boulder. "Company men," he called to Penhurst. "Even to the credit cards. Well, well." He looked at the big man. "John Cornish your real name?"

The man said nothing. Tarp kicked the wounded foot and the red face paled.

"Answer me."

"You sadistic sonofabitch!"

"Is John Cornish your real name?"
"Yeah."
"How long have you been with the agency?"
Cornish looked away. Tarp kicked the bleeding foot again.
"Now, I'll put a bullet in the other kneecap the next time you don't answer. I don't want to dick around. Understand me? *I don't play fair and I don't waste time*. How long have you been with the agency?"
Cornish cleared his throat. He looked as if he might weep. "Two years."
"Who's your officer?"
There was a hint of stubbornness as he watched Tarp's gun point at his knee. "Mr. Norbert F. Hacker."
"Hacker!" The name made Tarp smile. "Oh, my. And why did Hacker the Hack send you way up here to the wilds of Maine, John?"
Cornish licked his lips. "I need a doctor. Are you going to get me to a doctor?" His voice was going up in pitch. He would be good for only another question or two.
"That depends on your answers."
"That goddam bullet's still in there!"
"It's only a .22, John. You've got a real big foot. You'll be okay. Now, why did Hacker send you up here?"
"He wants to talk to you and the Englishman," a voice behind Tarp said. It was the other man, who was still kneeling on the small, rounded granite rocks. "Mr. Hacker wants to talk to you."
"About what?"
"About Sir Hamish's visit."
Cornish's face was shiny with sweat. "It's true. That's all. He just wanted to talk to you. And Jesus, you *shot* me!"
"Without warning." Tarp smiled humorlessly. "Remember that the next time you carry a weapon. The world is full of bad people who shoot first when they

think somebody with big feet is walking on their turf." He picked up the two machine pistols and lofted them one by one into the river. "Just to keep you honest, gents."

"What are you going to do with us?" the kneeling man said. He did not seem to be frightened. "You're in pretty deep already, Tarp."

"Oh, you're warning me?"

"I'm just telling you. The agency won't forget this."

"Good." Tarp looked at the river. It swirled down through the boulders, two hundred yards wide, an awesome natural force. "What I'm going to do is, I'm going to send you back the way you came."

"That's smart," the kneeling man told him.

"Fix up Cornish's foot. But don't do anything silly." Tarp climbed to Penhurst's side. "Can you watch them for a bit?"

"Of course. Let me reload." Penhurst brandished the steel tube that he had taken from the walking stick. The walking-stick handle made a saw grip; beyond it were eighteen inches of chamber, action, and barrel. He pulled forward on the barrel, ejecting a shell and bringing a second into the chamber from a recess in the grip. He inserted a fresh shell there. "Be gone long?"

"Minutes."

Tarp went to the little lake, swung the old canoe up to his shoulders, and trotted back. Minutes later, he had it in the river next to the aluminum freighter, rigged to tow. "Get in," he said to the two agency men.

"You're coming along?"

"Partway. Get in."

Tarp started the motor when the canoe was floating free. Fending off his own canoe with a paddle, he reversed into a backwater and powered out into a tongue of current that pushed viciously at the bow, trying to slam it back against the shore. The big motor surged and they moved steadily into the river with the bow angled upstream so that their progress was almost directly across. The two agency men sat in the bottom, ignoring the spray that lashed at them from the upstream rail.

In the main current, Tarp swung the motor over and pushed upstream around a dozen rocks in order to move into a deceptively smooth glide whose force swept them down again alongside a rock the size of a small house. Just below it, he applied power, and the big aluminum canoe surged over the turbulence and pushed into the smooth, slowly circling water below the rock. There, in an eddy as big as several backyards, spots of foam floated on a surface as smooth as a polished floor.

"Grab a paddle," Tarp said.

He bent low, felt over the engine until he found the engine mounts, and quickly unscrewed them. The heavy outboard was awkward to lift by himself, but he had only to clear the transom and then let it go, and it sank instantly into the tea-colored water.

"Jesus Christ!"

Tarp hauled in the wood-and-canvas craft and untied the rope. "That's Canada over there, where you came from. My side is the U.S., where the sheriff will be looking for two men who came on my property with guns. Maine sheriffs aren't afraid of the agency. Upstream there's a lot of dams and class-four water; I wouldn't go that way. The ocean is about two hundred miles downstream." He climbed into his canoe and held theirs by the gunwale. "If you both paddle like hell, you'll be all right."

"We could be killed!" the man he had shot wailed.

Tarp ignored him. "Tell Hacker to get off my ass. Tell him this is none of his business." Tarp started to say something else, then he stared down at his big hand on the gunwale, and his face looked suddenly bleak and bitter. "Oh, the hell with it."

He pushed away. He knelt near the middle of the

sixteen-footer, his weight a little to the downstream side so that the canoe presented some of its rounded bottom to the current as he put the bow into it with force. A few powerful strokes took him downstream of the cluster of boulders; he swung in and moved up in their shelter, picking his way from one boulder to another. He rested behind one to look across the surging water at the big canoe, which still sat behind the big boulder. The two men in it simply stared at him.

Tarp took out the Colt. His first shot ricocheted from the granite with a nasty whine, and they looked at him in astonishment. The second shot sent the smaller man for his paddle, and the third got them moving downstream. When Tarp holstered the gun, both men were splashing at the river, whose force had driven them out of the eddy. The stern of their canoe swung downstream until it was even with the bow and it looked as if they might go down rear end first, but some feat of paddling by the smaller man got them right again, and the last Tarp saw, they were speeding around a curve and down toward the rapids called Crossbone Rips a half mile below.

Tarp stopped in the near-shore eddy to dive into the cold water and retrieve the two Ingrams.

"Never know when you'll need these," he said. "I wouldn't want those two to know I had them, of course."

Penhurst looked pained. "Those two men could drown, Tarp."

"Oh, yes." Tarp looked hard at the old man. "There's always the risk of drowning in their line."

Penhurst looked down at the needle-strewn rock, pursing his lips. "You rather put them in jeopardy unnecessarily, didn't you?"

"No." Tarp waited until Penhurst glanced up and their eyes met. "I put them in jeopardy *necessarily.*"

Penhurst made a face that said clearly that he disapproved.

"I'm not a gentleman," Tarp said relentlessly. "Every game is played for keeps. They should have known that when they got into this wretched business."

"Should they?" Penhurst said almost sadly. "Do you think that Hacker told them what to expect from you?"

Tarp bent and put his hands on the thwart of the canoe, the thumbs turned to point at each other; with a grunt, he lifted the canoe to his thigh and then swung it up to his shoulders. "If he didn't, he isn't doing his job."

"Dear, dear—you lack compassion, my boy."

"Did you have compassion when you made a deal with the Nazis to blow up your supposed ally, the Yugo *partizan*?"

"Ah, well—that was *business*."

They walked back through the woods, and Tarp stowed the canoe in the crawl space under the porch and buried the Ingrams in the woods. When he returned to the cabin, he found the inside put to rights; Penhurst was waiting on the porch, ready to leave.

"You *are* coming back to England with me, aren't you?"

"To go into China after your dotty physicist?"

"Yes."

"It will have to be *business*, as you call it."

Penhurst nodded. "That's understood. I can offer a hundred thousand dollars plus incidentals, payable half now and half on completion. You're expected to meet expenses out of that."

"Funds from Her Majesty's gov?"

Penhurst shook his head. "The money will come to you through a private bank."

"Her Majesty's gov doesn't trust you anymore?"

"Rather the other way round. There have been leaks."

"Give me a little while to pull things together."

It took him twenty-three minutes. He turned on the electronic sentry, locked the front door, and joined

Penhurst on the path to the river. "Do we cross the river?"

"My aircraft is at Queen Anne reserve field. I've a car at the lumber camp over the river."

"I'll get the canoe again. They can keep it for me until I get back. Assuming that I do get back."

Penhurst was quite unperturbed. "You always have."

chapter three

"Norbert F. Hacker," Tarp mused. He was slumped in a window of the corporate jet that had brought Penhurst to Canada. "What set Norbert F. Hacker on us?"

He pictured Hacker as he had known him at the agency ten years before: an already balding, overweight timeserver who seemed to be going nowhere. Hacker had seemed the consummate good ole boy in those days before the New South and Jimmy Carter and cornpone Christianity. Hacker could have been cast as the sheriff in one of those cheap movies about cars and moonshine. He had a round face made rounder by fat, small eyes under colorless eyebrows, and a forehead deeply furrowed by some counterfeit of thought, as if the plow of intellect had tried very hard to cut the soil there.

"Still, he was very political," he said to his reflection in the plane's window.

"You're mumbling, Tarp."

"Hacker was very political. Or what's now called political. We used to call it brownnosing."

"An inelegant term for an inelegant man."

"Yes, indeed." Hacker was certainly inelegant; his idea of manners had been to hold up a napkin while he picked his teeth. "Still . . ." Tarp uncoiled his legs and swung around toward Penhurst, who had ensconced himself in a vast swivel chair of claret leather in the middle of the cabin. "Still, Hacker must have some clout now if he sent those two amateurs to see us."

"The gossip is he's next in line for Clandestine Operations."

"*Hacker?*" Disgust brought Tarp upright. "Jesus, the last time I checked, he was riding herd on the supply of erasers."

"But he hung on, you see. A man like that has one strong suit, Tarp—stamina. It's the quality that makes even stupid men dangerous. A hold like a bulldog."

"I'm not sure I'd call Hacker stupid," Tarp said slowly. "Not exactly stupid."

"He outlasted Nixon, and he outlasted Carter. In fact, the story is that he was able to set up a little empire while better men were being fired or were quitting in disgust. Now he's in line for head of Clandestine Operations."

"And finding out what we're up to would be a coup for him." Tarp glanced shrewdly at Penhurst. "Better yet, grabbing Arthur Beecham and his magic disintegrator ray would *really* be a coup." Tarp pulled on his lower lip. "He has access to some of your sources, yes? So he might already have heard about whatever it was that happened to the Chinese hospital. He could work out things pretty easily—you come to see me; I'm an old China gun, in some ways an obvious choice for a job; you want Beecham out of British pride. Or maybe to rid yourself of the taint of suspicion that you're a Soviet mole."

Penhurst was offended. "It's hardly a 'taint of suspicion,' my boy! It was a sensational accusation by a most untrustworthy journalist."

Tarp ignored him. "If Hacker is *not* stupid but is really a pretty shrewd good ole boy, then he'll have the sense to go easy with any story about a particle beam, which sounds like science fiction at best. He won't want to mount an operation and risk bringing out a crazy old Limey who thinks he's Dr. Zharkov in *Buck Rogers*. So checking me out is a pretty good idea—if I'm really going in, then it makes sense to let me be a damned fool and not him. And it's cheaper, too." He slumped in the seat again and crossed his legs so that his knees were now higher than his head. "I'll need a feasible cover, Hamish. Not necessarily an airtight one, but something that Hacker could chew on so he won't bite right down on me."

"Ye-e-e-s." Penhurst shifted a little uneasily. "I've been thinking something of the same sort of thing. Ten days ago, the American aircraft carrier *Eutaw Springs* lost an attack fighter in the Mediterranean—went overside on a night landing."

"That didn't make the newspapers."

"No. The U.S. has been trying to keep the Soviets—and Khadafy—off their backs while they try to do something about it. It was one of the new F-19s, you see."

Tarp nodded slowly. "And it must be sitting on the bottom, and American intelligence is sweating because somebody else may try to raise it."

"Exactly. It's really quite close in to the Libyan coast, and your navy can't sit there and fish for it. Word of the plane's loss will get out when the *Eutaw Springs* hits port, but until then it just might be believable that a free-lancer like you would go looking for it."

"Working for England?"

"Well, it could be. Here's the scenario: Her Majesty's gov don't have the F-19 but would love to look at one. They don't want to upset Washington, however, so they come to me—retired old poop—and ask me to hire a free-lancer to make some dives and bring up what he can. And then I go to you because of our old friendship and because you used to have a frogman's rating. . . ."

"I haven't dived in years."

"We want a feasible story, Tarp, not a perfect one. And I come to you to set it up, and at that point Hacker's two duffers come on the scene."

"Why isn't American intelligence trying to do something about the plane?"

"Perhaps they are. Aha! Perhaps naval intel have come to me and asked me to hire you to dive for the aircraft, thus keeping the U.S. in the clear. How's that?"

"And Hacker and the agency don't know about it?"

"Stranger things have happened."

"Indeed they have." He pulled on his lip. "Yes, the airplane will do for a cover. We'll have to set up a trail that seems to take me to the Med."

Tarp slouched deeper in the seat. Nothing was said for fifteen minutes, except once when he touched Penhurst's knee and said almost accusingly, "We'll not make the mistake of assuming that Hacker's stupid." Then he stared out the window, watching an iceberg in the incredibly blue water forty thousand feet below. After five minutes more he said, all business now, "Where to when we land?"

"Glynn—my country place."

"I need to be in London."

"Oh, dear." Penhurst looked hurt. "I'm afraid my town house is taken up with my granddaughter Gillian just now. She's a debutante, of all things. Did you know there are debutantes again? Just like my coming of age before the war. In fact, there's a party this evening." He looked at his watch. "Starts in another hour or two, London time."

"All the better. I'll go into the house with the guests and nobody has to know I'm there. I'd like twenty-four hours before Hacker's boys find me. All right, here's what I want done: I want you to send a message ahead to a man named Craik—I'll give you the address—and have him meet me at the airfield with a car and evening clothes."

"I don't much care for your going off on your own bat right at first."

"It's what you hired, Hamish. I won't kill anybody. Craik will have to find someplace to wait—you coordinate with the air base where we land—so I'll need transport from somewhere out along the runway to wherever Craik is. Best have an emergency vehicle meet me—I can slip out of the plane easily in the dark. Then march one of the crew through customs in my clothes. Oh, yes—and get my passport stamped, will you?"

Penhurst had decided to be aloof. "Would you like champagne laid on in the emergency vehicle?"

"Don't be arch, Hamish, it doesn't suit you." Tarp handed over a slip of paper. "There's Craik's contact data."

"Good God, is this *Eddie* Craik?"

"It is."

"But good God, Tarp, he was one of our people and he got cashiered because of a ball-up in Lebanon. He's got quite shady, I hear."

Tarp was settling his head against a pillow. He opened one eye. "Yeah—a fallen-away gent. A traitor to his class. Just my sort of fellow." He closed the eye and was almost instantly asleep.

He woke as the tires screamed against the asphalt of the military runway in the south of England and the engines began to roar as they strained to slow its headlong rush. Penhurst was sitting in the same easy chair.

"Everything set?"

"Exactly as you wanted." Penhurst was definitely not pleased. "I don't like losing touch at this early stage."

"I'll be in your own house, after all. Are the phones secure?"

"All my telephones are tapped, as you must know."

"Well—we'll be in touch. You can have me tailed, if you like." He stood up as the jet came to a stop. " 'Bye for now."

Moments later, he was in a small fire truck headed for a dark part of the air base; shortly after that, he was in the rear seat of a roomy London taxi that was moving toward a rear gate. At the wheel, a rather rakish-looking blond man of about forty was steering with the expert and slightly contemptuous ease of a professional.

"How've you been, Eddie?" Tarp said as he wriggled out of his pants in order to put on the evening clothes that had been laid out on the seat.

"Damned poor!" The driver gave a coarse laugh. "Gone to seed, Tarp, gone to seed!" He slowed the car and waved a pass toward the soldier on guard, who saluted and waved them on. Once on the highway, the taxi accelerated with an ease and quietness that suggested that there was something quite unusual under the hood. "This trip is going to cost you good, chum!"

"That's all right. Debts?"

Craik gave his coarse laugh again. "To the ears!"

"I'd like to hire you all day tomorrow, Eddie. Then I'd like you to do some digging for me and generally be on call for a week or so."

"How much?"

Tarp pulled a wonderfully silky sock over his right foot. "A thousand—pounds."

Craik's grin reflected in the windshield like a flash of diamond. "I'm yours, chum. For a thousand pounds, I'd go back to my wife! Actually, I'd do it for less; my own cooking's a caution."

Craik had chosen the evening clothes well. They fit and they were not new. Craik and Tarp had once shared a cave for six weeks in Uigur, and they knew each other's tastes fairly well. Their main difference was that Craik's tastes sometimes ran to adolescent boys, and two of them had been his undoing.

Tarp gave a final tug to his tie. "Ever hear of a company called Dammeco?"

Craik shrugged. "Can't say. Maybe in the stock pages."

"I want you to check it out." The plane on which he had flown across the Atlantic with Penhurst had been invoiced to Dammeco; Tarp knew, for he had looked in the air-control office in Canada.

Craik downshifted as he ripped into a curve, accelerated out, and shifted up again. "How far?"

"Until it looks dangerous. No risk to be taken."

"Fair enough. Anything else?"

"Book me a seat on tomorrow's Concorde to New York."

"Oh, la!" Craik leered. "Miss the girls at Times Square, do you?"

"Mind your manners, Eddie. Over and back tomorrow. Book it in the name of Haig."

Tarp climbed down within sight of the brilliantly lighted doorway of Hamish Penhurst's town house. Limousines lined both sides of the narrow street, and two policemen were directing traffic. Young men and women in evening clothes moved up and down the curving steps. Tarp, pretending to pay for the cab ride, leaned in and said, "I'll need a meeting place. The Embankment?"

"Good in the A.M."

"Day after tomorrow at seven, then—below Somerset House. Cheers."

He passed into Penhurst's mansion with half a dozen other people. Nobody seemed to care that he had no invitation. It was midnight, after all, and the guests were passing from this party to several others in adjacent streets, and back again. Tarp moved through a swarm of overexcited adolescents, going from one reception room to another, enjoying the odors of perfume and the appraising looks of a number of attractive women. He felt distant from them, as if he were an invisible observer there to study them scientifically, yet the looks they returned assured him that he was very visible. *Are you the one?* some seemed to ask. *Shall we?* asked others. One young woman, turning toward him suddenly and mistaking him for somebody else, put her bare arms around his neck and lay against him with her eyes closed. She smelled wonderful—perfume with a slight overlay of champagne and just a tint of excitement and exertion. When she opened her eyes, she said "Oh" in a child's voice. But she did not let go.

"I believe there has been a mistake," he said. "Regrettably."

"Oh." She studied him. "Oh, no." She kissed him. It was a young and meaningless kiss that rather gained momentum as it went on. "Oh, I say," she breathed. She leaned back from him and grinned, the sides of her mouth pulled quickly down in mock fear of having done something wrong. Her tongue touched her upper teeth and her chest rose with a very deep breath. It was quite a beautiful chest, Tarp thought, and beautifully framed between a low-cut dress and a diamond choker.

"Could I put you on hold?" she whispered. "Until about two?"

She was all of nineteen or twenty. Tarp was shocked, in a way, for he was so much older. "I believe I shall be in bed at two," he said.

Her tongue touched her teeth again. "I'll just bet you will," she said, and she laughed. He laughed with her. "You're rather too good to be true, you know," she said in a throaty voice that was still colored with her laughter. "I'm awfully tempted. . . ." Her eyes swung past his face. They were very wide set, rather sweet eyes; they looked dark in the light of the party, but in the daylight they would be gray. Her hands slipped down to grip his forearms. "I've a million people I've simply got to see," she said with exaggerated sadness. "Perhaps you'd care to trail about after me."

"Not at all," he said, but with a smile.

"I didn't think so." She touched her lips to his chin and slipped away, and he was left looking at a rather foolish-looking young man who watched her go with such obvious adoration that Tarp hurt for him. *He will trail after her*, he thought. *And maybe he'll enjoy it*. He made his way past the young man and then upstairs, where a servant was found who could lead him to the private apartment where Mrs. Duffus, Penhurst's housekeeper, presided. Tarp had brought her a note from Penhurst.

"I realize it's dreadfully late to show up like this."

"It's no trouble, sir." Her eyes were very blue and her Lowland Scots voice was very soft. In her mid-sixties, Mrs. Duffus ruled her domain with easy authority. "I'll just show you to your room, sir."

"That would be very kind of you." He found that he had become meek because of her. She was, for all her physical fragility, a formidable woman.

He was shown a large, rather chilly room on the third floor. The party thudded its way up through the house; footsteps pattered along the corridor, and there was a cascade of giggles. After half an hour, he knew that sleep could wait, and he went down to the party again.

The girl was dancing in the largest of the reception rooms. From arched niches around the walls, Roman emperors frowned down on her beautiful frivolity, as if they were the spirits of Labour politics trying to save the nation. Lively young men in evening clothes surrounded her. Tarp joined them and danced with her for seconds, then was cut in on and withdrew to the feet of one of the emperors to sip champagne. The same lovestruck young man he had seen earlier was standing next to him.

"She's absolutely the loveliest girl in London," the young man said. Tarp understood that the words came from sheer adoration rather than from any desire to communicate with Tarp. Still, they were uttered with a rather equine laugh as if to apologize for them. Tarp supposed that the young man laughed like that a good deal. He was just slightly bucktoothed, rather chinless, very polite, probably rich—a thoroughly nice, decent, silly young man of a dying class.

"I don't believe we've met," Tarp said. "I'm Andrew Haig." He had a passport with that name on it in his pocket, an extra that he had brought from the Maine cabin.

"Oh, jolly good!" The young man showed his teeth and laughed. "Johnnie Carrington. So very nice to meet you, sir." They watched the girl, who had changed partners twice more while they talked.

"She *is* lovely, sir," Johnnie Carrington said, as if Tarp were somehow to be congratulated for her—as if he might be her father or her uncle, perhaps.

"Indeed."

"I suppose you've known her for simply years and years."

Tarp guessed that the young man might be fifteen years younger than he. Did the difference give him the right to speak of "years and years"? The girl, after all, was hardly old enough herself for *anybody* to have known her for "years and years." Tarp decided to avoid the matter altogether. "And you?" he said.

"Oh, *me*." The young man seemed to dismiss himself as too silly to be borne, and at that moment Tarp decided that he liked him. "I've only known her for ten months. Nine and a few days, actually. Seventeen." He glanced at his watch; Tarp feared Carrington was going to count off the hours and minutes.

"Well, look at it this way," Tarp said, "she's only known you for nine months and a few days."

"Oh, she doesn't know that I exist!" Johnnie Carrington laughed out his horsey laugh and then turned his attention to the champagne. When Tarp next noticed him, he was across the room, standing in line to dance with her.

Tarp wandered away through the rooms, which were emptying of guests now as if a tide were going out, leaving on the beaches the wreckage of the party—a forgotten scarf, clumps of glasses, clots and clusters of diehards who were trying to make the evening last, three oddly morose people staring at a wall. Sleepy servants tried to stifle yawns and looked grateful when he refused their drinks and food.

"Bloody party's over," a red-faced young man told him at the foot of the staircase.

"Indeed."

"Bloody party's over for poor old England!" A mad, visionary gleam appeared in the man's eyes. "All washed up!" There was a gust of laughter from the ballroom, as if a door had been opened. "Let them laugh, if they can. They're dancing on their graves!"

"Are you Labour?" Tarp said.

The young man drew himself up with drunken dignity. "I am Communist!" he proclaimed. His black tie was askew and he had spilled champagne on his black-studded shirtfront.

Tarp straightened the tie. "The Party likes neatness," he said, and passed on. At the top of the stairs, he was passed by two musicians carrying instrument cases, and he saw three more coming toward him. There was another burst of laughter and he looked over the stair rail and saw the girl come out of the lower reception room with a half-dozen other young people, Johnnie Carrington behind her like a faithful dog. Still laughing, they swept through the foyer and out the great front door and were gone.

The party was over.

Tarp walked quickly through the empty rooms, cursing himself for having stayed up so late. He needed sleep. He came down the staircase for the last time, meaning to pass through to the back of the house and climb the private rear stair to his bedroom.

She was standing in the very middle of the foyer, quite alone. A cluster of party debris surrounded her, as if she were a statue—perhaps a minor but lovely goddess of partying—around whose feet the debris had blown.

"I thought you'd left," he said.

"Oh, no." She looked at him and only then recognized him. "Oh, it's you!"

"Do you need somebody to take you home?"

She giggled. "Of course not. Whatever are you doing here still?"

"I'm staying here. I'm a guest of Sir Hamish Penhurst."

Her tongue touched her upper teeth. "Grandfather does think of simply everything!"

"Grandfather?"

"I'm Gillian Penhurst. It was my party. I *live* here."

His smile was very pleased. He held out a hand. "Let's go to bed, then."

She smiled back, beautiful in her weariness. "Oh, yes. *Let's*."

chapter four

Tarp woke to the soulless chirping of his wrist alarm and slipped out of the antique bed. Behind him, Gillian Penhurst stirred and made some sound, like a child in its sleep. Early light gave the room a fantastic, underwater air, and he moved through it like a slow water creature, unsure of his footing, moving toward the white telephone he had noted three hours before. When he reached for it, her voice came from behind him.

"Hello."

He looked over his shoulder as if he were shielding the telephone. "Good morning."

"You have a gorgeous naked body."

"You're awfully outspoken."

She slowly pushed back the sheet and rose to her knees, shaking long, fair hair as if she were shaking off the ghost of sleep. She was broad-shouldered, like a swimmer, with the sleek muscles of those adept at that sport, and she had beautifully shaped breasts with a pinkness at their centers that seemed too vivid for the underwater light.

Tarp held up the telephone. "Private?"

"Oh, yes. It was only put in for my deb season."

"I'm going to make a call." *And hope that MI-5 haven't bugged it yet.*

She rushed past him toward her private bath, kissing his shoulder as she flew by. "Give you a bit of privacy," she whispered.

He dialed the secure telephone that Craik maintained and waited through five rings and the recorded briskness of Craik's voice telling him to leave his message at the tone.

"This is Tarp. Bring the cab to the rear entrance at one. Open the near-side door, wait twenty seconds, and then drive off. You'll probably be followed. Lead them around for an hour. Park at some kind of shop. Stay thirty minutes. Then drive around again and return. See you tomorrow."

His clothes were piled carelessly on a chair. He felt under them for the Colt, made sure that it was hidden in the pile, and then stood by a tall window that looked down into a rainy back street.

"Am I intruding?" she said.

"No. Am I?"

"God, no."

"Sometimes," he said slowly, "people are different in the morning. One wants them to go away."

"You look even better." She put her hands on his shoulders and leaned against him. "I hope I do."

She made love the way happy children are supposed to play, with joy and great concentration, chuckling sometimes. "Oh, my," she purred. "That was lovely. Does all that come naturally, or have you taken courses?"

"I believe it's instinct."

"I thought that the only way Americans knew things was if they took a course. That confidence that if you've been lectured at, you're educated."

He pushed himself up on his hands and looked down at her. "You're lovely."

"Oh, that sounds so serious. What is it?"

"I've got to leave soon." Her eyes were indeed gray in the daylight, a rather dark gray like wet stone, with a tint of violet. "How would you like to drive me out to Heathrow?"

"You're going—just like that?"

"Only for the day." He sat up. "I don't want anybody to know I've gone. Can you keep a secret?"

"Sometimes."

"Let's get me downstairs and out of the house without being seen."

She seemed delighted. Everything was play to her. He crouched on the floor of her little Swedish sports car while she drove out of the garage, and when they were on the streets she nudged him, giggling, and he sat up. "Won't you feel awfully silly, traveling in evening clothes?" she said.

"I hadn't thought about it."

She drove with more enthusiasm than skill, and it was an effort for him not to grab the wheel as she took a sharp turn in front of a bus. He found at last that it was best to get a good hold on her left thigh with his right hand and to keep his eyes on her chin, so that he wouldn't have time to say something derogatory if they were about to be killed. Astonishingly, however, she got them to the Concorde terminal safely, and he climbed out quickly and then put his head back into the little car. "You really are lovely," he said.

Her smile was glorious, but it faded quickly. "I've been thinking—I feel an awful little tart—I don't even know your name."

"Tarp."

"Just Tarp? All right." Her eyes narrowed as if she had to look into the sun to see him. "Am I going to see you again?"

He hesitated. "I don't wear very well."
"That's for me to decide, isn't it?"
"You're awfully young."
"You're not awfully old."
Again he hesitated, then took the pistol and its soft holster from his breast pocket and laid it on the passenger seat. "That's the secret. Take care of it for me. And you haven't driven me to Heathrow, and you didn't spend the last part of the night with me, and as far as you know I'm still asleep in a bedroom in your grandfather's house. All right?"
"Absolutely. Hurry back, darling."
The Concorde delivered him into Kennedy in time for a New York breakfast, had he wanted one, but he went instead to a car rental. A clean-shaven young man found him more interesting than Tarp liked and followed him; Tarp noted him and went on. He drove to a shopping mall for clothes and left the evening dress with a cleaner.
"You need these for the weekend?" the Puerto Rican woman said.
"Not that soon."
"Pick 'em up thirty days or we sell 'em."
Thirty days. I think I'll make that.
He drove farther east on the island and out to a cluster of scruffy docks on the sound where head boats berthed. He found a diving shop where they knew him and where he spent some time ordering diving gear that he would never use, then he turned back toward New York City and threaded ugly streets until he pulled up outside a jewelry store near the Grand Concourse.
A young man he did not know stood behind the counter.
"Yes?"
"My watch has stopped."
"Yeah? Digital. A battery, always a battery."
Tarp handed over the watch, from which he had already removed the battery. He was not surprised that

this young man had not recognized an old password. *Time takes. Time changes.* But he thought of Penhurst and his interest in Arthur Beecham, those two old men who had once been young.

"Hey, there's no battery in here." The young man had special lenses attached to his eyeglasses; they could be pushed up out of the way or lowered to serve as a loupe. He was squinting through them with an expression of great suspicion. "There's no battery in this watch."

"That's why it stopped."

"Geez."

"Yeah." Tarp leaned on the counter and turned so that he could look out the store window. The young man from the airport car-rental area was in a car across the street. "I thought I might find Mr. Steinberg here today," he said.

"Oh, yeah?" The young man looked at Tarp as if he expected him to pull a gun and hold him up. "Mr. Steinberg, my father?" His accent was excruciating—*fawthuh*. "He gave up the business about three years ago."

"Oh." Tarp looked outside again. The young man was talking on a radio. "How is *old* Mr. Steinberg?"

"My grandfather?" *Moi graan-fawthuh?* "He looks at the TV, you know? The soaps, the game shows—that's his life. Maybe that was always his life. He never got no excitement."

No, of course not, Tarp thought. *Shmuel Steinberg, aka Maurizio Berg, the leader of a Lithuanian resistance cell until the Russians almost killed him.* "I'd like to pay my respects," Tarp said.

"To my graan-fawthuh?"

"I used to know him."

"Geez." He pointed the way up the stairs behind the counter, then watched closely to make sure that Tarp was not a thief who was going to steal the boxes of cheap watches and thinly plated wedding silver that stood along the shelves. At his pressure on a button, a buzzer sounded above and Tarp pushed on the door and went in.

There was an old, old man sitting in a chair in front of a color-television set. He wore glasses so thick they looked like the ports on an undersea vehicle, and his face was permanently screwed up into a monkeylike squint. When Tarp spoke, he moved his head, but the thick glasses seemed to point at a spot several feet to the left of Tarp's face.

"My watch has stopped," Tarp said.

The old, old man leaned forward with the slow care of age and turned down the volume of the television, and then he got up and shuffled slowly toward Tarp. His body was a little twisted to the right, as if he were carrying a package under that arm. "If you got the right kind watch, it never stops," he said.

"But time moves quickly."

"Men move faster."

His mouth stayed open, even when he was not speaking. He looked as if somebody else had dressed him, for his jacket did not match his trousers and both were too big, left over from the days when he had been a large man. *And he killed an SS colonel with his bare hands, they said*. Steinberg was a little old man now, and that large, lethal Steinberg was gone. But he remembered the old passwords.

"I need some papers," Tarp said.

The old right hand made gestures in the air, writing words that could not be deciphered. "I don't do that no more."

"Maurizio, you knew me in the old days. You made me an ID kit for China in nineteen sixty-one."

"I don't remember so good. It don't help to remember too much."

"You made those papers by hand so that they looked engraved, even under a magnifying glass. They were works of art. I wanted to cry when I had to burn them."

The old head nodded. "I told you to burn them." He

put his tongue against his flaccid lower lip and pushed it out as if he were getting ready to spit. "Art! The papers I made in those days—nothing! Long ago—the boys and girls I helped. That was art!" He shook his head again, slowly. "Leah died, couple years ago. My Leah. You, she always liked. Cancer. She always said I'd go first and leave her with a broken heart, and here I am. I got so mad at her, dying first! My Leah!" He tried to clutch Tarp's arm and got a grip on the stiff material of the new shirt from the shopping mall. "I don't do papers no more like that. My eyes are gone."

"I need four sets of papers. One to take away with me, one for you to show the people who will come snooping after me, and two to send on. I can pay ten thousand."

The right hand, which before had written words in the air, now moved as if to erase them. "Money is no consequence. It's the eyes. Four sets papers just for you?"

"Two for me, one to show the snoops, one for an old man."

"You got photos?"

"You can do photos of me with the polaroid. I'll have to guess at the old man—give him glasses and a mustache. Irish passport for him, if you've got one."

"Sure I got Irish, what d'you think? And you—what kind you want?"

"Australian or Canadian to take away with me. The other one French or Italian—businessman."

Steinberg mumbled to himself and said again that his eyes were gone, but he led Tarp toward an inner room, gripping the cheap shirt from the shopping mall in unsure fingers. There, with a slowness that another man might have found maddening, he unlocked a cabinet and swung away a board where old pocket watches were hung and revealed a safe, which he opened so slowly that it appeared he had forgotten the numbers.

"Leah liked you," he said. "Leah *lusted* after you, in fact." He tried to chuckle; his shoulders moved, his mouth smiled, but no sound came out. "A funny thing, an old woman's lust. Not easily satisfied. She used to say, if you was a Jew, she'd have made a sin." He fanned passports and identity cards in his hands like a magician about to do a trick. Most of the papers were obsolete—museum pieces, some of them. Tarp, however, began to pick over them.

"I need one right away. I've got forty-five minutes."

"What you need?"

"Canadian or Australian, Egyptian visa."

It took only half an hour, but that was time enough for the young man from downstairs to come up twice. The old man dealt with him with contempt. Tarp had touched a living place, and he seemed to grow younger and stronger as he worked.

"There." He handed over a Canadian passport with an Egyptian visa. He looked larger. "And the others?"

"I picked them out. For the old man, the Irish journalist; for me, the French one. Plus the East German with the Libyan stamps, that's to stay here with you but have my photo in it—there'll be somebody along to ask you what I was doing here. Show them that."

"What, invite a charge I'm breaking the law here?"

"No, no; they'll be agency people. They already know all about you." He gave the old man Eddie Craik's secure number. "I need these in forty-eight hours. Send them to London and have the courier call this number."

"Courier!" The old voice had enough force to laugh now. "In four, five years, I have no use for a courier."

"Find one. Send the kid downstairs."

"Hah—that one!" He dismissed his grandson with a gesture. "I got a nephew, he's a travel agent, he'll know somebody."

"Fine. And when the agency people come, tell them you made me one passport that I took with me and the East German one. They'll want to know where you're to send it; give them that phone number." He wrote down Hamish Penhurst's private number.

"*Give* it to them?"

"Sure. They'll really think they're hot stuff—it's unlisted."

The old man saw him to the upper door. "I used to do it all with my hands. Stamps, papers—even once, I faked a photograph, all by hand. Little dots, you wouldn't believe. That's how my eyes went. But I saved lives!" He clutched again at the sleeve. "I do like you ask, don't worry. Don't worry. Old don't mean stupid."

The young man was waiting at the bottom of the stairs. "You were an awful long time," he said suspiciously.

"I have a lot of respect for him."

Outside, the clean-cut young man was still waiting. Tarp drove off without looking at him.

There was a stretch of broken street in the depths of Queens where going more than twenty miles an hour meant a broken spring or a blown tire. Warehouses lined the road on both sides; there were no people. A dog, staring at the empty pavement, was the only suggestion of life. Tarp drove almost angrily, hating the potholed street and the rented car, and as soon as he passed the worst of the holes he accelerated to put it behind him. His tires squealed and the softly hung car swayed and surged with false power.

Behind him, a blue light flashed and a siren wailed and fell silent.

Tarp groaned.

"Get out of the car, please."

He was a young policeman, square-faced, his clothes so neat that he made Tarp's teeth ache. Tarp got out very carefully; the young cop's hand seemed nervous as it rested near his huge revolver.

"Walk ahead of me to the patrol car, please."

"You know, I didn't think I was speeding. . . ."

"Walk ahead of me, please, sir."

There was another neat policeman in the back seat of the patrol car. He was wearing dark glasses, and it was impossible to see whether he was asleep or crazy or bored or dead.

"Get in."

"Shall I get my license?"

"Get in."

He got in and the door closed behind him with a solid click. The other policeman turned his dark glasses toward Tarp. He reached up and took off the glasses, and then Tarp could see that he was actually the smaller of the two agency men who had tried to interfere in Maine. The last Tarp had seen of him, he had been splashing down toward the ocean in a canoe.

Not good.

The smaller agency man preceded him into a plain building near the Kennedy cargo terminals. The other policeman walked behind Tarp. Tarp's hands were behind him because of a pair of handcuffs. The three of them walked in file down a short corridor and came to a door where the small man simply waited while the other one came up and opened it.

The small agency man in the dark glasses went in.

At a touch on his shoulder, Tarp went in.

The small man turned and planted two powerful blows into Tarp's body, the first low in the groin and the second higher in his gut. Tarp was not quite surprised, but he was shocked by the small man's strength and his obvious rage. Pain spurted up through his abdomen and drove the breath from his lungs. He contracted instinctively, trying to protect the hurt places, but the man behind him punched him in the kidneys, and he could not keep from straightening. Then the small man struck him twice more, once with his hand and once with the nightstick that had dangled at his waist. Tarp went down and stayed down.

There was blood on the tile floor by his head, blood in his mouth. He waited for a kick. When none came, he counted to twenty and put his head up.

Norbert F. Hacker was sitting open-legged on a straight steel chair in a corner. He nodded to the first make-believe cop, who knelt down and went through Tarp's pockets as if they were attached to empty clothes. While he searched, Tarp probed his mouth with his tongue, tasting the blood and testing the pulpy lacerations.

Hacker looked quickly through his papers. He lingered for some seconds over the Canadian passport. He got up then and came toward Tarp. Movement of any kind took on importance when performed by Hacker, for he was overweight and looked as if he believed that activity was dangerous. Too, he always frowned as if he was thinking of unfortunate facts. Hacker was wearing a short-sleeved white shirt with a little alligator on the pocket, and green slacks and a green tie that was pulled tight at the folds of his fleshy neck so that he seemed to be choking.

He knelt in front of Tarp.

"There are some things that I believe we need to share together," he said. He had a Maryland accent. It was like a meeting at the watercooler or in the coffee shop, the prelude to a conference arranged by their secretaries. "In fact, I wanted to meet together with you a couple days ago."

Tarp exhaled noisily. His abdomen and his mouth hurt, and he did not like lying at Hacker's feet with his hands cuffed.

Hacker's face took on its most important and thoughtful expression. "You been seeing Sir Hamish Penhurst," he said.

"He came to see me."

"Well, see, I got to ask you why he did that. That's what we got to talk about together."

"May I sit up?"

"Why, sure!"

"I don't want him to hit me with that nightstick again." Tarp sat up slowly. His head seemed to rise several feet above his shoulders when he changed position. Hacker, who could not maintain his crouch any longer, signaled for his chair. Sitting, he was still above Tarp, who was sitting on his buttocks on the tile floor.

Hacker leaned forward with his hairy hands on his green slacks and said solemnly, "You just tell me in your own words what Sir Hamish Penhurst wanted."

"He's an old friend."

"We got good reason to believe he's a Russian plant."

"That's bullshit."

"Now, you don't have access to the privileged and secret data that I do. On balance, I believe that he is a Russian agent. Now what did he want, in your own words?"

Tarp had to seem to hesitate and then give in. He glanced at the two men in the police uniforms and then at Hacker, and he said in a near-whisper, "He wanted me to do some diving."

"Where would that have been at?"

"The Med."

Hacker nodded, as if to say that he had suspected as much. He took the Canadian passport from his shirt pocket with the cute little alligator on it and opened it to the Egyptian visa. "This part of the Med?"

"More or less."

"How come Penhurst didn't supply the paper?"

"I wanted something he didn't know about in case I had to bail out."

Hacker did his best to look sly. His eyes almost disappeared into their lids. "You mean to say you *don't* trust old Hamish Penhurst."

"I don't trust anybody."

That was a telling point with Hacker. He might not be very bright—or, then again, he might be very bright indeed—but he depended upon other people's trusting natures. When he heard somebody else say that he trusted nobody, he was impressed, because that was exactly the number of people he trusted, too.

"Where'd you spend the night?"

"London. Penhurst's."

"Word I got is a cab stopped at Penhurst's awhile ago to take you off into the country. What's all that?"

"I didn't want him to know where I am."

Hacker tapped the fake passport on his lime-green knee. His white shoes winked at Tarp and his white belt rippled with reflections of the flourescent light when Hacker's body moved. "You're goin' after that F-19 that went in off the *Eutaw Springs*, now ain't you?"

"Is that what you believe?"

Hacker looked as solemn as a man posing for his picture. "Now, Tarp, I don't think you understand the seriousness of this situation. This is very big medicine, all this kind of business, and here you are messing around with a questionable figure like Sir Hamish Penhurst. You're not in a very good position here, Tarp. I'm not convinced you realize that yet, and I want to tell you this for your own good—*for your own good*—that this is very big, serious medicine. Now I want you to take a minute and then I want you to tell me which side you find yourself on in the bigger issues here."

Tarp felt over the inside of his cheek with his tongue. He was thinking, but not about the big issues; he was thinking about Gillian Penhurst. *She probably likes hard rock and soft ideas*, he was thinking. *She probably thinks the* Star Wars *movies are art. If she thinks.*

"Now, Tarp, what side are you on?"

"I'm still an American, Hacker. Even if the agency did treat me like garbage."

Hacker shook his head. "Just hate to hear things like that. I just hate to hear those things said!" Hacker pounded on the chair between his lime-green thighs. "Someday, I hope you will be mature enough and fair enough to admit that your own behavior and your own record had a little something to do with your ass gettin' run out of the agency."

"Sure. I was arrogant and independent and—let me quote—'an uncontrollable operative who is no longer trustworthy because of early-life experience in China.' Okay, but I'm still an American. Good enough?"

Hacker was nodding. "I sincerely hope and pray it is. I sincerely hope so."

He stood up and signaled to one of the counterfeit policemen, who unlocked Tarp's handcuffs and walked away. Hacker looked into the Canadian passport again and then took out a business card and put it into the passport. "There's a couple phone numbers on that card. You just give me a call, anytime of the day or night, whenever there's something going down I ought to know about. You hear me?"

Tarp did not want to risk standing up just yet. He sat cross-legged, like a kindergartner at story time, looking up at the bright green high rise of Hacker's legs and his white belt and his shiny green tie and his pink sweaty jowls, and he said, "You going to try to run me, Hacker?"

Hacker's eyes glinted at his two helpers. "I guess I'd just about know better than to try to run somebody that the agency in its wisdom has said is uncontrollable. You ain't a team player, Tarp, and that's a fact."

Tarp sighed. He rolled to his knees and hands and then slowly, very slowly, pushed himself erect, as if he were the first ape giving *Homo erectus* a try. "That's a fact, indeed." He took the passport back. The room tipped and slid away from him like running water. "So what am I supposed to telephone you about?"

"About whatever you think is worth me knowing. About old friend Penhurst, there. About the F-19. And all like that. Now, are you going to do that thing for me?"

Tarp sighed again. "If I don't, I suppose you have something in mind for me."

"Well, now, Tarp. . . ." Hacker cleared a roll of bulge from his tight collar and stuck out his chin as if he were doing a Mussolini imitation. "We at the agency believe that a man is to be held accountable."

"Um." Tarp put the passport in his pocket. "I suppose I've missed the goddam Concorde by now."

"They agreed to hold the flight for a few minutes while you and me had this little talk. You can walk right aboard now. Enright, take Mr. Tarp here over to the Concorde departure lounge, will you? He's pressed for time."

"Yes, sir, Mr. Hacker."

Tarp ran his tongue over his bruised gums. "I had a car."

"That's all taken care of. One of the boys here will drop it off for you so's you don't have to delay. Hey, you want us to pick up that tux you dropped off at the cleaners?"

"Thanks a lot. No, I'll be back for it. I'll be in touch, Hacker."

Hacker tried to smile. His dislike for Tarp was too strong to let him. "You do that."

The small man who had been in Maine, the one Hacker had called Enright, had taken off his dark glasses. He looked almost young and embarrassed without them. "Let's go."

Tarp came close to him. Enright flinched slightly, expecting some vindictive gesture. Quietly, Tarp said, "Are you and I even now?"

"Why—I guess so. Sure."

"Be *real* sure. Being even means starting clean—no anger, no revenge. Sure?"

Enright swallowed. "We're even."

"Good. Don't forget." Tarp walked out of the little room. When he glanced back, Hacker was patting his face with a white handkerchief and staring at the place where Tarp had lain on the floor as if some important clue to the secret of things had been left there.

chapter five

Amplified rock music from Gillian Penhurst's room thudded into his ears. He had left her there with her white telephone and her noise, fleeing her giggles and her rock stars as if he feared contamination. *Too old,* he thought again. Now he was pulling the skin on his temples and cementing small, wispy patches of transparent membrane with an organic cement. The pull elongated his eyes. *Not as good as inserts,* he thought, *but not bad. Not bad.* His skin had begun to change color because of the pills he had started taking when he had come back from New York the evening before.

His face lacked the roundness of the supposedly typical Chinese, and it was lined with a very Western set of worries. Yet China was a huge country, with many racial types. Colored and with the eyes altered, his face might not seem Chinese to an American raised on Charlie Chan movies on late-night TV, but in China itself he would arouse no curiosity—especially when he had finished dying his hair and settling his body into the slightly stooped posture and the short-striding walk he knew so well.

His tongue touched the inside of his cheek. The damage done by Hacker's people was very slight.

Tarp looked over the suit that Hamish Penhurst had supplied. It was too classically Maoist—dingy fabric, careless needlework, a label from a factory in Hunan province. China was changing more than this suit suggested.

Tarp put it on and slipped his feet into worn leather shoes. He took a pair of eyeglasses from a table and carefully threaded the wire bows over his ears. He let his shoulders sag. His hands went to his sides out of habit, the thumbs touching the trouser seams. He bowed to himself in a full-length mirror. *Mr. Xiang, I presume?*

There was a rapid little knock at the door, and before he could speak, Gillian rushed in. Seeing him, she pulled up quickly.

"Yes, miss?" he said in the hoarse voice he would use in China.

"Oh, I'm sorry . . . I . . ." She stared. "God, darling, is that *you*?"

"Close the door, please." He straightened and took off the glasses. "I want you to promise me you won't tell anyone what you just saw."

"All right."

"You could get me killed, you see."

"Are you joking?"

"No. This has nothing at all to do with you, you see."

"You looked positively—well, Chinese."

"I was born in China." He took off the suit jacket and began to pull one of his own shirts on. "My parents were missionaries, odd as that may seem."

Her lovely face contracted into a frown as she tried to make a calculation. "But that was during the second war, wasn't it?"

"I was born in a Japanese prison camp. My parents died there. Until I was nine, I spoke, ate, thought

Chinese—I *was* Chinese." His smile was both apologetic and proud. "I was a runner in Mao's headquarters when they drove out the Nationalists."

Her frown deepened. He was talking of ancient history to her.

"Mao," he said. "Mao Tse-*dung*. It doesn't matter

"Are you angry with me, darling? You look angry."

He hesitated. *No. I'm simply older than you by too much. My life happened before you were born.* "No, I'm not angry at all. I feel a little—*distant*—maybe."

She came to him. "Don't."

"Can't help it. Generational *angst*." He kissed her forehead and moved past her. "No good being gloomy! Let's talk about something else. Tell me something cheerful. What have you been talking about on that white telephone of yours?"

"Oh, I've been talking to that awfully silly Johnnie Carrington! He's such a bore. You're lucky you don't know him."

"Oh, but I do. He's madly in love with you."

"I know—but he's so *wet*!" She threw herself on his bed. "How do you know wet Johnnie?"

"Met him at your party. He laughed a lot."

"Johnnie has the most awful laugh in the world. However, he makes up for it by having almost no chin."

"He's crazy about you."

"Won't do a bit of good!" She was propped up on her elbows, lying on her back with her feet toward him. "The family think he's impossible."

"A damned sight less impossible than I am. Johnnie Carrington's exactly the sort of man you'll wind up marrying."

She picked at the bed cover. "I know. But not for years and years. Johnnie asked about you."

A little warning signal flashed in Tarp's consciousness. "Oh?"

"I suppose he's jealous. He wanted to know if you were staying here."

Jealous—or professionally inquisitive. "What does chinless Johnnie do?"

"He's something at Whitehall. Something quite silly, I'm sure."

Tarp slipped on a dark blue, double-breasted blazer and bent over the bed to kiss her. "I've got to go."

"*Why?*"

"Things to do."

"I thought I was being awfully alluring, lying here."

"You are. See you in a couple of hours."

He started out the door and then turned back. "Johnnie Carrington seemed a thoroughly nice young man, you know. It's no good, this thing with me. Fact of life."

He walked down toward St. James's and found a red telephone box. He dialed Craik's secure number, listened to the recorded voice, and then said to the device, "Find out what you can about a man named Carrington, John, age middle to late twenties. Upper class, probably Foreign Office but could be MI-5 or another service. Meet me at five on the Embankment."

When he stepped out of the box, he saw a man who might have been a bank clerk standing twenty feet away with his face in a newspaper. Tarp had already marked him near Penhurst's house. *English. Maybe one of Hacker's people. Time he earned his money*. He started to walk.

Hamish Penhurst was waiting for him on the other side of the Thames, near that area where Shakespeare's Globe had once stood. *Faded Glory. Once, the Globe; now, empire the sun never rises on*.

"I had a tail for a while, Hamish."

"You got rid of him, I trust?"

"Oh, yes. Could have been MI-5."

Hamish Penhurst looked vague. "Let's stroll a bit before we go in." Penhurst pointed with his beautifully rolled umbrella, and Tarp fell into step with him along an unappetizing street.

"Everything set, Hamish?"

"Everything. Once you're outfitted, we're ready."

"Anything new on Arthur Beecham?"

"No more melted hospitals or anything of that sort. No indication that anybody else is interested."

"How's my cover story going?"

"Very well, indeed! We've leased a trawler out of Malta and have sent down a good bit of diving gear. I'm spreading about the notion that I'm interested in the F-19 thing."

"My kit for China?"

"Ready to go. Maps, papers, false orders, substantiation—everything will be on board your aircraft. One set of papers will certify you as a middle-level bureaucrat from a form of center for unexplained phenomena. You're to be flown to Delhi, where you'll change to a Hedgehopper and go in at night. Parachute, of course."

"Of course."

Tarp had not told Penhurst about the papers from Steinberg in New York; in fact, he had said nothing about the quick trip to New York and back. The habit of keeping things in separate compartments was very deeply ingrained.

They turned back toward the point where they had met.

"You've checked the clothes I sent?"

"Yes. They're fine. A little out of date, but I think that's okay for my character. I'd like some pencils with Chinese markings."

"Pencils." Penhurst pretended to groan. "You're really much too careful about detail. Fanatical." He sighed. "I wish I'd had ten like you at MI-5. Maddening but quite wonderful." He paused at a warehouse door. "Final instructions will be on board the aircraft. I've provided you with three contacts—a primary in Western China, fairly near the prison, who can get you and Beecham out, and two others as reserve. I have this quite carefully planned, my boy, so please don't do things on your own bat, will you? The primary contact can call in the Hedgehopper to pick you up, and you can be flown out to Delhi in a matter of hours. If it goes well, it will be quite clean and very quick."

Tarp grunted. He sounded unconvinced. Operations were seldom either clean or quick, he seemed to say.

Penhurst leaned on his umbrella. "You will go soon, eh?"

"As soon as I'm ready."

"Ye-e-e-s." Penhurst ground the point of the umbrella against a chip of wood. "We really must move it along, my boy. The implications of the thing are enormous." He had mentioned nothing about Gillian, but Tarp knew that he was a very suspicious old man who was adept at entertaining possibilities.

"Let's go in," Tarp said.

The warehouse held an unofficial supplier to several British government agencies, a former armorer from Enfield who could do things with weapons that were almost magical. Among other things, he was a legendary pack rat, and the warehouse held as remarkable a collection of guns as could be found outside a museum—and more remarkable in some categories than any museum.

"Will Kerwin?"

"Yes."

"I used to hear about him. Trustworthy?"

"Absolutely."

Will Kerwin was a short, muscular man of sixty who had just the suggestion of fat around his middle. He wore military fatigues; his rolled-up sleeves revealed sinewy, almost hairless arms and thick wrists. His handshake was quick and firm.

"Glad to meet you, sir. Sir Hamish has asked me to fit you up for a trip abroad. Got a shopping list, sir?"

"A short one, yes. Rifle, pistol, two grenades, two self-contained flares, ammo."

"Knife, sir?"

"I'm not much with a knife."

"I do recommend one, sir. Even if you don't like one for social work, you can always keep your nails clean. I've got several are very nice and light. And the rifle, pistol, grenades, and flares—that's it? Got some lovely clandestines in just now, sir—stainless steel crossbow, for example—no? Little throwing ax, an American Indian would—no? Quite. Come this way, if you please, sir."

Hamish Penhurst hovered behind them, his professional interest evident.

"What sort of rifle d'you have in mind, sir?"

"I want accuracy and firepower. Something light."

"HK-91's still a nice piece, sir. Done a lot of good work."

"Lighter. Parachute stock. I'd really like Chinese marks, if you can."

"Mm." Kerwin rubbed an eye. "Chinese. Dear, dear. Not awfully good on superior, lightweight weapons, our Chinese friends. Hold on, though—step over here, will you, gentlemen? I do have one thing—got it donkey's years ago, really keep it as much for the oddity of it as anything—only a specialist like yourself might appreciate it, sir. . . ." He unlocked a cabinet and selected a short, all-black rifle that looked almost daintily small compared to the bull-pup assault rifles around it. "Curiosity, eh?"

Tarp examined it. "Copy of the Mini-14."

"After a fashion, yes. But scaled down." Kerwin laughed. "Almost a lady's gun, you might say. But you can cut down a tree with it—.223 ammo, lots of punch, auto or semi-auto. A prototype, I've always believed—maybe something they were looking at for insurgency use in Africa. But expensive to make. Now, I'll admit the finish could be better—*lots* better—but she's a lovely little shooter. Dead on. A *little* tendency to jam, but I've installed a fore-grip pump for fast clearing."

Tarp hefted the rifle. It felt much too small. "I'll need to fire it."

"Oh, certainly! We'll take it downstairs. I'll just pull a couple of double-thirty clips for it, and a ten to carry in it."

"Sold."

"Very good, sir. Now for the pistol. Coarse work or fine?"

"Coarse. Very coarse. Last resort."

"Big, then. American .45's good for close work. Still—maybe something in nine millimeter. Let me see. . . ." He squinted down an aisle of steel shelving with weapons on both sides, ticketed and lying flat. Tarp was startled to note a *jezail* partway down on one side. *Something for everybody. Nothing too obsolete.*

Kerwin folded his arms. "I got a Czech VZ-52 someplace," he was murmuring. "Lovely, smooth action, although it's almost an antique. Still, it's 7.62—maybe a little light. Then there's heaps of Makorovs in their nine millimeter, even some of the Chinese Type fifty-nines, same weapon—but they look like they were carved out of old potatoes by a drunken sailor."

"They shoot," Tarp said. "One of them'll do."

"Well. . . ." Kerwin wrinkled his nose. He smiled happily. "I've got just the pistol! Funny it didn't come to me before. A Browning High Power that the Canadians made for China in the second war. Perfect, sir! You know the HP, of course—damned reliable, powerful weapon. Well, this is every bit as good as the Belgian FN. Made over in Toronto, got Chinese markings, there must be hundreds of them still kicking about in China. Just the thing! How about it, sir? Eh? Really a fine old weapon—may I fetch it for you?"

Half an hour later, Tarp was putting the guns through their paces. He found the rifle deceptively delicate, for it was a punchy, accurate weapon whose one real defect—

fragility in prolonged combat use—did not worry him. He hoped not to have to use it at all, and prolonged combat would be almost unthinkable. When he was through at the firing range, Kerwin put two clumsy, tin-can grenades on the table next to him.

"They match your outfit, sir." He chuckled. "Type forty-two, copy of the Soviet. Frag sheet inside the can, pressed TNT—about a three-second delay after the ring is pulled, but don't count on it. About a twenty-five meter frag range. Bit like throwing a can of peas at the mother-in-law, what?" The grenades were, indeed, like slightly squat tin cans, with large rings and a right-angle lever at the top.

"Serviceable," Tarp said. "Put them with the other things."

Penhurst looked at the ugly grenades with distaste. "Would you like something with more finesse, my boy? A fountain-pen gun—belt-buckle explosive . . . ?"

Tarp patted his shoulder. "You're a Romantic, Hamish."

Penhurst signed several forms and watched as the weapons were put away in camouflage bags. "Someone will stop by for these within the hour, Mr. Kerwin."

"Very good, Sir Hamish." He nodded to Tarp. "Pleasure to do business with you, sir. Oh, if you can—bring that little Chinese rifle back, would you? Never find another like it."

"I'll do my best, Mr. Kerwin."

They moved out into the afternoon light. Penhurst pointed their way west and north. "I've bought another set of weapons in your name from a free-lancer. Russian and Libyan marks, the sort of thing you'd use down in the Mediterranean. That word will get around. Kerwin's solid, however—absolutely secure."

"Good."

"When will you go, my boy?"

"When I feel ready."

Penhurst gave him a telephone number. "They'll be

waiting to hear from you. One call, and off you go. Don't dillydally for any, ahem, personal reasons, will you?"

Again, Tarp thought of Gillian. "Not for a moment."

Craik's taxi came slowly toward him, and Tarp, recognizing it, pretended to flag it down and climbed in. Along the Embankment, the man who looked like a bank clerk ran for a telephone, but he was already too late.

"There's a package on the seat for you," Craik said. "Damned pretty little stewardess person dropped it off." His manner implied all sorts of indecencies about the stewardess. Tarp slit the package and pulled out the passports that Steinberg had made for him. One had a blurred photo that was old and caucasian and that might just pass casual inspection for Arthur Beecham—whatever Arthur Beecham looked like—and the other had Tarp's face in it and identified him as a textile executive from Arras, France.

"What have you found about Dammeco, International?" Tarp said as they entered the wheel of traffic around the palace.

Craik presented his profile so they could talk. "Conglomerate, mainly energy-related tools and such. Started as a mud-drilling business in the fifties. Founded by a South African named Adrien van Damme. Didn't show a farthing's profit for a while, and then the company got very frisky. After OPEC began to act up, Dammeco had so much cash they started merging with everything that moved. Not one of the giants, mind you, but they're damned well off. Got a skyscraper in Paris; got two airlines, one a cargo outfit operating out of Singapore and one a short-run passenger line in East Africa; got three or four big blocks of mineral leases, again mostly in Africa; lots of tools and forging, offices in South Africa, Germany, Brazil, Singapore."

"Where does Hamish Penhurst fit in—how come he used a Dammeco jet to pick me up?"

"He doesn't fit in the business—not on any of the boards or anything like that. However, there was an occasion when MI-5 hired Adrien van Damme and Company—this was before they became Dammeco—back when Penhurst was first heading up MI-5."

"What for?"

"Don't know. Actually, I didn't turn up that last bit of gossip, old boy; I remember it from my own days under the old goat scrotum's aegis. I *think* we leased van Damme's cargo line for an operation in Malaysia."

"Straight operation?"

Craik glanced into the rearview mirror, his expression ironical and mocking. "We never did anything *quite* straight, Tarp. There was a faint odor to it—can't remember quite what of; they'd kicked my arse down into comptrolling by then, preparatory to cashiering me altogether, so I didn't get a lot that was going on—but there was something, something—can't quite recall it."

"Drugs?" Tarp suggested.

"By God, maybe so! How'd you come up with that?"

"There was a scandal about some MI-5 types when I was coming out of China in the mid-sixties. Word was they were ferrying opium into a pipeline that wound up in a lot of American veins. It was all hushed up, but the American version was that some private parties were making a bundle at Uncle's expense, and the British version was that they were simply supporting the price of a major cash crop from one of their former colonies and were dumping the stuff at sea. Any of that sound familiar?"

Craik smiled to show his big, bad teeth. "Dear old thing, if I'd known of a scheme like that, I'd have had a piece of it. Believe me, I was in complete ignorance—otherwise, I wouldn't be driving a taxi now. I say, you don't think the great Penhurst was involved!"

"I don't think anything." He scowled at the London

traffic. "Keep after this, will you, Eddie? Find out who Adrien van Damme was or is—find if there's any tie to Penhurst. But be careful."

"I'm never anything but, chum—never anything but."

They drove in silence for a minute. "Is that it, then?" Tarp said almost languidly.

"Only if you don't want to know about Johnnie Carrington."

Tarp leaned forward. "Damned fast work."

"Not work at all, chum. I know Johnnie Carrington. To speak to, I mean. Better than that, I was pretty close to his sainted pa." Craik's eyes met his again in the mirror. "Tommy was MI-5. He recruited me, in fact."

"And his son?"

"He's MI-5, too. Rather low on the ladder so far, and may stay there. Too nice a fellow by half, Johnnie—far too decent to get ahead; rather like one of those characters in Dickens who screws up everything and then gets rewarded at the end with a loving wife and five rosy-cheeked kiddies. Now, Tommy Carrington was a different sort altogether—lots of imagination, not too many morals, incredible stamina. Got a cross just at the end of the second war, when he was only a wee sprig of a thing. Would have had a hell of a career if he'd lived."

Tarp leaned forward again. "Line of duty?"

"No. Tacky little killing right here in Lunnun Town. Cops said he'd been done in by a pimp. Found him behind a Paki curry shop in Soho, slit from his pecker to his ears. Most incredible job with a knife I ever saw."

"You *saw* him?"

Craik was silent for some seconds. "I identified him. Cops found his MI-5 'Don't touch' card and called the office. I got sent because I was on duty and I knew him." Craik shook his head. "Never saw anything like it in my life."

"Did they get the man who did it?"

"No. Paki or Indian job, they thought. One cut, Tarp—in just below the ribs with the blade up in the heart, a twist that almost cut the heart in two, then straight down right to the pubic symphysis. You can't gut a chicken that well with one cut. They brought Tommie in on one stretcher and his guts on another."

That crude picture was Craik's way of dealing with a horror that had not left him, Tarp knew. "Is that why Johnnie's MI-5?"

"I suppose. He was in school at the time—practically still in short pants. Death made Tommie a hero, although between you and me he'd been a bit of a bastard at times. Ambitious as hell, Tommie was. Wanted to be head of the outfit and often said so."

"What did Penhurst say to that?"

"Nothing. You know Penhurst. They weren't pally, if that's what you mean. But that went way back. They'd been on an operation together at the end of the war—Tommie used to make these rather bitter, veiled remarks about it. . . ."

Tarp made a guess. "In Yugoslavia?"

"Yeah. How the hell'd you know that?"

"Coincidence." Tarp had remembered Penhurst's tale in the woods back in Maine, that story he had told to distract the two agency men. *There were three of us out there with all those Yugoslavs, and our task, you see, was to get this fellow Djadlik killed. . . .*

"There were three of them on that operation," Tarp mused.

"Really? Tommie never talked about anybody but himself and the Grand Cham Hamish."

"No matter. Two men who didn't like each other from the first, I suppose. Odd. I've always liked Hamish—can't put myself in the place of somebody who didn't. Odd." He gestured toward a street corner. "Pull over, will you? I'll walk back from here." Tarp stepped out of the cab and then thought better of it. "Go after more details on van Damme. I don't like mysteries. Put somebody else on it to help out, if you need to. Got somebody good?"

"If you don't mean 'good' in the moral sense. It'll cost you."

"Do it."

Craik grinned up at him, his ruined face a devilish, merry mask in the early evening light. "You're rather a lot like Tommie Carrington, you know? Straight as a seam and mean as sin—and you never let go." Craik looked down the empty street. "Always chasing trivia." He put the taxi into gear. "See you round the 'varsity, old thing." He accelerated away as if he were starting a grand prix race, his arm in the air like a signal.

Tarp walked slowly toward Cavendish Square. He made his mind empty because nothing made very much sense.

Gillian was going out to other debutantes' parties. As she seemed inevitably to be before such evenings, she was excited and pleased and more beautiful than ever. Tonight it angered him that she liked what was to him wasteful frivolity.

"Enjoy yourself," he said churlishly as she was leaving his room to dress.

"Oh, do come with me!" she sang.

"God forbid."

"You'd be awfully welcome, you really would! You're an ideal extra man!"

"I may have that put on my tombstone."

"Are you angry with me, darling? You look angry."

"My suit's at the cleaner's. No, I'm not angry. I'm—thinking about something else." It was like the first time he had seen her; by forcing himself to turn away from his annoyance he could see her youth, her remarkable radiance. "I'm being stupid. You go out and have a wonderful time."

She kissed him. "I've got to dress. Did I tell you Johnnie Carrington's picking me up?"

"No." He was quite casual. The warning signal had sounded in his head again. "His idea?"

"Oh, yes, he *begged*!" She turned away. "Forgive me, darling. I've got to dash."

"Gillian!" She looked back at him, perhaps startled by the violence of his voice. More quietly, he said—for he had been about to tell her he was going away, and he had caught himself only in time—"Have you still got my gun?"

"Of course. Why?"

"I just wanted to know it was safe."

"It's under my clean panties—safe as the Bank of England!"

He watched her hurry out; she left a dizzying scent behind her. Tarp packed the Chinese suit and the shoes and glasses; in his bathroom, he hacked at his hair with a pair of scissors, giving it the look of an uncut lawn, and then he dyed the remaining hair black. When he heard Gillian pass the room, he went quietly to the corridor and then to the top of the stairs so that he could look down into the large foyer where he had first seen her.

Johnnie Carrington, in evening clothes, was waiting for her. He was grinning foolishly. "Oh, I *say*!" Tarp heard the young man exclaim as she came toward him. *But he's not such a fool,* Tarp thought. *Not by half*. He watched the young man's pleasure as he took her arm. Coldly, Tarp was appraising the likelihood that Johnnie Carrington was more interested in Gillian's grandfather than in Gillian herself. *Following in his father's footsteps. Studying his father's enemy*. Tarp turned back to his room.

He was wondering just what had happened a generation ago in Yugoslavia when Penhurst and Carrington and some third man had betrayed a *partizan* to the Nazis.

"I'm going out, Mrs. Duffus."

"Very good, sir."

"Don't wait up for me. I have my key." In fact, he had copies of Gillian's keys to the garage and the security system, made without her knowledge.

"Very good, sir. Good night, sir."

He walked through the dark streets, already experiencing that heightened awareness that was the preparation for action. He felt alert, energized, impatient. Already, he was putting Gillian into a little compartment far back in his consciousness.

He found a coin box and dialed the number in Washington that Hacker had forced on him.

"Nine, two, five, seven thousand," a woman's voice said. "Go ahead."

"I've got a message for Hacker."

"Yes, all right. Go ahead, please."

"Tell Hacker that his friend from Maine is going on a cruise. He plans to do some diving. He'll be in touch from Cyprus."

"Thank you, sir."

Tarp hung up. He stood in the silent telephone booth. *How stupid is Hacker?* he wondered. His life seemed suddenly plagued by questions: How smart is Johnnie Carrington? What happened in Yugoslavia? What is Dammeco, International? He seemed to be allowing questions to intrude that were not, at least on the surface of things, relevant to his mission. He had a disciplined mind that seldom allowed such wandering. The experience allowed for two possible conclusions: either he was losing his discipline, or the questions were so important—despite the appearance of irrelevance—that they could not be ignored.

Tarp made an impatient gesture. He took out the card that Penhurst had given him earlier and dialed a number.

"Good evening."

"Business call."

"Identify."

Tarp read the numbers from the card. There was a pause of several seconds, then the voice on the other end said, "Identity accepted. Message?"

"Go."

He hung up. Thirteen minutes later, he was speeding north through London's evening streets toward a military airfield.

chapter six

Dropping through the night sky was like being born again. He had no sense of place or will, only that fall through darkness with the air hissing in his ears like blood; and then he opened the chute and the thin fabric trailed behind him like a veil of blood trailing from the gills of a wounded fish. There was the familiar hard tug at the harness and then he was swinging slowly below the open parachute.

He let go of the drop pack and paid the cord through his gloved fingers until the bag swung in its own shorter arcs thirty feet below him. He looked up. There was only lack of light; the dark chute blocked out the paler black of the overcast sky.

The Hedgehopper aircraft was already gone. In order to drop him, it had roared to altitude and cut its engines to glide sharply down, banking at once when he was clear. He dropped toward China; it glided back toward India.

He could smell China now. The odors rose as if to

welcome him, dung and dust, pine and standing water. He was dropping out of the new world and into his childhood, out of time and into memory—out of the luxury of Gillian into the rigor of his infancy.

The drop pack hit the ground and its automatic release let go. Tarp relaxed himself for contact. He hit, rolled, came up.

Black-gloved hands pulled in the lines like fisherman's hands hauling nets; they gathered the billowing black fabric, which wanted to cup the air and which, holding it still, erupted between his arms in huge blisters. Punching them down, he bundled the parachute into an unruly mass and lay on it to force out its captive air. When it was under control, he touched a button on a small box attached to the front of his black jump suit; a light winked on the drop bag a hundred feet away.

Tarp rolled the parachute up. It made a small package—smaller than the roll of clothes in the drop bag. He took off the jump suit and put on the Chinese clothes he had tried on at Penhurst's; when he buttoned the jacket, he realized that his hands were trembling and his arms were weak. *China. Old mother.* He had to stop to urinate. *Excitement. My God, I'm like a kid.*

He checked the things to be left in the bag—map case and maps; emergency food for two days; the little rifle, with full clips and a hundred extra rounds; the pistol, one full clip and twenty extra rounds; the two grenades. He put the parachute into the bag and zipped it shut. In Chinese characters on the outside of the bag it said, GOVERNMENT USE ONLY. DO NOT TOUCH. LEAVE THIS BAG AS YOU FOUND IT. Many people would obey that instruction.

He had landed in an area of rolling, scrub-covered hills that were marked at irregular intervals by pine forest. There were vast expanses of open land in western China, and nomadic herdsmen still used them. Half a dozen miles away was a village with farms run by a peasant collective—or so said Hamish Penhurst's intelligence—but the drop area was grazing land. The chance of anything's being found was small; nonetheless, Tarp buried the bag carefully. A hundred yards away, he implanted a tiny, transistorized directional beacon that would respond to a signal from a button inside his scruffy briefcase. The beacon would lead him back to the bag when he needed it again.

From a low knoll, he saw the glow of the distant town. He made mental note of it and of the winking red signal far across the wasteland where the railroad ran. He knew he could find his way back.

He headed toward the town. Two roads and the railway met there.

"Priority," he said in Chinese. He needed no reminder to use the old language. It was enough to be there, to see the familiar Oriental faces; language came like water from a spring.

He kept any hint of officiousness from his voice. He displayed a document that said that he was to be accorded level-seven priority.

"Thank you, Comrade Xiang." The haggard station master had already thanked him four times. The rudeness of the Cultural Revolution seemed to have given way to a new courtesy, to Tarp's slight surprise. In turn, he tried to be polite himself. "Thank you," he said.

The station master was a harried, skinny man who looked as if he was dying of some degenerative disease. His hands trembled. He panted for breath. Yet he had a face of compelling intelligence and sensitivity that was not at all compatible with his job, as if imminent death had transformed him into a poet. "I can do nothing for you, comrade, until the Achievement of All the People comes through at nine-seven." Tarp understood that the Achievement of All the People was a fast freight.

The station master raised his pained eyes. "A place can be made for you in the soldiers' car."

"So long as I am at Qer-Li today."

"Oh, yes. Yes. The Achievement of All the People reaches Qer-Li at four-thirty-one. As for your car, comrade—."

Tarp waved the fingers of his right hand impatiently. It was a gesture he had learned from the teacher of a revolutionary school when he was nine—the gesture of a harried functionary. "Not my car; the People's car. As for what is to be done about it, that is not your affair." He had told the station master that his car had broken down outside town.

"No." The station master seemed relieved.

"To each of us, the task he has been given," Tarp rasped. He pointed a finger at this sick man as if accusing him of having betrayed the maxim.

"Yes, yes, of course. Would you like to rest in my office until the train arrives, comrade?"

Tarp jerked himself erect. "Surely that will interfere with your work, Station Master!"

"Ah, no—no—that is, not this once—."

"Your office was given to you, I am sure, to make work efficient. For me to use it 'this once' would make you less efficient. Unless you did not need the office in the first place."

Perhaps, having seen the face of death, the station master had become patient with such bureaucratic silliness. "There is a waiting room," he said quietly.

"Good." Tarp picked up his briefcase and his bag. "Show me the toilet first."

Tarp was grateful for this chance to practice Comrade Xiang Bo-jok before he had to face someone more dangerous than the station master. Tarp felt that he knew Comrade Xiang very, very well: an upper-level bureaucrat, a few years past the age for promotion into the highest echelons and therefore just a bit officious, a stickler for form and a rather tedious spouter of the most conventional sort of wisdom. Comrade Xiang walked with a slight stoop; Comrade Xiang had the habit of wrinkling his nose as if at a bad smell and of looking up at the ceiling every minute or so; Comrade Xiang was just slightly unkempt because he wanted to show everybody, and especially those below him, that he had no reactionary ambitions toward elegance.

Comrade Xiang Bo-jok was a senior inspector with the National Program of Energy Physics. His papers were perfectly in order; his clothes were right; he was perfectly convincing—even to the shoulder bag that he carried, which had been made in Japan and which he would tell anyone who asked had been a gift from co-workers at his last promotion. The bag was now a little seedy because his last promotion had been some years ago.

Tarp—or Comrade Xiang—sat alone in the waiting room with his brief case on his knees and his shoulder bag next to him. Peasants on their way to the next town eyed him covertly. He was a different physical type from them and therefore an outsider—and therefore a curiosity. They told each other that he was from the north, from Manchuria or even Korea. Women held their children back from going too close to him, and when one child backed against his knee, its mother ran forward to rescue it.

Tarp paid no attention. Yet he followed everything that went on around him. These people wrenched his heart—it was that simple. He had not been in China in fourteen years, and then he had been in the coastal cities. These people and this country were like the China of his childhood.

Think of something else! he scolded himself. He tried to think of Gillian. He could not call up her face; he could not even think what hour of the day it would be in London. Was she sleeping? Laughing, still dancing at the party? Had she found another lover already? It was no good; even trying to imagine her with somebody else was not powerful enough to distract him from this vivid China that so assaulted him.

Think of something else! He tried to imagine the murder that Craik had told him about—Johnnie Carrington's father. *Brought him in on one stretcher, his guts on another*. The story disturbed him, not because of its gory detail but because of its connection, however faint, with Penhurst. Yet he was sure that Penhurst need never have stooped to murder to remove a rival for the leadership of MI-5. *But it was such a long time ago*. Then he thought of himself, sitting there trying to suppress his own memories of China. *It never matters how long ago it was. Past is present.*

"Comrade Xiang!"

He had almost swung into sleep. He tried to stare at the station master as a sleepy Xiang would have stared, openmouthed, cross.

"The Achievement of All the People is here, comrade."

"Ah."

There was a bad taste in his mouth. He had been sitting with his head fallen to the side and now there was a pain in his neck. Perhaps the station master had had the pleasure of seeing Comrade Xiang almost asleep with his mouth open like a peasant, his head twisted painfully to one side. Tarp hoped that he had.

The station master held out a flat metal box. "The comrade will need nourishment," he said apologetically. The box was made of aluminum, two nested rectangles held together by metal clips. It was a little lunchbox.

"I have an account for my food," Tarp said in Xiang's harsh Han dialect.

"It is from the railroad kitchen." The station master blinked at him. "There is plenty."

Tarp muttered something mean-spirited about waste, but he put the box into his shoulder bag with a grudging thank you. "Tea?" he demanded.

"The soldiers will have tea on the train."

"Good." Then, like any good bureaucrat when he has

been treated well, he bestowed a feeble compliment. "This is a properly run station. I will put it in my report."

The station master looked around the ugly room. "Thank you," he said so softly that the words hardly reached Tarp's ear.

The soldiers of the freight train's guard unit were not very impressed by Comrade Xiang. They ignored him, in fact; he had to ask for tea, and although it was brought to him the first time he asked, he had to get the second cup himself. He drank it and ate the station master's lunch, rice and crisp, fresh vegetables, tastier than anything he had found in London. As he ate, the officer in charge of the guard unit glanced at his papers.

"You are not from this province," the officer said. He wore the red stars of the army on his standing collars, but no other mark of rank. Such was the People's Army, where a private and a colonel were uniformed exactly alike—except, of course, they were not, for everybody was able to tell them apart with ease.

"Obviously not," Tarp grunted.

"Going to Qer-Li."

"I am."

"About the prison hospital? Funny business that. Eh? Oh, don't look so shocked; you're the third one to go look at the place since the fire. If it was a fire. Eh? Funny, funny business." His eyes met Tarp's. Tarp—as Xiang—gave nothing back, not the faintest admission that he was indeed going to the prison hospital about "funny business." The officer persisted. "I went out there the next morning, you understand. We're barracked there—in the town, not out at the prison. They called us in, naturally. I was one of the first on the scene."

Tarp looked at him, wiping a crumb of rice from his lower lip.

There was no silencing the officer. "I will tell you what I think it was, comrade." He was one of those men who loved his own pet theories. "It was a meteorite." He seemed proud to know the word, the concept of meteorite. He sat back against the hard railway bench and held up Tarp's papers to shield his eyes from the light. "What kind of thing is it, when you get destruction without explosives, eh? I am not guessing, you understand; I am speaking from considerable experience. What am I to think when I am shown a building knocked to pieces and a long trench in the ground leading up to it? Eh? A meteorite, exactly! Just what I think, too. Because"—he leaned toward Tarp—"there was lots of heat, lots of noise, but no explosive. Everything falling in, nothing blowing out. Meteorite."

He waited for a response. Tarp merely looked at him.

The officer stood up. He grabbed a seat back because of the swaying of the train. "Your silence is commendable, comrade. You should be in military intelligence." He held out Tarp's papers. "These are in order. Thank you." He gave a cursory salute. He had the professional's disdain for civilians, a disdain that was probably increased by the great distance from Peking. The Chinese military still carried memories of the old warlords like secret, pornographic photos in a wallet—forbidden fruit, the stuff of dreams.

Tarp said carefully, "Thank you, Commandant. Your theory will be given careful attention."

The officer swayed over him. He gave a small snort of laughter and swayed away up the aisle, chuckling ambiguously. Two minutes later, he was bellowing at several of his men about something quite different.

The train strained to reach thirty miles an hour across the desolate terrain. Two diesel engines were pulling a mile of freight cars; they seemed to stop at every signal and road. Once they backed up for twenty minutes, then went forward in a series of neck-snapping jerks. Yet it all seemed to be routine. The soldiers were calm, and the train pulled into Qer-Li at the time the station master had said it would. There was sudden activity around Tarp and the car began to empty. Soldiers carrying duffle bags pushed out the rear door; thirty seconds later, other soldiers—their replacements—came in the front, slinging bags into the overhead racks and flinging themselves into empty seats as if they had been knocked there by unkind destiny.

The officer went out last, shepherding ahead of him one of the men he had been scolding, who was laden with files. "This is your stop, too, comrade," he said.

"I know." Tarp rose, adjusting his glasses. "Civilians should not get in the way of the People's Army."

"And why not? They're slow and crude, most of them." The officer looked disgusted. "Intellectuals, a lot of them. The stupidest people in the world, intellectuals—especially when they're eighteen. All they dream of is getting their hands on a pair of American cowboy pants."

Blue jeans? Tarp thought. *Well, if Pepsi-Cola comes, can jeans be far behind?* He almost smiled. The young men pleased him in their wonderful, bumbling innocence about cowboys and America.

Tarp fell in behind the officer. "I have been giving your meteorite theory much thought, Commandant," he said, keeping his voice low as if it was important that no one else hear. "I have to look at the evidence myself, of course. But it is very—tantalizing. Was anything seen out there?"

The officer climbed down the steps of the railroad coach, his arms so full of papers that he could not hold on to the steep rails, forcing him to go awkwardly like a lame, old man. "Like what?"

"A streak of light—fire in the sky?"

"Some peasants reported a bright blue light that lasted for several seconds." He shrugged. "But you know—peasants—eh?"

Tarp cleared his throat. " 'The common wisdom of the workers is the thinker's star,' " he quoted.

The officer nodded but looked unhappy. Gazing at the roof of the concrete-block station, he said, "Half of them intellectuals and half of them morons. Find me some wisdom there!"

"I would like your idea in a memo," Tarp said. "I know you officers are busy men—overworked. . . ."

He had found the commandant's vanity. The man nodded and then said generously, "Like you, I am sure, comrade."

Tarp lowered his voice again. He pretended not to notice a bulging file that was slipping farther and farther from its place inside the officer's left elbow. "I wonder sometimes, Commandant, if people without war experience even understand what real work is."

The officer jammed his elbow against his ribs. "You served in—?"

"Korea," Tarp lied.

"Combat?"

"Liaison with the Soviets. Translator. I have a little Russian in me, as you can see." He put out a hand and caught the file just as it was about to tumble loose, hugged it to his own chest in a gesture meant to emphasize his sense of inferiority to the officer.

"Ah, I wondered. No offense. But your eyes, I thought, maybe Manchurian—."

"Many people think Uzbek." Tarp did not elaborate. "I must be going on. Let me help you with these files as far as your car."

They trudged across a dry gravel parking area that had been raked that day so that the curving sweeps of the rakes had left a pattern like that left by a mason's trowel in wet plaster. There were only four vehicles in sight—three military trucks and a Russian-made command car.

"You are being met?" the officer asked.

"I had my own vehicle, but it broke down. I had better find a telephone."

"Going out there tonight?"

"Time is essential in my work."

The officer pursed his lips. "I can get you a car. You

know what military vehicles are like—not spoiled by civilian limousines, eh?"

Tarp heard experience with other spoiled civilians in that statement. Other inspectors had come through, of course, other civilians who had demanded cars and who had complained about rough rides and surly drivers. "I can ride a motorcycle, if need be," he said in Comrade Xiang's proudest voice.

"No need for that. Get in." They piled the papers on the seat between them. As the car began to move the officer said, "How many copies of my meteorite theory would you like?"

Tarp was given a twelve-year-old Ziv sedan that looked like a 1950 Buick; with it came a military driver whose coastal accent was so strong that Tarp had trouble at first understanding him. The driver was big but young, a child in a man's body, and he was outspoken about not liking having been called out from his warm barracks. A few words from the officer silenced him, however.

"One of our morons," the commandant said. "The only thing that would have been worse is if they had given you one of our intellectuals. What ever happened to soldiers?" He was holding a pen that had been made in Rumania. "When will you be back? Tomorrow? I have to write that idiot a set of orders."

"The day after, at the earliest. I will send him and the car back."

"No need. I will put him on detached duty to you for three days. And put him to work when you get out there—send him out with the peasants to delouse their cattle. He needs educating." The officer made marks on a form and put it into an envelope. "My report will be ready when you come back."

"I look forward to it." Tarp gave a civilian version of a salute. He snapped at the driver, who clashed the gears together as if he were playing cymbals, and the car moved off as jerkily as the train had.

Some miles into the empty country beyond the town, Tarp tried to remember what distractions had entertained his mind when he had first landed. Those first hours seemed very long ago now—a story told to him by somebody else. It was as if he had seen the parachute drop in a film, had read somewhere of the station master, who must be long since dead by now.

Gillian. She returned to him with a little shock. She seemed like fiction now, too.

He let her go. He was entirely in China now, past and present. He was home.

chapter seven

"Welcome to the Qer-Li Departmental Center for the Correction of Social Incorrigibles, Comrade Xiang. I am Do Qing, deputy chief administrator. The chief administrator is occupied just at this time and begs your forgiveness a hundred times that he is prevented by such a press of work for the good of the People that he cannot meet you in his own person firsthand."

Miss Do was a hunched, fierce woman in her forties with passionate eyes behind magnifying eyeglasses, and a body that looked as if it had been shaped by angry and disagreeable forces. A small dowager's hump already marked her shoulders; her mouth was pushed forward as if by pressure on her cheeks; one hip was a little higher than the other so that she walked with an awkwardness that suggested suppressed pain. Throughout her little speech, she had kept her face raised to Tarp's as if he was expected to bend down and kiss her.

"I appreciate the chief administrator's diligence and hope that all of us are such models in our devotion to the work of the Revolution," he said dutifully. "Anyway, we are too easily corrupted by empty forms of courtesy."

They shook hands. "You came by train," she said.

"My car broke down beyond Cherchen."

"I saw a military car, I think."

"The People's Liberation Army were sensible of the importance of my mission."

She gave him an abrupt nod and began to hobble quickly along a corridor. The bad hip rose with each step and she had to swing her right leg out to the side to plant the foot for the next step. She would be, Tarp knew, bad-tempered and harsh in her judgments, as people in pain were justified in being.

"You were not expected," she said.

Tarp said nothing. Mr. Xiang was the sort who made visits that were not expected.

"We have no fancy lodgings," she said. She was breathing hard from her exertion but she did not slow down; they went out a door and down four concrete steps to a paved yard. A cold wind was gusting through it as the night came on and the temperature dropped.

"Snow tonight," Tarp muttered.

"You know Sinkiang then," she said. She laughed harshly. "The snow was over that doorway six weeks ago!"

"I know the province only by reputation."

"I know it by experience." She pulled at the handle of a heavy metal door and wrestled it open before Tarp could help her, and as she went through it blew against her and pushed her shoulder into the steel jamb, and she cried out. When Tarp came through, he saw a face set in rage against the world. "I am sure you will want to meet your colleague as soon as possible," she said maliciously.

Comrade Xiang offered a baffled smile.

"From the Geophysical Phenomena Center at Yü-men. I would think one inspector would be enough and you could share reports, but nobody cares what I think."

"We have no common criteria," Tarp muttered.

They walked down a dimly lighted corridor where their heels clanged on metal grating and unpainted concrete block flung the sound back at them. Tarp saw neither prisoners nor guards; the atmosphere was more that of a deserted factory than a prison.

"Where are the prisoners?" he asked.

"Women to the south, men to the north. The factory block in between." She led him up flights of stairs with iron-pipe railings. Everything was quiet, seemingly deserted. He saw a metal gate through the grilled glass of a door, and beyond it, solid metal doors standing open to reveal cells within. She saw his curiosity and said, "We used to have twenty-seven-hundred prisoners. Now we have eleven hundred and fourteen. We will get no new ones, is the decision at the central administration." She was panting, but she managed to laugh again unpleasantly. "This is the terminal station of the system. We release nobody, except to death."

The Qer-Li prisoners were incorrigibles because they were politically impossible. Revolutionary society had no place for them—the old, the foreign, the out-of-date. The regime would not send them to the firing squads but would let them die, like an unwanted, vanishing species.

Arthur Beecham would be an incorrigible—an embarrassing vestige, a small, no longer dangerous dinosaur.

"Your prisoners are old, then," Tarp said.

"Most of them. Still, they cause trouble. Sex!" She wrinkled her nose in disgust—a child of Mao and the Cultural Revolution. "It never stops with some of them. An intelligent person has enough of that at a certain age, but I can tell you from bitter experience, for some of them, intelligence does not function."

"Well," Tarp said placatingly, "old men—."

"Old women!" she cried. "Old women are the worst! They play with themselves, did you know that about old women? We have to put tranquilizers in all the food. It has cut factory production, but what can we do? The chief administrator agrees with me on this point absolutely!"

Somebody else had been talking to him about old women and sex. *Who?* He remembered; Steinberg, the man who had made the passports. *Only day before yesterday. No, more because of the time change. But it seems like years. . . .*

One block of the top floor had been converted to Spartan guest rooms by painting the concrete block white and replacing the steel prisoners' bunks with hard wooden beds. The sense of imprisonment was still strong. A photograph of Deng Xiaoping brooded down from one wall. Mao's red book, once as common in such places as the Bible in American motel rooms, was missing.

"The staff dining room and kitchen are closed," she said. "I can have food sent up, if you must eat. Cold food."

"No tranquilizers in it, I hope?" He tried it out as a bureaucratic joke. She gave him a sour smile, like a drop of acid rain. "The staff kitchen does not put tranquilizers in the staff's food. The chief administrator is married."

"There is no need for me to eat."

"I will have cold food sent up. If I do not, I will be criticized."

"I do not need food."

"Then leave it."

He tried to make another bureaucratic joke. "Then *I* will be criticized."

She was quite serious. "Yes, the man from Geophysical Phenomena might put it in his report. The toilet is down the corridor; you can flush it down there." Tarp took this advice as a sign that she approved of him.

"Thank you," he said.

"You are welcome a thousand times. I advise you not to stay up late. Our day begins at five—a bell will ring."

"That will be helpful in getting up."

"Indeed. Good night, comrade."

"May the Revolution prosper," he said.

"What? Oh, yes." She hobbled away, rubbing her bruised shoulder. She had been stuffed full of injustice.

In the morning there was snow in the courtyard, and by daylight there were already a hundred prisoners there with brooms, sweeping it away. The bitter wind, blowing colder now, kept sweeping it back behind them as if it were a broom, too, but they came stubbornly on, this sweeping of endless snow a metaphor for their lives.

A copy of the *People's Daily* arrived with a bowl of steaming rice and a few flecks of gray, salt fish. He ate greedily. The food was the food of his childhood—but better than the food of his childhood had been. *Once Mao himself tousled my hair while I was eating. He said, "The children of hunger will grow up strong." He meant those of us who survived.* Tarp ate and read the newspaper, which was as dull as any newspaper anywhere. He wondered if there could be, in fact, "news" anymore.

"I have set up a tour of the prison for you," Comrade Do said.

"Yes. I want to see the site of the accident, of course."

"I supposed you wanted to see the whole prison, so you could make comparisons. I know *I* would!"

"Just so." Tarp raised his collar against the wind, for they were standing in an open doorway by the immense courtyard. "Yes, a tour will be fine."

"You want to meet your colleague from Geophysical Phenomena first."

"Oh? Oh, of course I do." He sighed. She smiled. She knew that two bureaucrats on more or less the same mission would despise each other. It pleased her to push them together.

A man came toward them across the courtyard. He was walking the long diagonal from a doorway that she had pointed out as that of the administration offices. The sweepers were gone, and the man was isolated in the midst of that field of concrete. He was either a very plump man or he was very heavily dressed because of the weather; as he came closer he proved to be both plump and swaddled. He had round cheeks that looked shiny, as if with grease or sweat, and his round face was framed comically in a fur-lined hat that came down over his ears and met his upturned, padded collar. He looked roly-poly and almost jolly.

Tarp supposed that the man was, like him, an operative.

"So!" the man exclaimed, exactly as if he were an Oriental in a Hollywood film—Charlie Chan's number-two son. "Ah, so, Miss Do!" He giggled.

"Here is Mr. Xiang of the Energy Physics Program," she said to the plump man in a voice that suggested that they were sharing a joke.

"Yes. Yes!" The man shouted the word. He pumped Tarp's hand enthusiastically. "Terrible weather here—terrible! You should see it at Yü-men—it's worse!" he giggled wildly.

"This is Mr. Qiu Bo-da, from Yü-men," she murmured. They all stood with their hands clasped in front of them as if they were about to have a group photo taken. Tarp decided it would be a good idea to shake hands with Qiu again and they did so, smiling and nodding. They might have been two men demonstrating how the Chinese have taken to the Western custom of shaking hands.

"So," Tarp said. There was a silence. "We have something in common, comrade."

"Yes. Yes," Qiu said. He smiled. *He knows I'm a fake,* Tarp thought. Qiu himself was too good to be true, however—he seemed so clearly to be impersonating somebody that it was unimaginable that he could be as false as he seemed.

"Like me, Comrade Qiu, you are here because of this, um, incident."

"Oh, yes."

"What do you make of it?"

Qiu giggled. He tossed his head almost girlishly and glanced at Miss Do as if something very naughty had been said. Tarp pressed on. "I have heard it suggested that a meteorite hit this place."

There was no containing Comrade Qiu's merriment. Tarp wanted to smother the man in his padded clothes.

"*Not* a meteorite, in your view, I take it," Tarp growled.

"Could be. Could be." Qiu giggled. Miss Do did not join him, however, and he desisted.

"Well," Tarp said, "I am glad to have this scientific chat." He clapped his gloved hands together. "I believe I am ready for the tour now, Comrade Do. Comrade Qiu, will you join us?"

"Oh, I had my tour yesterday!" Qiu smiled. "I am ready to write my report." He bowed. "I leave you to your investigations, Comrade Xiang."

Tarp bowed. "I leave you to your report, Comrade Qiu."

They walked away in opposite directions. When Tarp looked over his shoulder, he found that Qiu was looking over his shoulder at him. Tarp wanted to wink, but he doubted that it would carry at that distance.

An aged prisoner was assigned him as a guide. A guard went along as well—it seemed to Tarp that the guard alone would have sufficed, but he guessed that this was a way of keeping the prisoner busy—and it was actually the prisoner who hectored them along, nagging the guard about opening doors and boring Tarp with unwanted data.

The prison was as big as some towns, although drastically underpopulated now; the factory still had its own railroad siding. The machinery was antiquated, some of it belt-driven as if it might at one time have been water-powered. An enormous foundry building was quite empty.

They climbed to the top of a central water tower. There were rooms up there that had once been used by administrators and guards, but they were unused now The guard jangled his keys impatiently, but the prisoner droned on and on.

"What is that building?" Tarp asked. He was drowsy and bored.

"The laundry."

"And that?"

"Guards' housing. Guards' family housing, that is; unmarried guards are over there beyond the—"

"And that? The long building beyond the wall?"

"That is the Slum."

"What is the Slum?"

A wisp of white moustache fell over the grinning old mouth. "My woman lives there. Children. Dogs. Prisoners' people."

It looked like a squatters' town anywhere in the world. There were wood fires burning in the open, clothes hung to dry, a confusion of temporary walls. Beyond the building itself was a high fence with guard towers.

"Then they're prisoners, too," Tarp said.

"Oh, yes. Yes. But they choose to be."

"How often do you see your woman?"

"Visiting days."

"How often are you with her alone?"

"Oh, never. That is not allowed. But she sends in food for me and washes my clothes, and we talk through the fence."

They left the tower. On the long climb down, Tarp had time to think about living voluntarily in this unkind climate, a willing prisoner in a squatters' hovel. The idea was not pleasant.

* * *

Whatever phenomenon had destroyed the prison's hospital had been selective and almost neat. Unlike a conventional explosion, which would have caused progressively less damage away from the center, this had been virtually total for as far as it had reached—and then it had simply ended. There had been fire beyond the principal area of destruction, to be sure, but most of that had been quickly put out, and Tarp could see where the fire had been merely secondary. The main area of destruction looked as if it had been blown apart by a long chain of very small charges, all except for one large section of a cell block that looked as if it had been cut with a hot knife, leaving walls with uneven, shiny surfaces of melted rock and concrete.

Melted, he mused. That was the report that Hamish Penhurst had received. *Melted stone*.

The damage had been done in a long, almost rectangular zone whose midpoint seemed to be the hospital's emergency-generator shed. The shed itself was undamaged, curiously, but deep scars had been gouged in the pavement on both sides of it, while to the east, the hospital wing and the cell block had been obliterated, and to the west a length of twelve-foot-high stone wall and a section of barbed wire beyond it had simply disappeared. The pattern was explained, it seemed, by the commandant's meteorite theory, for at first glance it did look as if something had crashed in from the west, taking out the barbed wire and the wall and then slamming into the hospital wing.

"Do you believe it was a meteorite?" Tarp asked Miss Do, who had come along for this part of the inspection.

"I think nothing," she said. "I was not here at the time."

"But you have read the guards' and prisoners' reports."

"They contradict each other."

"Could it have been some kind of escape?" Tarp

asked. She snorted. "Seventeen prisoners are missing," he said.

"Yes—our oldest and feeblest, eleven of them bedridden in the hospital. How do you suppose they would have got through the outer perimeters of wire? It is still intact!" She folded her arms, closing herself like a book. "There are land mines out there. None of them went off."

They walked down to the emergency-generator shed. There were two large jet engines inside that had been reworked to drive a generator. "Big engines," he said idly.

"From a Russian IL-28."

"Lots of electrical power."

She shrugged. "Our electricity goes off every time it snows."

"The engines were hot when the guards got here after the, um, incident," he said.

She cackled. "*Everything* was hot!" she cried.

He stood at the end of the generator shed and looked to the right and then to the left—first toward the melted edges of the hospital wing and then toward the gap in the high wall, across which barbed wire had been crisscrossed since the event. The exposed edges of the stone wall were like those of the hospital walls, shiny, waxlike. Tarp stood there for several minutes.

He might have stood just here. Having trouble with the weapon—whatever it was, if it existed—gouging the pavement there and there—blasting the hospital wing. . . . But why? Why? And then, after that, yes, could be that his power was failing, or he turned the power down maybe. Yes, that's why the edges melted instead of exploding, less power; yes, after the hospital, he turned the weapon on that wall, gouging the pavement in that direction because he couldn't aim the weapon very well. Cutting his way out through the wall and through one wire fence. And then. . . .

It could have happened. If there is such a thing as a

particle beam. If Arthur Beecham really invented one and was really here.

"I would like to see the files of the missing prisoners," he said to Miss Do.

Miss Do was relieved when, an hour later, he excused himself, taking several of the files with him. She had two new clerks and she wanted to bully them in private, so she was glad to get rid of him. It was the end of the mid-afternoon rest period; he could hear the prisoners moving in slow march-step to their afternoon adjustment lecture. They were incorrigible; they had been abandoned; but they were made to sit twice each day through lectures on the political philosophy that they had already been judged incapable of understanding.

Tarp shook his head.

A guard led him around the high wall that loomed over the scant remains of the hospital and the cell block and down to the gap in the stone wall. Tarp looked carefully at the gap and at the barbed wire that had been strung across to fill it. The hole was big enough for two trucks to drive through side by side. *If this was Arthur Beecham's particle beam, he certainly couldn't control it very well.* Tarp looked through the wire at the gap that had been melted in the first fence.

"Take me to the Slum," he said to the guard.

The guard was not stupid, but he was stubborn. Perhaps he had been sent to Qer-Li because, like his prisoners, he was incorrigible—narrow-minded, mulish, utterly unimaginative. "There was no damage at the Slum," he said. It was like hearing a cow speak.

"That is correct," Tarp said. Comrade Xiang made it very clear that he did not take advice from stupid guards. "Take me there at once. That is an order."

The guard wore a gray uniform that was exactly like the green uniform of the People's Liberation Army. It was rumpled and it did not fit very well. His Kalshnikov sub-machine gun was brightly polished and very efficient-looking, however. He drew great comfort from that weapon, Tarp saw, for now, ordered to do something he did not want to do by a civilian, he gripped the gun more tightly.

Still, he obeyed the order.

They trudged stolidly back along the high wall. Tarp could smell wood fires. The wind had shifted and the sky was dark with snow clouds.

"Do you go to the Slum sometimes?" he asked the guard.

"I may."

"Can you get a woman at the Slum?"

"Does the comrade want a woman?"

"Certainly not! I ask if *you* get a woman there."

"I think it would be against regulations."

Tarp grunted. "I suppose you can get a sausage cooked there, though, if you take it to them. Eh? Or a fish?"

The guard said nothing as they took several paces along the wall. Then, as if he had just discovered speech, he said in a rush of words, "I shot an antelope last summer up in the forest east of here and I brought it down and me and two friends we took it to the Slum and they roasted it for us and we all ate real good." He gripped the Kalshnikov as if it were a holy relic. "I had a permit for the hunting and my officer said yes it was all right to let the Slummers cook the antelope."

Three steps more. "You are not married?"

One step. "No, comrade."

Two steps. "Tell me the truth. This will not go in my report. Man to man: do you have a woman there sometimes?"

Three steps. "Yes, comrade. My officer says it is a dialectical question, which is the greater evil, taking a Slum woman or engaging in reactionary masturbation. He says taking the woman is less an evil." The guard looked miserable. "My officer says I am an animal."

Tarp made Comrade Xiang's voice very sincere. "At a certain stage of revolutionary development, comrade—I mean, in the development of the revolutionary individual—an act that frees the mind to dwell on socialism becomes a good act, although by itself it may seem an evil act. I would suggest that in the future, each time you go to a Slum woman for relief, you engage her afterward in a dialogue on the inevitable movement of history. That way, you will convert an act that was an act of selfishness into an act that becomes part of the revolutionary struggle."

The guard actually smiled. "Do you really believe so?"

"Totally." Tarp cleared his throat. "Have you ever seen an ethnic woman at the Slum, comrade? Not Han Chinese—more like an Uzbek, maybe, or an Afghan?"

"There is one. She is no good. Nobody has her. The young girls are good."

They came to the edge of the Slum and Tarp was able to study it. At some time in the past, it had been simply a supporting building connected with the prison—perhaps a storage shed or even a garage. It looked like a large Quonset hut left over from World War II. Long since, however, other buildings had been built up against it, some of them made out of oil cans and big food cans hammered flat, some out of scrap wood. Tents of many kinds and colors of cloth had been rigged, too, and there was a confusion of structures that almost obscured the half cylinder of the original building.

Tarp saw children in rags, big-eyed and somehow placid. There were dogs and a remarkable number of cats. And there were women of all ages. The only men were off-duty guards, strolling among the fires and joking with the women.

"Where does the ethnic woman live?"

The guard shrugged. "I have not seen her in a long time. Maybe she is dead. Maybe she is inside with the old women. I never go in there."

"All right, comrade. I am going inside. You wait for

me out here. You may buy something to eat but do not find yourself a woman because I may want you."

"I am supposed to stay with you."

"No—forgive me for correcting you, comrade—you were supposed to show me whatever I needed to see. You have shown me. Now I do not need to be shown. Wait out here."

Like a well-broken horse, the guard was accustomed to yielding. "Will you explain to my officer if I am seen here?"

"Of course. I will be responsible, comrade."

Tarp walked through the Slum in the character of Xiang. Guards watched him with poorly disguised curiosity. Women moved away from him, afraid of his civilian clothes and the danger he might pose to the very fragile legitimacy of their presence in the prison. Turning the corner of the Quonset hut, Tarp almost collided with a pretty girl who started to grab his arm; for an instant, because she was very young and she was laughing, Tarp thought of Gillian Penhurst. Then the girl saw he was not a guard and she scowled and backed away.

A fat old woman tried to block his way into the building. He moved her aside with a slow, powerful push of his left arm.

The building stank. It was like a sewer.

It could have been an Indian longhouse of centuries before. There were three big, open fireplaces situated down the long axis of the building. Makeshift walls formed a wide corridor. If there were any windows, they were blocked up or hidden by the walls, and what little light there was came from the fires and from the smoke openings overhead.

Tarp moved slowly down the central corridor. He peered into each of the filthy cubicles. He saw old women who were dying of disease and loneliness and simply of time; he heard senile mumblings; he smelled fresh excrement and urine and unwashed clothes.

He kept his eye on a curtained entrance partway down the walls to his left, for it was there that the pretty girl had disappeared, only to come out again and slink away. He pretended not to have noticed.

When he got to the hanging where the girl had gone in, he put his left hand on the makeshift curtains. They were filthy and felt grainy and greasy. They were many layers thick, like the accumulated hardships of the women who lived there.

He moved the hangings aside.

A dirty woman stood in the middle of the cubicle. He knew that she had a weapon because of the way she held one hand behind her, and because of the weapon he knew that he was in the right place. He looked past her to see in the gloom a still dirtier and older woman squatting on a coarse, lumpy bag that must have served as a mattress. He was aware of crates and of drums and boxes, some with military markings in Russian and Chinese, of an oil lamp hanging from the tin-can ceiling, of a few chipped dishes on the floor.

He stepped inside and let the hangings fall.

The young woman tensed. One step more from him and she would use the weapon.

Tarp tried to ignore her. He twisted his body so that he could look around her at the old body on the mattress.

"Arthur Beecham, I presume?" he said in English.

The old face broke into a huge smile.

"There, you see!" a cracked voice said, as dry as the creaking of an old hinge. "I told you Winston would send somebody for us, Sheila."

Tarp looked at the younger woman. He spoke to her in Chinese. "You are Beecham's daughter, I think. I am a friend. I have come to help him."

He took a step to the side, not taking his eyes off her, and when his foot touched a wooden surface he bent and felt over it, found it to be a box, and sat on it. The woman never took her eyes off him, nor did she change her stance—her right hand behind her right hip, the weapon hidden by her dirty layers of clothing.

"Mr. Beecham, I've come from Hamish Penhurst," Tarp said in English. Still, his eyes were in firm contact with the woman's.

The old face broke again into a grin. "Oh, yesh." He seemed a little surprised at the English that came to his lips. He partly covered his mouth with a hand as if to hide the sounds. "I—I am afraid I have put my teeth shomeplace," he said slowly. Indeed, there were no teeth in his mouth.

"Hamish Penhurst wants me to take you home to England, Mr. Beecham."

"Oh, jolly *good*!"

Tarp smiled just as engagingly as he could.

"Hamish Penhurst would also like you to bring your particle-ray machine to England, too, if it's convenient. Could you tell me where it is, sir?"

The toothless old man who was dressed in women's clothes looked at Tarp with wonderful, wide eyes. His "S" sounds were made slushy by his lack of teeth. "You're shitting on it," he said happily.

chapter eight

The young woman had taken the old man's teeth from her pocket without a word and had withdrawn into a corner of the tiny space, leaving her still within a few feet of Tarp, whom she continued to watch with open hostility. She crouched like a frightened animal, distrustful and dangerous. All that could be seen of her face and head was an area not much larger than a fist, and it seemed to be hiding in the cave of ragged cloth with which she had swathed herself.

Arthur Beecham, after saying a few more words to Tarp in his singsong English, had put in his teeth and then fallen into a silent, dreamy trance.

Tarp looked at the woman. "You are Mr. Beecham's daughter, are you not?" he said in Chinese. She stared at him.

"I read the file in the prison," Tarp went on. "It said that he had had a daughter by a Russian wife. I guessed that you might have followed him here. It is very important that he go back to England. Will you help me get him out?"

"I will do anything to get out of this hell!" She spat the Chinese words with such passion that Tarp was shocked. Her voice was quite deep and strangely hollow, and it was almost as if the words had been spoken by another voice—perhaps a masculine one. Her accent was that of a north-central peasant, and it sounded graceless and uncouth.

A new problem, he thought. *The old man will want me to get her out, too.* "Do you speak English?" he said.

She shook her head. "Get me out of here!" she hissed in peasant dialect. *Like that guard,* Tarp thought. *Like having a dog talk. A moron,* as my friend the commandant would say.

He tried to assess what it would be like to take her with them. Her layers of clothes effectively prevented him from guessing what sort of body she had, but he hoped there was strength and solidity there, at least. Her face was pasty and uninteresting. From habit or from fear, her eyes were narrowed, and she looked very much like the Oriental peasant she seemed; she had the sullen expression of the guard. Her cheekbones were high and broad, her mouth very wide.

"Will you get me out?" she said with the same intensity.

"Of course." He was probably lying, he knew. At this stage, lying was easy. His responsibility would end with Arthur Beecham and Beecham's invention (if, in fact, there was one). Tarp had made no contract for a brute of a daughter. "Of course," he said. He smiled.

"How will you do it?" Beecham said in perfect Han Chinese.

"I am thinking about that right now."

"Good. I do not know about such things. Neither does Sheila."

"I will do the thinking. Thinking about getting out of hard places is my profession."

"What is your name?"

"Call me Xiang for now."

"And you are a subordinate of Hamish's?"

"A colleague."

"Does Hamish know I have perfected the proton beam?"

"He thought you might have."

Arthur Beecham had bright blue eyes with lines at the corners that crinkled as if he had spent a good part of his life smiling, despite imprisonment. "The beam is very crude just now," he said. "The next model will be much improved. I know already how I shall improve it."

"You fired it from the emergency-generator shed, didn't you?"

"Oh, yes! I had to have all that power, you see. As it was, the generator faltered and I only melted some things. The first model is quite, quite crude, oh, yes!"

Tarp shifted his weight and felt the splintered wood of the box under his buttocks. It was time to get moving, time to get Arthur Beecham out of China, but he had another question. "You destroyed the wall so you could be with your daughter, I know. But why did you destroy the hospital?"

"Oh, because that's where I put the accelerator and my special capacitors together! I had to leave so much behind, you know. Any intelligent scientist could have reconstructed my processes."

"In the hospital?"

"In the hospital laboratories, yes. I worked as the head technician."

"Ah." Tarp shifted his weight again, getting ready to stand up. *I may have to get rid of the woman*, he was thinking, but out loud he said, "And why did you destroy the cell block?"

"Oh, well." There was great sadness in the old voice.

"I had friends there. Their lives were quite, quite hopeless. I gave them release."

Without asking for their views in the matter. Or perhaps he did.

Tarp put his hands on the box and started to get up.

"Just stay right there, Mr. Tarp," a new voice said—in English. The filthy hangings moved and Mr. Qiu's round, oily face floated into view. He seemed less roly-poly, because he had taken off his padded overcoat so that he could roll it up and hold it in front of the PPK that he held in his left hand. He made sure that Tarp saw the pistol, and then he held the rolled-up coat in front of him so that it would serve as a crude silencer. "Hi, folks!" Qiu said brightly to Beecham and Beecham's daughter.

"She doesn't speak English," Tarp said.

"No shit!" Qiu looked at the daughter. "You're one smart fortune cookie, Tarp, I got to give you that. I been here two days and I didn't tumble to her."

"How do you know me?" Tarp's voice was a growl—a warning sign of building anger that the man who called himself Comrade Qiu was quick to notice. "I recognized you this morning. They told me you'd show up. My people, I mean." Qiu's eyes swept over the cubicle. "Where's the Buck Rogers ray gun?"

"I'm sitting on it."

Qiu giggled. "Don't shit me, man! I want it, no kidding. I want it and I want the old man, but you and the dog-faced girl don't make the trip."

"All right, I'm not sitting on it. It's parked in a garage on the other side of the prison. I hope you've got a big truck."

"No sweat. I can get three trucks if I need them. *Don't do it!*"

Tarp had shifted his weight, drawing his heels in tight against the box to get more thrust so he could move fast. Qiu had seen the move and was watching him now, but Tarp was watching Beecham's daughter, whose face showed the animal rage he had seen before. Her hand was down behind her hip again, and he knew that she was dangerous now, and he was telling himself that *Maybe two birds with one stone, maybe Qiu and the woman at the same time, maybe they'll get each other. . . .*

Tarp moved his head. The pistol swung to follow, and Beecham's daughter, sensing the movement, swirled toward the short Chinese with a speed that was as hard to follow as a martial-arts fighter's short punches. The filthy rags went into eddying movements, like buckskin fringe, and only the flash of a knife blade marred the circular patterns in shades of brown. Qiu saw that flash as the knife came from her right hip, crossed her body, and started the transfer to her left hand, and he fired once into the rolled-up coat while the gun was still pointed in Tarp's direction. The pistol made a plopping sound, as if a frog had jumped into a pool of water, and Qiu was trying to spin to his left fast enough to put the pistol into the woman's midriff.

Tarp had pushed away from the box toward Arthur Beecham. He watched Qiu and the woman with fascinated horror.

She shifted the knife into her left hand. It was moving with dazzling speed now—into Qiu's abdomen just above the navel, going up and across as she put it in with the tip elevated. Qiu yelped. She had a powerful wrist that stuck out of her rags like a thick brown branch. The knife tip rotated and the blade twisted in his heart and moved three inches in a cutting arc, slicing the heart muscle and then curving down and around so that the lower third of Qiu's heart was severed from the rest and the cutting edge was now pointed down.

Then she did the thing that horrified Tarp.

Beecham's daughter had used her right hand to fend off the pistol. Now she put that right hand on top of her left wrist and pushed down with all the strength of both hands, even rising to her toes to get more leverage, and the blade ripped down through Qiu's belly with a sound like tearing cloth.

A smell like wet grass spread in the cubicle.

Qiu's insides flowed forward to his feet like blue-green sausage. Blood began to spill over them from his lungs, the brightest and gayest red in the body.

She retreated to the rear of the cubicle to watch and to shield her father, bloody knife still in her hand.

Tarp stood up.

Qiu's eyes appealed to him. *Why?* he seemed to say. They looked down. The horror of death and the horror of that way of dying were mixed. His right hand had dropped the rolled-up coat and was flailing behind him, trying to find support on the dirty curtains; Tarp grabbed the arm and then the other shoulder, reaching around the man's back because he did not want to hold the dying man up by clutching his spilled bowels.

He spun Qiu away from the doorway and laid him down. The dying agent's legs, thumping like the tail of a fish in a boat, tangled in the mess on the floor. Tarp leaned over him.

"Who's running you?" he asked. *"Who's running you?"*

Qiu wanted to say something. He opened his mouth, but blood from his lungs filled his throat and escaped in a spray and then subsided as the last, pent-up air sighed out with an odor like leaking gas. Then he simply lay there dying, trying to guess at the answer to that same question. *Why? Why like this?*

Tarp picked up the PPK. He looked at the woman and the old man. He felt nauseated. "Get his clothes off," he said to her. "We'll need his clothes. Can you do it?"

She looked down without disgust. "Why not?" She was like the butcher who has just killed the calf with a hammer blow, like the peasant's wife who has slaughtered the pig that has lived in the house all summer.

Why not? That was her answer to Qiu's dying question. But perhaps she had some scruples, for she said in the voice of a child, "He was a bad man, was he not?"

Tarp looked down at the round face. It had turned a pasty, dusty color that was almost lavender. and all the oil seemed to have gone from the skin. He wanted to say, *We are all bad men,* but he knew she would not understand that. "I suppose he was," he said.

"A Russian, was he?" she said.

"Or American. It is all the same." He sighed. "Get his clothes off."

She had put the knife away in her clothes, and with it, the animal fierceness that had transformed her, that had made her for an instant—he had seen it—wildly beautiful. He caught her arm. It felt muscular and lean, like a man's arm. "I know how to get you out now." He jerked his head toward the doorway. "Can you trust the others?"

"Yes."

"Can they take care of the body?"

"They get rid of things so they are never found."

"Can they get a guard's uniform for us?"

"Oh, yes. How many?"

"One, only one. Get the clothes off that body and then get rid of it. And get a guard's uniform from the women." He bent over Arthur Beecham. "Are you all right, sir?"

"Oh, yes, thank you, quite all right." The old man seemed to come back from some distant place. "Did you see what my Sheila did?" He said it with wonder, twisting his head up to look at Tarp. "That was quite remarkable."

"Yes, sir. I've never seen anything like it." *But I've sure as hell heard of something like it!*

He went to the doorway. The smell of the dead man made him dizzy. "I'll be back as soon as I can. Both of you stay right here until I come back."

He went out and through the filthy building, where

crones bent over the fire pits like witches and watched him in the shifting light.

Something is wrong. Something is very, very wrong.

It made no sense at all, but he found himself wondering where Sheila Beecham had been when Tommie Carrington had been murdered with a knife thrust that had gutted him like a chicken—behind a Pakistani restaurant in London, when she had been about twelve years old.

He spent twenty minutes searching the tiny room next to his own. There was nothing there but furniture like his own and the small nylon suitcase that had been the dead man's. It had no false bottom and nothing hidden under its cheap lining, but behind the unsmiling picture of Deng Xiaoping—twin to the one in his own room—he found a set of identity papers that Qiu had brought for Arthur Beecham. Tarp pocketed them. He found, as well, a Chinese government-issue emergency kit in the suitcase, something that a scientist of a certain level might have carried. It contained squeeze-tube hypos of atropine, morphine, and an anesthetic. Tarp took that, too.

He packed his own meager belongings in the Japanese shoulder bag and put it on his cot. The PPK was in the waistband of his trousers, snug in a makeshift holster in the lining. Tarp sent for the young military driver who had brought him out from the rail head.

"Put Comrade Qiu's bag and my bags in the car. Then meet me by the southeast gate of the big courtyard."

"With the car?"

"Of course not. You can't get a car that far."

"You want me to meet you on foot?"

"Exactly." Tarp heard the driver sigh. He was very young and he was not very energetic. "Later on, we will want the car."

"Later on?"

"In an hour or two."

"But that will be evening mealtime."

"You will get fed later."

"But it will be dark then."

"You can eat after dark."

The driver sighed again. Tarp wanted to slap him. "Go get the bags and meet me by the southeast gate."

The driver moved away. Slowly.

Tarp went looking for Comrade Do. She was still bullying the new file clerks, who looked harried and who were, he thought, already looking for reasons to quit. "A million pardons for interrupting you at your work, Comrade Do! Much as it grieves me—."

"What is it?"

"Comrade Qiu and I will be leaving. We have decided to, um, join forces. 'Two dogs that pull together can do the work of an ox,' and so on."

"You will require a prison vehicle?"

"No. He will go with me in my military car. We think, um, we will make the most of time and gasoline in this, um, difficult era."

"I thought you went in opposite directions."

"The situation has changed."

Comrade Do looked pleased. "The chief administrator has not had an opportunity to offer you a meal in his apartment."

"My grief is without boundaries, but time is, um, the lubricant of the great machine of, um, of, um, of the Revolution."

She looked at him with contempt. "The chief administrator will be *very* put out." That idea seemed to cheer her. "Well, if you want to go, then you will go, of course."

"Thank you, comrade. I would like to go once more beyond the inner wall, with my military driver, to select samples from the walls and the paving. For examination. And evidence."

"As you like." She snapped at one of the file clerks, who had leaned against a desk to rest. She turned back to Tarp. "You do not suspect negligence in the prison administration, I hope?"

"None."

"No dereliction—no sign of official mismanagement?"

"Nothing of that sort. A well-run, efficient, and productive facility, comrade. A model of its kind."

She nodded unhappily. "Yes, a model mortuary. Well, you understand, comrade, if there was to be any criticism of my part in the work here—I would prefer not to have any ugly surprises—."

"None whatsoever!" He moved closer to her and lowered his voice. "Comrade Qiu and I agree, your treatment of us has been impeccable. It will be mentioned in the reports. The chief administrator, on the other hand—we never set eyes on him—a certain suggestion of, um, not caring about what we thought. . . ."

She was very careful not to seem disloyal. Still, she was pleased. "Shall I mention this to him, comrade?"

"No. It is only a minor criticism. Minor." On such criticisms, he knew, careers were brought to an end.

"I am so relieved."

They shook hands. He looked back at her from the door of the big office and saw her standing there, snarling again at the two clerks, a bitter woman trapped inside a body that she hated. Trapped inside this prison, inside this China, inside this life.

She, too, had a problem of getting out.

Dragging his young driver with him, he again pretended to examine the area of destruction. He had asked for a wooden box to hold samples, and after rejecting two, he had picked one that looked like that on which he had sat in the cubicle. The driver was carrying it. Tarp poked about, picking up pebbles, broken reinforcing rod, big chunks of blasted cement block. When he thought he had enough, he led the way along the wall, past the ruined hospital wing, around the outside of the main prison block. The soldier was sweating because of the heavy box.

"Your coat is unbuttoned," Tarp said.

"I am hot."

"You do not look like a soldier. Button up your coat before one of the guards sees you and reports you. Suppose there was a Russian here—or an American? What would they think of the great revolutionary army?"

The boy sighed. "What would a Russian or an American do here?" he grumbled.

"Spy on the readiness of the army."

He took one end of the box and they carried it along under the shadow of the cell blocks. The wind whistled along the wall and blew up under their coats. Because of the heavy clouds, it was darker, and flakes of snow were beginning to blow into their faces and swirl in angles of the wall. It felt like Boston in February.

"I have to go to the place they call the Slum," Tarp said. "I have more samples there." He pulled the soldier along by yanking on his end of the box. "These people are thoroughly disgusting and utterly nonrevolutionary. Most of them are women. You must be alert."

There was a fire burning in a cut-down oil drum near the entrance of the old Quonset hut. Near it a fat woman was breaking up cardboard packing cases with her feet and ripping the crushed cardboard into pieces, which a girl of ten carried to the flames. Through the cracks in the huts he could see other splinters of light from little fires and oil lamps.

"Put the box down here," Tarp ordered. "You wait for me."

Three young women materialized, as if from the wind, and began to giggle with the driver. Tarp stepped inside the Quonset hut. The soldier was laughing now, distracted, and behind him the box of rocks was being covertly dragged away by the little girl while the fat woman put Arthur Beecham's wooden box in its place.

There was no sign of Qiu's body in Sheila Beecham's cubicle. She was squatting over a five-gallon can in which some coals glowed feebly; her father squatted on the far side of it, ludicrous in the uniform of one of the prison guards. Thirty years in China had taught him how to sit and stand and walk like a Chinese, and he did not look at all like an Englishman now, but rather, like an Oriental beggar in stolen clothes.

Tarp touched her shoulder. "The dead man's clothes," he said. "You must wear them." She looked vacantly at him. "Put on the dead man's clothes over your own. You must look fat." Bending near her, he realized that she smelled.

She got up slowly. Qiu's clothes were taken from a hiding place behind the mattress. They had been more or less cleaned of the blood and the great rent in the coat had been sewn up. She handed a bundle of papers from the pocket to Tarp and began to pull on the trousers. They were too big around for her and too short, but she pulled at them and at her own clothes, and when she was done she did not look too bad. Tarp gave her a pair of sunglasses from Qiu's suitcase.

"It is too dark for these," she said.

"No. He was that kind of man. Fancying himself a film star." She seemed unable to make anything of "film star." She put the glasses on, hiding her eyes. Tarp pulled Qiu's hat down over her dirty hair and yanked the ear flaps to pull it low; it was too tight because she had so much hair, and he ripped the lining out of the hat and put it on her head again with angry, impatient jerks. With the collar up and the ear flaps down, as Qiu had dressed, Beecham's daughter was almost entirely hidden.

"Swing your arms when you walk," he told her. He demonstrated Qiu's funny walk. "Bounce a little on your feet. Like a ball. He was one of those people who try to impress everybody with their energy. Yes, like that."

"I will call attention to myself," she complained.

"Yes, but they won't see *you*. They'll see him."

He pulled the old man to his feet. "You must be a guard now, Mr. Beecham. Try to say nothing. Keep your hair covered and your face down so those blue eyes of yours do not show. You are going to carry one end of the box that you say has your weapon in it, and a very stupid young soldier will carry the other. Say nothing to him. If he talks, grunt." He looked at Beecham's daughter, then at Beecham. "If something goes wrong, drop to the ground."

"And then?"

"And then wait to be killed."

They went outside. The fat woman was broiling meat over the fire of packing boxes, and the driver was standing nearby, legs apart, arms folded like the soldier-hero of an opera about the army. The girls were still circling him and still giggling. Snow swirled in the firelight like moths spinning around a lamp. From the huge bulk of the prison wall, thirty yards away, a single small rectangle of light marked their goal.

"Time to go." Tarp raised his voice. "Time to go!" The soldier looked around, the heroic expression still on his face, and then it metamorphosed into his usual bovine stolidity, and he came slouching over. "You and the guard carry the box," Tarp said. "Comrade Qiu and I have matters to discuss."

The soldier sighed. He hardly looked at Arthur Beecham, who was standing there with his hands inside his sleeves, seemingly enjoying being a guard after so many years of being a prisoner. "Well, pick it up!" Tarp snapped. "Be alert now, both of you—I have my eyes on you and everything I see goes in my report!"

They started across the windy space. Tarp's hand rested on the butt of the PPK. If things went bad, the gun would allow him to do only one thing: kill Arthur Beecham so that he would be of no use to anybody.

"Swing your arms," he whispered to Beecham's daughter.

"I cannot. I have gone all stiff."

"Laugh. Giggle." Tarp laughed as loud as he could. The sound seemed to terrify her. "Laugh!" he said. She tried to laugh with him, and the sound was like a gurgle in a water pipe. Tarp made a gesture with his left arm as if emphasizing a point. "Very good, comrade!" he said cheerfully. "Very, very good!"

Arthur Beecham had placed himself on the side away from the lighted guard's booth that they would have to pass. The opening in the prison wall was wide enough for a small truck, and there was a tiny office connecting to it by a door, outside of which a guard with a Kalshnikov on the sling waited. He had been on duty when Tarp and the driver had gone through with the empty box; perhaps he had seen Qiu in the days before.

Their deception had one important advantage: they were going into the prison, not out of it, and so they were not very suspect.

The guard stared at them and at the box. He looked at the papers that Tarp and Beecham's daughter held up but he did not ask to examine them. He saluted.

Tarp's grip on the pistol relaxed.

"Move along with that box," he said impatiently. "I could carry those rocks faster by myself!"

They moved into a tunnel that cut through the prison block; because it connected at both ends with the outdoors, it was cold, and the wind boomed through it with added force. The tunnel was lighted by overhead bulbs in small wire cages, which were projected on the walls like the shadow of imprisonment itself. "Not much farther now," Tarp said when he could see the black rectangle of the tunnel's end ahead.

"Can't we set this box down?" the soldier whined.

"Are you a soldier or a revisionist weakling?"

The driver sighed. "I am a tired man," he said.

Arthur Beecham never wavered. He was like the old

farmers Tarp had seen as a child in the rice fields—always weary, always strong. After thirty years of labor, carrying the box was easy.

The old Ziv sedan was at the very edge of the parking area nearest to the big courtyard. There was very little light there. The soldier started to put his end of the box down on the ground, almost dropping it in his hurry to be rid of it; Beecham, however, handled his end with patient care, for he knew what was inside. Before Beecham could forget himself and scream at the soldier, Tarp put his hand over the old man's mouth and bellowed at the driver himself. "Fool! Idiot! Moron! Lazy piece of dog excrement!"

"It is only rocks," the boy whined.

"To *you*—to *you* it is only rocks! To you, the whole world is only rocks. You are a stupid pile of dog excrement—no, you are a stupid little puddle of puppy piss. You are *nothing*!" Tarp thrust a hand forward. "Keys!"

"But, comrade—."

"Keys!"

Tarp opened the bulbous trunk. He grabbed one end of the box and the soldier hurried to pick up the other and they put it into the trunk. Tarp straightened quickly and said, as if with horror, "My notebook!" He pretended to look on the ground behind the car. "My notebook!" To his surprise, Beecham's daughter picked up the cue and, swinging her arms as he had taught her, began to walk about with her eyes on the ground.

Tarp jerked his head back toward the courtyard. "Go look for my notebook, Puppy Piss."

"But, comrade. . . . Yes, comrade. What sort of—?"

"Small, black, government issue. Be quick! Go to the end of the tunnel and come right back!"

"Yes, sir, yes, comrade."

He trotted off with his face turned to the ground, glad to be free of them. As soon as he had turned the corner Tarp motioned the old man into the car's trunk, and without complaint, Arthur Beecham lay down with the wooden box. Tarp closed the trunk and locked it.

"Into the car."

When the driver returned, Tarp and Beecham's daughter were sitting in the black rear seat. "Comrade Xiang," the young man whined, "I could not find the—."

"I found it," Tarp said. "Drive on."

The young man sighed. "Where?"

"Out of the prison, of course."

"Then where?"

"I will tell you when I think you need to know. Drive on."

The car moved slowly. It took them several minutes to make their way through the prison roads, passing under bridges and crossovers, winding along passages with high walls on both sides. The driver went with extra slowness because he was afraid of getting lost. At last, however, the main gate came in sight, brilliantly lighted by overhead lamps that put everything in a pitiless, corpselike greenish brightness.

Tarp handed his papers and Qiu's to the driver. "Take them into the guard."

"But. . . . Yes, Comrade."

He disappeared into the guard's kiosk. Seconds passed. A minute passed. Tarp kept himself very still to hide his concern. Next to him, Beecham's daughter stared straight ahead through her dark glasses. Tarp could smell the sour odor of her clothes. *She needs a bath. Several baths.* He thought of Gillian. *Another life.*

He could see the guard talking on a telephone, holding their papers in his hand. Tarp put his hand on the PPK.

Beecham's daughter moved. "I will not let them take me back," she said viciously. "I will die before I will live that way again!"

Tarp agreed silently. *Yes, she will die.*

Headlights were bright behind them and came on very fast. A car was speeding toward the gate.

"*Do nothing!*" Tarp growled at her as her hand moved toward the door handle. The car stopped directly behind them with a quick little scream of its brakes, its headlights illuminating the car's interior harshly, and at the same time the guard's kiosk opened and the guard came out on the step, their papers in one hand and the other up on the strap of his shouldered submachine gun. Footsteps sounded beside their car.

There was a knock on the window next to him.

With one motion, he drew the pistol and leaned forward to roll down the window with his other hand, shielding the pistol from sight. "Well?"

The man was not in uniform. Behind him, however, were two guards with guns.

The man saluted. "Compliments of the chief administrator, comrades."

Tarp stared at him. It took him fractions of a second to understand what the man had said. He raised his head to look beyond the man as he moved aside to reveal that the guards were carrying between them a metal cylinder as big as a ten-gallon can.

"If you would be good enough to unlock your door, comrade. . . ."

Tarp pulled up on the button. He hid the pistol under his coat.

The guards grunted as they swung the cylinder into the interior. There was plenty of room for it, for, besides the bench seat on which Tarp and Beecham's daughter were sitting, there were two jump seats folded up against the partition, and room on the floor for them and their occupants. The cylinder was put into this roomy space. The civilian and the guards waited expectantly, like parents who have given a child a wrapped package. Tarp raised the lid of the cylinder and saw plates, utensils, metal cups, a flat little teapot, all resting in a tray with handles that just fit inside the cylinder. When he lifted out the tray, he found a covered dish with hot, spicy noodles in it. There were other covered dishes nested below that one.

The civilian handed him a bottle with a florid label. "With the chief administrator's profound wishes for a successful mission of inspection, comrades."

Tarp took off the cap and sniffed. *Chinese vodka, by God!*

"Thank the chief administrator in the names of both myself and Comrade Qiu. Tell him we take *special* notice of his thoughtfulness and will remember his keen efficiency and devotion to duty when writing our reports."

The civilian bowed. "Thank you, comrades." He would be one of the chief administrator's cronies, perhaps a protégé. His relief was the chief administrator's relief.

Tarp closed the door and rolled up the window. The driver got in and handed their papers back. All around the old sedan, guards were saluting.

"Drive on," Tarp said.

As they passed through the outer perimeter of barbed wire, Tarp began to take circular metal dishes from the cylinder. Wonderful smells spread through the car's interior—chicken, vegetables in mustard sauce, fish-head soup with dumplings.

Tarp uncorked the vodka.

"A toast, comrade!" he said to Beecham's daughter. "Let us drink to bribery in a revolutionary society!"

chapter nine

"Stop the car."

"Comrade?"

"Stop the car."

The ancient sedan swayed gracefully to a stop, more like some ship coming to berth than an automobile stopping, and the young soldier turned to stare into the darkness of the rear seat.

"Where are we, Comrade Xiang?"

"How would I know that, idiot? We are on a road."

"Why are we stopping?"

"Comrade Qiu and I want to relieve ourselves."

The young soldier turned forward again. In the dim green light of the dashboard, his sullen face looked cunning. "We are in the middle of nowhere," he said.

"Turn out the lights."

"Comrade?"

"Turn out the vehicle's lights. We will destroy the battery."

The soldier guffawed. "Comrade, this battery will last for—."

"Turn off the lights!"

He turned off the lights. Tarp and Beecham's daughter got out. Tarp opened the driver's door. "Stand in the road."

"Why?"

"I may get lost. It is very dark here."

"Then let me put on the lights."

"You will destroy the battery. Stand in the road, idiot."

The wind groaned through the stunted little trees beyond the road and pelted them with fine snow. The soldier huddled in his padded coat, yearning for the car's warm interior.

"Do you need to relieve yourself, soldier?"

"No, sir."

"Yes, you do. As soon as we are done, you will do so. Stand there until I call you."

He led Beecham's daughter off the side of the road and then made his way silently around the rear of the car and came up behind the young soldier and struck him once with his left hand just at the base of the skull, and the boy went down on the black road as if he had been dropped from the sky.

"Sheila!"

She came from the roadside. "Is he dead?"

"Unconscious."

"You will kill him now?"

"No."

He was taking Qiu's little medical kit from his bag.

"Why not?"

"He is only a boy."

"Are you afraid to kill him?"

Tarp flicked on the dashboard lights so that he could read the labels in the kit. He took out a tiny tube of anesthetic, unscrewed its long, conical cap to reveal a thick needle. "Get your father out of the back of the car," he said wearily. He did not want to talk to her about killing people.

He bent over the boy. *Too young to die for nothing*, he thought. He pulled down the coarse trousers and plunged the thick needle into muscle there and squeezed the tube. The dose would knock him out for hours.

The soldier's pockets held no secrets—hardly even any clues to a personality. A pack of Noonday Sun cigarettes, a manual on the disassembling of the KR-57C carburetor, a key, a bit of money, the temporary orders assigning him to Comrade Xiang. *No debutante balls for you, my friend. No glass slipper. No invitation to the palace.* Tarp tied the limp hands and fashioned a gag; he dragged the boy to the rear of the car and boosted him into the trunk with the wooden box.

"You are sentimental," Sheila Beecham said as she helped to lift the boy's shoulders.

"Very." He slammed the trunk lid. "That is why I am here."

"You are not tough enough."

"And you are not beautiful enough!" he rasped as his anger left his control. "We all have these deficiencies!"

"That was a petty thing to say." She did not sound hurt; on the contrary, she seemed saddened.

Tarp sighed. "I am sorry. I said a stupid thing. Forgive me."

"Why? It is quite true. I am not pretty."

"Ah, who can tell? With a bath and some clothes, you might be a new person. Look here. . . ." He started to say something about her use of the knife in killing Qiu, but he realized he was not ready to go into all that with her.

"What?"

"Nothing. We need to get moving again."

She shrugged.

Tarp dropped into the driver's seat with such weary violence that the old springs sagged and rocked under him and the car seemed to shudder from the shock.

Tarp could hear Beecham eating. "I am sorry we had to leave you in the trunk so long, Mr. Beecham."

"It was not so bad."

"You got hungry, though."

"Oh, yes." Beecham sounded quite matter-of-fact. "That is very good food."

"Oh, yes." He was still matter-of-fact. Perhaps he had lost his sense of taste, as old people do. He made plenty of noise, however, as if he enjoyed the act of filling his belly, and he ate very fast, like a prisoner who knows that his bowl will be taken away soon.

Tarp put the car in gear. "When you get back to England, you can have English food again." English food must be a peculiar memory to Beecham now, he realized. Perhaps all that he remembered was the food of wartime austerity—still, Tarp reasoned, there must be some fantasy of boyhood treats, even of a Pickwickian abundance that never was—treacle tarts and strawberry mess, beef and Yorkshire pudding and cider and wonderful hams. "Actually, you may find English food a little changed." He was thinking of the American fast-food places in central London. "Actually, the best restaurants in London now are Chinese."

He snapped on the driving lights and swirling snow appeared. The lights made a white tunnel down which the car seemed to charge. There were no other cars on the road, and the snow was beginning to pile up on the surface so that the world beneath their wheels was as featureless as that overhead.

"A good night for this kind of thing," Tarp muttered.

Beecham's daughter was riding behind him, next to her father. She moved to one of the jump seats so that she could lean forward and talk to him in a low voice, as if they had to keep things from the old man. "Where are we going?" she murmured.

"A town called Jing-jen. Down toward Cherchen. Maybe a hundred miles." He had picked up her conspiratorial tone.

"Why?"

He hesitated. *Should I tell her?* He was going to make contact with the person whose name Penhurst had given him. *Who is she, after all?* He looked at her reflection in the windshield. *She could be anybody. Informer, mole*. He thought of her murder of Qiu. *Trained agent*. Tarp entertained all possibilities: Russian operative, Chinese secret police, CIA agent, even a British mole. Or she might be simply what she said she was—Beecham's daughter. "I have to see somebody there," he said.

"You mean you do not want me to know."

"I do not want you to know more than you need to know."

"Ah." She gave a chuckle. "The stupid woman does not get told much, is that it?"

"Do you not speak English?" he said abruptly.

She hesitated. "I used to do so."

"Try now."

"It has been a long time. Even with my father, Chinese is easier." She looked at her own reflection in the windshield and said very slowly and tonelessly in English, "How-do-you-do-I-am-very-pleased-to-make-your-acquaintance." She looked at his eyes in the glass. "How was that?" she said in Chinese.

"Textbook perfect. Not a very convincing demonstration if you mean to be taken for an Englishwoman, however." The accent had been quite perfect—as perfect as Hamish Penhurst's or his granddaughter's, with the same upper-class tones as theirs and old Beecham's. But the words had been spoken without the native speaker's easy acceptance of their worth, and so they had been mere sounds. "Your mother was a Russian agent," he said. He said it flatly, as a fact and not as a question.

"She was Russian."

"Not an agent?"

"I do not know such things."

"She was in prison?" He had read it all in Beecham's file, but now he wanted to hear it from her.

"Oh, yes. That is why I am not like most people. I was born in a prison!" She met his eyes. "Why are you smiling?"

"Was I? I am sorry. I was born in prison, too."

She hunched forward. "Where?" It was the first show of interest he had seen except for that flash of passionate and beautiful hatred when she had moved to kill Qiu.

"In China," he said.

"In China!" She seemed astounded. "Like me!" He thought she might scramble over the seat back in her excitement. "Where? When?"

"Just at the beginning of the second war. In a Japanese camp. Tell me about your mother."

"Oh—!" She made an exasperated sound. "She was in prison and he met her there. They were allowed to live together."

"Where was that?"

"Mukden."

"The Physical Research Center at Mukden?"

"The prison."

"No. Mukden is not a prison. Your father would have been under guard, but he was a scientist. Your mother was probably a Russian agent who was put there to report on him."

"How do you know that?"

"It is one of the things I know. Was your mother a scientist?"

"She worked. I was brought up in those days in the care center."

"And then what happened?"

Her face was obscure now, brooding. She took off Qiu's cap and began to scratch her scalp, as if she were pretending to be a peasant in the act of thinking. "My father got very sick. I was seven. My mother said they took him away to a hospital and we could not live there anymore."

"Your father had a mental breakdown." He had read that much in the report, which had called it "a return to mental decadence." Apparently, Beecham had simply stopped working.

"What is mental breakdown?" she said.

"It means you stop thinking the way people believe you should. What did your mother do?"

"She did what they told her to do. We went to the women's prison at Lan-Jo. I was there for five years. Then one day—my mother was gone. They told me she had been sent back to Russia with a lot of others, and that now I was going to live with my father again. So they took me on a train to Chu-chou and then in a truck to a place out in the desert. He was there. He was very different—much older. Like now. I took care of him for three years there, in a nice little room in a row of cells where other people lived with families, too—most of them foreigners."

Tarp's eyes were narrowed against the bright snow. "The Rocket Design Program in Koko Nor," he mused.

"And then. . . ." She stopped. She laughed strangely. "This part will be hard for me to tell. I have told this part only to a woman. It is very hard for me." He heard her take two deep breaths, as if she were preparing to dive. "I was fifteen. The Red Guards came. Everything was in a mess for several weeks. One day some Red Guard girls came and . . . they came into our room and chased me out and they crowded around me and said bad things and called me names. And they took me out . . . with a dozen or so other girls from that place and . . they put us in a truck and drove us out, out, way out . . . into the far villages and. . . . There were farmers and herders out there who had no wives. They gave us to them. To be their wives. I was given to a man about forty whose wife had died. I married him."

Tarp concentrated on the road, the car, the snow. *Let*

her tell it, he thought, *it's her story.* But he knew peasants and he knew that brutal country up close to the Mongolian border. Life was hard; men were brutalized. They were not of the twentieth century, many of them. He told himself, *Let her tell it*, but he was filling in details despite the warning.

"He was not so bad," she said as if the fact surprised her still. "But I could not cook the way he wanted. Or do many things right. I knew nothing about his pigs, his animals, his little field. It was a commune, but each man said 'mine' about certain things. They had a collective but they were very grasping. Then I did not—get pregnant. He beat me. That is what it became, after three years. He beat me. I looked forward to working in the commune's fields, so I would not be beaten. Another woman told me to find a younger man and—you know—so I would get pregnant and then he, I mean my husband, would not be shamed and he would stop beating me. I could have done that. I was not so bad to look at then. But I did not."

The stubbornness in those words impressed him. He had never been made to feel different or inferior in China; indeed, his memories of his childhood there were often happy ones. Her pride was like the pride and the strength of some gnarled, battered, but living tree that has sunk its roots down through crevices of rock in order to grow, however dwarfed and bowed by the wind.

"How did you get to Qer-Li?" he said.

She passed her hand over her dirty hair. Her chin was on the padded seat back behind him, bouncing with the motion of the car. "My father sent me letters every year or so. I knew where he was. When my husband died, I went down there. It was a good time to get away with such things—Mao had just died and there was a lot of confusion. I could not stay in my husband's village; the other men wanted his pigs and his tools. They all thought I wanted them and wanted to cause trouble. I was so glad to go away! I ran away at night and came to Qer-Li because other women helped me along the way, and one who had a friend in the Slum helped me get in there."

Tarp believed that she told him the truth. There was no way yet of checking the story, and so he reserved a grain of doubt; yet, to hear that deep, weary voice, to see those spare gestures and that bereft expression, one had to believe her. She had touched him.

Tarp cleared his throat. Almost angrily, he said, "Now look here. . . ."

"Yes?"

He had to clear his throat again. "About Comrade Qiu."

"Who? Oh, the man at the Slum. Yes?"

"I have never seen a knife used that way before." He waited for her to say something. When she did not, he said, "Did somebody teach you how to do that?"

"Yes."

"Who?"

"My mother." Beecham's daughter was riding now with both forearms on the seat back and her chin on her hands. "She taught me that at the women's prison. They were very hard there. She said I needed to be able to take care of myself."

"And she taught it just that way—? Just where to put the knife in, the twist, that business of using both hands for the downward thrust?"

"Yes, just like that. She made me practice."

"Does it take a special knife?"

"A heavy blade, very sharp."

"Where did you get such a knife at the Slum?"

"I brought it with me. I always carry it."

Tarp concentrated on the road, which was getting slippery. He tried to make his next question casual, but he could not because the moment had become so highly charged. "Where did your mother learn to use the knife like that?"

"In Russia, I think. All she ever said was, 'They taught us this,' or 'They taught us that.' I think she always meant in Russia."

Tarp was sure now that the mother had been a Russian agent, although this piece of training was not familiar to him. Beecham's file had mentioned only that she had committed "crimes against the people," and he supposed she had been planted at the Physical Research Center to report on Beecham and had been caught. *But they taught her some very fancy knife work in Russia, and the same kind of fancy work showed up in London in the sixties when Carrington was killed. Now her daughter can do the same stuff. . . .*

"When did you say your mother left you?"

"When I was twelve."

"How old are you now?"

"I think I am twenty-eight."

Could her mother have left China and gone to England? Too much coincidence. But the dates might match. Have to check. Find a source. Who would know about all this Russian stuff after so long . . . ?

"Have you ever killed anybody else that way—with the knife?"

"My husband," she said after several seconds.

So there were a farmer in the north, and Johnnie Carrington's father, and Comrade Qiu, who had nothing in the world in common except their way of leaving it. A technique that had been taught in Russia decades before—before this twenty-eight-year-old was born—and that had left them savaged and dying, and terrified by the horror of it, and with a question in their eyes: *Why? Why?*

"Do you believe me?" she was saying.

"What?"

"Do you believe me?"

"Which part?"

"All of it."

"I have no way of checking your story."

"But do you believe me?"

"I cannot believe until I check."

"Yah!" She struck his seat back with her hand. "A man who trusts nothing is a stone!"

"A man who trusts nothing stays alive," he said.

"Why?" Her face was bitter. "Why do you not believe me? Is it because of my mother—because she was Russian? Do you think I am a Russian spy?"

"Well, I think somebody is. Ever since I got to China, I have been waiting for a Russian to show up. I hoped that Comrade Qiu would be my Russian, but I believe he was working for an American named Hacker. I cannot believe that your father is the Russian. And so, if there is to be a Russian in this business, from what I know right now it either has to be you—or it has to be me."

chapter ten

Tarp had parked the old sedan fifty yards off the road in scrubby woods above the town of Jing-jen, and then he had waited for the light to walk back along his tracks to see how revealing the tire tracks were in the snow. He was tired: little needles of pain danced along his shoulders, and the dryness of his eyes made him squint. The sky, heavy with clouds, was like the underside of a cooking pot. Only a few snowflakes drifted down now. The wind had blown itself away.

There was less snow under the trees than he had expected. The ground was even bare in places; with an improvised broom of long-needle pine, he smudged the tire tracks and mixed pine needles and dead oak leaves with the snow.

Safe enough for a few hours. Barring the inevitable miracle. Hamish Penhurst had lectured him on "the inevitable miracle" when they had met in London in the sixties, Penhurst as head of MI-5 and Tarp as an American wildcatter covering China. Penhurst had recognized his value and had tried to recruit him, tried to make him a double agent for England and the United States; and between recruitment pep talks he had lectured about "the inevitable miracle." He meant the unpredictable and purely chance collision of events that could be explained only by a belief in magic or in amoral gods. Inevitable miracles, he had insisted, were the ruin of many good plans, the *terminus ad quem* that always had to be planned for. "Always have an alternative, my boy," he had said in a London club. "The inevitable miracle always trips you up if you *don't* have an alternative, and it often does even when you do."

Tarp walked softly back toward the Ziv sedan. A thorny vine scraped on his padded jacket with a sound like tearing paper. *Tearing flesh. Poor Qiu. Ripped open like a fish.* He looked into the car. Beecham and his daughter were asleep, sprawled like victims of carbon-monoxide poisoning. Tarp opened the trunk and checked the young soldier, who was alive but who looked feverish.

Tarp opened the car door and touched Sheila Beecham's shoulder. She woke instantly and lay just as she had slept, twisted in the seat, her wide eyes puffy.

"I'm going down to the town," he said. "You must stay awake now. If anybody comes, tell them that something happened to the car and your driver has gone for help. The papers for the car are in the glove box. There is a set of papers for your father—not very good, but they were the best that Comrade Qiu could offer."

"All right."

"You have papers of your own?"

"Old ones, from my marriage."

"You may be better off pretending to be a man and using Qiu's. The only people you will have to worry about are the rural militia. They are very stupid and very dogmatic. Now, remember that the boy is in the trunk—let nobody look in there. I will be back in three hours, I hope. If I am not back by night, then I will not be back at all. Then you will have to go on alone."

"How?"

"Leave the car here. Move at night, sleep by day. If you have to make contact, make it only with old people. Sometimes, they are compassionate."

"Where would we go?"

He looked at her puffy eyes for some seconds. "Your father can trade his machine and his knowledge for a very good life in China."

"No!"

Her violence offended him. He still had great affection for China. "Then you must try to get over the border to Pakistan. In Peshawar, there is a woman named Peri Krishnamurti—she runs a place called Peri Kri's. A lot of war groupies hang out there. She would help you."

"What are 'groupies'?"

"In this case, they are people with enough money to get close to a war but not enough guts to fight in it. They like the thrill of being just close enough to hear the biggest guns." He rubbed his sandy eyes. "Tell Peri Kri that I vouch for you."

"And then?"

"Then go where you want."

"My father wants to go to somebody named Winston."

"He may have to go to hell to find him. That's where most of Winston's friends wound up, and his performance at Dresden probably got him in, too. Perhaps you'd better ask for the Queen, instead. Well, I'm off. There is still food in the canister."

He cut into the woods below the car so as to slice across a broad curve in the road and descend into the broad, arid valley where Jing-jen lay. As he went down, the forest thickened, and the trees, mostly pines, got bigger. He found the walking easier than in his woods in Maine because the ground was hard and dry and free of ferns; he moved quickly, down the slope and then up the shoulder of another hill and down its other side. When his path was intercepted by a gully, he cut to his left along it and came to the road again; from a wide curve, he was able to look over the stunted treetops into the valley. The railroad and a procession of electrical towers, like giants striding across the landscape, crossed at the town; there was a wood-pulp mill where the smoke rose from a bark shredder and the faintly sickening odor of the pulp was spreading in the air.

Thirty minutes' walk brought him to the outskirts. Jing-jen was a planned and sterile community put up after the Nationalists had abandoned this country. Where a bridge had been put up to span the dry riverbed, the Communists had put up a town of identical and uninteresting buildings that looked as if they had come from a processing plant like so many tin cans. *Russian*, Tarp told himself. *Only the Russians are this dull*. The buildings began abruptly where the forest left off, as if this was all the town that was wanted and all there ever would be. There was a school nearby where children were singing, and it looked very much like the spool factory in the next street, which looked very much like the dwelling units on each side. There were signs of the new China, however, in backyard pens for chickens and ducks, and even several small, boothlike shops put up with obviously free enterprise.

He asked his way of a man on a bicycle. Several squares farther on he had to ask again, this time of two urban militiamen who carried old bolt-action rifles on their shoulders, copies, as nearly as Tarp could tell, of the American Springfield. One had a type-59 pistol stuck into his belt.

"I am looking for the Culture Park by the truck repair facility, comrades."

One of them was overweight and tough-looking, probably a military veteran. "What park?" he said rudely.

"The Culture Park."

The man stared at him. He was of that older generation for whom good manners had been a betrayal of socialist integrity. "You are not from here," he said rudely.

"Of course not!" Tarp said with equal discourtesy. "I am from the National Energy Program. I have just come down from Qer-Li." He offered his papers. The younger of the militiamen, as if to make up for his partner's rudeness, took them with elaborate shows of gratitude.

"You're a long way from Qer-Li," the older one said.

"Indeed."

"The papers are in order," the younger one said. He seemed to have been too polite to examine them closely; indeed, he had merely glanced at them. "The truck repair is two streets ahead, one street to the right. A big cement building with a cracked front. The Culture Park is just beyond."

All the buildings have cracked fronts, Tarp thought. *Russian work*. "Thank you, comrade."

The older one scowled. Perhaps he had a hangover or an ulcer. He let Tarp go a few steps before he said, "I saw no car you came in!"

Tarp looked at him coldly. "I am not surprised." He walked away. When he looked back from the next crossing, they were far down the street, going the other way. *An unhappy man, trying to stick his trouble on somebody else like a burr. An inevitable miracle in the making*.

When he saw the uninteresting facade of the truck repair, he passed it on his right and turned again, and ahead of him, the park gate stood out by virtue of its tawdry and quite fake gaiety. On a sunny day, it might have seemed more in keeping with the slogan that framed the entrance in three-dimensional characters: SO THAT ALL THE PEOPLE WILL GLOW WITH HEALTH AND BEAUTY! But some of the paint was missing, and some of the characters were loose and hanging down, and the place looked sickly, like an old spa that has been turned over to the spiders.

Inside the park walls, there was some landscaped grass, a low hill or two, and a tiny pond with a bridge and a teahouse. *Russian again,* he thought. *Designed in Smolensk by an apprentice who never got closer to China than his school library. They probably put the same bridge in every new town in China.*

There were two old women in the teahouse. They looked disappointed to have a customer.

"A copy of the *People's Daily.*"

"Tea?"

"No tea today, thank you." He looked over their rickety table of knickknacks and inedible foods. *Something blue. Supposed to have something blue.* "That pair of shoelaces, please."

"Those are for an infant."

"Exactly."

The shoelaces were wrapped in crinkly blue paper like the paper that firecrackers come in. It had dust on it; its creases had been bleached almost white by time.

"No tea at all?"

"Not today, thank you, Mother."

He crossed the barren terrace above the unnatural lake and crossed the bridge. There was a cast-aluminum urn there, just as he had been told there would be, and he took the crackly blue paper and wadded it and dropped it in the urn.

Tarp sat on a bench under a leafless tree. The sun tried to burn through the clouds to warm him. A middle-aged man in a dark blue jacket pushed a wheeled ash-can up to the bridge and removed the wadded blue paper and trundled away without looking at him. The man was supposed to look in the blue paper and find the code words that Tarp had written there. The procedure had sounded very simple when he had memorized it back in London. Here, in this barren place under that feeble sun, it seemed like the gibbering of a lunatic.

Fourteen minutes later, another figure appeared down the path. Tarp had timed the interval. The newcomer was a woman. She wore trousers and a short jacket, and a long coat that was unbuttoned as if it was too hot because she had been walking fast. She went past him and over the bridge, circled the teahouse and came back and threw herself on the bench next to him.

They looked at each other.

"Exercising?" Tarp said.

"Every day. From my office to the teahouse and back." She took a deep breath. "I saw three cranes this morning," she muttered.

Bingo. "High or low?"

"Two low and one high."

"I am sure that is a sign of coming happiness."

She sat very straight with her hands on her knees, exhaling noisily, as if she were still doing an exercise. "I did not expect you until tomorrow at the earliest," she said. "I am not ready for you."

He paid no attention to her complaint. "I want you to make contact at once. I am ready to move out."

"You have him?"

"That is not your business. I want the plane to come in and pick me up. I want to know where the pickup will be made, and when. That will be the end of your involvement."

"No, no." She seemed vexed. "I am supposed to hide you, feed you—care for you."

"That will not be necessary."

"I have orders."

He studied her. She looked frightened. *Something is wrong*. "What is it?" he said.

"What is what?"

"You are frightened."

"I have never done this before. Calling in the plane."

"There is more than that. What is wrong?"

"Nothing. Nothing, nothing!" She tapped her fingers on her knee. She was lying, he was sure.

"The sooner the plane picks me up, the better for both of us."

"Ai!" She sounded like an actress. "Was there trouble?"

"What kind of trouble?"

"Getting him out. I have heard nothing."

"Good. You're better off that way. Call in the plane and set a place and time. Tonight or tomorrow."

She stared at him, driven by some inner anguish, her eyes popping as if from a disease. "I am only a courier."

"It will go very quickly if you do your job. Meet me here this evening to report."

"You will be seen!"

"Yes. I have not learned how to be invisible yet."

"Let me hide you. *Please.*"

The hair rose on the back of his neck. Like the badger, he betrayed his sense of danger that way. "No." He stood up. A vagrant shaft of sunlight found him and warmed his shoulders. "Here—tonight—six-thirty. I want everything to be ready then." He looked around as if he expected to find watchers, half hidden by the leafless trees. There was nobody. "I try to take care of myself," he said to her. "So, I am very suspicious. I will kill anybody who tries to follow me. Just mind your own business." He walked off, weary and troubled. Perhaps she was only a coward; perhaps she was something worse—a self-doubter, a lunatic. Perhaps it was a sign of Penhurst's age or of England's collapse that this untrustworthy woman was his contact—somebody who might have been a good courier ten years ago but was now either fearful or unstable. *How long since Hamish had to depend on this one?* he wondered. *Hamish, what have you left me with?*

He went back along the same road and out of the town, turning into the woods on a curve and then waiting ten minutes in case anyone was following; then he went on to the gully and up over the hill along the same route he had followed earlier.

A hundred yards from the car, he made a circle. Partway around, he found Beecham's daughter leaning against a tree with her eyes on the sedan. He came up behind her quietly—silently, he thought—but when he was three yards from her she turned, and her hand was under her coat and he knew she was holding the knife.

"I thought it was you," she said quietly.

"A good thing you do not have the gun," he said. Fatigue made him grumpy. "You are what Americans call 'trigger happy.' "

She was hurt. "I thought I did the right thing."

"Of course, of course." Too late, he realized that she wanted praise from him—a fact remarkable in itself. "Yes, you did very well. But not all problems are solved with the knife. What if there had been two people?"

"I knew there was only one. I saw you, way over there."

"I must be tired. I am going to sleep. Give me two hours—four, if you can."

She walked with him to the car. "When are you going to trust me?" she said. "Hey? When?"

Tarp got into the front seat and put his head back. "For a beginner, you know some good questions." He closed his eyes and was instantly asleep.

When he woke, a brassy sun had scattered shadows through the woods, and she was sitting in that dappled light thirty feet from the car with her back against a tree. Beyond her, Arthur Beecham was sitting cross-legged, making marks in the dirt with a stick.

"Is your father all right?" Tarp asked her. He was carrying one of the metal dishes, which had cold, rather greasy rice and limp vegetables in it. He ate with his fingers.

"He has nothing to do. He misses the prison routine."

Tarp crouched in front of her. "Have you eaten?"

"Enough. The soldier is restless."

Tarp filled his mouth with grains of rice and wiped his fingers on dry leaves. "We will get rid of him tonight. The car, too. The military will begin to miss them both tomorrow. We may need it tonight, and then we will get rid of it."

She watched him eat. "Where are we going?"

It was like the old days—squatting on his heels, the smell of pine woods in his nostrils, pushing cold rice into his mouth. Very basic, very direct. Survival. "I will know after I go into the town again."

"Is it dangerous?"

"Everything is dangerous now. Do I look too Western to you?"

"No. But you do not look very Chinese."

"That is bad." He was worried that the membrane cemented at his hairline was slipping. He gave the soldier another injection from the medical kit and then he spent half an hour in front of the rearview mirror, repairing the tension at his temples. As he worked he thought. The inevitable miracle might come about when Comrade Do and the commandant met by accident or spoke about some entirely different matter on the telephone; one or the other would be reminded of the visitors, and they would discuss them and then they might realize that the car had left the prison but it had never arrived at the railroad. Or some woman in the Slum, more venal than the others, would betray them. Or something else would set a hunt in motion: messages would go out, the rural militia would be called, farmers and herders would be alerted. They would be very good at hunting out here.

Got to ditch the car. And the boy.

And Comrade Xiang. Not good for more than today. Same with Qiu. Other identities are in the drop bag. Can get that tonight.

Beecham and the woman are unknowns. Nobody missing them yet. So that's all right. If anybody tumbles to me, they'll think I travel alone. Or with Qiu. Two foreign devils. Running dogs. But I can get away with Xiang today if the miracle doesn't happen. But better to serve up Beecham and the woman as what they are. Foreigners. Hide them by making them obvious.

Tarp studied his face in the elongated mirror. The eyes looked better. Maybe it was simply the effect of fatigue.

Tarp went to the trunk, opened it. The boy's eyes were halfway open. His skin was clammy now. His body lay against the long wooden box that Arthur Beecham insisted contained his particle beam. The box itself had been used to ship X-ray parts to the prison hospital, and the markings were still legible on it. The box had come from East Germany by way of a broker in Hong Kong. It was about the size of a case of rifles, made of rough, cheap wood. It did not look like a weapon that could revolutionize warfare.

The trouble is, Tarp admitted to himself, *I don't believe it's a particle beam at all. I think either the old man's crazy or I've been had.*

He boosted the box to the ground. Using the car's tool kit, he began to pry up the top of the box. Its original nails had been pulled and then some of them had been hammered back into the same holes; along one side, other nails had been used and they had been put in clumsily, splitting the wood and coming through like claws. Tarp put a screwdriver under the lid and pried, wiggling the tip to lift and move the tool along one side. When he could get his fingers in the opening, he began to use the board itself as a lever to lift the nails.

The box was crowded with electrical wiring. There was a steel tube at the junction of one side and the bottom, running the length of the box. It looked as if it had been cannibalized from some other device. Heavy cable in silver sheathing snaked along the other long side and down the left end; the central space was jammed with color-coded wires and the copper plates of transformers and a fiberboard plate with wires spraying from it like the legs of a centipede. Tarp recognized a row of transistors and two solid-state boxes, again cannibalized from other equipment.

Along the underside of the top of the box were fourteen plastic packets filled with what seemed to be a translucent gel, four of them amber and the rest a pale and poisonous blue. They were linked by a golden mesh.

"Don't you ask permission before prying into my business?" a waspish old voice said behind him. It was Arthur Beecham, who looked quite insane at that moment.

"I had to know what I was dealing with, sir." They were speaking Chinese; the syllables came out as cold and menacing.

"You deserve exactly what would happen to you if you touched any of that."

"I have touched nothing."

Beecham looked down into the box. His mood turned around; such was the action on him of his own work. "It is such a beautiful piece of thinking," he said softly. "So elegant."

Tarp's reaction was different. *If I was going to convince somebody that I'd made a death ray out of chewing gum and old coat hangers, this is about what I'd come up with. Rube Goldberg in a packing crate.*

Tarp pointed at the bags of gel. "What are those?"

"Don't touch them!" Beecham grabbed Tarp's wrist. "They'll blow you to kingdom come, my boy." Oddly, he had switched to English for the warning. "They hold a residual charge, I think. Not sure, of course. Untested theory. They're the heart of my solution, you see."

"Bags of jelly?"

"My breakthrough. Absolutely genius." Beecham beamed on his handiwork. "Anywhere else in the world, they'd need a building the size of Westminster to house what's in those little things."

"What *is* in those things?"

"Ah, my boy, that would be telling!" Beecham squatted on his heels. "One thing one learns in prison is never to tell what one knows. It's like food—one always saves some. If they give you ten bowls of rice, you eat nine; if they give you five grains of rice, you eat four. Always hold something back."

"And if they give you no rice at all?"

"Have you been in prison?"

"If they give you no rice at all, you eat the rice you have saved, and then you live on the memory of rice. But if you live on the secret memory of your machine, Mr. Beecham, then it may never get to England. What if something happens to you?"

Beecham played with a twig. "Then things will be as if I had never thought of it. Then it will be my secret forever."

Tarp looked into the wooden box. Its messy circuitry, its borrowed parts, its fragile-looking plastic sacks, like so many containers of shampoo—was it a secret worth dying for? Or was it a dotty old man's hoax?

"I'd like a demonstration of your machine, Mr. Beecham."

The old man did not look up. "Fine with me. Find a power source."

Tarp got into the car and emptied out Qiu's suitcase and ripped up the bottom, which was only cardboard under a rather flashy layer of blue nylon. He cut a rectangle from the carboard. Two pages of the *People's Daily* were torn into four-inch strips, and then the strips were torn almost all the way through at quarter-inch intervals to make lengths of what looked like fringe for party decorations.

Tarp searched through the car—under the hood, inside the trunk. Finally, under the driver's seat, he found what he wanted: a repair made with cloth-backed adhesive. When he pulled it away, it left a black strip to which dust and hairs quickly clung.

Tarp rolled the cardboard into a two-inch cylinder

and fastened it with the tape. He put the strips of paper fringe together, not quite overlapping so that the tears were staggered. He rolled and spiraled these and fed them carefully down into the cardboard tube and taped them in place, so that, when he was done, he had a tube filled with interwoven layers of narrow paper strips, row after row that projected into the center and tangled together like the soft spokes of a surrealistic wheel. When he looked down the tube, he could see only hundreds of thin pieces of paper with torn edges.

He fitted one end of the tube over the barrel of the PPK and taped it in place. He made a flat package with the rest of the cardboard and the *People's Daily*, putting the PPK and its makeshift silencer in it; when he was done, he had a flat, innocuous-looking package that he could carry under one arm. He left one end open so that he could put his hand inside and grasp the pistol. He left the package on the seat and went to Beecham.

"Mr. Beecham, I'd like you to put on my clothes. I'm going to turn soldier."

He stripped off the boy's uniform and put it on and put the few possessions back into the pockets, buttoning the soldier's orders and his papers into the tunic. Beecham dressed himself in the droopy suit that Tarp had brought from London. The result was laughable.

"You look just right," Tarp said. "You're supposed to be Irish, anyway, so nobody would expect too much." He made Sheila Beecham take off Qiu's clothes and then, piece by piece, try on her own tattered garments until something vaguely resembling Western dress emerged. "I want you to look like an Irish Socialist's secretary. At the moment, you look like a cross between a ragbag and a wolfhound. I suppose that's just about right. Into the car."

When they had settled themselves, he turned to face them. "Now, let's get it straight. Mister Beecham is an Irishman named Toole—can you both say that? *Toole*."

They both said *tool*.

"Miss Beecham is his secretary named Sheila."

"Oh, jolly good! That's her name, you know!"

"Now, Sheila—hereafter, you are to speak English. All right? *Speak English!*"

She closed her eyes. "I—have—no—papers," she said in her wonderfully articulated, hollow English.

"None of us has papers. If anybody tries to talk to you, speak English! Both of you!" He caught Beecham's eye. "Will you talk to your daughter in English while I drive, please?"

"What about?"

"About anything."

"But why?"

"It's part of the disguise."

"But it isn't disguise. We *are* English."

"That's the idea."

"What? Oh. Oh, I see! Like that old story. 'The Something'd Letter.' Purloined. 'The Purloined Letter.' Oh, jolly good."

"I—do—not—understand," his daughter said.

"Oh, well, m'dear, we speak English so we won't seem to be Chinese, you see? Because we don't look sufficiently Chinese in the daylight, but if we speak English nobody would bother to guess that we're *pretending* anything! Or something of that sort. Is that how it goes?"

Tarp smiled. "Bang on, sir."

The old man chuckled. "Oh, what fun!" Tarp started the engine and the old man put one hand on his daughter's and said, "Now, my dear, we must speak in English. Understand? In English . . ." Tarp smiled again. Beecham was shouting, exactly as if he were trying to communicate with a foreigner.

Sheila Beecham was blushing furiously. Father and daughter could talk volubly in colloquial Chinese, but they were embarrassed to deal with each other in this different language. It was as if they had confronted each other naked.

"Oh, dear," Beecham said. He looked appealingly toward the rearview mirror. "This is very difficult," he said in Chinese.

"Speak English!"

The woman opened her mouth and tried to speak, but no sound came out and she put her hand to her eyes as if to hold back tears. "I don't know who I am in English!" she cried in that language.

"Just so," her father said. He patted her hand. "Oh, dear, oh, dear. Let's press on, Sheila—press on, my girl. . . ."

Tarp let the car coast down the long curve toward the town. He knew that he had to go through the town if he was to return to the drop bag, so he had decided to take the Beechams with him to his meeting in the Culture Park. There was only one road going south, and they were on it now.

"I'm going to stop the car outside the gate of a little park," he said to them as he drove. "Then I want you to get out with me and walk to a teahouse in the park. I'll order tea for you—you can't speak Chinese, remember—and then I'll have to go away for a few minutes. I don't want to leave you in the car because I think you're more exposed there than in the park. Anyway, there's a chance that they'll be looking for the car by now. You just sit there and drink tea—eat if you want to, it'll be your last chance today—and then when I come back, get right up and join me and we'll leave. Is that clear?"

"I hope so," the old man said. He looked unsure of himself. *He looks like an old con*, Tarp thought. "Sheila, is that clear?"

"I hope so," she said in English. She seemed a little more sure of herself now. Tarp found himself wondering if she would be able to handle her knife as well in English.

He let the car roll over raked gravel under the wall of the Culture Park and then over pine needles and cones as he put it up close to the concrete. He got out, opened the rear door, and saluted.

Arthur Beecham looked startled. Sheila Beecham was concentrating very hard on speaking English and looked almost intelligent.

"Very well, Father," she said slowly. "Let us exit from the motor at this very nice park."

"Exit from the motor? I don't think one says 'exit from the motor,' my dear." He started talking to Tarp as he clambered out. "Surely you don't say 'exit from the motor,' do you? It sounds like—"

"Father!"

"My dear?"

"He does not speak English, Father."

"Oh, nonsense, my dear, he speaks it better than you or— Oh, I see what you mean. Oh, dear." He put his hand over his mouth in a schoolboy's gesture. "Oh, naughty me!"

Sheila Beecham took one of her father's hands and put it on her forearm in a gesture of perfectly natural affection. "The driver will close the door, Father," she said in her perfect English. Her eyes met Tarp's and glided right on by. She seemed hardly to recognize him.

Tarp saluted again, shut the rear door, and got the flat package from the front seat. He put it under his right arm and closed the door.

The Beechams were twenty feet ahead of him. Other people were walking along the road in the dying daylight. From the park, the sounds of a delighted child, of the low thump of a kicked ball, of a woman's laughter, reached his ears like siren calls from his childhood.

Here we go. He could feel the hard shape of the PPK through the newspaper. *Here we go*.

chapter eleven

He thought that the two women in the teahouse were not the same as the two he had seen that morning; this pair seemed to enjoy their work. The place smelled better, too.

Sheila Beecham was working very hard at seeming not to understand Chinese. She had asked her father what he wanted in English; now, with the loudness and excessive clarity that her father had used earlier in speaking to her, she was saying to Tarp, in English, "Tea. *Tea.* Do you understand, driver?"

He tried to stand like a Chinese soldier. *Hell of a soldier, pushing middle age and not ranked yet. A real moron.* "Two teas," he said in Chinese to one of the old women. She looked hopefully at a tray of foods, urging him with her eyes to buy more.

"I want rice cake," Arthur Beecham said. He sounded insulted, as if somebody had already told him that there would be no rice cake for him that day. "I truly would *like* a piece of rice cake."

"Oh, Father," his daughter said like a bad actress with a speech impediment, "you shall have rice cake then."

"Oh, jolly good!" He turned to the other of the two old women and said, in the clearest possible Chinese, "One rice cake, Mother, a thousand thanks."

"Rice cake, yes, rice cake!" Tarp said very loud. He tried to smile at Beecham like a teacher who has just heard his pupil say something brilliant. He nodded his head vigorously. "Very good, Irish friend of the People, very good!"

"What? Oh. . . ." Beecham switched guiltily to English. "Oh, damn." He put both hands over his mouth this time.

"Very good," Tarp said again and pushed him gently toward the door. Tarp snatched up several things from the food table—canned fish and canned bean curd and a small dish of cold noodles—and urged the Beechams on ahead while he paid.The canned goods looked like relics of the Manchus, for they were dusty and their labels were faded.

There was unusual movement outside the door, and it caught his eye. He saw a man hurrying toward the gate, against the normal flow of people—a man who was staring back at the Beechams.

That's trouble, a voice said in his head. He squeezed the PPK under his arm, assuring himself that it was still there.

The Beechams sat at a table and spread their meager supper in front of them. Local people passed on and stared in open curiosity at these exotics.

"Smile," Tarp muttered through set jaws. "You love it here. This is all fascinating."

"I am frightened," Sheila Beecham said.

"So am I. Now, I'm going up that path there over the little bridge. I'll be only a few minutes. If anybody comes near, *speak English*. Act stupid. You know nothing about identity papers." She nodded, biting off a corner of rice cake with big, white teeth. "All right, dismiss me."

"What?"

"Tell me to wait over there. Westerners do that with their servants."

"Oh. Oh, I see." She pushed another piece of rice cake into her mouth with a faintly dirty finger and extended the other arm to full length in a gesture worthy of a funerary statue, at the least—Grief pointing the way to Eternal Bliss. "Wait there!"

Tarp made a little bow. The newspaper crackled against the PPK. He smiled.

He ignored the locals. Somebody was snickering, probably at seeing a soldier of the People's Liberation Army dismissed by a foreign devil. He was worrying about the man who had hurried out of the park; he had recognized the Beechams, somehow.

Tarp sat on the end of the same concrete bench as in the morning. The PPK was pointed to cover the rest of the bench, and he had only to cross his arms, resting his left hand on the pistol butt, to use it. By bending very slightly forward, he could look under the absurd little bridge and see part of the Beechams' table.

Tarp was nervous. He was always nervous when things were coming to a head like this. It was a form of fear, he thought—not fear of being hurt or of being killed, but fear of seeing things go wrong, fear of some stupid error or some stupid coincidence that would make all the plans and all the work pointless. Fear of the inevitable miracle.

And here comes a possible error right now. His contact was coming down the path with short, quick steps, looking at the ground as if she had been trained in humility. Tarp glanced under the bridge and saw only the Beechams. *So far, so good.*

"All right, make it quick," he said before she could even sit down.

"It is impossible," she said. She let her body down

on the bench with a violence that suggested extreme self-hatred. "It will not work. It is—"

"Do not waste my time. What have you got for me?"

She took a deep, shuddering breath. "They need more time. The airplane cannot be ready for—"

"The airplane is supposed to be standing ready at all times. Do not talk nonsense to me. Tell me a time and a place for the pickup."

Her eyes were tormented when she looked at him; they were dry and heavily lined at the corners. "Where is the man? Where is the device?"

Tarp looked under the bridge again. There was a new pair of legs planted by the Beechams' table. *The inevitable. The error. Goddam!*

Tarp kept his eyes on that pair of legs as he snapped his words at her. His anger crackled around her like static. "I ask you once more, woman, and then I will leave here and you will not see me again. If that happens, I will report you so that you will be out in the cold so fast you will freeze to death. Now: where is the pickup and when?"

She began to cry. Tears plugged her nose almost at once—Tarp realized that she had been crying recently, as well—and he felt foolish, like a man locked into some endless wrangle at the end of a love affair. "The old military airfield beyond Cherchen. Two miles west of the road to Xi-Pan—bearing one-nine-eight from Cherchen center. Map coordinates—EP7, AR9. . . ." She had to keep sniffing back her tears.

"I can find it," Tarp snapped. "Enough! When?" He had leaned forward so far he could have touched the gravel of the path with his left hand if he had wanted to take it off the butt of the pistol. He could see two pairs of legs now, one of them Sheila Beecham's and one the stranger's.

The woman was almost ready to crack. *Somebody's pushing her. A husband or a son—maybe for more money. Maybe wanting her to turn us in. Patriotism or greed. Or guilt.* She sniffed again. "Tomorrow night, two hours after midnight, *but the plane is not ready*!"

"Tell them it has to be ready. If the plane is not there at that time, I will find another way."

"No—stay here!"

"You are a fool."

He was striding very fast along the gravel path. He did not dare to run, did not dare to call attention to himself, but he moved with lunging strides. He could not see the table now because of the hump of the bridge, but they could not see him, either. A few feet from the bridge, he cut to his left, went down along the side of it and over the ankle-deep, sandy trickle of water at the bottom and up the other side.

He came around the end of the bridge.

There were two men with the Beechams. Both they and Beecham and his daughter were behaving very decorously, and the effect was of a bizarre but very formalized dance. One of the two men had Arthur Beecham by the left arm and was trying to pull him away; Beecham was complaining, but without raising his voice. Closer to Tarp, another man, burly and low-browed, was backing very slowly away from Sheila Beecham, who was a little bent over. Tarp knew from her posture that she had just been struck with a very hard, very short punch in the belly. Tarp could see five other people near or on the terrace. In the semidarkness, their faces were pale and a little unreal. Clearly, they were keeping away from whatever was happening at the table.

Tarp came on at the same ground-devouring pace, up the slope from the stream so quickly that the low-browed man was caught by surprise.

Tarp passed Sheila Beecham on his left. He heard her gasping for breath; still, she was trying to disguise her pain. *Good,* he thought, you're good at this. He moved one step to his right to have a clear view of the man who was trying to pull Arthur Beecham away.

The low-browed man was about a yard and a half on the other side of Beecham's daughter. Beecham and his assailant were about four yards ahead of Tarp.

The man with Beecham made the mistake of hesitating. He wanted to do two things at once—to hold on to the old man and to pull something from his coat—and he could do neither well. In that instant of hesitation, Tarp turned his body to the left and, without taking the package from under his right arm, pulled the trigger once.

The makeshift silencer was good for one shot. Paper strips blew out like confetti and began to drift among the five of them like snow; the pistol shot was reduced to an unearthly snap, as if the limb of a distant tree had cracked. Or it might have been something dropped in the street beyond the gate; or it might have been a sick man's cough.

The man who had been trying to kidnap Beecham sat down on the stone paving. He seemed to be watching the pieces of the *People's Daily* flutter down in front of him.

Tarp would not risk a second shot without a silencer. He squeezed the pistol against his right side, and as he saw the low-browed man begin to move at an angle to him, heading so as to pass wide of him and go toward Beecham, he spun and took a long step with his left leg, like a fencer's lunge, and rammed his big fist into the side of the low-browed man's low-browed head.

The man went over with an abruptness that made it seem that he had slipped or tripped. With the same speed that had unleashed the blow, Tarp's fist recoiled and he became again a soldier of the liberation army, one concerned for his Western charges. He took Sheila Beecham's right elbow in his left hand and pulled her toward her father.

The man who had tried to grab Beecham was sitting on the ground staring at the shreds of paper, while a red stain widened on his chest. As Tarp passed him and gathered in Arthur Beecham the man sank slowly on his back and looked up at the sky.

Tarp pushed Beecham's daughter ahead and clutched the old man's skinny arm. "Come!" he said.

"Oh, Right-o." Beecham had learned in prison that there are times when one does not argue. One simply goes.

There was movement on the fringes of the terrace. People were moving cautiously. They were unsure of just what they had seen, but they knew that the hero of the little drama was a soldier of the People's Liberation Army, and therefore the two men on the ground must be the villains.

"Move," Tarp hissed. "Don't run . . . move . . . good. Act as if nothing has happened . . . nothing has happened. . . ."

A family group watched them go. They passed under a lighted lamp. The man of the group, who was about thirty and who had three children and a very pretty wife, said anxiously. "What happened, comrade?"

"Reactionary thugs," Tarp said. "Black marketeers. Call the militia."

The man and his pretty wife nodded at each other as if they had known as much. They began to explain it all to their children, kneeling next to them and pointing down at the terrace where the two men were lying as if asleep. ". . . and the brave soldier defeated the bad men who wanted to steal from the people by—."

Tarp turned to his right, and the roadside gravel ground under his feet with the sound of breaking glass. He held each of the Beechams by an elbow. "Get behind me," he murmured.

It was almost dark, but he could see movement at the rear of the car. Somebody was prying open the trunk. Tarp began to run.

The box—don't open the box, Jesus God don't touch the box! Oh Christ he's found the soldier, the fat's in the fire. . . .

There was a man waiting at the rear of the car. He had been bent over the trunk and he straightened and turned, holding a wrench to defend himself. Tarp slowed and set himself as if to launch a kick at the man's middle.

The wrench swung in a vicious arc.

Tarp swayed back, then pushed the man's arm on around in the same arc, slamming it into his shoulder and then slamming his weight into the body, forcing him back against the trunk. He pushed the muzzle of the PPK deep into the man's midriff, deep into fat. *The mafia hit men used to use a pillow for a silencer*. He pulled the trigger. *Fat makes a good pillow*. He reared back and pulled the man out of the maw of the trunk and swung him against the concrete wall of the park, where he collapsed and gasped and began to whimper.

Gut shot. I'd whimper, too.

Somebody else was coming out of the car. Tarp was too late to stop him, too late to kick the door closed; the man was quicker and kicked it open. Tarp's foot met the door in the wrong way. He was knocked backward into the road, but he kept his balance and did not fall. The other man had the advantage, however. He was small and would not come at him foolishly—*a tough adolescent*, Tarp thought as he saw the wink of a blade—and then another and another as the youth made sweeping cuts in the air between them.

He did not want to use the gun again. He did not want the noise.

The knife sang through the air once more, and then the youth turned aside and there was a harsh inward breath. Tarp saw Sheila Beecham there, and he kicked up into the man's groin and then rammed him against the side of the car with such force that the window gave with an audible crack, and where the head had hit there was a spiderweb of cracked glass.

Tarp spent a second bending over the fallen young

man. He had been cut along the upper arm and the shoulder.

"Are you all right?" Tarp said quickly.

"Yes," Beecham's daughter said.

"Your father?"

"Quite fine, thanks," a voice came from the dusk.

"Get in the car, quick." He went to the trunk and satisfied himself that the box had not been disturbed.

End of the line, soldier boy. He dragged the unconscious soldier out on the road. *Time to grow up.* He left the half-naked body by the gut-shot man. *They'll be so confused they won't know what to make of you. Nor will you.*

Tarp scrambled behind the wheel. "Ready?"

"Yes, go, go!"

The old car crunched forward over the gravel. Using no lights, Tarp turned a corner and then another, narrowly missing cyclists who screamed after him in fury. He reached the main road and snapped on the lights.

"Who were those men?" She was on the seat behind him, her mouth almost touching his right ear.

"They were after your father. Not me and you. Your father."

"I know! They used his name! They said, 'Are you the Englishman, Beecham?' "

That gave Tarp something to think about. *Nobody* was supposed to know that Beecham was even alive.

"I think that the men in the park and the men by the car were together. If they knew your father's name, then they probably knew about the device. I think they had planted somebody in the park to watch for him. That means. . . ." Tarp trailed off.

"Yes?"

"That means that either somebody recognized me this morning—or the whole operation is blown and they knew enough to wait there for us—or there's a leak someplace." He thought of the woman's hopelessness.

when he had talked to her on the bench. *Maybe she knew. Maybe she knew it's blown.*

"What do we do?" Beecham's daughter said. She was speaking English, and the language had more conviction and more substance to it now. And the *we* had force.

"We press on, as your father would say."

He spun the wheel to the right and the big car swayed around a curve that took them out of the town. There was traffic in the other direction—three long-haul trucks coming up from Cherchen and then a Chinese Jeep with soldiers in it, their weapons sticking up like spines on some prickly sea animal, silhouetted in the lights of the following vehicle. Tarp drove carefully until they passed the chain-link fence around a tractor depot at the far edge of settlement. Beyond it was only forest and darkness.

Tarp put his foot to the floor and the big car began to purr.

chapter twelve

Tarp cursed with relief when he found the hiding place of the drop bag. He had needed the marker beacon even to come close to it in the dark, and then it had taken him another fifteen minutes to find the bag itself. It was cold in this wasteland now; the wind blew like a knife that seemed to cut all the way from the Pamirs, where it had its start, across the Takla Makan, bringing cold and snow like the dust of the ancient caravans. There was no moon, not even a star.

They had left the old sedan in a dry streambed under the road where a former locomotive boiler had been used as a bridge. The car had just fit in there, with hardly room enough for Tarp to open his door and wriggle out. Somebody would find it in a few days—a search party out looking for them, or a hunter going up into the hills for antelope, or a herdsman. *Or a flash flood, coming down from the Altin Tagh. They'll wonder what's made such a fine dam under the bridge!*

He flashed the light three times and then waited with

the PPK in his fist. Beecham and his daughter were supposed to bring the box up when they saw the signal. Tarp squatted on his heels with his left hand on the slick fabric of the bag, feeling for the hard outlines of the rifle. *One minute, then I'll have to get out the rifle and the grenades and go down there. . . .*

Beecham's weary breathing was the first thing to reach him, and then he saw the woman's head, silhouetted against the almost black sky, moving darkness against still darkness. *Should have brought night goggles. Too damned risky, this way.*

"Over here," he said in a voice no louder than he would have used in a small room. He flashed the light into his hand, and for an instant a shape like the inside of a pink shell glowed.

They set the box down carefully and Beecham folded up into a sitting position. Sheila Beecham sat down more slowly. "Heavy," she said. He saw her move a hand but could not see the purpose of the movement—to wipe her forehead or to sweep back her hair.

Tarp moved close to them and they all bent together over the box so they could hear him in the wind. "It's about twenty miles to the airstrip," he said. "We have to be there by two of the morning after this—about twenty-six hours from now. There are two riverbeds to cross, but I think they'll be dry. But it's rough going—no trails. I'd like to put ten miles behind us before we sleep. Can you do it?"

Beecham's daughter still wanted to get out of China. "I can do all of it tonight, if I have to."

"Mr. Beecham?"

The old man said nothing, and Tarp listened to the wind moving through distant trees in an unrelenting whisper. "Once," the old voice said, "the Red Guard made me walk all day and then all that night. Round and round my laboratory, which they had wrecked. When they said I could stop, I went on walking, to show them I could do it. Yes, I can walk there tonight."

"Good." Tarp unzipped the bag. "There's food here if you want it, such as it is—energy bars, they call them. Like sawdust with carbohydrate mashed in." He began to chew on one. They each accepted one, and Tarp began to peel off the soldier's uniform so that he could put on the black jump suit, which he had worn when he had parachuted in. *Years ago. Falling out of England, into China. Out of the present. Out of Gillian. Into—?*

The jump suit was made of a fabric that made no noise when it moved across itself. It had a zippered pocket on each thigh and another high on each arm; it closed with black nylon zippers at ankle and wrist like a wet suit. He put the extra sets of ID papers and passports into the sleeve pockets and then buckled the Browning HP around his waist.

"I've got a sweater in here, if you're cold."

He rolled up the uniform and thrust it into the bag. He strapped the knife on his right calf and zipped the pant leg down over it, then put the grenades into a shoulder bag, pulled it over his head, and put the PPK and the extra rifle clips into it.

"The box needs handles if we're to carry it all that way," Beecham's daughter said. She sounded tired, almost hopeless.

"Are you going to make it?" he said.

"Of course!" Angrily, she got to her feet and stood there, shivering in the harsh wind.

Tarp tied the box in parachute cord and rigged handles at each end, padding them with the shoulder pads from Comrade Qiu's overcoat.

"I'll carry one end. You two trade off on the other." He hefted one end of the box. It weighed sixty pounds, at least. If Beecham were to be believed, he had got it down to the prison generator shed all by himself.

"Let's go."

When he had first crossed this terrain on his way to the railway station, he had thought it easy walking, but then the daylight had been coming and he had been able to pick his way. In this dense darkness, however, the ground seemed cruelly uneven, and there were roots and thorns at every step. Tarp walked first; Sheila Beecham followed him with the other end of the box, which joined them like a bond of guilt. *Like marriage.* She never complained, and sometimes she walked with her father's hand on her shoulder to lead him. When they stopped to rest, Tarp said to the old man, "What would happen if we had to leave the box?"

"You would have to leave me, too."

"I was only asking."

First light found them on a ridge in the foothills of the Altin Tagh. To the west was a hazy view of mountains; to the north was the depression of the Takla Makan. Tarp led them farther up a slope into a grove of tormented, stunted little trees and took them into the tangle of their gnarled trunks, where there was just room for them all to lie down. He had filled the fabric water bottle at one of the "dry" rivers, which had been crotch-deep with snow melt. He dropped in tablets and moved the fabric bottle in idle circles, and by the time he was ready to offer them the medicinal-tasting water, they were both asleep. Tarp piled extra clothing on them and then unfolded the thin ground cloth from the drop bag and spread that over them. They slept together like children. *Hansel und Gretel.*

The old man even looked childlike in his sleep. His daughter, however, looked old and unhealthy, as if sleep was hard work for her. *Who are you?* Tarp wondered. Was she really nothing more than this man's child, or was she something more—she who was the daughter of a Russian agent and the product of a hostile China? *You're a very good killer, whatever you are,* he thought.

He took up a position thirty yards above them and sat against a tree with the rifle in his lap. At eleven in the morning, he came down and sent her up to stand watch.

At three o'clock, he went on alone. Unencumbered by them and the box, he could move at an easy jog that ate up the miles. He found a game path and followed it until it ran into a sandy lumbering road, and he took that at a better pace until his compass told him he had gone too far south and then he struck into the woods again. At five-thirty, he was looking down over the old airfield: there were the remains of three hangars, the barely visible outline of the encircling taxiway and seventeen aircraft bunkers, and the broad field where P-38s and P-40s had snarled and roared and swooped into the sky. All was silence now; the brave fighter planes had faded, like the caravans, into the wind. Now the incoming aircraft would have to cope with wiry brush and a few small trees in the landing area.

Tarp planted the beacon in a dirt-filled crack between two rocks and turned back.

At ten, he started them toward the airfield.

"How far?" Beecham said.

"Less than last night."

"I can make that, then."

He carried the other end of the box for a short distance and then his daughter took it from him.

"How will we know when we're there?" she said.

"I left a marker."

"How will the plane know to come to the right place?"

"That's not my concern. If they do it alone, they'll drop flares and take a big chance. If they have somebody on the ground, there'll be lights."

"Who—on the ground, I mean?"

"That's not my concern, either. Except, after that ball-up in the park, it *is* my concern. We have to be careful."

"What if the people on the ground do it wrong?"

"Then the plane won't land."

The box swayed between them. "What if the plane can't land? What do we do then?"

"We find another way out."

"Is there another way out?"

"There's always another way. The trick is recognizing it."

They reached the beacon shortly after one-thirty. Tarp put the box down and Arthur Beecham sat on it. They passed the water bottle around and the remainder of the food from the bag, and he said to the woman, "Can you use a gun?"

"No."

He took the clip out of the PPK, palmed the round out of the chamber, and handed it to her. "This is the safety lever—when it's like that, the gun won't shoot. That way, it will. Keep it the other way until you absolutely want to shoot somebody. Understand?"

"Yes."

"All right. Do it a few times. Move the safety, aim, pull the trigger. Aim at that tree trunk; at least you can see it. Good. Close your left hand over your right like this to steady it. Good. When you shoot, another round will come up into the chamber and it'll be ready to fire again, as fast as you can pull the trigger. Each time you fire, the gun will climb in the air—force your hand right up. So push down. All right, run through it again."

She did it over and over.

"Why will I need it?"

"To protect your father. I'm not going to be with you for a little while."

"*Why?*"

"I want to check the plane out when it lands. I'll leave you two here. The plane will come in over our heads because of the wind and will stop at the far end of the field, and then turn and come back here. I'll signal if it's all right. During that time, you'll have to be ready to use the gun."

"Why don't you trust the airplane?"

"I don't trust anybody—remember?"

He put the clip into the PPK and handed it to her, warning her not to chamber a round until the aircraft landed. Handing it to her, he had that feeling that always comes with turning over a weapon, even to a friend. Yet he knew that if she had meant to kill him, she could have done it a number of times with the knife. Whoever she was—whatever she was—at that point she should have the gun.

"Do you want more water?"

"No. Let me be by myself now. I am frightened."

Tarp sat on the box with her father. Beecham watched the faint shape of his daughter's body disappear up the hill in the darkness. "I am sorry to say," Beecham murmured in a conspiratorial voice, "that I don't believe my daughter is a pretty girl. *Is* she?"

"Ah—well—."

"No, not pretty." He had answered his own question. "Rather what at best used to be called 'handsome.' Don't you think?"

"Ah—hmm—."

"Or so it is to be hoped." Beecham sighed. "I should very much like to see her happily married one day. A pretty woman has a much easier time of it, you know, getting married and having babies and so on. But what I think is, if a woman is well-to-do, she immediately takes on a great deal of prettiness. Wouldn't you say?"

"Prettiness is overrated, Mr. Beecham."

"Well, that's all very well for you to say. Now, I've known one or two really quite homely girls to get absolutely smashing husbands because they were well-off. Years ago, mind you. It's my belief that if I had a bit of money, Sheila would be more attractive to men. Do you believe my particle beam is worth a million pounds?"

"If it does what you say it does, it's worth a great deal more than that."

"Yes, well, there you are, you see. I'm not a mercenary man. I'm a scientist, but I'm a father, too. I believe I shall say to Winston that I should greatly appreciate getting a million pounds for my discovery, not for my own sake but for my daughter's. Would the nation have a million pounds, do you think?"

"I believe so, yes."

"They were still on austerity when I left."

"There's always plenty of money for new weapons, Mr. Beecham."

"Just so. So I shall settle the million on Sheila, and she'll overcome some of her disabilities. Would you, for example, consider marrying my daughter if she had a million pounds?"

"I'm not really the marrying sort, sir."

"Oh? Oh, what a pity. I rather like you. Oh, well, I daresay you know some eligible young men, eh? Do you go to dances?"

Tarp smiled. "I went to one just before I left London."

"Oh, good! Where was that?"

"At Hamish Penhurst's house."

"Capital! Well, as you've no interest in Sheila yourself—and I quite understand, I really do. Perhaps, when I get the million you could make some introductions, eh?"

Beecham's was a selective dottiness, Tarp decided—and a rather endearing one. "I think it's fair to warn you, sir, that getting married and having babies isn't thought quite as necessary as it was when you left England. Many women get along without all that now."

"Oh? Well, I'm sure she'll be able to use the million anyway. Lord knows *I* wouldn't know what to do with it."

They sat comfortably together on the box until the first sound of the plane's engines reached them.

It came in almost directly overhead, sliding down from the hilltop just at tree level. As its engines roared toward them two rows of high-intensity light blinked along the abandoned field. The plane corrected its path and the lights came on to stay, guiding it in; they were like the lights of a city street in the empty valley below. As it pulled level to let down on the field the plane turned on its own undercarriage light to reveal the wiry growth in white, sickly brilliance.

"Chamber a round and put that pistol on safety. Let's go, let's go!" Tarp had the box on his shoulder and was starting down the slope. He had already pulled Beecham to his feet, and the old man, hand in hand with his daughter, was scrambling down behind him. Tarp looked overhead for a telltale reflection of the lights on the high cloud cover. "Come on, come on!" he muttered.

The plane's wheels ripped through the little bushes as it touched down and raced up between the two rows of lights. The engines bellowed as the jet props fought to slow it.

"Down!" Tarp yelled. "Down!" The plane was turning and starting its run back to their end of the field. As it did so the field lights were extinguished and they were in an astonishing darkness again.

"All right. Once we've got a foot on board, they'll take off. These will be very, very nervous men. They won't waste a second."

"Then let's get on board!"

"No, I'm going to have a look first. Stay put—both of you! Mr. Beecham, keep your hands on the box so you'll always know where it is. Sheila, have the pistol ready. When I come back, I'll say, 'Hail, Mary.' If anybody comes and doesn't say that, shoot them. I'm off."

He was running, stooped over like a baboon, the rifle carried in his right hand and the tough little plants flicking at his knuckles. He went up a low knoll and down the other side, and he could see the sparks from the aircraft's engines.

There must be people nearby, he knew. He thought of the almost hysterical woman in the park. *Ready to crack. Dangerous contact.* Yet she had brought the plane in on time. The organization of the pickup seemed good. *Maybe it's all right. Maybe it's all right.*

He rounded a wing and came up hard against the edge of the open door.

"Good King George sent me."

"Yeah, I've had you covered on a night scope since you came over the hill, mate—all right, let's go."

Night scope. Very smooth.

"Let me see your face."

"Shit, mate—!" A light came on. He saw a caucasian face, lit garishly from below, a Halloween mask of a face.

"You weren't on the crew that brought me out."

"No. Whole other crew."

"I asked for the same crew."

"Shit, man, this is Communist fucking China! Let's get out of here!"

"I have to get somebody else."

"I know that, I know that! Let's go! We got to make a judgment on weight—priorities, mate, that's what I was given, first the old man, then his device, then you, and the woman last. This is a tiny little bird, this craft, she don't like heavy loads. All right, let's go!"

Something, something, something wrong . . .

"Now you're talking!" the man cried. Tarp whirled and saw Sheila Beecham and her father struggling toward him, the box between them. He leaped toward them. "I told you to wait for me!" he screamed. But Sheila Beecham's face was transformed with that lust for freedom he had seen before.

"Goddam you!" he roared. But the crewman from the plane was wrestling the handle of the box from her hand and was pulling it and Arthur Beecham toward the plane. The old man had to trot now to keep up, and then the crewman lifted the box shoulder-high and flung it at the opening in the side of the airplane, looking, in the red glow of the aircraft's lights, like an ant flinging food into a mysterious maw.

"In you go, sir—get in, Mr. Beecham. . . . Let me give you a hand. . . ."

The crewman was inside the plane now, and he bent down and hooked a hand under Beecham's armpit and boosted him up. Tarp was trying to hold Sheila back, he was not sure yet why, and then he flung himself forward toward the black opening of the door, dropping the rifle as he moved so both hands would be free.

"Go!" he heard the crewman shout. "*Go!*"

The engines screamed and the plane began to roll forward.

The two rows of high-intensity lights came on.

In their pitiless glare, he saw the crewman begin to lean around the doorframe, a machine pistol in his left hand. With what seemed an unreal slowness, he aimed it down beside the plane. Sheila Beecham was there—trotting now to keep up with the plane's first forward movement.

He's going to kill her, Tarp thought quite clearly. Then he understood what was wrong. *He knew about her. He said "the woman." Nobody knew about Beecham's daughter. Except the men in the park.*

Tarp's feet were off the ground, but by so little that he could feel the little bushes whipping them. Next to him, Arthur Beecham was lying on the floor of the aircraft, his feet still well outside the door opening. The box lay between them.

Tarp heaved himself farther inside as the machine pistol began to bang over his head. His left hand groped in the shoulder bag, found what it was looking for. The machine pistol fired again, and the plane began to gather speed. Tarp wrenched at the grenade he had pulled from the bag and hurled it to his right, away from him, over his own body toward the pilot's compartment, at the same time grabbing Arthur Beecham's jacket at the small of the back with one hand and a rope handle of the box with the other, pulling them toward him with his whole strength.

"No. . . . Jesus God!" The crewman saw Arthur Beecham drawn toward the doorway.

Tarp swung his legs out and down. The riveted steel of the doorframe was just above his groin. The swing of his legs gave him momentum; like an acrobat beginning a back flip, he swung out of the opening with his knees jammed against the metal, pushing, thrusting, forcing the aircraft away from him.

He felt the box teeter on the edge and fall over, and he let go of it.

He gathered Arthur Beecham close to him, like a lover, and fell backward, landing with crushing force, rolling over and over with his arms around the old man to protect him, making himself a shell to guard this precious old egg.

He heard the man in the aircraft shout. The machine pistol fired once.

Then the grenade blew.

The crewman sailed out the doorway of the plane into the white stare of the high-intensity lights, a brilliant rectangle of orange silhouetting him for an instant, and the plane's engines roared like animals that had been hurt; the craft surged forward and ground-looped, went up on the left wing and the nose, and exploded into fire.

"She's going to blow," Tarp heard himself say. The voice sounded clear, even dispassionate, but he was not aware of having spoken.

"My goodness. . . . oh, my goodness. . . . oh, dear me, my goodness . . ." Arthur Beecham's voice went on and on. Tarp could feel a vibration on his chest: the old man was shaking. He lay partly on top of Tarp, still clasped in his arms. "My goodness. Oh, dear, dear. . . ." There was a pause. His voice came from somewhere different; he had raised his head. "Whatever happened to my airplane?"

Tarp tried to make his left hand let go of his own right wrist. It finally did so, although clumsily. He found that he could, with difficulty, move the arm off

Beecham's back, but there was remarkable pain when he did it.

"Sheila!" Beecham moaned. "Where's my Sheila?"

Beecham was trying to free himself from the grip that had saved him. He pushed at Tarp's body now, repeating his daughter's name and thrusting with his fists, pummeling Tarp, wriggling free. Tarp let one of his pushes roll him over.

Now Tarp could swivel his eyes to the left and see Sheila Beecham against the landing lights. She was stumbling along the improvised runway, weeping, moaning as if the whole universe had died, but whether for the loss of her father or for the failure of her escape from China, he could not tell. Tarp knew that if she stayed out there in the white light much longer, somebody would kill her. Already, a hundred yards away where the plane was burning fiercely, human figures were gathering, probably bewildered and frightened, probably rushing about in contradictory paths but looking from this distance like dancers around some ceremonial fire.

"Hail Mary," Tarp heard himself say.

She gave a gulp and a kind of hiccup, and then she saw her father. She bent over him. Tarp could see the bright lacquer of tears on her cheeks. There was a terrible joy there, too, an instant understanding that the old man was alive. "My father," she said again and again in Chinese. "My father. . . ."

Tarp wanted to tell her that he was alive, too, but he could not make the machinery for speaking operate; and at that moment the gas tanks of the burning aircraft exploded, and a wave of heat and concussion swept over them, and she collapsed on him, weeping happily, and Tarp passed out.

Consciousness came hesitantly, crossing over from the ragged dreams of sleep to the silence of the wasteland, where the rush of the wind was not unlike the sound of his coma. He knew that he was awake when he felt pain. He remembered the last moments on the aircraft and then what had followed, and then he knew why his neck and his upper back hurt so much.

"Beecham?" His voice was a hoarse whisper.

"Quiet—you must be quiet or they will find us." Her lips were close to his ear. She was squeezing water over his mouth from a cloth.

"Your father?"

"On watch."

"How long since—?"

"Maybe an hour. Can you move?"

"Where are we?"

"On the hillside above the airfield."

He looked aside at her without moving his head. He did not want to move it because of the pain, and he was afraid to try to move it because he might find out that he could not. Behind her head, the sky was very faint, not from the landing lights but from the first leaden touch of dawn. "What happened?"

"After the plane exploded, a man came running down past us, picking up the lights. Somebody else was shouting at him, and there was a man screaming where the explosion was. Father and I lay where we were. Where you were. When the people were gone, we pulled you up here. We heard a helicopter come and go away, and then trucks came, and a helicopter again. I think maybe they wanted to put out the airplane fire but they did not. It burned itself out. There was some shooting, so maybe they found the man with the lights."

Tarp tried to sit up. Pain almost put him out again. "The box," he gasped, "the box. . . ."

"I have the box," she said simply. "Father told me where he thought it was. I got the rifle, too."

"*You* did?" He looked at the broad face. "Good for you." He lay still for several seconds. "Help me sit up." She managed to get him to a sitting position with his back against a rock. "Not good," he said through nearly clenched teeth. "Get the shoulder bag. Will you?"

"Yes." She was back with it within seconds.

"There's a medicine kit. There is a packet with four pills wrapped in foil. They have a depression in one side like a thumbprint."

"Yes, I have one."

"Give me two of those."

"What are they?"

"A painkiller. But not a brain killer. They take the edge off the worst of it."

The pills were a strong endorphin that did not have the side effects of morphine. They would block some of the pain without slowing him.

"Where's the rifle?"

"My father has it. He says he can use a rifle."

"Your pistol?"

"Under my coat."

"Good. When daylight comes, they may decide to search. You must have left a trail, dragging me up here." He moved his head a fraction of an inch. The pain was muffled but definitely there. "We've got to move."

"My father is very tired." She lowered her head so she could look at him. "You could not lift that box now, could you?"

Tarp could not sustain that level stare. He muttered something about more painkiller, and then he felt over his hip for the Browning HP and checked it over. She continued to look at him.

"What happened on the airplane?" she said. "My father says he thinks you blew it up. He thinks maybe we should not trust you anymore."

"Yeah, I blew it up. They were the wrong people. They were going to fly him to the wrong place."

"Russia?"

"Yeah. Or Afghanistan, then Russia."

"How do you know?"

"Because they knew about you. Nobody should have known about you, except the men in the park. But they shouldn't have known about the plane; only the woman who was my contact knew about that. So either she was busted, or she was in with the men who tried to kidnap your father. I'm beginning to think that she was. And that means that this whole operation is busted—maybe has been busted almost from the beginning."

"Are you *sure*?"

That was the question he always hated. "No," he said reluctantly. "No."

"Then they could have been English!"

"Yes, there's a chance that they were. But I have to go with the likely thing." He allowed himself to meet her eyes. "If I waited until I was sure, I'd have been dead a long time ago." It was getting light. The outline of the valley was becoming clear below them. "I did what I had to do," he said stubbornly. Her face was set in a mulish, angry expression. "Help me up," he muttered.

"Can you stand alone?" she said when he was up. Clearly, her tone said, he could not.

"When I have to. Get your father."

"And then?"

"We'll get out of this."

"Oh, of course."

"Are you going to argue with me?"

"Our chances are not very good."

"Our chances were never very good. Nothing has changed."

"Nothing has changed! How can you say it? There are soldiers down below; my father is exhausted; you are hurt. . . ."

"And most people think we're dead. Whoever was on that plane *is* dead; that means that his—their—superiors will think both they and we are dead. In a day or two, the English will think we are dead because I do not intend to contact them—because there is a leak someplace. And if the English think we are dead, so will the Americans, because English intelligence is a sieve, and the Americans stand under it and catch what falls through. I think our chances are quite good, and I intend to get out of here—I'll walk out, if I have to. Or crawl on my gut or roll downhill if that's the only way. Now, you go talk to your father—he doesn't trust me and you don't like me, so you two decide what you want to do. In half an hour, I'm moving out. You two decide if you want to come with me."

She sneered. "I thought it was your job to get my father out."

"It was—until that airplane blew up. Now the operation's busted. Go talk to your father."

Tarp leaned against a tree and studied the valley below. Nausea came up in waves from his abdomen, and he kept his balance by putting his weight with both hands on the tree trunk and leaning forward against it with his face pressed to the rough bark.

There was enough light now to see the shapes of two vehicles about a hundred yards from the charred wreck of the aircraft and, beyond them, a small helicopter. *Evac*, he thought. *Medical chopper*. Zone military headquarters was sixty miles away, and the helicopter probably came from there; the vehicles might be either armed militia or PLA.

She came back from talking to her father with her head down and a pouting look on her face.

"Well?" he said without taking his eyes from the valley.

"We go with you."

"Get the army uniform from the black bag."

"Why?"

"Don't ask questions."

When she brought him the rumpled clothes, he unzipped the black jump suit. "Help me get those on."

"What are you going to do?"

When he stripped off the jump suit, the air bit coldly. He hoped it would make him more alert. He had had little sleep. The cold, however, felt muffled, like the pain in his neck and back, more like a memory of cold than the sensation itself. "Pardon me." He was naked except for briefs. "You will have to help me with the trousers. I can't bend over."

"What are you going to do?"

He had to lean against the tree with his left hand while she pulled the trousers up over each leg, one at a time. The jacket was easier, although he could not put his arms behind his body to get them into the sleeves, and he had to hold his arms out at shoulder height so she could pull on one sleeve and then feed the other in.

He was wearing his jump boots, made of a vapor-barrier fabric and cushioned, studded soles. They were not like the issue boots of the People's Liberation Army, but they would have to do.

He looked up at the sky. It was almost full daylight.

"They'll move up soon."

He studied the two vehicles in the valley. *Old Soviet GAZ-69s. My God, from the Gorki Plant. Mid-fifties.* They were slow four-wheel-drive cars that were supposed to carry five men each; the Chinese seemed to have got eight aboard each one. The farther one had hauled a trailer from which the soldiers had taken two heavy machine guns that were now set up at each end of the line of vehicles.

Tarp searched the hillside above him. High up and to the right, the silver-gray trunk of a dead pine looked bright in the morning light.

"See that dead tree?"

"Yes."

"Can you get your father and the box up there?"

"Yes."

"When I tell you to go up there, go up. When you and your father and the box are up there, fire two shots, about two seconds apart." He bent down by flexing his knees and picked up the web belt with the

Browning on it and the shoulder bag. He put the automatic into the bag and hung it over her shoulder. "That will give you a second weapon if you need one. I'll want the rifle."

"What are you going to do?"

"I'm going to go down there and borrow their helicopter. Then I'm going to fly up here and pick up you and your father and the box and go looking for a friend." He grinned—a crooked, pained, rather ragged grin that asked for her companionship. "I think we have a good chance."

But she still looked mulish. "I want to believe you," she said. "But what if it was the English who sent the airplane, after all?"

"It makes no difference. The airplane is burned. The men are dead."

She stared at the hard ground. When she lifted her face, there were, astonishingly, tears in her eyes. "I thought I would be in England tonight," she said. "I thought I would eat real English food."

"I'll buy you a real English dinner if we get out—I promise."

She shrugged. She was very tired, too, he realized.

He swung the rifle to his shoulder and, taking the thirty-round clips from the bag, rammed one into place instead of the short clip. "All right, start for the tree now. Fire the two shots when you get there."

chapter thirteen

Tarp came down the slope through the wind-twisted trees with the Chinese Mini-14 in the ready position. He needed to look like an officer who had been in a firefight and who wanted help. He touched his forehead, where half an hour before she had sponged dried blood from a gash. There was a lump there now and the puckered edges of a cut that had stopped bleeding. *Good detail. Nice bit of makeup.*

He did not want to be shot by a trigger-happy armed militiaman as they came up the hill toward him. He was wearing the green of the PLA, but he was sure that if these men were militia, they would be shooting at trees, each other, and anything else that moved. Through an opening, he could see them down there now between the vehicles, gathered around a slender man with a map. Four of them were guarding the downed aircraft, probably because other troops—regular army from corps zone headquarters, probably—were on the way.

He waited until he was almost at the edge of the trees. There was a vertical drop of about twenty feet in the remaining hundred and fifty yards to the soldiers, a slope steep enough so that he would try to run, and the jarring of the motion would cause him more pain.

Tarp began to shout in Chinese. "In the trees! Stay in the trees!" There was sudden activity by the vehicles, and both of the heavy machine guns swung in his direction.

"Keep good order and hold steady!" he shouted up the hill. "Fight for the People—fight for the People!"

Just before he left the cover of the trees, he tore open the gash on his forehead with a fingernail. Then he stepped into the clear and began to run toward the vehicles with his rifle held over his head.

"Comrades! Do not shoot! Comrades!" Pain pounded at the base of his skull, and he waited for the machine guns to fire. He was in the open and running through calf-high grass. He heard the bolts of rifles click. *Armed militia. If they're using bolt actions, they're not PLA.*

Tarp stopped. He swayed—not to imitate a wounded man, but because his balance was poor. He turned around and shouted back to the woods, "Hold firm! Relief is coming!"

Again, he ran toward the line of troops, stumbled, caught himself, and trotted on. He could see the man with the map quite clearly. He had come out from behind the vehicles and was holding the map under his left arm. His hands, palms turned back, were pointed out and down in a gesture meant to keep his men from firing.

Tarp drew up. He was panting. "Comrades!" The young man was twenty feet away, hardly farther than the length of a living room, but Tarp saw him as if at the end of a long corridor, diminished to pinhead size but as clear as a drop of blood under a microscope.

The man began walking toward him. He had a pistol

in his hands—a revolver, not an automatic. An old British Webley.

The man's eyes were moving over Tarp, over his uniform. Taking in the rifle, the red collar stars.

"Xiang Zhen," Tarp shouted before the man could speak. "Political officer, 115 Division!" *Dear God, Lin Piao's old outfit. Where did that come from? I'm going crazy.*

The slender man nodded. He was quite young, quite good-looking. He was worried about how he was to deal with this business of a clandestine British aircraft that had crashed in his territory. The armed militia were supposed to keep order and be ready to repel invasions, but this was a decidedly unusual incident.

"Your men look to be in good order," Tarp said. His voice was shaky. "You are in charge here?"

"I am the commandant." The conflict between the military and the political officer were summed up in those words. This young man could be very stiff-necked, Tarp decided. He gladly went with the force of the young officer's own preference.

"I am a thousand times grateful to see you, Commandant. I had thought that help would never come." He hurried on before the young man could speak. "We think there are seven of them up there . . . chased them in the dark, thought there were only two . . . firefight . . . bad business! I have two wounded up above. I must get medical help for them."

"You have been here—how long, comrade?"

"We heard the aircraft explode! Heading for Cherchen in my car . . . the flash in the sky was quite clear . . . trouble getting here because of no road, but . . . found them . . . infiltrators. They spoke Russian. Commandant, I must have medical help for my men."

The young man pointed his revolver at Tarp's head. "You are bleeding, comrade."

"A fragment—shattered bullet, I think. . . ."

Two shots sounded on the hill. Every man but Tarp

and the officer flinched. Tarp groaned. "Again! Or maybe it is my men who are firing. Can they have local support from reactionary elements, do you think?"

The officer shouted commands. Tarp advised him to go slowly, but he need not have worried; he was putting his men back behind the vehicles. Tarp stumbled through the line of militia and cut between the vehicles to head toward the helicopter. Behind him, the militiamen moved with sounds like a cavalry unit preparing to charge, clanking their metal canteens and ammunition boxes, rattling their bayonets. Like most armed-militia units, they were haphazardly armed; six of them wore only arm bands over civilian clothes to distinguish them, and their weapons ranged from ancient Springfields to Kalashnikovs. One had a butcher knife stuck in his belt.

But soldiers, nonetheless. Killing is killing.

"Comrade!"

The hair on Tarp's scalp felt as if it had been brushed the wrong way. He tried to turn and had to pivot entirely around on his feet. "Commandant?"

"Am I to support your men, comrade?"

"Let me get my wounded out. Then, if you would, proceed slowly up the hill. But remember, Commandant: your first responsibility is to guard this airfield!" Tarp tried to look very knowing. "They may try to land another plane."

He turned and tried to make himself run to the helicopter. The young officer would begin to ask questions very soon. Tarp did not want to be there when he did.

"I have two wounded up on the hill," he shouted.

The helicopter pilot was tough. Tarp knew it the moment their eyes met. The man had been somewhere—Vietnam, Angola—somewhere ugly and dangerous, and he had the eyes of an old mercenary who has been corrupted by war.

"I have to wait for the convoy from zone headquarters." The voice was firm. It made it very clear he did not intend to move.

Tarp tried an implied threat. "I am the Political Officer of the 115."

"I take my orders from the commandant of the Four-Four-One."

The chopper was a little Russian HKL-20, originally designed to be a form of airborne command vehicle and then put to better use as a small medical chopper. So rigged, it could carry two stretchers below the fuselage and two more inside, besides the pilot and a medic, although it was overloaded in that configuration and an easy target. This cynical flier with the dead eyes must have flown it that way many times, listening to men in pain and waiting for the ground fire that would kill him. Tarp glanced at the medic with him, who was still in his teens and who looked very nervous.

Tarp knew that he would have to move quickly. He was also trying to think far ahead to a time when it might be useful to have these two think of him as a dedicated Chinese officer instead of as a Western infiltrator. "My men are more important than your orders," he said. The pilot was going to snarl something back, but Tarp aimed the rifle at the middle of his chest and he closed his mouth again, staring into the black eye of the muzzle and sucking in cigarette smoke from a damp butt between his lips. Tarp pushed the rifle an inch forward. "Take me up the hill."

The man was so fatalistic that Tarp was impressed despite himself. Without another word, the pilot hoisted himself into the bubble cockpit of the little craft, making no move toward the pistol at his waist. He was simply going with the strongest force; he had stayed alive this long by knowing how to recognize such force and then by yielding to it—the wisdom of despair.

"Not you," Tarp said to the medic. "No room. I will be going direct to the nearest military hospital with my wounded. Where is it?"

The medic stared at him and then looked in anguish at the pilot and then at Tarp's gun. In a stunned whisper, he said, "The zone military hospital. Sir. Comrade."

"Good. As soon as your unit commandant arrives, tell him that I will be found there. I will make explanation at that time." He jerked his head toward the militia vehicles. "I am not accountable to those people."

"No. Yes. Comrade. Commandant!"

Tarp one-handed the rifle and pulled himself into the helicopter, feeling vertigo as he moved too fast. He fell into the right-hand seat with too much force. The pilot merely looked straight ahead as if Tarp were not there and no rifle was pointed at him.

"Take it up." Tarp felt that he was going to vomit. He concentrated very hard on the place in the pilot's neck where he would have to shoot him if he disobeyed. When the man had flipped several switches and the rotors were starting to spin, Tarp managed to reach over and take away his pistol. Through the pain, he found a small fragment of amusement in the fact that the pistol was a Browning HP, the twin of the one the man had issued him in London.

He managed to fasten part of his seat harness before the helicopter leaped into the air.

The pilot was very, very good—a professional of the sort Tarp liked to be with, as friend, as colleague, as enemy. His motions were spare and clean, his decisions quick.

"Where?" the man shouted.

"Up the hill!" Tarp pointed with the Browning. When the chopper headed out over the militia, he turned the Browning over and saw that the clip was in place; he ejected a cartridge to make sure there was a round in the chamber. He pointed again. "That big dead tree. The silver one."

The craft rose abruptly.

"Any ground fire expected?"

"No."

He circled the tree once. Tarp could see Arthur Beecham, seated on the box; his daughter, foreshortened to a pale face and broad shoulders, stood behind him, shielding her eyes as she looked up. Tarp pointed down.

There was an open space among the trees thirty yards from the silver trunk, and he set it down there as gently as if he were landing on newly laid eggs.

Tarp signaled through the bubble. Sheila Beecham had followed the descent with the muzzle of the PPK, which she held in both hands as if she thought militiamen would erupt from it when it touched. He waved again, and the pistol came down and she nudged her father. The old man roused himself with difficulty and tottered toward the helicopter. When he reached the side of the craft, he simply came to a stop, like some sort of underpowered mechanical toy that had bumped into a wall.

"In," Tarp heard her shout at him in Chinese. "In, Father!" She ducked low under the blades, dragging the box. *"In!"*

Tarp could not bend down to help him. He had to concentrate on the pilot; he knew that his reactions were slowed by pain and endorphins. When his daughter pushed him from behind, Beecham got in. He was slow about it, and he crouched against the basketlike frame of a stretcher that was lashed to the metal bulkhead. She put one end of the box up into the chopper by herself, then pushed the thing in and got herself in after it, like a clumsy, aquatic creature crawling up on the land.

"Up!" Tarp said when she was in. He lifted the muzzle of the Browning to signal. The machine lifted; they spun in the air like a dancer and sailed out over the treetops.

"Hospital?" the pilot shouted. Tarp nodded; however, when they had put another, lower hill between themselves and the armed militia, he signaled again with the pistol. "West!"

"Not the hospital?"

"West!"

The machine headed west. When they were skimming low and fast over the stunted landscape toward the distant mountains, the pilot said wearily, "Are you going to kill me?"

"No. Why would I kill you?"

The pilot jerked his head toward the compartment behind them. "They are not wounded soldiers."

"No." Tarp wondered how much to say. "They are political prisoners," he said. He watched the empty, barren land speed by. "Just do as I say."

They flew on. The pilot kept the craft low, as if he knew that he was supposed to stay under any radar net. The land they passed over was almost desert, and the chance of being seen from the ground was small. Far to their left now were the highlands of Tibet, true alpine desert and snow-covered mountaintops; to the right was the sink of the Takla Makan and its meager fringe of population. There was no railroad here and no regular air traffic. The only roads were seasonal ones.

"Can I smoke?"

"Yes."

The pilot lit a Work Together cigarette with a match while he controlled the chopper with his knees, flicking the dead match out the big opening in the bubble without looking, like a truck driver flicking it out the window of a ten-wheeler. He breathed the smoke deeply and did not look at Tarp. "I was in Angola," he almost shouted so he could be heard over the engine. "Three years. Flying Cubans and their cannon fodder out of nowhere places. We turned one of these little dragonflies into a gunship; I had a flamethrower under the fuselage; I could spray flame straight down. Like American napalm. We used to go in and wipe out these villages of mud huts." He drew in the smoke and let it slide back out of his mouth like an uncoiling snake. "Very heroic work, that."

Tarp had found a position for his head that seemed to keep the pain at a bearable level. "I was a child when we beat the Japanese in the north. We used to strip them and send them walking like refugees because we wanted the clothes. The peasants would stone them to death afterward."

The pilot drew on his cigarette and flung the butt away into the noisy air. "The world is shit," he said.

"The world is all right," Tarp said. He thought that over for a while. "People are the shit." The pilot did not answer, and perhaps Tarp had spoken too low to be heard. He watched three antelope run from the noise of the helicopter; they bounded over the low trees and kicked up puffs of dust from the hard earth. When they were gone, Tarp pointed down with his thumb. "Take it down!"

With a very small shrug, the pilot let the craft drop and slow, and it seemed to swing at the end of a long chain, curving down toward the earth and then touching very lightly. The man sat as he had been sitting, one hand on the controls, his eyes looking ahead.

"Get out," Tarp said. The man swung his feet out and slowly turned around and climbed down, keeping his head low because of the rotors. Only when he was on the ground did he look up at Tarp.

Tarp moved into the pilot's seat. He tried to keep his head the way he had held it so the pain would not return. When he was in place and had buckled himself into the harness, he slid the clip out of the Browning and ejected the round from the chamber and tossed the pistol beyond the pilot. He threw the clip out the other side into some dry grass. Their eyes met. Tarp lifted his right hand a few inches—apology, salute.

He took the controls, and the helicopter slowly lifted and moved forward. He made it move clumsily, but as he increased speed he made it more graceful and more willing, and after thirty seconds, it lifted as if a weight had been dropped and rushed away.

He brought it in low over the eastern gate of a little walled city, over the gate that had been called the Emperor's Eye until the last emperor had been removed, along with the concubines and the spoiled princesses and the bureaucrats two thousand miles to the east. This little city had been an administrative center in the Djagatai Empire; Marco Polo had passed north of it but had not bothered to detour to look at its thick red walls rising from the mountainside. When other cities like it had vanished, trade had kept this one alive, an outpost on the silk route. The people who lived there now thought of themselves as special, as survivors, because the city was a survivor. They tried to make themselves tougher than others: they still acted as if they were an outpost of empire and not merely a subadministrative center for seven rural cadres.

The city lay just on the inner edge of the Western Military Zone. Beyond the outer edge was the Soviet Union, although the people of the city still called that mountainous region Tadzhik, and they still taught a local history in which Samarkand, which was now in Russia, was an important trading partner. Politics came and went, they seemed to say, but the city and the land remained, and it was the land and not men that gave the laws: laws of survival, laws of communication. Men set up boundaries that made good lines on maps, but it was the land that created real boundaries and therefore real identity.

The Emperor's Eye still looked east toward Peking. But Peking was so far away!

The helicopter had come in along the Low Penetration Corridor that was clearly drawn on the military maps in the aircraft, and it had cut out of the corridor seven miles south of the city to zoom north at a still lower altitude. Its passing spooked a small herd of the half-domesticated, hairy cattle that throve on the dry plants of the place, and they lumbered toward a dry streambed in slow panic.

Skimming lower than the cranes that arrowed in toward a marsh two miles away, Tarp found the two-lane paved road that connected the city with the rest of China; he turned the helicopter to follow it to the city gate.

Pain held his neck and shoulders like a brace. He did not turn his head to look at Beecham or Beecham's daughter. She had spoken once, to ask if he wanted water. The old man had said nothing.

The red-walled city looked from the helicopter as if it had been made by a very skilled and imaginative child working with red clay and a putty knife. The city walls were thicker at bottom than at the top, and from a distance that extra thickness seemed to be a buttress that supported everything within the walls as well as the walls themselves, as if it were one single structure cut from clay slabs. At the corners and over the gates were squat towers. Inside the wall, the city climbed the mountain in terraces; within each terrace, buildings were seemingly piled together without order or pattern. Streets and buildings seemed to have gone wherever there was space; when there was no more space, the buildings had been made higher, then higher again. Set back and overhung, towered and winged and galleried, they looked like an impossible clutter of verticals within the weight-bearing city walls.

Tarp crossed that wall just above the Emperor's Eye and slowed the chopper there, putting it into a wide arc that took him away from the city's center. He was looking for a place that he had never seen, but he believed he would recognize it when he saw it. He made a pass over the western gate—called the Eye of the Snake because it had looked along the caravan route—and came back over the jumbled rooftops. He was cutting the city into corridors in his search.

On his third pass, he saw it: up the mountainside, beyond a low red wall, there were trees. Within the trees were lower walls, and within those, the flash of water. Fountains splashed there; within their circle, incredibly, was a swimming pool, as regular and blue as any in a California backyard.

Here we go again. He was grim-faced with the pain. *Dropping in on an old friend*.

The chopper settled down among the trees as if it was tired. It came down lightly, slowly, gently, like a bit of falling fabric, touching and then seeming to collapse from weariness as the rotors slowed and stopped and their tips settled.

Tarp did not turn his head. "This is going to be rough," he said in English. "Don't say anything. Let me do the talking."

Men in gray uniforms were running toward the chopper. They kept themselves low and had their weapons ready. They were fit and knowledgeable, veterans of somebody's war; although their uniforms were not the PLA greens, they were far too well equipped to be militiamen. Most of them carried the silenced type-64 sub-machine gun, and scattered among them Tarp saw several H and K squad machine guns. *Nothing but the best. Always the glass of fashion*.

The helicopter had PLA markings, but these tough soldiers took no chances. They used available cover and surrounded the aircraft; squad machine gunners were down with their weapons on bipods while Tarp watched. They had a quality added to their toughness that made them truly dangerous: they were paranoid.

Tarp waved a greasy white cloth out the helicopter bubble.

An officer shouted at him. The attempt to be loud distended his vocal cords and made his face hideous.

He had a huge voice, but the effort of shouting destroyed the words. Tarp could understand nothing.

He waved the white cloth again.

The officer screamed something at a man beside him and he fired a three-round burst from one of the silenced type-64s. Coming immediately after the officer's bull-like voice, the silenced gun seemed eerie. The shots passed over the helicopter, zinging into the sky to fall far beyond the city wall.

Tarp waved the rag again. *Maybe they'll get the idea we don't want to get out.*

The officer approached the open hatch, still bellowing. Because his words were utterly unintelligible, it was like watching a silent film of a man shouting; the sound might as well have been music or a crashing tide. His mouth worked horribly. He gestured with both arms. His eyes bulged. Like his men, he wore a uniform of silver gray; unlike theirs, his had silver stars on the collar and very discreet black marks on the shoulders. If the days of the warlords had not been over, and if private armies had not been forbidden by the People's government, one would have sworn that he was a member of a warlord's private army.

He stood directly below the open hatch. One of the silenced type-64s was pointed at Tarp's chest. He managed to make a single sentence understandable: "This is a forbidden zone!"

For the first time since he had started down the hill that morning, Tarp realized how exhausted he was. Pain is a very wearying thing. He hardly felt able to lift his arm in a salute.

"This is an emergency, comrade."

"This is not a hospital!" The officer began to shout again. Tarp understood an order to get out and the repetition of the statement about the hospital. The fact was that the officer had such a thick Korean accent that he was hard to understand even at a normal conversational level.

"I had to land here, comrade."

"This is a violation of the agreement of November seventh!"

That was news to Tarp. "I am grieved by a thousand regrets, comrade, but I had no choice. I have business with the illustrious Sun Dai-Qing."

"Who dares to say he has *business* with General Sun?"

General Sun! So—a general now! Tarp focused on the officer's submachine gun. He was having difficulty concentrating. "Tell the illustrious general—if you will—tell him. . . ." Tarp blinked his eyes. "Tell General Sun that Tarp would like to speak with him."

"*Tarp?*"

"Tarp."

"That is a name—*Tarp*?"

"That is *my* name."

The officer howled at a man standing fifty feet away, and he dashed up with a walkie-talkie; the officer jabbered into it, keeping his eyes and the type-64 on the helicopter hatch. He strolled back, then hoisted himself up into the bubble. He seemed to be posing heroically there, perhaps so that his men could admire him. "You are not alone," he said. He made it an accusation. "You have an old man and a woman here!"

"The old man is exhausted."

"He is Western! Is he a spy?"

"He is a journalist from Dublin, in the nation of Ireland, the center of the Western world. He has come to do an interview with General Sun."

The officer slung the submachine gun from his shoulder, muzzle down, and pulled his weight into the helicopter so that his left foot, which had been swinging in the air, could take some of his weight. "The woman looks like a monkey," he said. "What is she?"

"She is the secretary of the great journalist."

"She is very ugly to be the secretary of such a great man."

"Irish standards are different."

The officer looked down at Tarp. He had begun to enjoy himself. "Why did you bring them in a medical helicopter?"

"There was an accident."

"Accident victims go to hospitals."

"The great journalist wanted to come here."

The officer backed out of the hatch and stepped down to the ground. "You do not even have a flier's suit," he said contemptuously. He would have said more, but there was chattering on the walkie-talkie and he wheeled to take it. "Well?"

Tarp heard words. Murmurs. He wanted to lie down. He wanted oblivion.

"You are to leave your aircraft and follow me!" The officer looked angry again.

"I must have your word that the helicopter will not be entered or touched."

"You must have *what*?"

A huge hand seemed to be squeezing Tarp's head, closing the eyes, crushing the skull, filling his ears with a ringing clatter. "Not to enter—the heli—or touch. . . ." Tarp swallowed. It was an effort to look out at the man now.

There was another conversation on the walkie-talkie, longer and more violent this time. In the end, the officer gave up. He looked up at Tarp with disgust. "All right. Your aircraft will not be touched. *For now.*"

Tarp left the rifle and the shoulder bag. Slowly, he inched his way across the seat, managing to turn his body so that he could back out of the helicopter. In doing so, he had to turn his head; pain shot up over the back of his skull. He heard a soft little cry, realized that it was his own. It helped him to concentrate, however; climbing down, he could focus on each movement of his legs and his hands. The pain struck twice more before he was standing in the lush grass beyond the circle of the rotors.

"*You* are wounded?" the officer said.

"There was an accident." A soldier took the Browning HP from his holster. "I have a knife strapped to my right leg," Tarp said. The knife was removed. Beecham staggered down, hardly awake enough to stand up straight, and his daughter came after him. She put his right arm over her shoulders and steadied him. "Give him your pistol and your knife," Tarp said to her. She glared at him, but there was a soldier already going toward her. She handed over the weapons.

"More?" the officer said. "You will have to go through a metal detector. More?"

"No more," Tarp mumbled. He was trying to remember all the weapons they had carried, trying to think whether or not he was right.

The officer walked next to Tarp across the grounds, keeping four feet of space between them. Two soldiers carrying silenced type-64s marched ahead, two more behind. For all that it still looked like winter here, the grounds were impeccable, without that sodden look that the withdrawal of winter leaves behind. Here were signs of work and care: raked gravel and newly turned earth. The pines looked fresh and green, and beyond them were the fountains and the swimming pool, already filled with water despite the season.

There was a generous compound of pink and red buildings in the middle of the park, their tile roofs almost golden in the sunlight that had appeared. This was the former palace of the territorial sub-governor of Yarkend, built in 1636 by the Western calendar. Now it was a museum, according to official news releases of the People's Republic—the Popular Repository of Caravan Route Antiquities, Yarkend Division.

Just inside the gate were two American M2HB .50s on tripods. Ammunition boxes were neatly piled behind a screen of shrubbery, so that, except for the crews, the two weapons might have been modern versions of Foo lions set there as symbolic, not actual, guardians. They passed between the machine guns, went up a flight of pink stone steps, and passed through an intricately carved doorway. Just inside, as the officer had promised, there was a metal detector exactly like those in use at airports. Several soldiers in the same gray uniforms came smartly to attention as they stumbled through.

Should have shaved. I'm a mess. These people look like real soldiers. Tarp tried not to wince when his neck moved.

Visitors to the Popular Repository of Caravan Antiquities might have been forgiven for thinking they had come to the wrong place. The interior looked more like a busy regimental headquarters, for there were uniforms and weapons everywhere, and the antiquities were hidden by mounds of military gear. Tarp counted four kinds of assault rifles from as many nations, two ceiling-high piles of boxed light machine guns, both Russian; a waist-high stack of cases of grenades with Russian and Egyptian markings; and ammunition for a number of weapons. Because this long hall seemed to be a busy place where men came and went on business matters that had to be dealt with quickly, the presence of the equipment suggested vast stores of it elsewhere, of which this was merely the overflow.

"This way!"

The officer led them to a twelve-foot-high doorway whose double bronze doors were green with age. It took two soldiers to push one of the doors open, and they stepped through—into a different world. Carpets of great rarity lay on the polished floor, heavy silks hung at the few windows, and the lustrous red of lacquer was everywhere.

"Here." The officer stood stiffly by a farther door. *He's afraid of that door*, Tarp thought. *He doesn't dare go through that door*. Tarp started over the carpets toward it and found the softness underfoot treacherous for his balance, which he had maintained so carefully over the stone paving and the hard floors they had already crossed.

A soldier opened the door for him.

Tarp passed through, listening for the Beechams to come through after him.

The door closed.

A row of ceiling-high windows ran the length of the room on his left and, through some trick of architecture, looked out over the city and a two-story drop to the ground, although they had not climbed any stairs. Intersecting beams overhead were lacquered red and gold. Against the long wall on the right were two suits of Yu'an armor. And except for the carpet that stretched across the pale wood floor, that was all that the room held. It was stark, pure, as arresting and harsh as a sudden glare of light.

Tarp prepared himself. Again he regretted that he looked so slovenly.

At the far end of the long room, a door opened and a soldier stepped through. This was a different kind of soldier, more austere than the others, and taller, too; his uniform was gray but was made of something other than cotton, some space-age fabric that had a soft sheen. He did not look at them but stepped to the side of the doorway and put his submachine gun at the ready. A second soldier slipped through the door and took up a position on the other side.

A slender man, also uniformed, came through the door, which closed behind him as if of its own accord.

He was two inches shorter than Tarp and at least thirty pounds lighter. His head had been shaved. The stiff collar of his uniform held his head high in a disciplined posture that suggested a religious more than a military order.

He came forward without haste, his eyes on Tarp's

face. Ten feet away he paused. He put his hands behind him and spread his feet a few inches. Muscles clenched and unclenched in his lean cheeks, sending ripples of movement along the jaws. "Is it you, then?" he said in Han Chinese.

"What's left of me."

"How am I to believe you?"

"I pulled the thorns from your paw."

"Are you injured?"

"I have done something to my back."

"Have you no place else to go?"

"None that I trust."

The man ended his questions. The muscles along his jaws moved. His thin, brooding face was without warmth. "I am not sure I am glad to see you."

"I took that chance."

The man looked at the Beechams. He looked at Tarp again, seeming to savor his fatigue and his pain. "Do you work for the CIA now?"

"Not for some years."

"But you are still an American. Not a Chinese with an American face. You made that choice long ago." He was temporizing. Delay did not suit him, and he made his discomfort clear. "I cannot pretend that certain things did not happen, Tarp."

"Neither can I."

The cold eyes met Tarp's. They seemed to want to enter his eyes, to penetrate him, to explore. Tarp made an effort and focused on those eyes, not to accept or to share the look but to resist. The other's eyelids flickered almost imperceptibly and a curtain seemed to come down. "You may stay—for now."

"I am on the run, Dai. The helicopter—it should not be found here."

"Very well."

He seemed to want to leave the room then. Tarp, however, spoke again and made him stay. "There is a wooden box in the helicopter I must have."

A slight widening of the nostrils betrayed the man's anger. His voice remained cool, almost ironic. "You ask a great deal—considering our history."

"I came here because I thought—perhaps—our history is the thing that lets me ask so much."

The other's forehead seemed to rise up into the shaven scalp, lifting his eyebrows, opening his eyes a fraction more. "Makes *me* the debtor?" he said incredulously. "That is an idea worth thinking about. And worthy of you. You are welcome, then—and your friends—and your *box*." He said the word with venom, as if it was the box that symbolized his sense of being imposed upon. "At least—you are welcome until I make up my mind about your remarkable idea."

He turned about smartly and walked the length of the austere room. The soldiers came to attention; the door opened; they passed through. The door remained open, and some seconds later a young man came to them.

Within minutes, they had been led to a suite of rooms whose doors opened on a little courtyard. A single peacock paced through the splashes of end-of-day light. Old male servants in black moved silently around them; a doctor and a male nurse appeared and began to examine Arthur Beecham. Huge stacks of black towels suggested that baths were imminent.

Beecham's daughter watched the doctor suspiciously, but she had enough curiosity to whisper to Tarp, "Who was that man?"

"He's in charge here. Sun Dai-Qing—General Sun, he calls himself now."

"What did he mean—all that about thinking it over? About debt?"

"We are old friends."

"*But what did he mean?*"

A servant was beckoning to Tarp from a doorway. He

was holding two enormous towels in his arms. "He tried to kill me once."

"In a war?"

"No, no. Nothing like that. The oppposite, in fact."

"What is the opposite?"

"Love." Tarp started toward the man with the towels. "He was in love with me."

chapter fourteen

Tarp lay in a stone tub filled as high as his ears with water so hot his skin was bright red. There was a wooden support—hardly a pillow—under his head, and he had found a position where the pain could be kept away. After half an hour, the doctor and the male nurse came in and lifted him out of the tub and put him on a quite modern medical table made of tubular steel and black vinyl. Face down, he felt the doctor's hands moving over his back and his neck; he mumbled sleepy answers to the muted questions about his injuries. A third man came in with a case of acupuncture needles and inserted seven of them in his shoulders, and later the male nurse manipulated his spine and his right arm under the doctor's supervision. After forty-five minutes, they put him back in the hot water like a helpless lobster that had not cooked enough.

When he was helped out, it was all that Tarp could do to pull a cotton gown over his body. He was utterly drained, and he could not raise his head.

"Two more treatments and you will be well, Commandant," the nurse told him.

"What is wrong?"

"You hurt your back."

A servant helped him shuffle along a corridor. In the cotton robe and paper slippers, Tarp felt like some ancient prisoner of a nursing home. The corridor was cold, and unable to raise his head or move more quickly, he felt that he was getting a foretaste of old age. It was not very pleasant.

There were bottled-gas heaters in the rooms. His own room was bright and very warm, and he felt cared for and almost infantile.

"The old man?" he murmured.

"In that room, Commandant," the servant said, pointing across the little courtyard. He was truly old and slow and fat, with a stubble of silver on his plump cheek like the sheen of oil. "He sleeps."

A young, thinner servant came in and shooed the old one out of the room. "The meal will be here directly, Commandant," he said with a jerky bow. "General Sun excuses himself tonight but asks that you be available to discuss with him in the morning."

Tarp yawned. "Thank General Sun." He wondered if he wanted to wait to eat. There was a narrow bed against one wall; if he lay down on it, he thought, he would probably be the happiest man in China. But he would not eat. He yawned again. "Call me in the morning."

The man made his awkward bow again. "The household servants rise at four, Commandant. The general rises at the same time. For meditation."

"Does the general eat then?"

"He takes tea only. At six."

"Call me at five-thirty."

When the man was gone, Sheila Beecham came into the room from the courtyard. Like him, she wore a cotton robe, hers of very dark blue with a white cotton rope at the waist. She had been bathed, too, and her face looked ruddy and polished, but most astonishing of all was her hair. Washed, it had become electric: it stood out from her head in a thousand filaments, each projecting like a wiggly wire for about a foot before bending of its own weight and falling back to make a billowing, light mass around her face. Within that buoyant mass, her monkey's mask seemed wise and small.

"That man said I would get food in here."

Tarp swung his torso so he could look at her. His head was bent as if he were a grotesque in a horror film. "Food. Oh, food, yes."

"I have my own room! Next to this one. It is as big as five rooms at the Slum!"

The Slum. The prison. He was falling asleep standing up. "Oh, yes?"

"There is a bird out there that screeches like an old woman."

"A peacock."

She took two steps toward him. "I had a bath! I had not had a bath in six years!"

"Good."

The bath seemed to have waked her up, while it had almost put him to sleep. She bounced a little on her toes. She folded her hands in front of her. At last she said, "Would you like sex?"

Tarp twisted again to stare at her. He burst into laughter. "I can hardly *move*!" he said. "Why—would you like sex now?"

She seemed surprised. "Oh, I never liked it." She frowned. "Some of the other women told me it was possible to like it, but I never did. I thought it was just something my husband wanted, you know." She smiled. "What I would really like is some food!"

"Yes." He had decided that he was hungry. If he could keep himself awake, he would eat, he thought. "It's a matter of"—he yawned—"priorities."

He decided that he would lie down until the meal arrived. That decision was the last thing he remembered.

General Sun Dai-Qing took his morning tea in the highest room of the highest tower of the ancient palace. The sun, rising out of the desert plain to the east, thrust its first ray through the room's single window like a sword. If there were clouds, the bright spot of silver where the sun rose brightened the room, nonetheless, and turned it the color of sand.

Sun Dai-Qing sat with his back to that window and watched the progress of the sunrise on a blank wall. This morning, Tarp sat with him. Both were cross-legged on an intricately figured carpet from Herat, far to the west.

"To understand my past, and to live with it intelligently, that would be wisdom," Sun said. "Not to put the past away—that is the mark of a fool—but to know it and to make it my own. America cannot do that; America has no past. China has too much; the past is a burden for China, and China is not wise." He lifted a cup to his lips, put it down. "You seem to accept your past, Tarp. You are the only wise man I have met in sixteen years."

"Your past seems bearable, Dai."

"I try. I try." Sun embraced himself, and his long, powerful fingers dug into the muscles of his bare upper arms. "But my past is like winter—I have to stand naked in it to toughen myself. And I never adapt. It is always bad weather."

"But why?"

"I am a deviate."

"Surely no man's a deviate to himself."

"I used not to think so. *Deviate*. That was the sign they painted on my uniform in prison. I spent three of those years in solitary confinement because I was homosexual. The guards were of the lowest kind—peasants—apes. They said they would castrate me because

I was not a real man. They said they would send me to live with the old eunuchs of the Imperial Palace. They made me perform oral sex on them—because they were real men and I was not, they said. I got very tired of them. I killed one of them. Then they tried to kill me—they were going to throw me out a window—but an officer came and stopped them. The prison committees were trying to be understanding—it was the time of the Hundred Flowers, just before the Cultural Revolution—and they said they wanted to bring all deviants into the Revolution. Mostly, the deviants were political criminals, but I was one, and so was a man from Szechwan who had practiced cannibalism. So they put me ino solitary confinement for three years." He sipped his tea again. "I toughened myself, but I paid a price—isolation. Solitude. *Deviation*."

"But you were rehabilitated."

"Well, I was very loyal to certain people. Deng. Lin Piao. When the wheel came round and Mao and the gang were discredited—I was rehabilitated! I am very useful, after all."

Neither spoke. The outline of the window moved across the wall. The room was cold, but Sun, bare to the waist, did not shiver. His external self was controlled; underneath, Tarp was sure, he raged.

As if to prove him right, Sun said passionately, "I must talk to you about those days!"

"Yes?"

Sun's eyes were accusations. "I loved you!" He said it as if he meant just the opposite. "I loved you as they say that men love women in those stories that the world is so fond of. Romances!" Perhaps he had meant, or at least hoped, that his voice would be dispassionate, but it expressed all the anguish of that past that so troubled him. He was like a monk for whom the flesh was still the devil. "When you refused me. . . . It still chokes me to say it—you hear? I was going to kill both of us. You do believe that? I would have killed myself after I killed you, but . . . I wanted to see you dead! Because when you refused me you said . . . *'Deviate!'* That's what that action said."

"I saved your life once," Tarp said gently.

"Yes." Sun passed a lean hand over his face. "Yes, of course."

Sun was four years older than Tarp. Just before the Nationalists had been driven out of Peking, a band of their soldiers had caught Sun, who was then a runner for Lin Piao. They had tortured him for two days and then had left him in a barn, standing on the crosspiece of a truss with his feet nailed to the wood. Tarp had found him.

Sun put his hands on the carpet in front of him. "Why should I help you? Why? Because you told me I am something offensive? Am I to thank you for that?"

"It was twenty-five years ago, Dai."

"So?" Sun's voice was hoarse with emotion. "My past is alive. In here!" He jabbed at his head with a tense finger. He put his fingers back on the carpet and said more calmly, "I must learn discipline. All my life, I have tried to teach myself discipline. But—!" He held his bare right arm up. It was bent at a perfect right angle at the elbow; the index finger was extended. It looked like a weapon. "*But*—I will not use the easy way that satisfies most men. 'Time heals.' That is the fool's way. That is not dealing with the past; that is simply *forgetting* it. I want to be able to *use* it. You see, Tarp, it is not that you have come back here and that suddenly that old emotion has become alive again; not at all. You are foreign to me now—you are coarsened, old, utterly different. No. It is not that you have come back. It is that you have brought *me* back!"

His hands clenched the thick pile of the carpet, and when Tarp looked at the nails he saw red fibers of the carpet wool caught there. "You want me to do things for you, Tarp. You ask, 'Why not help me—we were close once?' I ask, 'Why should I not kill you—we were close once?' "

There was a soft knock at the door. It opened; a young man came in quickly, wearing the same silver-gray uniform. Smiling, he stepped past Tarp and knelt to embrace Sun. He and Sun looked intently at each other, hands on the other's forearms, and he rose and went out as quickly as he had come.

"My son," Sun Dai-Qing said. "Or so I think of him. They are all my sons now." He was much calmer. "I was rehabilitated before I left the prison, you see. They castrated me."

He clapped his hands together and then put them on his knees. The change in position seemed to signal a change of mood; he became businesslike. "So, tell me why you are in China. What sort of threat are you?"

Tarp lifted his cup. The tea, gray-green, pale, smoky, gave up its flavor grudgingly. "I have to get the old man out of China," he said.

"Who is he?"

"A scientist."

"Who is after you?"

"Perhaps nobody. He is supposed to be dead; nobody—almost nobody—knows that I am in China. But sooner or later they will put things together. There was an incident yesterday—an aircraft that exploded. . . ."

"Ah, was that you? I received a message about it. We were warned to stand alert for possible large-scale sabotage." Sun shook his head. "The zone military command are very fanciful."

"What did they say about the aircraft?"

"British type. Hedgehopper model. Common airplane, of course—Malaysia, Sri Lanka, several African nations."

"And the crew?"

"One body was found. No identification given. The alert, however, was for *Russian* infiltrators. You are not working for the Russians now, are you, Tarp?"

Tarp made a face. "Not knowingly." He massaged his

neck, which was noticeably less painful this morning. He could move his head again. "Will you get in trouble for harboring me, Sun?"

"Oh, no." A cruel, proud smile appeared. "I am too useful."

"This is not *really* a museum."

"Oh, yes, *really*, as things *really* go, it is a museum. It is even listed as a museum. I am *really* listed as the director of the museum. Of course, we allow no visitors because we are not yet ready to open. Besides being director of the museum, I am also the chairman of the Urban Commune, a member of the Presidium of the Seven Rural Cadres, and secretary general of the party for this region—all of which means nothing, for what I *really* am, my friend, is a warlord of the old sort who is willing to run an insurgency school here for the tribal chiefs who want to fight the soviets in Kirghiz and Afghanistan. I also devote much of my time and my fortune to moving small arms into Afghanistan."

"I saw them. You seem to have a good stock."

"Oh, very. Russian, most of it, a lot of it the material they left behind in Egypt. Some that the Israelis captured. Also, I buy independently on the world market. I have an agent in Munich and an agent in Singapore. I am *really* a very valuable person to modern China, which needs somebody like me, a former convict who is conveniently hidden away from journalists and diplomats."

"You seem to have plenty of money. You could live in the West."

"Ah—the West." Sun stared at the square of sunlight, which was now low down toward the floor. "Just as China needs me, you see—I need China. China is in my bones." Again his mood changed quickly. He seemed to have shaken off his anger. "This old man—is he important?"

"To me, yes."

"Internationally important?"

"Maybe."

"To America? To the Soviets? Oh, I see—it was for the old man that the Soviets sent in the airplane! Ah! Does Peking want the old man?"

"Not at all."

"And the wooden box you made me take from the helicopter. What is in it?"

"Maybe nothing. Maybe—a device."

"Made by the old scientist?"

"Yes."

Sun put out a hand, the fingertips brushing Tarp's sleeve. "Stay in China with me."

Tarp was surprised. "For good?"

The fingers rested on his arm. "You are more Chinese than American. I would give you part of my army. A joint command. You can be rich, powerful—you can have women. All that means nothing to me now. There is a palace thirty miles north of here—you could have it! You can have everything, Tarp—a very good life. Power." His eyes were hypnotic. "My friendship."

"And the old man?"

Sun made a small gesture of dismissal. "We will stage a crash of the helicopter. There would have to be bodies in it, anyway."

"Is that how you would accept the past?"

"Yes! By making it the present."

Tarp studied the fingers that touched his arm. "I can't," he said with real regret.

Sun took his hand away. "You are not so wise as I thought." He slapped his hands on his knees again and became brisk. "Very well! I have two choices: to turn you in to Peking, and thus win the applause of the Central Committee and revenge myself for our past. Or—to help you get out, and thus make you my debtor—and revenge myself in a different way for our past." He nodded almost dreamily. "Or I could kill you. Or put you in a cage for life. Who is the woman?"

"The old man's daughter."

"Is she your woman?"

"No."

"Too bad. I could have her raped by a hundred soldiers while you were forced to watch." He looked gravely at Tarp. "I am joking, of course."

"Of course."

Sun put his elbows on his knees and placed a finger on each side of his lower lip, pushing it out into an exaggerated pout. He looked at the blank wall with such intensity that an invisible hand might have been writing his decision there.

"I will help you get out, Tarp. As you must have known I would all along. Maybe you are wise, after all. But I can only help you as far as Afghanistan. I am sending a shipment of small arms in three days. It will go through the military zone in trucks and be transferred to ponies in the mountains. The crossing is made at night. There will be a band of Afghans going along—trainees, wounded who have recovered. The shipment has to go up over the Kush to Faizabad. There is a battle going on in Faizabad now—the rebels will lose, in time, but they are trying to punish the city for not resisting the Soviets as strongly as they think it should. If you take the arms to Faizabad, I believe that they will help you get out to Pakistan."

"I can't go direct to Pakistan?"

"I can move anything I want into Afghanistan, but Pakistan and Kashmir are closed to me."

"What if I could call a British plane in to pick me up?"

"Never! Much too dangerous. Much."

Tarp considered the offering. A border crossing high in the mountains, which would still be snow-locked; a run through Soviet-occupied country; a battle. "What about the border crossing?"

"Thirteen thousand feet. Very cold. Two of the Russian officers are bought. The patrols will have to be killed; they falsify the reports. It is always bloody, but we always get through."

"And the Afghans?"

"There is a self-styled general named Ghulam Kashti. A good, murdering bandit. A thief, an egomaniac, a soldier. He will probably take you to Pakistan, but he will probably ask you to help him first."

"How?"

"My intelligence reports that he is after some Russian gold that is hidden in Faizabad. Everybody else is after the Faizabad power station. He wants to hold the area long enough to get at the gold. I suppose he will ask you to help him."

"Can he be trusted?"

"Of course not."

"And the gold—does he know where the gold is?"

"It is supposed to be in a bunker."

Tarp had an idea. "How close is the bunker to the power station?"

"I have no idea. Why?"

Tarp shook his head. "Only a thought. I might work something out if there was electrical power. I will work something out, anyway."

Both men let time pass. Tarp could hear the chant of soldiers far below, like the chant of soldiers everywhere. He understood the attraction of such a life for Sun: the sense of purpose, the discipline, the smoothness of its edges.

Sun, as if pursuing his thoughts, said lightly, "You will not join me, then? You will not be a warlord?"

"You know I cannot."

"Yes. But, just as you have to refuse, I have to ask. And I have to dress and begin my day." Still he did not get up. He made a fist of his right hand and laid his muscular forearm on Tarp's knee. "Look at my skin. All those tiny wrinkles, thousands of little wrinkles, like silk. I am getting old. That is what all this talk of the past is, in the end. I am getting old."

He stood up. A moment later he was talking about insurgency weapons and about training guerrillas, and Tarp knew that he had said the last words that he would say about his private self or his private past.

There were three days of intense activity. Tarp interviewed six Afghans who said that they were officers, a word that meant usually that they believed themselves leaders. He picked one of them, a mustached young man named Mahmud Khalq, to be his lieutenant. There were forty Afghan soldiers altogether, a ragtag lot of recovered wounded, political exiles, and former smugglers let out of Chinese prisons. Tarp made lists—equipment, weapons, codes. He studied maps, memorized names, read biographies of Russian officers. Sun had a major and a lieutenant colonel on his payroll. There were sheafs of reports on the Afghan situation.

With rest, both he and Arthur Beecham seemed to thrive. The old man's eyes got back their boyish life. Tarp summed up their situation for him. "We're going to travel hard and fast, sir. We'll have vehicles partway up the pass, then ponies. You can have a litter. Once we're in Afghanistan, I'll hope to find a truck."

"I have two good legs, you know."

"The cold will be terrible up there. It takes all your strength."

"Sheila will be there?"

"Oh, yes."

"Then I shall be perfectly all right. You're sure this is the way to get my invention out to Winston, are you?"

"I believe it is, yes."

"Well, then of course we shall do it. We shall simply do it!"

Tarp outfitted himself from General Sun's generous supplies. He sent Sheila Beecham to the palace's firing range with the PPK and the Chinese Mini-14 and an instructor; he drew a new silenced SMG for himself.

"Am I to keep these now?" she asked him. Her monkey face was screwed up excitedly.

"Until we're safe in Pakistan."

"Good!" Something had been done to her hair—it no longer burst from her head like wires but lay more softly, if unrestrainedly, on her head—and she looked quite different.

Not pretty, no, he thought, remembering the conversation with Beecham. *Handsome? Doubtful.* He watched her handle the rifle. *Interesting, though. Damned interesting.*

chapter fifteen

The battle in the pass was short and dreadful. It lasted hardly twenty minutes. Tarp had never tried to fight under such conditions—metal sticking to damp flesh, the wind like a hot coal laid against the skin. It was night—that low hour of the morning, in fact, when peaceful men die in bed.

There were six men in a tiny hut and another eleven out on patrol, and those in the hut should have been able to defend it until they could call in support, but the communications had been cut by the bribed officers and Tarp's people had the code for entry. They cleaned out the hut with the silenced type-64s and then ambushed the patrol as it came out on an exposed snowfield; yet the Russians fought with a tenacity that was astonishing until he remembered that surrender meant death and a wound meant death, and their only hope was to behave like supermen and fight and run and fight and run until they were off the snowfield and could take cover in some ice-covered rocks. Five of them could, at least; the rest were already dead. When they tried to hold the rocks, Tarp ordered the Afghans in with grenades and the heaviest automatic fire they could lay down. There were no Russian survivors—the Afghans did not leave survivors—and Tarp lost nine of his own, including two "officers."

"Bring our bodies. Leave the rest."

There were two vehicles by the communications hut, a winterized tractor and a UAZ with a truck body and Afghan regular-army markings. Tarp ordered Beecham and the box put into the UAZ along with three wounded men; Mahmud Khalq oversaw the loading of horseloads of ammunition on a sled behind the tractor. A gravel road, hard as steel now with ice, led down from the mountain outpost—down to the comforts of the fire base where the bribed Soviet officers had earned their money. Led by an Afghan who knew the mountains, however, Tarp's train of animals, men, and vehicles turned away from the base and cut down the mountainsides.

A rendezvous had been made with Ghulam Kashti forty miles inside Afghanistan. Tarp found the rebel leader at a stone hut that had been used by herdsmen for a hundred years and more; Kashti looked like a fierce tribal chief from some British romance—"one of the chaps who are our nemesis on this side of the Khyber Pass." Tarp took it as a compliment that Ghulam Kashti made himself even fiercer after he had seen Tarp.

A real bad dude, Tarp concluded. *The baddest man in the whole damn town*.

Ghulam Kashti got slowly to his feet. *Very macho. Honor very big thing here*. Ghulam Kashti spat something yellow very close to the toes of Tarp's black jump boots. "You *American*?" he asked, making the word sound like an insult.

"None of your business." Tarp spoke Farsi well enough to make his point.

Ghulam Kashti smiled—truly a horrible thing to watch. His round cheeks seemed to lift in order to expose his teeth, around which his lips coiled upward. "Bang-bang? *Soldier of Fortune* magazine?" Several of Kashti's men tittered. "Playing soldier?"

Tarp shook his head. "Playing nursemaid to your guns."

Ghulam turned the horrific smile to a mask of rage. "The Afghan people's battle against the Soviet thugs needs no nursing from play-pretend Yankee soldier boys!" The men cheered.

"I have sixteen light machine guns, twenty cases of grenades, and a lot of other gear. I lost nine men coming over the border. I need to talk to you privately."

"I could have come over the border and lost nobody! Ghulam Kashti comes and goes over the border like a ghost!"

"I need to talk to you privately."

"Ghulam Kashti has no secrets from his brave soldiers! Ghulam Kashti is a general who shares the pain of his loyal boys! Ghulam Kashti—!"

Tarp leaned close to the brown face. "*Gold,*" he whispered.

Ghulam Kashti, caught in mid-rhetoric, had one arm raised dramatically to score some point that he had already forgotten. He stared at Tarp, his mouth still open.

"*Gold in Faizabad,*" Tarp whispered.

Ghulam Kashti got his arm down and looked around. He took a step back from Tarp and put his hands on his hips. Without warning, he pulled out a Russian pistol and fired three wild shots in the air. "Ghulam Kashti welcomes the support of his Chinese friend, General Sun Dai-Qing!" he screamed. "Unload the shipment!"

Afghan insurgents began to scramble down from the rocks above the hut. Others began to wrestle with the feisty, mean little ponies that carried most of the gear. Ghulam Kashti posed in the middle of this activity, hands on hips, pistol still in hand, his legs spread and a venomous imitation of a grin on his face. Ghulam Kashti was a curious figure, for he wore a Russian military tunic with the markings removed, an impeccably clean turban, and the trousers from a very old civilian suit of Western cut. His shirt had once been white with thin stripes of brown and green, and it had been intended to be worn with a tie. Ghulam Kashti did not affect the tie, however.

He waved the pistol toward Tarp. "Inside the hut," he muttered. He led the way inside. The hut had no roof except in one corner, where it provided enough shade to keep a drift of snow from melting. A folding table had been set up in the hut; around it were several incongruous folding stools in bright colors. There were maps on the table.

Ghulam Kashti slammed the pistol down on the maps. "War is bloody theater!" he said in English. He tapped his chest. "I have been to the theater, so I know." He stared at Tarp. "Sit down." Without waiting for Tarp to sit, he dropped his own weight on one of the stools. "I tire of all this drama," he said self-importantly. "All this acting."

"I wasn't sure it was acting," Tarp said. He sat down with care, expecting the stool to collapse.

"Everything is acting," the Afghan said. "Everything but Allah, food, and the prick. From Allah comes all goodness; from food comes all life; from the prick comes all pleasure. The rest is acting." He folded his arms. "Well?"

Tarp had decided to keep it simple. "I want to be got out of Afghanistan. Into Pakistan."

"I want to get out of Afghanistan into Paradise. So?"

"Me, the old man, the woman."

"Fifty thousand American dollars. Each."

"Bullshit."

Ghulam Kashti spat. "Then you will die in Afghanistan." The idea seemed to please him.

"Don't you want the gold in Faizabad?"

Ghulam Kashti leaned forward. His hand rested on his pistol. "What do you know?"

Tarp had already located the city on the map between them. It was an old British artillery map, years out of date but accurate in its distances and bearings. "When I left Yarkend, the Soviets still held the power station, the central mosques, and half a dozen office buildings in the center. Your people had cut the supply route from the north and had control of the roads, at least by night. The Russians were being supplied by air and had air support, but you had overrun their SAM positions and were making the air more difficult. There are two relief convoys pushing for the city, one down from Samarkand and one up from Kabul, but they're having very heavy going. Sun's intelligence estimated that it would take them four days, and your people would probably pull out by then."

Ghulam Kashti was disgusted by his knowledge. "General Sun must trust you," he said unhappily. He wanted to sound sly, but he sounded envious.

"What's the situation today?"

"They sit. Four hundred yards from the power station, which they hit with light artillery. It is all we have. So, we wait."

"For what?"

"Who knows? The idiot who calls himself generalissimo commandant of the Afghan Insurgency Collective may be waiting for his bowels to move." He tapped the pistol. "What do you know about gold?"

"I know that there are supposed to be twenty gold bars in a bunker east of the power station. Stored there by the Finance Bank of Kabul when the invasion came. Twenty-six-pound bars, worth about a hundred thousand English pounds each—call it three and three-quarter million dollars." Tarp smiled. "You want the gold but you can't get into the bunker."

Ghulam Kashti smiled back. "May Allah have your

testicles chewed with the teeth of rats." He nodded. "Yes, I have been sitting there, four hundred yards from it. All the other generals think about is the power station—it is a 'symbolic presence,' the generalissimo commandant tells us at the staff meetings. *Acting!*"

"So you know where the gold is, but you can't get into the bunker." Tarp folded his arms and leaned back. "I don't want the gold, but I can get into the bunker."

"How?" Ghulam Kashti jumped up. *"How?"*

"But I want to get out of Afghanistan. Remember?"

"How can you get into the bunker?"

"If I open the bunker so you can get at the gold, will you get us safely to Peshawar?"

The Afghan flashed his awful grin again. He had a natural flair for poses—he had been quite right; he was an actor—and he now put one foot up on his flimsy stool and flattened his right hand over his heart. "Dear American friend and ally, if you can truly open that bunker to me, I will conduct you personally to Peshawar. To Bombay! To London!"

"Peshawar will do." Tarp stood up. "I want three passes—journalists' safe conducts."

"After you open the bunker."

"Now. Just in case something happens to you, my dear Afghan ally."

"You will run away."

"I wouldn't get ten miles without your help. Draw me a map of the area around the bunker, too. I need to know exactly where the power station is. Then send me three men who have been up there; I want some first-hand intelligence. How far is Faizabad?"

"The rear line is eleven miles."

"All right. I want to go in at sunrise tomorrow—move along the roads tonight. I'll need some high-voltage cable."

Ghulam Kashti posed again. "I can get you anything!"

"I'll let you know how much after I see the map." He pointed at the table. "Write me those passes, will you?"

Tarp sought out Arthur Beecham. He found the old man sitting on the wooden box in a patch of pale, almost white sunlight, an enormous quilted comforter wrapped around him so that he looked like a large and rather genial caterpillar. Sheila hovered near him with the Chinese Mini-14, a high-tech Cordelia guarding her Lear.

Tarp knelt in front of Arthur Beecham.

"Mr. Beecham, push has come to shove."

"Eh?"

"Mr. Beecham . . . *Does it really work?*"

"What's that? What, my particle beam? Why, of course it works. Shame on you for doubting. Shame, shame!"

"I have to put it to the test, sir."

"What's that?"

"I need to use the particle beam so we can get out of here."

"Oh, jolly good. Though it's rather pleasant here just at the moment. This isn't China any longer, is it?"

"This is Afghanistan. But it isn't England. We want to go to *England*."

"England!" Beecham's face was transformed. Sitting higher than Tarp because of the box, he looked down with an almost royal smile. " 'Oh to be in England, now that April's there.' Eh?"

"Yes, sir."

"Is it April yet?"

"It's May."

"Oh, jolly good. Lovely month on the Downs, May. What is it you mean to do with my particle beam, exactly?"

"I have to cut through a concrete wall several feet thick."

"No problem there. Anything else?"

"We should be much admired if we could destroy a power station."

"Oh, yes, well, that's a piece of pie, as you Americans say. Don't you? I'm sure I heard an American say that during the war."

"A piece of cake, sir."

"What? Cake? Oh, I see, cake-not-pie. Hmm. Doesn't make much sense if you don't like cake. Where was I?"

"The power station."

"Yes, yes. Well, don't destroy the power station until after you've done the other thing, because you'll need the power, you see. The beam runs on electricity. Did I tell you that?"

"Yes, sir. How much power?"

"Rather a lot. Ten to the eleventh watts for a big show. I only had about ten to the seventh at the prison."

"All right, sir, now—if you'll show me exactly how to hook up the device, I'll leave you and Sheila here and I'll come back for you when it's over."

Beecham's voice became quite sharp. It allowed for no contradiction. "The beam is my invention. I will do it all myself. Forgive me, but I insist."

"I'd have to take you into a battle zone, sir."

Beecham drew himself up. "Oh, come!" he murmured. He not only looked like a king, he even sounded like one. Tarp got the point: Beecham's whole adult life was a battle zone.

When Tarp returned to the hut, Ghulam Kashti had the three passes ready. They would be useful only if Ghulam Kashti himself were removed. Tarp liked to be ready for contingencies, however. *Inevitable miracles*.

"The electric cable?"

"My men are looking for a suitable transmission line to steal, American friend."

"We can go at sunrise?"

"At sunrise, Great Ally of the Afghan Struggle. We will fight side by side."

Side by side would have to do, Tarp knew. He was sure that he did not want to try to fight with Ghulam Kashti behind him somewhere.

* * *

There was a one-story building about a hundred yards below the bunker where the gold was supposed to be stored. Three hundred yards away to the left, the power station sprawled across a downslope that ran to a freestone river. Tarp had been given a drawing of this cluster of buildings; he had studied it, questioned the soldiers about it, and then he had gone ahead to a forward point to study it through binoculars.

They had moved up in the predawn darkness. The air was bitter cold; the threat of snow was again imminent. The sky was still overcast when the sun rose, and the Afghans muttered hopefully that the clouds would keep the Russian gunships on the ground. But Tarp knew better. He supposed that they knew better, too.

At first light, the meager rebel artillery began to pound the power station as it had been doing for two days. Tarp and Ghulam Kashti moved up with their troops. The men who had come over the pass with him had surprised Tarp by asking to stay under his command, the battle at the pass having convinced them that he was lucky.

Mahmud Khalq had brought him the message after the men had voted. "There will be fighting," Tarp warned him.

"Good. Very good."

"They must take part of the power station and hold it for an hour."

"Very good. They want to kill Russians. They say you are lucky; you go where Russians get killed. Very good."

And where Afghans get killed, Tarp thought. *Not very good.*

The Russians were dug in on both sides of the river behind the power station and the city center. They had run their tanks up on earthen ramps to give them elevation for use as artillery; the Afghans believed that the Russians were short of fuel, and Tarp supposed they were right. Between the Russian positions and the rebels were units of the Afghan regular army, which was supposed to be loyal to the Soviets and their government in Kabul; obviously, however, the Soviets had put them where they were because they did not trust them.

The rebels and the Afghan soldiers were caught between wanting to hate each other on principle and wanting to join with each other because of nature. So the rebels had been waiting for the army to defect, and the army had been waiting for the rebels to go away. They shot at each other, but cautiously.

"Where is the Russian relief supposed to be?" Tarp asked Mahmud Khalq.

"One day away, maybe two. Coming fast."

"Air support?"

"The big gunships come every day; they fly in, bang-bang, rockets and a big machine gun. They say here that they shot down two helo transports, but they are afraid of the gunships."

Tarp could understand. He was afraid of the gunships himself.

He looked at the maps of the bunker. He wanted to put the particle beam inside the one-story concrete building and have a line brought up from the power station. He motioned Ghulam Kashti to his side. "Will the other generals send their men against the power station this morning?"

Kashti grinned. "Oh, yes, American friend! Now that they know Ghulam Kashti will send *his* men in, they are willing. Where the Tiger of the Pamirs goes, the rest will follow!"

"They must hold the station for an hour. All right?"

"And in that hour, you will open up the bunker?"

"Yes." *I hope*.

"You must be a magician, American ally! The CIA sends *big* magic around the world!"

"Yeah," Tarp drawled. He signaled to Mahmud Khalq. "Magic time!"

It was very basic, very old-fashioned war. The Russians had the high-technology weaponry; they had allowed the Afghan army only the most conventional arms. The rebels were even more traditionally equipped: assault rifles, old Thompsons from the days of Britain's empire, bolt actions back to the Ross and even the Martini. They had three captured armored personnel carriers and the tractor that Tarp had brought in, as well as two bulldozers.

The APCs and the bulldozers, their blades raised, spearheaded three assaults. The Afghan insurgents, turbans flapping, civilian clothes pulled tight against the chill wind, fanned out behind them. In their prepared positions, the Afghan soldiers—half of them recent conscripts pulled from their villages under Russian guns—squinted down the sights of their guns—and hesitated.

Afghan officers began to shout. Russian advisers bellowed into field radios, demanding support. Political officers shouted at both the Afghans and the Russians, threatening executions.

In a fortified strongpoint down the hill from the bunker, a Russian captain slapped an Afghan major who did not give an order to fire quickly enough when fifty rebels came trotting toward them.

An Afghan sergeant shot the Russian captain in the back with a burst from a Kalshnikov.

Grenades burst in front of the rebel advance. Three of the six strongpoints were strongly loyal and began to lay down deadly zones of fire; the others, however, were firing only sporadically. Without warning, a rebel flag went up over one of them, something that had been made by hand and hidden in a tunic for that moment, and the guns from that strongpoint began to fire on the next one. Farther along the line, the Russian captain's bloody tunic was raised on a pole; at the far end of the defense perimeter, a white flag waved back and forth with metronomic regularity.

"Keep them close to me!" Tarp shouted at Mahmud Khalq. "Move out!"

Beecham's daughter was right behind him with the

Chinese Mini-14, a woman at that moment indistinguishable from the men on either side. She had made herself into a shield for her father, who was being carried by two husky rebels while two more trotted behind them with the box and three more dragged coils of heavy cable.

From a position on their right flank, Ghulam Kashti covered their progress across the open ground to the concrete building.

Far to their left now, two bulldozers were pushing part of an earth wall down the riverbank; closer in, the tractor was burning, its driver lying half out of the seat like a bundle of old clothes. Two of the APCs lay shattered between the forward lines. Over two of the defensive strongpoints, however, the rebel flag was flying, and rebel soldiers had concentrated on the remaining one between them, from which they could make a strike down into the power station.

Tarp hunkered under the protection of somebody's garden wall and waved Khalq to him. "Where is our radio man?"

Khalq spread his hands. "General Kashti had none to spare."

"General Kashti is a lying bastard. Send somebody down to those strongpoints to see what the situation at the power station is."

Fifteen minutes later, word came back that the rebels were at the power-station fence and had breached it, but the Afghan troops inside were loyal and were fighting hard.

"We can't do anything without power!" Tarp roared.

Then the gunships came.

There were four of them, MIL MI-24s, big and fast and armed with weapons the rebels had learned to fear: laser-sighted missiles and four-barreled heavy machine guns. They made one pass down the battle line, catching the rebels in the open and skipping gasoline jelly at them. Because of a decision that had been made on the other side of the river, where everybody of any importance was Russian, they attacked every strongpoint in the line, apparently on the theory that if two of them had fallen, the rest would fall soon. They took out loyal Afghan soldiers and defectors and rebels with utter equality, and when they had finished their second pass, they had done more to swing the remaining Afghan army troops over to the rebels than any amount of persuasion could have.

When the gunships clattered away, the rubble was strewn with bodies, but Afghan regulars were turning on their Russian advisers and their political officers, and the outer perimeter of the power station was being assaulted by rebels backed by Afghan army troops.

Tarp sent Mahmud Khalq back to Kashti with a message: *Send radios or the deal is off*.

Two radio men arrived and Tarp moved forward, and seventeen minutes later he stood inside the gutted, one-story building with one of them while the other went down toward the power station. Arthur Beecham was giving orders to the men with the box and Sheila was standing near him as if she were the mother of this odd, frail child. And the child, whose prize toys were in the wooden box, was testy because he wanted to begin playing and the things weren't quite ready yet.

The concrete building had been cleaned out by flame on the first day of the battle. A burned-out truck body was the only object of any size in the interior, which was as big as a small church but much lower. At one end, a window twenty feet long, its glass completely gone, looked up the slight grade toward the bunker.

Tarp had sent Mahmud Khalq up to an observation point to study it, and he now said to the radio man, "Ask Lieutenant Khalq what is happening at the bunker."

After some static-ridden chatter, the man said, "He says there are loyal troops dug in there and they are shooting down toward the power station."

"How many?"

"Maybe twenty, he thinks."

"Weapons?"

"He thinks maybe two machine guns and two squad autos."

"Tell the lieutenant to place the men so that they can cover this building in case of attack from the bunker. I will be firing from here but I have no defense."

The cable was slow in coming up, and it seemed to Tarp that if the regulars in the bunker had any ambition, they would come down the slope and take over the building where he was, from which they could have fired on the rebel flank. The men in the bunker liked it there, however. The bunker had been built in the H-bomb 1950s as an atomic shelter for the Russian technicians who had overseen construction of the power station, and it was thick-walled and well-provisioned. Tarp supposed that no foot soldier in his right mind would have left it without a very direct order.

"Here comes your wire."

Sheila Beecham had been speaking to her father; Tarp had thought she had been talking to him, and he had started to give her a grateful smile, only to find that her back was turned to him.

Four men sweated the massive cable up the hill behind a little motorized wire runner, which normally carried a spool on its rear. One of the men was bleeding from glass fragments that had hit him down below, but he worked without complaining. Being accustomed to nothing but adversity from childhood on, these men were tough.

"No, no—not there! Not there!" Arthur Beecham was screaming at them in English, which they did not understand; still, he made himself quite clear. "I want it over here! Oh, Sheila, *do* make them put it over here—here, *here*!"

There was a steel-legged bench in the vast interior that had escaped complete destruction. The box had been put on its charred top, and Beecham was giving orders for it to be moved to the shattered window and the cable dragged up to it. Tarp broke in and had the table moved back from the window for security.

"How do we hook it up?" Tarp said.

"*You* don't!" Beecham snapped. He was in a thoroughly bad temper now. "I do!" He glared at the Afghans. "You must get these colored people out of here."

Tarp wanted to object, but it hardly seemed the time for a lecture on racism. "They're our people, Mr. Beecham."

"I don't care, I don't want them here. Out, out—they must go away! All of you—shoo—shoo! Sheila, do get them out of here. You there, boy, go away . . . shoo!"

"Mr. Beecham, they're on our side."

"But I don't *know* them!"

The men were pushed out, and Tarp's radio operator had to stand behind the burned-out truck while the connections were made. Not even Sheila and Tarp were allowed to watch, nor could Tarp get close while Beecham took out a three-way switch that had been secured inside the box and wired it up on the charred table like the remote switch of an electric train.

"Now you may look, I suppose," Beecham said petulantly.

"Did it occur to you, Mr. Beecham, that it might be useful if two of us could wire up that thing?"

"I don't like people hanging over me while I work."

Tarp looked at the box, the little switch, the snakelike cable. "Is it ready?"

"When they give us power, yes."

"And then all we do is turn this switch over?"

"And aim it, of course." Beecham pointed to the hole in one end, through which the metal tube that Tarp had seen inside the box now projected. "It isn't really very much like firing a gun, because the beam has to propel itself through the air and so you have to hold steady on. But you can see the beam, so it's a bit like a tracer bullet."

"Or a laser sight."

Beecham ignored him. "It would really be much better in a vacuum." He looked around vaguely as if he hoped he might find a vacuum eight or ten feet away. "One loses so much power exploding the air," he murmured.

More than a little crazy, Tarp thought. He looked at the box and the metal tube, so much like a piece of a vacuum cleaner, and the little three-way switch, which had been cannibalized from a heavy-duty buss box. *But I'm acting as if the thing will work—so I must be crazier than he is.* "In for a penny, in for a pound," he muttered.

"What's that?"

"Saying my prayers, Mr. Beecham." He went behind the ruined truck. "Tell Lieutenant Khalq I'm in the process of setting up my rocket launchers."

The radio man stared at him. Tarp could hardly blame him.

"My rocket launchers. They are of a new and very small and very secret type, which I brought here from Washington in my luggage. I am setting them up, tell him. Tell him also that I will be using a laser sight and that he and his men will see a shaft of light from it, and they are not to be surprised."

The radio man licked his lips. He was not from a culture where men argued with their superiors. The story about the rockets and the laser sight greatly troubled him, however. When he relayed the message to Khalq, he was hoarse with tension.

Tarp did not care what the Afghans thought he was about to use, so long as they did not realize that he was trying to use a particle beam. Inevitably, if the beam worked, the story of its power would spread; all Tarp could try to do was buy time by confusing the story with noninformation about rockets and lasers.

"Lieutenant Khalq says he understands, sir."

"Good. Now get in touch with the power station. Tell them to turn on the power."

"Yes, sir."

Nothing happened for six minutes. At the bunker, the regulars continued to pour automatic fire into the power station from their place of safety. Closer to Tarp, Khalq and the men who had come over the pass watched the bunker.

"Where the hell is—?"

The power came on with a noise inside the box as if two boards had been slapped together. Blue sparks jumped toward the ceiling and a powerful smell of electrical heat spread through the building. Where the cable entered the box, blue flame glowed as if a welder was at work. Tarp could smell burning wood.

"Oh, dear," Arthur Beecham said.

"What is it?"

"Well, it's such a nice lot of power, everything's burning up. Maybe it's not as bad as it looks. Mustn't see only the dark side, what?"

Tarp held his hand out toward the box. "Can I touch it?"

"Oh, yes . . . quite safe. . . ."

Tarp touched it, and an electric shock slammed through his arm and knocked him backward. He was aware that the wood had been hot to the touch. "*Jesus!*"

". . . but you may get a slight buzz from it now and again . . . a bit of leakage . . . it's only a prototype, you know. . . ."

Tarp was massaging his numbed arm. "Jesus!" He looked around the empty building. "I've got to fire this mother somehow." Behind the building was a pile of ruined tires. He cut sections to put under his feet and slabs that he could use as pokers to manipulate the box. The cut sections curled around his feet like oversized Turkish slippers and forced him to move in a strange, skiing fashion. He had to order the power turned off and on a number of times before he had the box properly into position, and then, leaning awkwardly along the charred bench, his feet in the bucketlike pieces of tire and the rear part of the box clasped between the slabs of rubber, he declared himself ready. "I hope," he said.

It had already been made clear to Arthur Beecham that Tarp, and not he, would do the actual firing. Beecham's feelings were hurt and he was quite defensive. "It isn't my fault that they're sending too much power," he said petulantly.

"No, Mr. Beecham."

"I didn't have this trouble at the prison," he muttered. "I had the right amount of power there."

"Yes, Mr. Beecham."

"Anyway, a little electricity now and again is good for one."

Tarp clutched the box between the thick pieces of rubber. Their acrid odor choked him as they began to burn. The wood of the box was black in two places already. Electrical leakage trickled along his arms despite the insulation.

God loves fools and madmen, Tarp had to remind himself. *With Beecham and me, we've got one of each.*

Sheila Beecham waited by the switch. She, too, used a heavy chunk of rubber tire to handle it.

Tarp sighted along the top of the box.

He told himself that that was what he was doing. *I'm sighting along a wooden box that is going to catch fire at any moment. I'm standing in shoes made out of rubber tires and I'm about to blow a bomb shelter to kingdom come. Oh, yeah.*

"Turn it on."

Seila's hand moved, and the wooden box, as if satisfied now that its proper moment had come, stopped vibrating and smoking, and a very fine blue line appeared between the metal tube and the bunker, as if drawn there in the air by an artist's pencil. There was a sound in the air like the deaths of insects in an electronic bug killer; bits of sparks unraveled from the blue line like fibers from a taut rope.

The gray face of the bunker erupted. There was no explosion as with artillery, but a sharp crack like that of a high-velocity rifle, repeated again and again so fast that the reports merged into an ear-jarring crackle. Molecules were being blown apart by protons, and as each molecule was shattered, the proton beam penetrated to another to shatter it. Solid concrete was not solid, after all; it was a structure of intricate, overlapping molecules, whose internal linkages the beam severed with a release of energy like little thunderclaps.

The face of the bunker shook and seemed to slide, and then was obscured by dust.

"Off!"

Arthur Beecham looked cross. "No!"

"I can't see!"

"Oh, bother seeing—just bang away!"

Tarp jerked his head at Shiela. "On!" The blue line was drawn again; the bunker erupted. "Off!" He let the dust settle. "On!"

"Off!"

"On!"

A huge excitement filled Tarp. He had cut steel with an acetylene torch, but it had not been like this. The sense of power between his hands was like nothing he had ever known, and he understood that if Beecham's device could be shielded and properly mounted, the man who fired it could use it like a scalpel to peel apart the universe.

"On!"

He was cutting a hole in the twenty-inch concrete that a bus could have been driven through. His arms were numbed as if he had been controlling a jackhammer, but he did not notice. There was a new smell in the building—burning flesh, as his hands began to stick to the melting rubber of the slabs—but he did not notice that, either.

It was like the rapture of the deep, the diver's euphoria that takes the good diver down and down, playing tricks on his blood to beguile his brain, sending him plunging happily to his own destruction in the deeps.

Sheila Beecham turned the device off.

"Hey!" He was enraged. "On—on!"

"It's enough!" She pointed out the wide window. "It's done!"

Tarp stared dumbly through the opening. Little was left of the aboveground part of the bunker. Khalq's men were firing happily down the slope at the regulars who had abandoned their safe refuge when its molecules had been assaulted and who were now trying to make their way down to the still-occupied part of the power complex.

"No," Tarp complained. "No. . . ." He was being pulled back from the deeps of destruction—and he did not want to come.

"No. . . ."

Ghulam Kashti and his personal bodyguard were going by the building at a run, and Ghulam Kashti was in the lead. It may have been undignified for a self-appointed general to run, but gold was the prize now, not dignity. Kashti passed the one-story building without a glance and broke into a full sprint for the remaining yards toward the enormous hole that Tarp had cut.

And then the gunships came back.

They went first to the perimeter of the power station, giving Kashti and Mahmud Khalq time to put most of their men under cover. Dropping more flaming jelly and urging their rockets into strongpoints, they passed over three times, their Gatling-like nose guns clattering. Ground fire popped like static on a cheap radio. Satisfied, two of the gunships turned for home. The other two, perhaps still having ammunition unexpended, came up the hillside.

Tarp saw them swing away, cross part of his line of vision, and then swing back, one behind the other in a line that a more battlewise leader might have avoided.

Tarp was awaking from his rapture—waking to scorched hands that could not free themselves from the rubber slabs, to arms numb to the elbow and aching above. But now he saw the gunships coming in, and without thinking, he was moving the box again, bringing it to bear on the two helicopters that were coming as one. Thinking, *They're too close together for their own good*. Thinking, *Maybe they're just kids. Fresh out of chopper school at Pyatigorsk*. The nose gun of the first ship began to pound.

"On!"

The blue beam missed the gunship and went on into endless space. *To Mars? To Saturn? To the edge of the universe?* Tarp moved the box with painful hands. The beam touched the lead gunship on the outboard end of its wing, anatomizing it with a sound like breaking crystal, and he moved it in farther and cut through the nose blister and the gunport and the forward observer's position, and the gunship blew up. The second gunship, coming too close behind, caught the beam and, trying to turn away from whatever had destroyed the first, took the beam near the tail and lurched down and forward and then spun crazily, to disappear behind the hill and end in an eruption of orange flame and a pillar of dark smoke.

"Off!"

Khalq and his men were crawling from cover, looking up into the sky where the gunships had been. Like men who have witnessed a miracle, they looked at each other and again at the sky, and then around them as if they suspected that the world had changed in a fundamental way while they lay seeking protection.

You want magic, you get magic.

Khalq looked down at the one-story building. He could not seem to get his mouth closed.

From the bottom of the hill, the wind brought a sound of cheering.

Tarp kicked his feet out of the rubber boots and

staggered to the place where the radio man was still crouching behind the truck. "Tell Lieutenant Khalq. . . ." Tarp tried to steady himself on the blackened metal and found that the palm of his right hand was burned. "Tell Lieutenant Khalq to cover everybody who comes out of the bunker, including General Kashti and his men. Nobody is to come to this building but General Kashti. Anybody else who tries it will be shot."

Ghulam Kashti came out of the bunker first. He moved slowly. His guards came behind him in single file, each with a rag-wrapped bundle on his shoulder. *Two bars of gold each,* Tarp was thinking. He was trying to peel melted rubber from his fingers. Every fourth man carried a ready sub-machine gun instead of the gold. *Trusting nobody. Taking no chances.*

Tarp wanted a weapon but could not hold one.

Kashti came down toward the building and signaled several men to follow, but Khalq called something to them and Khalq's men sat up in their sheltered places among the rubble and made their weapons very visible. Kashti shouted something and the young lieutenant looked scared, but he did not back down. Kashti sent the men with the gold on down toward the rebel position, put three of the men with sub-machine guns as close to the building as Khalq would let them go, and then came trudging heavily down toward it alone, grinning and swinging an Uzi as if he were about to do something wonderful with it for Tarp's entertainment, like twirl it or throw it into the air.

"Sheila. . . ." Tarp started to say. She already had the rifle in her hands. She put her father behind her and backed toward the bench and the particle beam.

Tarp moved the box as Kashti came on. *Hip shot.* "Stand away, Sheila," he groaned.

"I'm not afraid of him," she said. She had both hands on the rifle. The switch for the particle beam was across the bench from Tarp, out of his reach. He was going to shout at her in frustration when Arthur Beecham's bony hand appeared on the bench's black surface and hovered over the switch.

Kashti came close to the window and stepped up on a pile of rubble outside so that he loomed in silhouette against the bright sky like a statue of a military victor. "You did as you promised!" he crowed. His smile was ghastly. "You are magic!"

"Remove those men with the sub-machine guns, General." Tarp moved the box a fraction of an inch, estimating its aim from the place where he stood beside the bench. Kashti flinched at the movement, but he was watching Sheila's rifle, which was the weapon that he feared. His eyes swept the interior and then came back to the rifle.

"Where are your rockets?"

"Remove the men with the SMGs, General!"

"Tell your little lieutenant to remove his men, instead!"

"What, so you can murder us?"

"Death in war is not murder!" Kashti grinned again. His eyes began another sweep of the interior, looking for the rocket launchers.

"On!"

Arthur Beecham's fingers moved. The blue line glowed between the tube and Kashti's pelvis, and the Afghan bandit exploded. The building reeked of burned flesh and cloth.

"Off!"

Kasthi's legs had fallen inside the window. The rest of him was sprawled down the rubble outside as if it had been poured from a bucket.

Tarp bent over the mess. "Magic time," he whispered to the still-grinning face.

He kicked out the sparks in the smoldering cloth and, with burned fingers, ripped the Russian tunic from the torso. Belted into it were two gold bars. Each one was worth about a hundred and fifty thousand dollars.

Tarp called Lieutenant Khalq down to the building and gave him the problem of disposing of the rest of

Kashti. On the slope above them, the three members of Kashti's bodyguard were still standing under the guns of Tarp's Afghans, looking down to the place where their leader had so suddenly been cut down. "Keep those three isolated until I leave Afghanistan. Three or four days. And spread the word that General Kashti's bodyguard are carrying a fortune in gold bars."

"Gold, Commandant?"

"Yes. Kashti wanted it for himself, but I think you should tell the other generals that it is for the freedom fighters of Afghanistan."

Tarp carried the two gold bars in his shoulder bag. With difficulty now, he jockeyed the box around and turned the beam on the power station itself until the power went off because the generators had been destroyed. By that time, Tarp was finding it difficult to hold on to the rubber slabs, and he was relieved when he could order the box disconnected from its cable. Then he and Beecham and Beecham's daughter went back down the slope, hoping they were starting their trek toward Pakistan.

chapter sixteen

It is almost three hundred miles from Faizabad to Peshawar over roads that labor up the mountains and seem to hang over fast-running rivers like goat tracks. Snow and ice loom over the fragile roads—the Himalaya and Khyber peaks, pink-white clouds of mountain.

It took him four days to reach Peshawar. He found it like the early days in Vietnam: the rebels owned the roads by night and the Russians tried to patrol them, mostly from the air, by day. The second day after the battle at Faizabad, the weather turned sharply warmer and dense fog formed where the warm breeze breathed over snow, and for twenty-four hours the gunships could not find them or anybody else on the roads. Tarp drove the light truck he had stolen in the border pass; his Afghans followed in another truck and a bus that they had picked up in Faizabad. Tarp told Mahmud Khalq that they should leave him, but the lieutenant said the men did not want to. They wanted to accompany him, like a hero, to the Khyber Pass.

"What do they think of my missiles?" he said to Khalq, curious to see what rumor had made of the particle beam.

"Wonderful. Most wonderful!" Khalq seemed a little embarrassed. "Myself, until I heard it from your own lips, I did not think there were any missiles, Commandant."

"Oh, yes! Shoulder-fired."

"Most wonderful! I never saw the launcher, alas."

"Disposable."

"Ah!"

"A new design. Most secret, you understand. It is hoped to send them to insurgency forces. You understand, Lieutenant, that I was testing these missiles, but word of them must be kept secret."

"Oh, yes; by Allah, by my father's honor, by—"

"Very secret. Not only the missiles and the launcher, but the laser sight as well. The blue flame."

Khalq smiled happily. "Ah, the blue flame!"

"You saw it, then."

"*That*, I saw! In fact, I am ashamed to confess it, Commandant, I—I actually thought it was the blue flame that shot down the gunships!"

They laughed together. "That was only the laser sighting device," Tarp told him. "I prefer that you discuss it with no one."

"No one, Commandant! But the men—ah, well, that is another story. You know—rumor, gossip—they are good men, Commandant—."

"The best—."

"—loyal, courageous—."

"—good fighters, tough—."

"—but peasants, most of them. Uneducated. Much given to gossip and rumor. They will talk, Commandant . . . they talk now, they talk over and over of your missiles. They are uneducated men." They were in the front seat of the truck as it moved through the fog; Khalq peered ahead into the wetness. "I, on the other hand, am an educated man."

"Of course."

"I was to have gone to the foreigners' university at Moscow last year to learn local-government administration. Now I have devoted my life to exterminating the people who were to be my benefactors." Khalq glared at the gray vapor behind the whipping wand of the windshield wiper. "Life is not just, Commandant."

It was a very young man's discovery. Yet it was a valid discovery and one that could lead to real wisdom. "No," Tarp said kindly, "life is not just. But it has surprising pleasures, nonetheless. They will come to you in time."

Khalq looked aside at him. Perhaps he had found wisdom already. "I will be killed soon. Nothing will come to me 'in time.' Forgive me for contradicting you, Commandant."

Later, Khalq went back to one of the other vehicles to be with his men, and Arthur Beecham moved up into the front seat with Tarp. His left hand was bandaged because he had burned it, turning on the beam that killed Ghulam Kashti. It looked like a big white mitten, and he waved it almost gaily when he talked, as if it had become a badge. Tarp's hands were wound with gauze, too, and the palms had been smeared thick with an anesthetic goo. Perhaps this similarity of their wounds gave them an unusual sympathy with each other, for they rode together in mostly silent, mutual enjoyment. When Beecham asked a rather vaguely formed question, Tarp instantly understood what the subject was.

"What did you think of it?" the old man asked.

"Very, very dangerous," Tarp said.

"But the feeling of power!"

"That's what was so dangerous." Tarp remembered that feeling of near euphoria. "Rapture."

Beecham's face took on a dreamy look. "Yes," he whispered. "I felt that, too, at the prison."

The next day was clearer and the roads were unsafe.

They hid in the hills and moved on after sundown, clearing the nocturnal rebel roadblocks with the help of the passes that Ghulam Kashti had written. The night after that, they reached the Khyber Pass. Tarp turned the Soviet truck over to the Afghans and took, instead, a delapidated sedan that had been requisitioned in the retreat from Faizabad. It was an ancient 4-CV, the beloved "Quatre Chevaux" of postwar France, a car that had been noisy and cranky when brand-new and that was now a movable rust heap. Its pressed-metal sides were virtually without paint, and it bucked fiercely on any grade. However, it did not have Soviet markings, and that was its greatest asset to Tarp.

He took Lieutenant Khalq aside. They walked off the road and down a hillside treacherous with scree. In the shelter of an outcropping, Tarp unwrapped one of the two gold bars that he had taken from Kashti's body and shone his flashlight on it. "For you and for the men."

"Gold, Commandant?"

"Yes. So that maybe life will not seem totally unjust."

Khalq's eyes were shiny now. "The weapons that we would buy from General Sun!"

"Yes. It will also buy women or airplane tickets to Paris or hashish or even, if you want, a place at the foreigners' university in Moscow."

"I would buy weapons with it!" the young man cried. "I would lead these men against the invaders!" Tarp handed him the twenty-six-pound bar. "Do as you will." He wondered if Khalq's excitement was the same emotion he had felt when he had fired the beam—the rapture of power. "God help you."

The Afghan rebels whom he had brought over the pass from Sun's lined the moonlit road as he put the 4-CV into gear. As the rattling little car bucked forward Khalq, who was at the end of the line, saluted smartly.

"Everything but the skirl of bagpipes," Tarp muttered. "Tarp of the Khyber Rifles."

Beechman's daughter was sitting beside him. "I don't understand what you said."

He waited until the car had bucked again. "I'll take you to a movie one day. It's too hard to explain."

He nursed the 4-CV into Peshawar the next day. He had not been in the Pakistani city before, but he thought he knew what sort of place it would be—not its people or its crowding or its poverty, but its smell of war, for it was the jumping-off place for the conflict in Afghanistan. One would be able to buy anything there, or sell anything—especially guns or people who knew how to use guns.

Tarp was patient, and did not try to urge the car faster than the crowds in the streets. He hunched a little forward so that he could look out and up, enjoying the vigor of the place. Sheila Beecham sat next to him, expressionless; beyond her, old Arthur played with his lower lip and looked unhappy.

"What sort of place is this?" Beecham's daughter said. The noise outside the car was ferocious, much of it blaring from radios that young men carried on their shoulders.

"You're looking at it."

"It seems—very crowded."

Perhaps she had never seen so many people squeezed in together. Perhaps, Tarp realized with astonishment, she had never been in a city before. He leaned across her to look at her father and to try to cheer him up. "Mr. Beecham—what do you think?"

Arthur Beecham's face looked unhealthy, as if he might be coming down with some minor disease. He continued to work at his flaccid underlip with nervous fingers. He looked aside at Tarp and then looked out at the streets again.

More than they bargained for. He's scared. The sooner I get them out of these mobs, the better.

He had to ask three times for directions to Peri Kri's—Peri Krishnamurti's Harry's Venetian Bar and

International Restaurant. The people who knew the way were young and they carried guns. Peshawar seemed to have so many guns flowing through it, legal and otherwise, that some of them had overflowed and washed up on the belts of the locals.

Peri Kri's turned out to be one of a block of storefronts in a twisting street, its windows plastered over with signs in several languages and three alphabets. They advertized pizza and money orders, film and Real Madras Curry. Over the door, a cardboard sign said: PAWN SHOP. GUNS A SPECIALITY.

"End of the line, folks."

Sheila Beecham drew back against her father. "Why?"

"This is it. This is the place I've been looking for."

The Beechams huddled together. Tarp suddenly saw them as refugees, people who had been pulled from the sea and set down somewhere to be forgotten. "I don't like it here," Arthur Beecham said, his voice a childish whine.

"It's better than prison."

"No! I don't like the look of these colored people. They're very noisy. They are very, very . . . *brutal.* I can tell by their faces. I don't like them."

Tarp took the keys, stepped out into the flow of human beings, and squeezed around the back of the 4-CV. He opened the door on Beecham's side, diverting the current of people across the sidewalk. "These are very gentle people, Mr. Beecham. These people are Moslems, and their skin is brown, not yellow, but they are every bit as nice as the people in China."

"No . . . no. . . ." Sheila Beecham put her arms around her father, like an older sister protecting a child.

Tarp looked into the oncoming mob. He searched for a particularly pleasant face. "Pardon me . . . do you speak English? Pardon me . . . do you speak English? Pardon me. . . ."

The third man was delighted to be spoken to. His

fleshy lips came up in a broad smile to show perfect teeth. "Oh, yes. May I be of service to you?" He spoke English with a strong British note, only slightly touched by Pakistani.

"I wonder if you'd speak to a friend of mine," Tarp said.

"Oh, yes." The dark-skinned man bent down. A wave of cloying scent moved past Tarp. "How do you do, sir?" the man said to Arthur Beecham. "Welcome to Peshawar. Are you American?"

Arthur Beecham drew back still farther. "I'm English."

"Oh, yes! I have visited England. Five years ago, when I was a delegate to the International Congress of Motorcar Sales Representatives, I was in your lovely city of Manchester." He beamed. "I met your second underminister for trade, Mr. Hartwell-Sloane!" He beamed at Sheila Beecham. "I am myself the owner of three motorcar agencies."

"Rolls-Royce?"

The man giggled and rolled his eyes. "Oh, no! Toyota! What a jolly witticism. Oh, no, since the unpleasantness with our neighbor to the north, the demand for trucks and four-wheel-drive vehicles has been outstanding! But not the Rolls, oh, no!" He shook hands with Beecham. "Welcome to Peshawar, so nice to meet you." He shook hands with Sheila. "Welcome to Peshawar, so nice to meet you." He shook hands with Tarp. "Came down from Afghanistan, did you?"

"How can you tell?"

The man giggled again. "I know the signs. Going back? I have a very nice arrangement on Land Cruisers just now."

"Nothing down, four years to pay?"

The man giggled and giggled. "Cash only, my friend!" He put his mouth next to Tarp's ear; the scent was overpowering. "So many people don't come back." And giggling and bouncing with laughter, he stepped into the stream of the city and was borne away.

Tarp looked at Arthur Beecham. "Not a bad chap," Beecham said.

"I thought so."

"Dark-skinned, of course. But—courteous. *Very* courteous. Spoke English, too."

"I noticed."

Beecham put his hands on the doorframe. "I've got to relieve myself someplace," he said. Thus did his bladder overcome his fears.

Tarp opened a pathway for father and daughter by standing with his arms spread just long enough for them to scurry from the 4-CV to the doorway, their heads down and together like celebrities trying to escape a crowd of photographers. The moment they were across, Tarp dropped his arms and dived into the car to get his shoulder bag and the wooden box, which was now a charred relic. He sprinted to their side and hustled them through the door and through curtains of beads and jangling bells on the other side.

Inside, there was an open space about eight feet by twelve feet, separated from an arched corridor by a waist-high wooden barrier and a gate. One of the largest men Tarp had ever seen was sitting in a chair by the wall. He had a 9mm in a shoulder holster, but he looked as if he could stop bullets with his teeth and break armor with his neckless head. He looked like a Tibetan, but he spoke Farsi.

"You wish to enter inside, honored guest?"

"I'm looking for Peri Kri."

But he had already seen her. She was standing beyond the barrier, consulting with a sleek little man about a piece of paper. She must have heard his voice, for she looked up, and then he saw that she was working to overcome the disbelief at seeing him.

"*You*."

Her voice was a whisper. He had never heard her raise her voice. Her nostrils flared very slightly and her lips parted. She moved through the wooden gate on very short, quick steps that flowed smoothly together like the gait of the small-footed women of the Chinese Empire. "You bastard," she murmured.

"Can you put me up, Peri?"

She snuggled against him. She was small, and he had to bend low to kiss her. She wrapped her arms around him. "You old bastard," she whispered happily.

"You still give a great massage, Peri. Ow!"

"I learned in India. In India, they teach you to massage *everything*. You want me to massage everything?"

"You already have, Peri."

"Only once! Don't be so American." She was sitting naked on his naked buttocks with her calves pulled in tight against his body. By twisting his head, he could see her pale brown back and the plait of black hair that hung down so far it rested at the base of his own spine. Large-mouthed, large-eyed, she had ungainly hands and feet, as if she had been made up of pieces too large for her. Yet she was a beautiful woman.

Tarp stroked her calves. She kneaded the backs of his thighs with powerful thumbs.

"I want you to sell some gold for me, Peri."

"Okay. How much?"

"A bar. Twenty-six pounds."

"*Ai-ya!* Not just pocket change, love."

"Is it too much?"

"Oh, no. I take twenty-five percent these days, darling."

"Not from an old lover."

"Most definitely from an old lover. Especially one who owes me so much from the old days!"

Tarp rolled up and twisted at the hips so he could catch the thick braid. "Ten percent—because it's me."

She twisted, too. Her eyes were heavily made up in a more or less Western fashion—mascara, brown liner, peacock-blue lids. "Fifteen—because it's *me*."

"No discount for lovers?"

"Darling, the world is full of men who are lovers. But their secret is out—they all have about the same equipment, and none of them is worth a discount."

"Peri, you've gone cynical."

"Oh, sure. I haven't been living in a convent, you know." She swiveled and pulled her left leg over, and he rolled his hips at the same time so their bodies slid over each other. Bending forward, she rested her left hand against his face. "I was so much younger in Saigon, darling. It was so long ago."

He touched the hand. "Want me to go someplace else?"

"Oh, no!" She leaned still farther, putting her forearms flat on his chest, elbows below the ribs and hands on his shoulders. "But it isn't love anymore, you understand?"

"It's play."

"Well—a little sad kind of play, maybe. Because of all the time that's gone by." She kissed his mouth lightly. "I was crazy for you in Saigon, you know."

"No."

"Sure, you knew. You used it. But that's all right, darling, because I used it, too. I was still Christian then; I used to go to church at dawn and light candles and pray that nothing would happen to you. Because I was so crazy for you."

"It must have worked. Nothing happened to me."

She shook her head. "No, it didn't work. Things happened to *me*." She put her head down on his chest. "I got older. I never dreamed it would happen to me." She followed the line of his breastbone with her tongue. "I wish I was seventeen again with you."

They made love, then bathed and lay by a little stove. She brought out a bottle of oil that smelled like sweet fruit syrup and began to massage him again. "Who is the woman you brought?"

"Business. Her and the old man."

"You and her—are you anything to each other?"

"Nothing at all."

"You working for the agency now?"

"No." He spread the thin oil over his shoulders. "I need a secure place to stash the woman and the old man for a few days."

"Okay."

"*Absolutely* secure. Secure from everybody."

"I know a free-lancer in Sri Lanka."

"I'd rather it was in Europe."

"This is the best I can do. *Safe*. A thousand a day."

"Dollars?"

"Sure, dollars. But guaranteed."

"All right, take it out of the gold when you convert it."

"Sure."

"I'll want some papers, too."

"Okay. Oh!" She licked her lips. "This oil tastes good, you know?"

"What a good idea."

He flew to Sri Lanka to look at the place where the Beechams would stay. It was a former naval fort down the coast below Moratuwa where the British had once put heavy shore batteries that had become obsolete almost as soon as they were manned. Now the place was the home office of something called the Smiling Sunrise Import-Export Trader. Whatever it was that the firm imported and exported seemed to require an electronic warning system, double sets of airtight doors, and a highly sophisticated fire alarm.

"Your friends will be completely protected here. We guarantee security. We have no alliances and we charge so much that it isn't in our interest to sell out a client. You come very highly recommended. Are your people fugitives?"

"In a sense."

"Intelligence quarries?"

"Probably."

"All right. We sometimes do contract work for governments. You understand. It's very awkward for us if we have two contracts that are contradictory. . . . I mean, we don't want to agree to protect somebody if we've already signed up elsewhere to find that very person. In the long run, that sort of thing undermines client confidence. Now we don't contract with the Big Five. In fact, we prefer corporations and individuals like yourself. With that said, let me propose that you give me your name and some other data and I do a check through our data banks to make sure we haven't put ourselves on the search for you for somebody else."

He was a remarkably sleek man of about forty with beautifully manicured hands and hair that was combed back to hug his head tightly. His face was glossy and just slightly plump, as if to express his success. He might have been Lebanese or Israeli or Palestinian or Egyptian by birth, but he had long ago abandoned his national affiliations.

"My problem is," Tarp said cautiously, "if you find that you've got a contract on me, then you've got me. I mean, you wouldn't have to look any farther."

"That's so." The sleek businessman spread his lovely hands. "You'll have to make the decision if it's worth the risk."

Tarp thought for some seconds. "No Big Five work?"

"No. Too messy."

Again, Tarp needed time to think. He remembered the corporate plane on which he had first flown to England and the search that he had had Eddie Craik begin. "Have any contracts with a company called Dammeco, International?"

The businessman folded his hands on the polished teak of his worktable. "We don't work with Dammeco," he said with a new primness. "That, also, would be messy."

"Care to explain why?"

"Sorry—no."

Tarp told him who he was, and half an hour later the man reported that Tarp was clean and uncomplicated, as far as the Smiling Sunrise Import-Export Trader was concerned. "But somebody's been asking about you," he said.

"And?"

"That's all—one of our subcontractors got a query. American origin, he thought. Wanting any word if you were seen."

Tarp tensed. "Okay—have you seen me?"

"Certainly not. Not if we have a contract, you and I."

"Good enough." Tarp was thinking about the query with the American source. *Hacker. Almost certainly Norbert F. Hacker.* He had another thought, too. *Where the hell are the Russians?*

The businessman showed him an apartment deep inside the ancient fort where the Beechams would be housed. They would be protected by the automatic defenses plus twenty armed men who lived in the complex. About the only way anybody was going to get in was by cutting the place open with Beecham's particle beam—and that would be inside with him.

"Very impressive," Tarp said after the tour.

"We like it."

"I'll recommend it to my friends."

He flew back to Peshawar wondering what he would tell the Beechams. They were both uneasy still, the old man less so than he had been in the car; Sheila was tense and somehow embittered. And Tarp sensed that they blamed him for something they could probably not define themselves—he was their rescuer, to be sure, but in rescuing them he had also taken away everything with which they were familiar. That they were now in a strange land where they did not speak the language or recognize the faces was his fault. By saving them, he had made them refugees.

He went directly to their rooms behind Peri Kri's. There were guards at their doors and a marksman on a roof across the courtyard; Tarp had ordered them and was paying for them, despite Peri's own security. Seeing them, he knew what had embittered Sheila Beecham: she was in prison all over again.

Arthur Beecham still looked unwell. Tarp watched him for several seconds and then looked at Sheila, who was pacing up and down with her arms folded under her breasts. *Strung out, both of them. It's tough for them. They want to be in England. They think.* Tarp considered what sort of life Arthur Beecham would have if he actually got to English authorities with his invention. *Another government facility. Wherever he goes, they'll put him in a fortress. Wherever he goes, he'll be in prison.*

"I'm going away for a few days," he said.

Sheila stopped her pacing. "*What?*"

"I'm having you moved from this place. To a safer one. Down in—"

"You're *having us moved*!" she screamed at him. "We're not objects! *We're not like that box*!"

Arthur Beecham gave Tarp a sickly smile as if to apologize for his daughter. "When are we going to England?"

"Soon."

" '*Soon!*' " she said with disgust. "When? *When?*"

"When I believe it's safe for you to do so."

Her father wanted to speak, but she came at Tarp like an enemy, her face made ugly by her hatred for him at that moment. "Have you replaced our Central Committee? Are you God now? Who *are* you, to tell us what we can do and when we can do it? You said you were hired to get us out of China and to England. We're out of China now. Take us to England!"

"Not yet."

"Take us to England and then *leave us alone*!" She was sobbing. Making an animal sound of pain, she whirled from him and hid her face in her hands. Arthur Beecham stood up and took her in his arms.

"My dear—my dear." He patted her back awkwardly. "We have to trust our friend here."

"Why?"

Arthur Beecham made his sickly smile again. "Because there's nobody else."

"I *won't* trust him! He doesn't trust me."

"Of course he does. Don't you, Mr. Tarp?"

"No, sir. I'm afraid I don't."

They all looked from face to face, each trying to find precisely how he felt about the other two.

"I didn't want to send you someplace else," Tarp said. His voice was made miserable by his sense that he would do what he thought was best, no matter what they wanted. "But the operation's wrong. I told you that after the plane blew up. Everything we've done since then has been on our own, because I don't know what our situation is anymore. So I have to make some inquiries in Europe to make sure it's safe to take you back."

The old man pulled his daughter down beside him on a sofa. "What do we do if England isn't safe? Mr. Tarp, I can't go on too much longer. I know it's weak of me, but I—I feel very tired now and I'm *very* confused. I woke up this morning—and I found myself missing . . . my old cell." He looked shattered. There were tears in his eyes.

"If for some reason you can't go to England, there are people who could arrange for you to be very safe for the rest of your lives. You could barter your invention for any kind of life you want."

Arthur Beecham was not satisfied. He looked bereft.

"Sheila," Tarp said, "you must help your father. It will only be a few more days."

"I thought when we were out of China," she said grimly, "it would all be over!"

Tarp did not tell her that so long as her father's brain functioned, it would never be over.

* * *

He spent the night with Peri. She had currency and a set of Iraqui papers for him. She gave him a safe telephone number.

"Your friends from Sri Lanka will pick up the Beechams tomorrow, Peri. Once they've been turned over, nothing's to be done unless I personally order it. *Nothing*."

"Okay, okay."

"We'll refer to them as the Package. If a message comes in any other words, ignore it. He's the Big Package, she's the Little Package. Both of them are simply the Package. If you don't hear from me in five days, tell them they're on their own. Let your friend in Sri Lanka act as their agent."

"Where will you be?"

"Wherever it is, I won't care what's happened to the Beechams."

She kissed him. "I'll hear from you, all right."

"Prediction?"

"Faith. I lit a candle for you this morning."

"I thought you'd given all that up."

"I had. But you know, it made me happy. I feel young again."

chapter seventeen

The several days that followed were like an old film that had broken and been spliced many times, leaving only parts of scenes. Jerky and illogical, moments stood out, and the rest was blur. He knew this state; in fact, he welcomed it. He could save himself for the critical times and tune off for the rest.

Tieless and unshaven, his eyes hidden behind sunglasses, he flew to Rome as an Iraqui bureaucrat. He shaved in a men's room and bought a suit in an airport shop, changed, and flew to Paris using the French passport that he had got from Steinberg almost three weeks before. In Paris he bought shoes, a repellently French tie, and a pair of authentic French plastic sunglasses and found himself a telephone booth, from which he dialed Eddie Craik's "safe" number in London. It was Tarp's belief, however, that the number was probably no longer safe.

"Yes?"

"Double-blind coin-box call, Eddie. Ten minutes."

He found himself another kiosk and, after precisely ten minutes, dialed the number of a pub two streets away from Craik's mangy flat. They knew his ways there and kept his confidences. "Message for Eddie. Overseas Central forty-four."

"This is all a mystery to me," a squeaky female voice said on the other end. "A *com*-plete bleeding mystery."

"Good."

Tarp gave the number of the kiosk to the overseas operator and told her to place it with *numéro quarante-quatre à Londres*.

In fourteen minutes, the telephone rang. No Parisian had seen fit to make a call from the kiosk in all that time, perhaps because Tarp had put a handwritten sign on the door: *Cassé*.

"Hello, there."

"Tarp, is that you? Mother of God, man, what's all the mystification? You've made me the star turn of my pub."

"I supposed your safe line might be busted."

"You're kidding! Jesus, Mary, and Saint Joseph, man, I pay a fellow three-fifty a week to keep it jumping about."

"It may be okay. But it may not. How've you been, Eddie?"

"Oh, wizard, as we used to say at school. I've had three tails for the last week—American, English, and something unidentifiable. I think he may be a West German who's gone funny. If he didn't look so fucking strange, I'd have suggested we all sit down and play bloody bridge."

"You'll be all right. You were supposed to be getting more data on Dammeco and Adrien van Damme for me, Eddie."

"I know that."

"Did you?"

"Does the queen have tits?"

"Give it to me."

"Better you get it from the chap's doing the work. Just got back from Jo-burg a few days ago. Actually, he wants to be paid before he spills."

"Who is he?"

"Tough little queer named Jenny Barnwell—with a name like Jenny he'd have to be tough, yes? His place or yours?"

"Tell him to meet me at the Calais end of the hovercraft ferry. If he's tailed, the meeting's off. And don't have direct contact with him. Or have you already?"

"What d'you think I am, a bleeding beginner? We work through a drop. Jenny's clean."

"All right, get him going. The morning ferry tomorrow. And if anybody asks, Craik, you haven't talked to me. I've dropped off the face of the earth."

"Suits me."

Tarp found a little hotel on the rue Jacob and next day sped out to Calais on the early express. There were three ferries in the morning, not one, and Jenny Barnwell was not on the first. On the second, however, was a pinched-faced young Englishman who looked like a jockey and who kept sweeping the disembarking crowd with mistrustful, glittering eyes. Tarp picked him as the one.

"Are we looking for each other?" he said as the man came off the gangway. The man flinched; he was certainly tense about something. Tarp had already looked over the rest of the passengers and had seen nobody who was unduly interested in him.

"Are we?" the young man said belligerently. Ahead of them, the one-day shoppers were already vanishing into the express customs lines before they descended on the French markets.

"I'm looking for somebody just back from Jo-burg."

"I'm lookin' for a fella'll pay these bills." He handed a small envelope that was thick with scraps of paper to Tarp. "Pay first, if you please."

Tarp merely glanced at them—cheap round-trip airfare to South Africa, three nights in fleabag hotels, eleven telephone calls, including two to western Canada. "Plus how much for services?"

The man swallowed. "Fifty pounds a day. Five days."

Tarp quickly counted out the bills and pressed them into Jenny Barnwell's hand. "You never had it so good. There's fifty in there for today, too. All right: what have you got?"

They were waiting at the end of the customs line. Barnwell looked about himself constantly, still checking for a tail. "Dammeco, International is the real thing—solid financial position, credit the best, making money in the EEC and outside it. Really into minerals and drilling lubricants and all that lot. But your Mr. van Damme's a ringer."

Tarp felt something stir with excitement. "And?"

"He isn't Adrien van Damme."

"Who is he?"

They passed through customs separately and met at the documents gate, then went out into brilliant sunlight and strolled toward the town center. Barnwell would not talk until they were by themselves again, and Tarp had to repeat his question: "Who is he?"

"I don't know. Like Shakespeare, he's somebody else of the same name, as they say." Announcing that he had missed breakfast, the little man led Tarp into a café. There was no question about who would pay. Barnwell crossed his legs and leaned back against the wall. He seemed to be enjoying the role now. "I took all that stuff that Eddie told you and I ran it through again, just to make sure he'd got it right. He had, except for one or two things he'd missed—the fellow that calls himself van Damme lives in Paris and has several bodyguards, for example. And he isn't married—no kids. For the last six years he's had a 'relationship' with an actress at the Comédie Francaise. The gossip mags say they might as well be married—both faithful.

"Eddie had van Damme's military record Xeroxed and I checked that out first. It fit okay. I mean, it made sense in terms of years and age and where he was supposed to be when, and all that rot. No combat record because he'd been in a supply outfit. Wounded when a bomb hit a building and invalided home. Stuff that's hard to check, actually. I did run his outfit's roster for a couple years when he was supposed to be on AD, and the name was there. The *name* was there—get me?

"Eddie said I was supposed to check out the South Africa beginnings. That seemed a smart idea to me, too. So I flew to Jo-burg and snooped about, trying not to let on what was going down because I'd already decided that the chap calls himself van Damme would be quite ugly if he was riled. I could be in a spot of trouble—I mean, he's a multimillionaire, and those people are *bastards*! So I stayed with the public record, putting myself up as a solicitor's agent checking on an inheritance. And I found out that Adrien van Damme really was born in South Africa, and he was born at the right time for our chap, and was sent to school in the right years, and he'd had his smallpox vac and the whole kiddie route. Even been registered into the German Reformed Sunday school.

"But there was one oddity. I couldn't find his name on the fifth-year roster of his primary school. Name was on the fourth year and it was on the sixth, but not on the fifth. So I checked back in the daily papers for that year—nineteen twenty-eight. They'd had a poliomyelitis epidemic that year. So many kids were out of the schools that they'd set up official branch schools in the hospitals—special schools with their own records, see? Well, finding those records wasn't easy, let me tell you. You got some bills in that envelope for a night out in Jo-burg when I was working on this little librarian—archivist, she called herself—and I really had to diddle the poor thing before I could get at the records. I don't know if Eddie told you, but women aren't my specialty, so this was a bit of work. Although she was a bit sweet, really. Anyway, she got me into this attic where I found the records under about six feet of dust—and there was Master Adrien van Damme and a bloody bad case of polio. He spent a whole year in the hospital!

"It didn't jibe with the war record, of course. Nothing in the medical section about the polio, no description of any effects. So I figured what had happened was, somebody had known that the real Adrien van Damme was out of the picture somehow, but he'd lived and left a birth record and all that, and so they doctored up the rest and concocted a life for a ringer. What the present Adrien van Damme is, is a real good fake."

There were empty coffee cups between them now and the remains of several croissants. Tarp tapped his cup with the spoon and signaled an indifferent waiter for more. "That's deduction. Not fact."

"Oh, sure. But I found a record of sale of the real van Damme leasehold in nineteen thirty-seven—Mama and Papa van Damme leaving South Africa. Why? Couldn't say. To where? Well, they emigrated."

"To Canada," Tarp said, remembering the telephone bills in Barnwell's envelope.

"Right. Eddie said you were quick. God, you are. Yeah, they went out to Saskatchewan—*just the two of them.* I found the ship's manifest. No kid—no Adrien. Why? Because their only son had died in Jo-burg a year before they left. I know because I talked to their former pastor in Saskatoon.

"So, see, the *real* Adrien van Damme died in South Africa in nineteen thirty-seven. Somebody else picked up on him and faked a military record and gave him a rebirth after war two. And now we've got Adrien van Damme, multimillionaire and head of Dammeco, International—who's a fake." The little man leaned over the round table and tapped it next to Tarp's newly refilled cup, "It was an inside job."

"Oh?"

"Faking those records was a class act. No expense too

great, and so on. It was a *government* job. This wasn't some poor sod of a Nazi concocting a fake background because he wanted to keep his balls intact. This was a big operation. They missed the polio bit, but it was a niggling little detail that was really well hidden. It was a class act!"

Tarp sipped his coffee. "You did well. Thank you."

The little man looked disappointed. "That's it?"

"That's it."

"Here, don't you want me to follow up? We're dealing with a bloody imposter here, a fake. . . . You mean you don't want to know more?"

"No." Tarp stood up and dropped a bill on the table. "I know enough. You did a good job." He looked into the little man's eyes. "I don't want to hear ever that you talked about this to anybody or even that you told somebody you saw me today. Understand?"

"Sure, sure."

"I don't like to get screwed."

"Yeah, I know." He looked miserable. "Eddie said you were a hard case."

"Good for Eddie."

Tarp went back to Paris. He found a new hotel and telephoned a number in Neuilly. A maid answered, her voice high-pitched and cross and old; he tried to picture her and wondered if he had seen her years before.

"*La résidence Laforet*."

Tarp spoke French. "I would like to leave a message for the sous-ministre."

"Monsieur le Sous-Ministre is not here."

"That is why I would like to leave him a message."

"Monsieur le Sous-Ministre is in his office at this time, every day. He is not here at all during the daylight."

"I know. I would like to leave a message."

"He will not be at his home until half after eighteen hours or even later." Her voice was shrill, as so many Frenchwomen's are, as if in resentment of the oppression of men. Tarp thought he remembered her now—a woman who had been in the family's service for a generation. "Monsieur le Sous-Ministre works very hard," she said in a softer tone. Tarp was sure he knew who the woman was now—she had been the sous-ministre's governess.

"Exactly. If I might leave a message. . . ."

He heard her sigh. Perhaps she was really too old for service now. Perhaps taking messages was beneath her. With exaggerated patience she said, "I await your message, monsieur."

"Please tell Monsieur le Sous-Ministre that Monsieur Chimère has called and will call again after six."

He had to repeat *chimère* twice, but she got it. *Chimère*—the chimera of Greek myth, the monster—had been his code name in Southeast Asia in the early days, a play on *khmer* and on his monstrous behavior. Monsieur le Sous-Ministre, who had then been an intelligence officer in a French embassy, had suggested it.

Tarp checked the schedule of the Comédie Francaise and found that he could see Adrien van Damme's mistress that evening in *Le Cid*. He had lied to Jenny Barnwell—quite intentionally—when he had said he knew enough about van Damme. He had simply used Jenny Barnwell all that he cared to. Now he meant to do his own probing.

He went to the Bibliothèque Nationale and poked among the periodicals in several languages. There was not much on Adrien van Damme, and even less on Hamish Penhurst until the last year, when the latter's name had suddenly blossomed into the pages of the bibliographies. The accusation that the former head of MI-5 was a Soviet spy had been repeated over and over in every news magazine around the world, but there was really no more substance to the charge than had appeared in the original article by the journalist who called himself Viktor Balkan. His interest piqued, Tarp began to list the articles that "Viktor Balkan" had written over the years. He had been very active from about 1950 through 1963, always writing from the point of view of a defector and former Russian Communist who had seen the light. Then he faded, publishing only an article or two a year for fifteen years, until the late 1970s when he again became prolific. The article on Hamish Penhurst appeared at this time, as did a muckraking but ultimately vague article on Adrien van Damme.

Tarp recognized one truth, however. Vague though he might be when it came to pinning down accusations about his journalistic subjects, "Viktor Balkan" knew the facts of international intelligence. He was no amateur.

At six-thirty, Tarp went into a telephone kiosk and called the same number he had called earlier in Neuilly. "Monsieur le Sous-Ministre, if you please."

"Who is this, please?"

"Monsieur Chimère."

"One minute, please."

But it was not a minute. The voice he recognized came on almost immediately. "Laforet here."

"Chimère here."

"Yes?"

"Can we meet tonight?"

"I am going out until midnight."

"After that."

"Very good. Here? Or—?"

"There would be excellent. Thank you." Tarp hung up.

The actress named Adelaide Vitry was forty. Her interpretation of the young Chimène in *Le Cid*, however, was so overpowering that age was forgotten. She was an actress in the great French tradition, her mastery of the long spoken line complete. Tarp found it impossible not to think of opera while watching her, fascinated, for she was so much larger than life and her voice so seemed to want music to break into full expression. Studying her through rented opera glasses, however, he could see that she was actually a rather small woman with stress lines at her throat and a slight coarseness of feature.

Tarp had flowers sent back to her. "I was overcome," he wrote on the card. He signed the name that was on his French passport.

Tarp went to a brasserie across the river and sat alone in a little booth, gazing at food he had no intention of eating. He was waiting for midnight. He felt a need to fill up his time now—not to think, not to notice the humdrum flow of life, but to wipe his mind clean as if to ready it for crisis. If he stopped to think, he wondered what he was doing—and if he wondered, he knew. He answered his own wonderment: *I am being independent and uncontrollable. I am doing what I always did. I am looking for the truth.* If he stopped to think, he admitted that he was depressed, the cause unclear but somehow connected with Sheila Beecham. Her rage at his putting them away in the fortress in Sri Lanka. *Because the truth is more important to me than they are. Because I have to know. Because I cannot take them to England and turn them over to Hamish and walk away, not knowing the truth.*

The truth about what? he asked himself rhetorically.

Why, about everything. Every detail, every aspect, every facet. No stone gets to rest unturned. No end can be loose. No "I" can exist without its dot. *Not for Tarp.*

At midnight, he was at Laforet's door in Neuilly. A grouchy concierge conducted him through the courtyard and sold him a *jeton* for the elevator, which was big enough for no more than three people and looked as if it had been built in the thirties, for it had a rather rakish Art Deco look. Tarp had had to wait while she telephoned the Laforet apartment; while he waited, he was studied from a distance by two men in dark suits. *Les types du bureau.* Antiterrorist insurance, probably. The elevator moved rather eccentrically, as so many

French machines were wont to do, but perhaps riders were supposed to feel compensated by the decor. There was, too, a tantalizing but not quite identifiable hint of perfume, like a memory of better days.

Another man in a very dark suit opened the Laforet door. He might have been another bit of insurance but was only a butler. Tarp supposed that he had verified the caller on closed-circuit television and again through the bulls-eye in the door, yet he looked as suspicious as a shopkeeper being asked for credit. Perhaps it was past his bedtime.

"Monsieur le Sous-Ministre is expecting me."

"Monsieur—?"

"Chimère."

"*Ça suffit, Paul.*" The voice came from Tarp's right, from a point blocked by the heavy door. Tarp moved in around the butler and saw Laforet.

"*Merci, Paul. A demain.*"

"*Bon soir, monsieur. Bon soir, Monsieur Chimère.*"

Laforet led Tarp along a thickly carpeted corridor. Tarp was mapping the apartment in his head, watching himself move east toward the street, then turn north into a rich-looking little room where a wood fire was burning. *Northeast corner of the building.*

Jules Laforet was fifty-seven now. His hair was silver gray and combed very close to his head. He looked groomed, like an expensive animal, a show dog. Like many men who find their way to power in Europe, he was slender and very handsome. That evening, he wore a double-breasted suit cut rather more extremely than an American or a British tailor of the first rank would have made it, a tie of silk so thick it looked sculptured, and narrow shoes that appeared to be utterly weightless.

"Is this being taped?" Tarp said.

"Not in this room, no. I shall have to file a report of some kind, naturally." Laforet was one of the few men in the upper echelons of French intelligence who could be believed when he said this sort of thing; he had a reputation for honesty, and it probably explained why he would never rise to the very top of the service. Honesty was valuable, but enough was enough, at least in France.

"When I heard it was 'Monsieur Chimère,' I had a start."

"I am supposed to be either in the Mediterranean or in China, Jules. Who knows I am here?"

"Nobody else will make the connection of that name, I think."

"And your men downstairs? And the butler? Secure?"

"Absolutely." They were both aware that the "absolutely" was sheer exaggeration. "You are on a job, of course, Tarp. You have that look. As if you are hungry. I am not a station officer anymore, my friend—I may not be able to feed you."

"Am I unwelcome?"

"You will always be welcome—with Jules Laforet. Monsieur le Sous-Ministre is another matter. Monsieur le Sous-Ministre is ambitious, political . . . pragmatic." Laforet took a long cigarette from a marble box and picked up a matching lighter that looked like a marble column. "I did have you in China, by the way—that is where the reports make you."

"Oh, good. Whose?"

"Our own. There's a NATO line that follows you to Cyprus and has you doing something the Americans don't like in the Mediterranean, but that's so patently a screen that I am surprised you bothered."

"I didn't think it would take this long. The Med story was meant to be good for about five days."

"Ah, well, that's another matter."

"I'd prefer that it be kept secret—my being here."

"I shall try. No promises, I'm afraid."

That seemed to end a movement in their encounter. Laforet, as if to mark a change, waved them both to chairs, and then Tarp became aware of silence, and the sounds that nudged at it—that curious hissing, almost a hum, that some logs make in a fire, the repeated honking of a horn outside that went on and on, like a summons to duty. *The horn of Roland.* Laforet always made him think in French terms, for Laforet was quite self-consciously an *homme engagé* in the mold of Malraux, whom he had adored—half Romantic hero and half self-serving politician. Being with Laforet made the conflict between love and honor that he had just found so irrelevant in *Le Cid* almost believable.

"I saw *Le Cid* tonight," Tarp said impulsively. It was not what he had come to talk about, and Laforet raised a handsome eyebrow. Tarp pressed on in the same line, however. "Adelaide Vitry played Chimène."

"She is a little mature for the role." Laforet spoke with the faint boredom of a man weary of working up to the real subject of a meeting through the underbrush of small talk.

"They say she is the mistress of a millionaire," Tarp ventured.

"Multimillionaire," Laforet corrected. "That has all grown a little mature, too."

"Van Damme has thrown her over?"

The eyebrow rose again; the voice grew wearier. "You know his name?" Laforet came to quickly. "Ah, I see! Note how slow I have grown since I left fieldwork! It is van Damme you want to question me about, of course." Laforet smiled. Twenty years earlier, his smile had been charming; now, it was a little glib, as if he had used the charm too much and it had lost its magic. "Would you have a brandy? I mean to have one myself."

"Of course."

"Is it van Damme that brought you here?"

"Partly."

"We must be cautious; he is a friend of the old government."

"But not of the Socialists?"

"Well, he is a multimillionaire, and Socialists, at least

in theory, are levelers. However, even Socialists are human, and they admire van Damme for spreading his wealth among them—not exactly redistributing it, but—making it available to certain politicians."

"What is he?"

Laforet put a finger on top of an old bottle of Armagnac, Tarp nodded, and he lifted it. "Whatever he is, he is not an agent. He has lived in France for many, many years, and he was vouched for by the English government. He is exactly what he seems to be—a ruthless businessman whose politics are related entirely to greed."

"Have you investigated him?"

"No, but my predecessors did, twice. He is not very interesting. He had a business connection with MI-5, providing them with air transport in the East. You know that, of course."

"I've heard a rumor of drug smuggling."

Laforet gave a shrug that was so Gallic it must have been meant as a joke. "Eh, well—you remember what it was like out there."

Laforet had been at Dien Bien Phu in 1954 as liaison between military intelligence and the bureau. He had gone back to Indochina in 1957; three years later, Tarp had worked under him when the agency had begun to set up its networks in the area to replace the French. Tarp had been a beginner then, barely as old as most college students. It was from Laforet that he had learned the classic posture of the spy: how to focus on the task of intelligence and close out the distractions of idealism.

"I'm trying to follow up some kind of connection between van Damme and Hamish Penhurst," Tarp said.

"But of course! Hamish set up the contracts between MI-5 and van Damme's companies. Penhurst was a good intelligence officer, really *very* able; he saw the value of using van Damme. And got his money's worth."

"And yet now he flies around the world in one of van Damme's aircraft."

"My friend, *many* men get flown about in van Damme aircraft."

Tarp set down his glass. Hands on knees, he tried to convince Laforet of his sincerity, as if he were a boy again, learning the trade. "Jules, I'm trying to find out if Penhurst has been bought."

"Surely you don't believe that Viktor Balkan foolishness!"

"I don't *believe* anything."

Laforet looked as if he were posing for a photograph, something just relaxed enough to put in a glossy magazine with a caption about the sous-ministre at home. He had composed his body; now he seemed to compose his voice and even his breathing. "One hears all sorts of things about people. The higher a man goes, the more gossip there is about him. I will tell you candidly that I never heard a word against Hamish Penhurst that could be proven. The wits say that if he is *not* a mole, of course, he is the only man in recent history in MI-5 who is not; there have been so many revelations that it has gone from being a scandal to being a joke. Now—let me say that I *do* believe there is something peculiar going on with the writer who calls himself Viktor Balkan—and since Penhurst is one of the men he has written about, I suppose that Penhurst seems peculiar, too. What does it mean? Probably nothing. Journalists, especially faceless ones like Balkan, say irresponsible things. There is a mania for 'news' as it is called now; it leads to a great deal of irresponsibility. At any rate, I see nothing in Penhurst's relationship with van Damme to make you uneasy." Laforet picked up his glass again. "What is it you fear—that van Damme is a Soviet agent? That he is running Penhurst? That they are both moles? It is ridiculous."

"I have a feeling."

"Instinct?"

"Caution." Tarp sipped the wonderfully smooth and

fiery liquor. "Could you get a message to Repin for me?"

Laforet's expressive eyebrows went up most dramatically this time. "*Repin?* Well, you don't do things by halves, as the English say. *Repin!*" He seemed to savor some idea that the name suggested, finding it as arousing as the Armagnac. "They retired him, you know."

"No matter. Can you get a message to him?"

"He is in Tiflis."

"I want to see him."

Laforet stroked the crease of his immaculate trouser leg. There was still the sense of a pose about him, but he was wearing a little smile that, in its irony, suggested great honesty in his response to the situation—perhaps to the enormous strides that his former pupil had made. "Van Damme, Penhurst, Balkan, and now Repin—a multimillionaire, a former head of MI-5, a faceless journalist, and a retired KGB officer. What hunters call a mixed bag." He studied the trouser leg for an instant, tipping his head one way and then the other to enjoy some trick of shadow on it. "Repin was always a bargainer," he mused.

"I know."

"What do you have to offer Repin?"

"I believe I'll let him tell me that."

"He won't tell you the truth, you know, if the truth should happen to be that Hamish Penhurst is a mole. But he might tell you the truth if Hamish is *not*. For a price."

"It was always my view, Jules, that Repin would tell anything if the price was right and it wasn't his ox that was being gored. Repin was an Asian specialist; Penhurst was always completely outside his neighborhood. So he might. He *might*."

Laforet stood up and touched the logs with a brass poker, and as if he were a sorcerer whose touch brought life, flames jumped up. He looked at them, satisfied with his sorcery, and then sat down again. "This is big," he said with a sudden return to his earlier air of fatigue. He seemed to be depressed by the idea of a big operation.

"Yes."

Laforet held up a finger. "Be careful. The word is in the air—you know how it is when the wind sings in the wires?—everybody knows that something big is happening. But nobody knows what it is. There is a—*restlessness*. I have felt it all week. I have had to meet twice with the American military attaché, once with the Swedish military attaché, once with the cultural attaché of the German Democratic Republic—why? For no good reason—small talk and nervous gestures. To hold their hands. Because something is in the air and they are restless. Everybody is waiting. I had no idea it was for you." He sighed. "You and Repin. It will take me a day or two to get word to him. I think I can go through a funny fellow in Ankara. How shall we communicate?"

It was Tarp's turn to sigh. "Coin boxes?"

"Oh, if we must. You make me young again, Tarp!" It was the second time he had heard that recently.

When he got up to go, Laforet put an affectionate hand on his shoulder—the gesture of the mentor whose protégé has outstripped him. "Would you like to see van Damme up close?"

"God, yes!"

"There is a gathering at the Palais Chaillot—an EEC cultural celebration of some sort. Adelaide Vitry is to perform, I think. Van Damme is on a committee and will be there, probably scouting the Socialists for new recipients of his money. Where shall I send an invitation?"

"I'm on the move. New hotel each night."

Laforet smiled tepidly. "Like a tour. How very American of you!"

* * *

At every door, and at intervals along every corridor of the Palais Chaillot, there were guards in uniforms that looked as if they were left over from an operetta. They contrasted strangely with the fifties' modernism of the decor. In the hall where the reception was held, there were a dozen more of them. Tarp was more interested in the somber, seemingly humorless men here and there who were too obviously plainclothes watchdogs. In glasses and a mustache, Tarp felt both silly and conspicuous, and he expected the plainclothes *flics* to see through his flimsy disguise and arrest him as a terrorist. One of them, however, actually smiled at him as if they were acquaintances, and while Tarp thought it possible that he actually did look like somebody the man knew, he thought it more likely that he still radiated the aura of the agency, and the smile had merely been an acknowledgement of his all-too-obvious profession.

He found himself a vantage point on a low terrace above the main reception area. He found Laforet, then the actress Adelaide Vitry in a kind of receiving line, and then, with his back to her, a balding man with remarkably sunken cheeks who had to be Adrien van Damme—or the man who called himself van Damme. The man had great authority, as they say of actors; like many wealthy men, he was accustomed to being listened to and he made the most of the respect accorded to his money. Just at that moment, he was holding the evidently rapt attention of three members of the Chamber of Deputies—and of one observer across the huge room whom Tarp recognized at once as Johnnie Carrington, whom he had last seen in Hamish Penhurst's foyer, watching Gillian come down the stairs.

And what in hell are you doing here, Johnnie? Tarp wondered. But he already knew the answer, for Johnnie Carrington was looking at van Damme with an open fascination that was unmistakable. *Not a very good field man, Johnnie; they ought to keep you behind a desk.* He looked very much as he had the first time Tarp had seen him, the night of his arrival in London, when Carrington had hugged the walls and watched Gillian with dog's eyes. *The specter at the feast.* Believing that Carrington would eventually see him, Tarp decided to go to him first; he went down two steps to the main floor and picked his way across it past bored diplomats and politicians; he passed within two yards of van Damme and was able to hear the slight accent—South African?—that marked his French; he was able to make a note of the two men near van Damme who watched him closely. *Bodyguards.* Van Damme did not take chances on something so flimsy as French government security.

"Hello, Johnnie."

Carrington jumped, exactly as people are directed to jump in plays and films to communicate surprise, although in life people rarely do so. He stared at Tarp, and Tarp knew that at first Johnnie did not recognize him. Then there was something else—some form of dislike, but not the dislike of the lover who believes he may be looking at his more successful rival; this was. . . . Tarp was surprised at the word he was entertaining. *Hatred.* No, that was not quite right. *Distrust.* Then a more conventional face replaced that one, like a liquid filling a vessel, and a foolish smile broke over his face.

"Hullo, there! Good Heavens, it's you!"

"In confidence, yes, it is."

"I thought you were in—" Tarp would have sworn afterward that the foolish-looking young man caught himself, but again, it was like an actor's doing so, as if it was meant to *communicate* self-correction. "—in Egypt," he said.

He was either the most ingenuous of young men or a superb actor. Tarp was beginning to favor the latter identification, and his assessment of Carrington was undergoing drastic revision. "I've done with that."

"Oh." Carrington's eyes swung back toward van Damme. Again Tarp had the sense that the force of that attention was every bit as intense as it had been the night of the party when he had watched Gillian that way, but here, the impetus was different. Not love, however callow. Something. . . . Tarp was appalled by his discovery. *Something very much like what he showed he felt for me. Profound suspicion—and disgust.*

"Seen Gillian?" Tarp said casually.

Johnnie Carrington jumped again. Bright, rather uneven spots of color glowed on his cheeks. "Oh! Oh, yes, right—yes, I've seen Gillian. Once or twice. Here and there." He gave his silly laugh, as if he were the juvenile in a thirties farce.

He's embarrassed. That was wrong. *He's guilty, by God!* Tarp had a moment when he disliked Carrington—disliked his youth, his put-on silliness (for that was what Tarp now believed it to be), his intensity—and then he had to laugh at the spectacle of himself because Johnnie Carrington was a decent young man, so decent that he felt guilty for seeing a great deal—it had to be a great deal—of the young woman who had so briefly been Tarp's lover.

Tarp decided to be wicked. "Give Gillian my best, will you?" he said.

"Oh, absolutely!" Carrington blushed again. He chewed on his lower lip and looked anguished. "Actually, you see. . . . I know this sounds a bit mysterious, I suppose, but. . . . this visit is rather, um, hush-hush. As far as Gillian and, um, her grandfather are concerned, I mean." Carrington giggled miserably, as if he had just discovered that his fly was open. "You've rather thrown a spanner in the works."

"Well, I won't tell if you won't. I'm rather incognito, myself."

"Oh, jolly good!" Carrington seemed genuinely relieved. Then a terrible thought seemed to hit him. "It's nothing wrong of me, you know—I mean, nothing Gillian couldn't know about in time—not, um, another girl or something. Or some tart. Or something. Actually, it's more or less—rather—a bit, um, official. . . ." His voice trailed off.

Tarp's mind was leapfrogging over this information to find a way of silencing Carrington. He did not want it known in London or Washington or anywhere else that he was in Paris just then. He saw his choices, and with that rapidity with which a man would choose among possibilities in a fraction of a second when his car is approaching a washout in the road, he said, "I'm looking for your father's killer, Johnnie."

There was no doubt of Carrington's sincerity this time. His face showed three distinct changes of emotion, like layers of a city turned up by an archaelogist. First, guilt, rather surprisingly. Second, that same distrust as before. And third, open astonishment.

"Don't say anything," Tarp said. "I can't explain now. But I'd like you to believe me. I've found somebody who uses a knife in the same way your father's murderer did. I'd like you to give me some breathing room by swearing to me that you won't tell anybody in London that I'm here or that you saw me."

Swearing might still be a potent item to Carrington. Some of the schoolboy shine was still on him; his word might still be his bond.

"No, I want to know. . . . I want. . . . How dare you talk about my father!" The reaction was quite remarkable. Tarp thought the young man was going to assault him. He had misjudged Carrington's intensity; some of it came from a profound inner tension. *He's on the hunt*, Tarp thought. He remembered what Laforet had said about his own look of hunger. *He's here on a hunt, by God!* Then the seizure passed, and Carrington became a red-cheeked juvenile again. "Do forgive me, sir. You gave me such a start! Talking about my father." He couldn't say the word *father* in a normal voice, try as he might. But he was much brighter and much more deceptive than Tarp had ever guessed, for it had been an act of will that had pulled him back from his outburst and made him adopt his fool's face again.

"Will you swear?" Tarp said.

"I—I don't understand."

"I don't expect you to. I'm on a track. I don't want to be thrown off by having London know what I'm doing. I think your father's murderer is along my track, too—just ahead someplace. Will you swear?"

"I should have to falsify a report." It was not an idle complaint; for Johnnie Carrington, truth was a valuable commodity.

"No, you won't. Reports get held up . . . typists, Xerox machine, internal mail. You can leave me out of your prelim and stick me into the final. That'll be a week from now."

"Five days," Carrington said miserably.

"A week; you've never before turned in a late report in your life. They'll give you the two days." Tarp knew he was right because the blush deepened. "If they ask you why I wasn't in the prelim, tell them you had a personal involvement. We're both seeing the same girl and you wanted to make sure you weren't reporting on me out of spite."

He had scored deeply. Carrington was breathing shallowly. His expression was that of an oft-kicked dog. "You're good," he murmured. "My God, you're good."

"Will you swear?"

Carrington watched van Damme for a moment. Perhaps something he saw down there decided him. "Yes. I swear. One week."

Tarp gave him a moment and then said, "You're good, too. Astonishingly good." He descended the two steps to the main floor and went straight to Adelaide Vitry and introduced himself as the man who had sent her roses after her performance in *Le Cid.* She professed to be *enchantée,* and she was at least entertained. Even a rather bumbling provincial admirer is better than no admirer at all.

He sought out Laforet. He pointed out Johnnie Carrington, who was still watching van Damme. "How did he get in, Jules?"

"Invitation, like everybody else, I suppose."

"He's MI-5. Desk man."

"Through their embassy, then. Perhaps they have a continuing interest in Monsieur van Damme, since he watches him so acutely."

"His name is John Carrington. Find out how he got in, will you?"

He visited the Laforet apartment again that night, and again after watching Adelaide Vitry at the Comédie, this time in a Marivaux play. He had gone back afterward very briefly, taking her the flowers personally this time. She had remembered him.

Jules led him to the little library again. The fire burned as before; there was brandy. When they had settled in their chairs, Laforet said almost casually, "I will have word from Repin tomorrow."

"You're a wonder, Jules. That's quick work."

"My man in Ankara is trying to overcome an indiscretion. He works extra hard."

"And the Englishman at the reception?"

Laforet removed a folded paper from the leaves of a book. "It appears that the request came through their embassy, but with the name of the guest to be supplied later. Carrington's name was sent over yesterday, an hour before the reception. All quite normal, except that it was Carrington who signed the request. That suggests that MI-5 had a sound reason for sending a representative, but Mr. Carrington had his own reason for sending himself. Is he a field man?"

"No. No, he was on personal business, you're right.

It must have hurt him to misuse his MI-5 connection that way. He's a very moral young man."

"Alas, poor fellow. I had trouble breaking you of that tendency, too."

"But you did, in time. It's youth."

"What was this moral English youth looking for?"

"His father's murderer."

"Ah, like Hamlet. An English obsession. And did he find him?"

"No. I think he's got the right scent, but the wrong track."

chapter eighteen

The house in Tiflis had once been set within a lawn and garden that were now paved over with macadam; it, in its turn, had begun to give way to earth and grass again, for it was cracked and potholed, and there were scruffy little plants growing now in the cracks. The house had been there before the Revolution, smug behind its gardens and its wall; the Reds had turned it into a hospital and then a school, and after that it had been a completely unworkable home for the old, a rationing center and a black-market depot. Now it was a whorehouse. During the day, washing hung on lines behind the house, and women lounged on the terrace where there had once been concrete urns and statues of a more or less classical sort. At night, bicycles and even a few cars parked next to the wall, and the neighborhood vibrated to the sound of American music of the fifties.

Tarp found the house in early afternoon. The day felt like autumn, cold and breezy; leaves left from the winter spun in corners and skittered along the walks. He went up on the terrace as he had been told to and knocked on the door that had been left when the French windows had been closed in years before.

"Not open yet. Come back at five."

"I have a friend from Irkutsk."

"What?"

"I have a friend from Irkutsk."

"What are you saying? Are you a Jew? You sound like—."

Another voice was speaking, commanding, too soft for him to understand the words. The woman who had opened the door turned her head to listen, dislike making her homely. When the other voice stopped, she screeched, "Irkutsk! He's some Jew from Irkutsk!" There was more from the voice, and the woman turned back to him.

"So, come in." Her face was sullen. "She says come in."

It had been a music room. There were a lyre and a pipe of pan in plaster above the blank where the fireplace had been. There had been parquet floors and embroidered wall panels; the floor had heaved and some of the blocks of wood were loose, some missing now, and the walls had been painted over or covered with tasteless hangings. Red and yellow light bulbs the size of onions hung from the center ceiling fixture, and a huge stereo took up most of one end of the room. The other end was given over to a bar with Polynesian touches in plastic.

"Irkutsk?"

The woman who was coming in was in her thirties and looked worn out. Hers was the voice he had heard. Like the room, she was hung in many fabrics, none of them very well chosen.

"I am looking for a friend," he said, as he was supposed to.

"Name?"

"Chimère."

She turned around, meaning for him to follow. She led him to a low-ceilinged room with whitewashed arches at each end and an enormous carpet, a copy of an oriental, he judged, from one of the Eastern European countries. The rug was so big that one side had had to be rolled under against one wall. There were pillows dropped here and there on the carpet and smaller rugs thrown over some of the pillows, and under the arched windows, built-in seats that were white like the walls. Tarp tried to think what the architect had had in mind, back about 1900—probably a bourgeois Russian's idea of an English Victorian's Turkish cozy corner.

"Wait here."

"Thank you."

"Drink?"

"No."

Twenty minutes later, Repin walked in.

Repin had always had a taste for English clothes and English shoes. The suit he wore now looked too big for him because he had shrunk with age and sickness, and its once impeccable fit was spoiled. He carried a cashmere coat folded over his left arm and a black homburg in his right hand, but he still did not look elegant, as he once had. He looked like a sick old man in stolen clothes.

Repin looked at Tarp and laughed.

Repin had a round face. When he laughed, he held his tongue up and forward so that other people saw a lot of it. His round face split like a melon and the tongue appeared in the center of it, bobbing with the rhythm of his laughter.

"Monsieur Chimère!" Repin laughed.

Tarp had stood up. "Well, Repin."

Repin's right eye had been covered with a flesh-colored disk behind the lens of his glasses, and to look at anything he had to twist his head so that the left eye could do the seeing. Oddly, this affliction made him seem alert and lively. "What in the name of the American God brings you to this hole?"

"I want to buy something."

Repin went on laughing. "Want to buy a girl? Some of Sophie's girls are pretty good. They do good things for my prostate." Repin looked around with disgust, turning awkwardly so that the left eye could see everything. "Doesn't this place look just *like* a whorehouse?" he said. "*Sophie!*"

Her voice came from far away, as if she had been waiting at a discreet distance. "Well?"

"Vodka! Vodka and something to eat!" Repin dropped the cashmere coat on one of the white window seats, placed the homburg on top of it, and then stretched, his hands pressed into his spine. When he had done that to his satisfaction, he cleared his throat with a horrible explicitness, looked for a place to spit, and finally rolled back the cheap carpet with one foot, spit under it, and let the rug fall back. "What do you want to buy?" he said.

"Information."

"You think I am a traitor?" Repin glared at him with the left eye, fierce as a hawk's. "You think Repin is a traitor now he is out in the meadow?" He waggled a hand between them to cut off any reply. "I hear you left the agency."

"Almost ten years ago."

"They kicked my ass out of Derzhinsky Square, did you know? They gave me a medal and kicked my ass out the door."

"Retired you."

"Retired, ha! Retired, shit! I made a mistake, they gave me a boot, and I sailed all the way through the air to Tiflis. A silly business in Turkey five years ago, a silly piece of disinformation. I had enemies." He put his hands behind him and closed his mouth very tight as the woman came along the corridor toward them. She set a tray on the empty window seat.

"Get out," Repin said without looking at her. She left, although not quickly, as if she wanted to show that she was an independent person.

"Is this place secure?" Tarp said.

"Not bad, not bad." Repin looked with great distaste at a dish piled high with herring. "Is any place secure? Have you ever been secure in your life, Chimère?" Picking up a bottle of vodka and a glass, Repin began to walk slowly around the room. "What kind of information do you want?"

"Hamish Penhurst."

The good eye glared at him. "Why him?"

"I have to know if he's a mole."

Repin made a sound of rage. "Because that pig's asshole Viktor Balkan says he is? You believe *that*?"

"It's something I need to know."

"And I will tell you—eh? Did I say I was a traitor? Did I say I would sell Soviet secrets? No!" Repin drank. "Go to hell."

"I'd like to look in your file. That's all."

"What file?"

"You always had files, Repin. Files on everybody, it was said. Somewhere in the world—a bank vault in Switzerland or Brazil—you must have a file on Penhurst."

"This is all romance, Chimère."

"I'll pay a hundred thousand dollars."

Repin looked at him. Repin laughed. His tongue rolled in his mouth like a wet ball bobbing on water. "Do you know how easy it would be for me to get a hundred thousand dollars if I wanted it? Eh? Do you know what my memoirs would be worth—anywhere in the world? Shit, I could get a hundred thousand and never violate security, never spill a secret."

He's old, but he won't let go. Tarp watched rage and pride change the old face. *They never let go.* Repin had run stations from Kabul to Malaysia; before he had been posted home to Moscow, he had been the terror of every Russian in Hanoi. He was still a legend in

China because of his work there in the thirties. Now here he was, old, half blind—and still fighting. *Never letting go.*

"All right, let me try something else. To make conversation. A good trader never gives up quickly. Have you ever heard of a piece of knife work that can cut a man from the breastbone to the crotch—disembowel him with one cut?"

Repin poured himself more vodka. "Now *this*—this is not a secret. To tell you this does not make me a traitor. Because this is history, is all it is. Yes, I know about that."

"Will you tell me?"

Repin looked playful. "How much?"

But Tarp knew that it was time to affect indifference. "Nothing. This is personal curiosity."

"Then I will tell you for free. I do not believe you, of course—you are not a *personal* man, Chimère; I remember you too well. But I will tell you, because it is not treason. Yes." He picked up a stubby little spreader from the tray of food. "The knife goes in"—he thrust at an imaginary victim—"twists, cuts across the heart, turns . . . then down, pushing *with both hands.*" He finished his vodka so he would not spill it and, glass still in hand, put the left over the right and pretended to cut his victim open.

"Yes," Tarp said quietly, "that's the technique."

"They taught it for a short time in a MKVD nursery—a training school, you know. Out in Novosibirsk. Women only. This is ancient history, Chimère—it was before the second war! It was a deadly technique, but a very poor one for an agent. They might as well have signed their names or left a card!" He poured more vodka. "There had to be an official order: no more teaching this technique, no more using it. Most of those girls are dead now anyway. In the war, most of them." He fixed Tarp with his good eye. "Why—you got a body?"

"Ancient history."

"Like I said." Repin set down his glass with a loud sound. "So! Are we done?"

Tarp could feel the moment slipping away. He was going to lose. "There must be something you want from a man like me, Repin."

"The idea, Chimère, that every man has his price is a capitalist one."

"What can I offer you? What could I bring you?"

Repin laughed. "Like the suitor for the princess in the fairy tale—set me to a task!" He shook his head. "I don't want any golden apples or any magic lamps." He snorted. "Yes—bring me my youth!"

"But you've had at least one capitalist desire, Repin—wasn't there something about drug dealing in Cambodia . . . ?"

"Lies! The lies of a pig's asshole of a journalist!" Repin poured himself another drink and, working himself up into real anger, began to stammer sometimes as he spoke. "You . . . repeating lies! Who are you, anyway? I am Repin! What could you offer me . . . bring me? What did you think . . . what, that now, because Repin is out in the meadow he will turn traitor? Or because a Western journalist writes lies about him he is *weak*?" Repin was shouting. He blinked the good eye constantly. "Because this . . . this, this . . . Viktor Balkan! . . . writes excrement about me and some, some long-forgotten stupid affair . . . *of which I was officially cleared*! . . . you think I am corrupt."

Repin took a step backward. His mouth opened and closed and Tarp thought he was suffering an attack and was about to fall to the carpet. Inexplicably, however, he began to laugh. The longer he looked at Tarp, the more he laughed. He pointed his empty glass at Tarp and laughed more and more. "I've got it, Chimère! That's it! *That's it!* I know what you can bring me."

He made a mock bow, catching himself as he straightened because he was a little drunk. "Bring me the liar who calls himself Viktor Balkan . . . and I will give you whatever I have on Hamish Penhurst." His pitch rose; he sounded playful again. "Oh, yes, there is such a file. Someplace. Maybe it has in it what you want and maybe it hasn't. That's the chance you take. It's like marrying the princess after you kill the dragon . . . maybe she's a lovely girl, and maybe she's just like her mother!" He laughed more and more. "Bring me Viktor Balkan and the file is yours!"

Tarp waited for some seconds for the old man to quiet. "All right," he said mildly, hiding his growing excitement. "Who is Viktor Balkan?"

"That's the hard part. Nobody knows who he is or where he is. You don't get a princess without a dragon, Chimère."

"And you'd trade your file on Penhurst for him . . . just because of an article he wrote?"

"Yes! I am a very, very proud man."

Tarp watched Repin march to the other end of the room and turn back. "I don't believe you," he said.

Repin halted. "*What?*" He looked as if he meant to throw the vodka bottle, which he was again carrying.

"It isn't just the article. We'd all heard that story before; it was an old rumor when I got to Indochina. There's more. What is it, Repin?"

Repin looked at him, looked away. He walked to a window and flung himself down on the window seat and poured himself a drink. "Viktor Balkan wants my files. He has one more thing about me he will print . . . one . . . indiscretion. This one is more serious—political."

"He's a blackmailer."

"*Yes*. These articles are like messages. They say: 'You see what I can do with information? Next time, it will be terrible.' He is a collector of secrets. He wants mine. I suppose he wants Hamish Penhurst's, too; that is why he wrote about him."

"But he must have insurance. If I find him, if I bring

him to you—surely he'll have some means of having his information about you published."

Repin waved a hand. "Ah! He doesn't know Repin! I am a very tough old horse. If I get him in the process, it is worth it. If I just hand him my files and get nothing—it is not worth it."

Tarp made himself wait. He wanted to seem cool and knowledgeable—even sluggish. He wanted to seem like a functionary. "If I bring you a man, will you know if he's Viktor Balkan?"

"Yes!"

"How?"

Repin was clearly debating whether to tell him. "I know who he *was*. Up until 1943. I got four fingerprints and part of a dental history. Don't ask me how I got them."

"He was a Russian, you mean."

"I don't commit myself on that."

"Was he ever in Yugoslavia during the war?"

Repin glared at him. Again, there was that threat of violence. Slowly, Repin said, "You know who he *is*, then."

"I've got a good idea."

"Who?"

"I'll tell you after I bring him in. Figure out where you'd like the delivery made, Repin. I mean to have that file on Penhurst."

From Ankara, he placed a call to Peri Kri in Peshawar.

"Get the Little Package ready to move."

"Oh, darling. That isn't anything personal, is it?"

"Of course not. Just get it ready to move. I'll pick it up myself."

"I lit another candle, darling."

"Don't, um, don't. . . ." His voice trailed off. He could not seem to choose among all the "don'ts" that presented themselves.

"Not to worry, darling. I won't."

He talked to Craik in London and then to Jenny Barnwell, going through tortuous shifts of numbers and times to do it, and then he tried to find a quick way of getting to Sri Lanka.

"But where are you going to take her?" Arthur Beecham wailed. "I don't want you to take her away!"

"I need her help."

"Doing what?" Beecham's daughter said belligerently.

"Kidnapping somebody."

"Oh, dear, oh dear," Beecham said several times, "Oh, that doesn't sound good at all."

"It doesn't sound *fair*, you mean!" she snapped. Her English was quite good now; she even had the separate tones of sarcasm and hostility under control. "We didn't leave China to become your accomplices in other crimes, Mr. Tarp!"

"This isn't another crime," he said wearily. "It's the same crime. What crime are we talking about, anyway? I'm not a criminal."

"You impersonated a Chinese official, stole an automobile, kidnapped a soldier, shot two people, stole a military helicopter, violated a border—"

"All right, all right! That joke's gone far enough. It *is* a joke, isn't it? I did those things to get you both out, after all."

"And now you want to involve me in something completely different!"

"It isn't completely different!" he bellowed at her. "It's all part of the same thing, you numbskull!" He thought she might strike him. If she did, he was going to strike her back. Instead, she turned her head—only her head—toward her father. "What is 'numbskull'?" she said.

"It's ah. . . ." Beecham, who was sitting, was able to glance up and catch Tarp's eye. "It means, ah, 'unfeeling person.' "

She snapped her head back toward Tarp. "I am not an unfeeling person!"

By that time, Tarp had calmed. "Sit down," he said quietly.

"I will *not* sit down," she said. She had the right tone for that, too.

"*Sit down*," Tarp insisted.

"I *will not—*"

"Oh, Sheila, for God's sake sit down!" her father shouted. They both looked at him. It was very unusual for him to raise his voice. "You aggravate me no end, both of you! Prison was a pleasant place compared to this room when the two of you are bickering in the middle of it. Now, Sheila, you be a good girl and sit right here next to me. And Mr. Tarp, stop badgering her and tell us what you mean to do." She sat down and collapsed into herself like a sulky child. "Really!" her father said. He looked at Tarp. "Shame!"

Tarp sat on an overstuffed chair the color of an oyster, facing both of them. "There is a man in Europe. . . ." He stopped to think. "Who has written bad things, lies, about other men. Another man wants me to kidnap the first man. If I do so, the second man will give me information that will let me judge whether it is safe for you to go to England."

"That seems straightforward enough," Arthur Beecham said. "Quite trenchantly put, I thought."

"Nothing *he* does is straightforward," Sheila said. She had pushed her mouth out angrily and squinted up her eyes.

"Sheila, my dear," Arthur Beechman said in the wispiest of voices, like a man who wishes to propose something outrageous, "I think that the strain of being here has been too much for you. I think it would be good for you to go away with Mr. Tarp."

"Ten minutes ago you said you couldn't live without me!"

"Well. Circumstances alter cases, and so on. I believe I can live without you for a day or two. It is only a day or two, isn't it, Mr. Tarp?"

"Three or four, sir."

"There, you see? Only three or four days. I really can live without you for that long." The truth was, as Tarp had already realized, that Arthur Beecham liked the quiet and the security of this apartment in the ancient fortress. Perhaps for him it combined the best of prison with the best of freedom: the opportunity to think without interference.

"Are you afraid to help me, Sheila?" Tarp said quietly. "Be honest."

Her spine straightened. "I am not afraid of doing any of the sorts of things you seem to like to do, Mr. Tarp! But, I confess, I am uncomfortable without my father now that I have been with him this long; and I am very uncomfortable in places where I do not know the language. But I do not mind discomfort . . . and I certainly am not *afraid* of it . . . if it is really true that this kidnapping of yours will help us to know if we can go to England."

"I give you my word. It will." *If it works.*

She spread her hands. The gesture was almost flirtatious—not with him, certainly; it might have been that she was practicing flirtation in front of a mirror. "Then I will go." A lugubrious note crept into her voice. "If I am not wanted here, then of course I will go."

Arthur Beecham screwed up his face in distaste. "Oh, Sheila, you *are* a numbskull!"

chapter nineteen

Sticking out below the purple beehive of the hair-dryer, Sheila Beecham's face looked small and feral. Her broad forehead was hidden by the colored plastic skirt of the huge machine, and unable to hear anything but the ridiculous music that the machine itself played, she stared resentfully at the wall opposite her. A soft sheet was draped around her; soft slippers were on her feet; her hands dangled in purple plastic bowls filled with liquids that would make them soft.

"Madame's hair must look like that," Tarp said to the attendant. He tapped a snapshot of Adelaide Vitry.

"Maitre Moumou says the style is wrong for Madame's face."

Maitre Moumou was a particularly nasty twenty-year-old who was the current rage of the Paris hair world. "This is what I want," Tarp said.

The young woman all but sneered. "Madame has the wrong-shaped face."

"But I have the right-shaped money."

The woman looked confused. In a business where money was so important, it was thought rude to name it.

From the hair salon, Tarp took her by hired car to a makeup specialist. Sheila Beecham was disgusted, but he ignored her. Putting the snapshot in front of the new artiste, he said in crisp French, "She must look like that."

"She has the wrong-shape face, monsieur."

"So do I, but one of us has to look like this picture. Would you prefer it be me?"

Adelaide Vitry wore very heavy makeup, off the stage as well as on. She had reached that age where her face owed more to art than to nature, so there was no attempt at milkmaid freshness or a newly scrubbed look. Her mouth was inevitably hard-edged and large and glossy; her cheeks wore heavy false shadows and shiny highlights along the bones; her eyes were as exotic as the wings of a new moth.

"Don't smile, or the whole thing will shatter," Tarp growled as he dragged Sheila away.

"*Now* where?"

"Designer dress house. Selon Cartouche. Vitry's dressmaker."

"I never knew women lived like this."

Paris was almost too much for her. As nearly as he could tell, she saw it and its occupants the way occidentals see Chinese cities: inexplicable warrens of odd-looking people who gabble in an unintelligible, perhaps inhuman, language. He tried to counter the effect of the city by keeping her on the move; now he dragged her from the car and propelled her through the baroque doorway of Selon (not "salon"; there was a pun in there) Cartouche, through whose portals many of the women of the Western world would have liked to pass—especially with a man who was determined to buy them a dress there—but at which Sheila Beecham balked like a mule. Two women coming out drew back from her, having first come too close; they had seen the coiffure, then the maquillage, and then they looked down and saw the man's trousers and the Chinese worker's shoes.

"Qu'est-ce que c'est, ça?" one said in wonder.

"C'est . . . c'est . . . le style nouveau, sans doute." Both had the high-pitched voices that Frenchwomen seem to learn as they are weaned.

"Le style nouveau! Oh! C'est . . . c'est . . . c'est remarquable, ça!"

Tarp smiled at them and pushed Sheila Beecham farther inside. "In!" he growled.

"I hate this."

"I never would have guessed."

He plumped her down in a delicate chair and held her there with heavy hands while models paraded past. Tarp knew some of Vitry's wardrobe from the evening he had spent in her dressing room in his character as the businessman from the provinces. (Rubber tires, based in Clermont-Ferrand.) "That one!" he said to the brittle woman who had been assigned to them.

"Monsieur has excellent taste."

Sheila Beecham was led off to a dressing room. Minutes later, a flustered dresser whispered to the brittle woman; she glanced at Tarp and then approached him almost cautiously. She cleared her throat.

"Yes?"

"May we furnish Madame with some underclothing, monsieur?"

"Why?"

"She appears to have worn none, monsieur."

Tarp smiled. "Good idea. Several sets. Money no object."

While the dress was having something done at the waist, Tarp took her back to their hotel, where she sank into her third hot bath of the past twenty-four hours. When the boxes arrived from Selon Cartouche, he put them on the bed in front of her and went off to his own room. He did not wear a dinner jacket tonight; instead, he put on a heavy, dark suit of the stiff material that van Damme's bodyguards wore. A bulletproof vest under the jacket gave him the bulk that he wanted. He bent his knees and slumped and became the shorter, heavier man he would need to be for several crucial seconds.

Tarp put a 9mm Walther in the vest's left-hand holster, up under the arm. Under the right arm was another holster; a small medical kit went into that one. *Courtesy of Jenny Barnwell. Money will buy anything.* He slipped a silencer for the Walther into another pocket.

She was ready when he walked into the living room. "By God!" he whispered.

"Don't make fun of me!" she wailed.

"By God . . . I mean, by God, Sheila, you look like a woman! If I didn't fear cracking that makeup, I could kiss you!"

"Because I look like somebody else?"

"No! Good God, no. No, because we're about to do something dangerous together, and . . . I'm grateful to you."

Her eyes stared out at him from the remarkable mask that was not Adelaide Vitry's face but that was enough like it. For the few essential seconds, she would do. "You may kiss me afterward, then. If we make it."

He took out the medical kit and put a small but thick disk, rather like a very fat coin, in her hand. There was a ring on the back with a green stone. "The disk goes in your palm. When the disk is pressed against something, the needle will puncture that rubber diaphragm in the center and pump the fluid. Anybody you touch will get a shot of it—including you if you close it in your hand." He pressed a cover over the dangerous side. "Leave the lid on when it's in your purse. All right?"

"Yes." Her voice was husky. "How long does it take to work?"

"Two seconds."

"That's a long time, sometimes."

"Yes, it is. The body can do a lot in two seconds. That's where you may have to use your strength."

He looked into her eyes past the thick fringe of false lashes and the thick mask of the makeup. She was not frightened. She was excited. He touched her bare shoulder. "You'll do very well. Just remember—once you start, you have to go right on through, as we rehearsed."

"Yes."

"If things go wrong, you must still try to go right through it. If there is shooting, or any of that."

"Yes."

"And if something happens to me, you have to get out of it and take care of your father. Peri Kri will give you the rest of the money from the gold."

"Yes."

"All right, say your words for me."

She looked away. She closed her eyes, opened them. "*Pour vous!*" she said in a high-pitched voice. "*Mouche!*"

"Good. Let's go."

He handed her a pale orange sari, and she draped it over her head and around her body, hiding the dress. Tarp put a red plastic dot with an adhesive back between her eyes and clamped a little gold ring into her left nostril.

"Keep your head down when you're in the theater."

"I know all that."

They went down a rear stair and out through the kitchen. A small, sleek car was waiting for them with Eddie Craik at the wheel.

"Problems?"

"None so far, ducks. Are we ready?"

"What about Jenny?"

"Gone bye-bye. Told him he was done, and he split."

"Good. Let's go."

Craik seemed to be as much at home in the streets of Paris as he was in London. He pulled up two streets from the Comédie Francaise and Tarp got out.

"Luck, old sport," Craik said. He flashed a grin.

"You, too."

Tarp settled down at a small café with a *noir* and a newspaper. He looked at his watch: one hour and twenty-seven minutes to wait. From his seat in the corner, he watched the rest of the café and the wet street outside. There were no signs of impatience; once he touched the holstered pistol and the medical kit, and that was the only indication he gave of having any other purpose there than to drink *café noir* and glance over a day-old copy of *Le Monde*.

At ten-fifteen he rose, folded the newspaper and placed it on the table.

He bought a half-dozen golden roses from the same young woman who had sold them to him before, and he turned up his coat collar and entered the Comédie by the discreet little actors' door that is hidden away in Palais Royal. At the concierge's booth, a beefy man smiled patronizingly and gave him an ironic salute.

"Still trying, monsieur," the man crowed.

Tarp fell into his character of provincial businessman. "Women love nice things," he said foolishly.

The man laughed. "Yes, women love *nice* things," he said, and in his tone was the cruel difference between a tire salesman and a multimillionaire.

Tarp knew the labyrinth of corridors and went directly to Vitry's dressing room. She would be onstage, for Jenny Barnwell had timed the performance. Tarp knocked lightly at the dressing room door.

"Oh. Oh, it is *you*, monsieur." Vitry's maid looked tired of him.

"Yes, yes . . . me!" He held up the flowers, but pulled them back when she put out a weary hand. "No, no, I want to give them to her with my own hands!"

"Madame is going out as soon as she comes off, monsieur."

"Yes, yes, but still. . . ."

"Madame is going to *him* tonight."

"All the more reason for me to give her my flowers first."

The woman shook her head, although not unkindly, as if she had some remnant of sympathy for this Romantic. She opened the door to him.

"You think I'm an idiot."

"You said it, monsieur, not me."

She was sorting through Vitry's dresses. Tarp went up behind her and put a saturated pad over her mouth, and when she was unconscious he put her body on the chaise in the inner room. Quickly, he administered a longer-lasting anesthetic, tied and gagged her with adhesive tape, and covered her with a ruffled throw.

Tarp checked his watch. Van Damme's bodyguard should arrive in four minutes, if he kept to his routine. Actually, he came in six. Whenever he called for Adelaide Vitry, he knocked at the door to tell the maid that he and the car were there, and then he faded away to wait in a shadow along the corridor. Tonight he knocked, and Tarp opened the door and put the silenced muzzle of the 9mm under his nose.

"Inside."

The man came in with his eyes trying to focus on the pistol, like a man in a cartoon who has a bee on his nose. Tarp put the needle of a squeeze-tube hypo into his neck, and the two of them looked at each other, as close together as lovers, until the injection took effect and he sank to the floor with a reluctant, and perhaps guilty, sigh.

Tarp pulled him into the dressing room. He took a scalpel from the medical kit and, without hesitation, cut the entire fleshy pad from the bodyguard's right thumb. He laid a strip of plastic gel against the exposed, bloody thumb and wrapped it in place. Spotting a half-full ice bucket next to Vitry's dressing table, he made an improvised ice pack and set the thumb in it before he slid the body under the chaise on which the maid lay.

Tarp took the piece of flesh that he had cut off. One

side looked exactly like the ball of a thumb, pink and whorled; the other side looked like meat. This, too, he laid against a strip of the plastic gel. He formed a cylinder out of a partly melted ice cube, put the gel on it, and had the facsimile of a thumb.

Seven minutes later, Adelaide Vitry flounced in. She was in a fury over something that another actor had done. "*Quel bêtise!*" she cried in her high voice. "*Que je m'étouffe de ça! Annette! Oh, cette sâle. . . .*" She saw Tarp. "*Oh. C'est vous.*"

Tarp spread his hands, the very picture of a fool. Then, brightening, he pointed behind her. "*Surprise!*"

Despite her rage, she looked where he pointed. She loved surprises, at least from men who adored her; they were inevitably nice surprises.

Tarp put the saturated pad over her face and held her while she gasped down the fumes. A minute more, and he had put her next to the maid.

"*Adieu, mon amour,*" he whispered when he had gagged and tied her.

He looked at his watch. Two minutes to go.

Applause came from the theater like the sound of a distant surf. Twenty seconds later, Eddie Craik and Sheila came through a green door halfway along the corridor.

"Well done," he said to Craik. "Get on with it."

"On my way."

Sheila was already taking off the sari. Tarp peeled away the red plastic dot and pulled the ring from her nostril. "Ready?"

"Absolutely."

He made himself walk like the shorter, heavier bodyguard. Sheila was also moving as he had taught her, tripping along with Vitry's short steps and holding the roses high to obscure her face. As they passed the concierge's desk Tarp pulled out a soft cap and began to adjust it on his head.

"*Bon soir, chère madame.*"

Sheila waved a gloved hand at the cubicle. The concierge went back to his picture magazine.

"Take little steps!" Tarp whispered.

"I am!" Her heels tapped on the wet pavement like the sounds of a woodpecker in a forest. Fifty feet ahead of them at the end of the wet sidewalk, van Damme's limousine was waiting, its driver silhouetted against the headlights coming down the cross street. He turned his head in a bored way, looked at them, and then looked away.

She knocked on his window. He looked up, surprised. He touched a button and the bulletproof window fell with a sigh.

"Madame?"

"Pour vous!" She thrust a rose through the window. When his hand came up for it, she pushed down with the disk, and the prick of the hollow needle and the prick of the rose's thorns were one. Tarp reached through the window and held the man by the hair when he began to struggle, and with his left hand he choked off any cry.

"Put that thing in your purse until we're in the elevator," he muttered.

Craik materialized from the shadow of a building. "Nifty," he said. He pushed the unconscious driver over, got into his seat, and unlocked the rear door. Before they got in, Tarp said to her, "No talking once we're in. It may be bugged." Only much later did he remember that the word "bugged" probably meant nothing to her.

Van Damme, like other wealthy men, feared terrorists and kidnappers. The limousine was armored, with gun ports in the doors.

As they passed through the wet streets, Tarp looked at Beecham's daughter. He asked a question without words: *All right so far?* She smiled. She actually seemed to be enjoying herself.

The car started down the concrete ramp into the garage under van Damme's apartment building, ahead of it a steel door and an automatic gate painted black and white. Next to the gate was an electronic scanner with a slot for a plastic card and a small plastic plate under which a blue light glowed, as if it were the ever-seeing eye that searched all night for van Damme's enemies. Jenny Barnwell had already found out what the plate was for.

Tarp gave Craik the skin from the bodyguard's thumb, which he had removed from its lump of ice and placed in his own palm to warm it. Craik had the plastic card from the limousine's glove compartment: the card went into the slot, the blue light turned red, and Craik, with the prepared thumb pad over his own right thumb, pressed it against the plastic plate. There was a fraction of a second's pause, and then the red light turned blue again and the automatic gate rose.

Craik coasted down the slope. The gate fell behind them and the steel door rose.

Tarp took back the thumb and the card as Craik brought the car to a silent stop beside a door marked *ENTRÉ AUX APPARTEMENTS*. Tarp got out and held the door for Sheila Beecham, acutely aware of the closed-circuit camera a few feet over his head. Exactly like Vitry, she did not acknowledge him, but crossed quickly to the door, and Tarp turned away from the limousine.

The bodyguard's thumb and the plastic card got them through the door and into the elevator, and they got the elevator started toward the seventeenth floor. They also, Tarp was sure, alerted van Damme's apartment that someone was coming up, for his apartment was the only one on that floor. The closed-circuit camera in the elevator stared down at them without judgment. Tarp pictured what was happening: another bodyguard, put on notice by a signal from the elevator, would be heading for the apartment door, perhaps shrugging himself into his jacket because he had been relaxing somewhere out of sight. He would glance at the screen of the television monitor out of habit, seeing that Vitry and her escort were there—seeing, as the hunter who shoots his friend sees the deer, what he was supposed to see, a man and a woman of a certain kind, in certain clothes. Perhaps he could not see her entirely clearly because she was checking her makeup in her mirror; perhaps he could not see the guard's face because he was bent slightly forward, rummaging in an inner pocket. No matter.

Tarp had mentally marked the moment when they left the elevator as one of greatest risk. He would have to check in both directions, and he would not know the terrain. If somebody was waiting for them—even innocently—that person would have the advantage. Tarp had studied an architect's plan of this corridor, but he knew that the exit from the elevator was risky.

He slipped his hand inside his coat as the doors began to open and positioned himself under the television camera. He had a sudden, powerful breath of her perfume. He screwed the silencer on the 9mm, and the doors opened with a sound like a tongue licking a pair of lips. He stepped out.

The corridor was empty.

She moved ahead of him and they turned to the right and walked ten steps to van Damme's front door.

The card and the thumb announced them. Tarp had the gun in his hand and he was thinking of where the apartment's other entrance was and what would happen if van Damme were near it and he botched this moment. Noise, warning—van Damme going out the other way—the opportunity lost. The *only* opportunity.

The door opened.

Beecham's daughter astonished him by giving a high-pitched laugh—it was Vitry's laugh, to be sure, but he had not taught it to her, and he realized that she had got it from hearing Vitry in the theater—and she pushed past the guard who was standing in the half-opened door. Holding the roses in her right hand so they were between him and her, waving them a little, chanting happily in a singsong little voice, "*Pour vous, pour vous, pour vous. . . .*"

Tarp came right behind her.

He put the silencer into the soft underside of the man's jaw, just where the carotid artery gives such an easily readable pulse. "*Doucement,*" he whispered. He emptied a squeeze tube directly into the blood supply to the brain.

Tarp held him as he began to sag. He had to watch the eyes and the hands; he had to keep the gun in the throat; he was screaming inside his head. *Go, get going Sheila, God in Heaven get going. . . .* The bodyguard's eyes rolled up under his lids and there was some attempt to make a sound; to speak, perhaps to protest. A bubble formed between his lips. His breath smelled of wine, of more wine than a man with his responsibilities should have been drinking. *Routine*. Tarp was lowering the body to the floor. *Routine. They get careless, thinking they're getting more efficient.*

He needn't have worried about her getting to business. She had not paused since she had started through the door. She was out of his sight now. "*Mouche!*" he heard her cry in that high voice, like a playful woman looking for her lover. She was entirely on her own now. "*Mou-ouche!*"

Tarp was still in the entrance foyer, from which doors led to left and right. To the right, the door was open and Tarp could look through a dimly lighted room with a ceiling-high bookshelf to another open door, beyond which was a white, brightly lighted corridor with tile walls. *To the kitchen. Servants' area.* The guard had come that way, leaving the door open because he was going right back, not bothering to put on a light as he came through the room with the bookshelf. *Done it a hundred times before. Routine*. He had put down his glass of wine, perhaps, knowing that his employer's mistress was at the door as she was at the door several evenings a week, year after year. . . .

Tarp took a Belgian Browning from the man's shoulder holster.

"*Mouche!*" She was far off to Tarp's left now. He thought that her tone meant that she had just found van Damme.

He heard a sound to his right, and he had time only to raise his own pistol before a big man with no coat on came through the lighted doorway beyond the dark room. The man was patting his mouth with a rolled-up cloth napkin, but he had a gun in his other hand, and Tarp shot him before the man could take in what was happening, before he could raise his own gun and fire it, before he could warn van Damme. He fell back against the white wall with blood erupting into his shirt and then tried to get up, his legs working and his gun arm moving upward, and Tarp shot him again. *Forgive me. You innocent. If anybody is innocent in this. You thought it was just a job, you poor innocent.*

Tarp went through the dark room and stepped over the dying man. There were two doors leading from the tiled corridor, one open and one closed. He poised outside the open one, listening to the noises of "Dallas" in French from a television beyond the door, and glided low and smoothly around the doorway and into the suite of servants' rooms beyond. The television set was in a small living room; there was an open wine bottle there, and glasses and a mostly ruined paté and two of the long loaves called *ficelles*, both partly eaten. And there was the dying man's coat, hung on a chair. Beyond the living room were four bedrooms and two bathrooms, all deserted. *One for each man. Driver, bodyguard with the sore thumb, man by the front door, man dying in the corridor. No women. Wise man, van Damme . . . no hanky-panky in the servants' suite, no jealousies, no triangles.*

Tarp came back through the rooms and looked along

the tiled corridor to see that the man had died; he turned and went through the corridor's other door, to find himself in a large kitchen that was lighted only by the glow of the city through high, frosted windows. Above him, huge pots and oversized forks and pincers were hung like the properties in a play about witchcraft.

He stepped over the dead man again and came face-to-face with Sheila Beecham.

"Done?" she said.

"You?"

They embraced. He felt guilty, sensing a surge of sexual excitement in both of them because of what they had done.

Van Damme was lying on his back in a crushingly opulent bedroom. He had on a vaguely Japanese gown of black and red over a black cashmere turtleneck and dark trousers. His body was contorted and his hands were clenched into fists, and a long hank of her hair was caught between his fingers like frayed rope. Tarp looked at her again and saw deep scratches on her left shoulder, and he realized now that there was a bruise high on her forehead.

"He fought you," Tarp said.

"Oh, yes."

Adrien van Damme wore a toupee. He also wore tinted contact lenses. Without those aids, he was an almost bald man of about sixty-five with pale blue eyes and a taut, gaunt body and a hideous, gaunt face. His breathing was very faint but his pulse was still strong.

"Are you going to be all right?" he asked her.

"Absolutely."

He gave her the guard's Browning. "Keep an eye out." He dialed the concierge, whose booth was just inside the high glass doors at the front of the building.

"At your service."

"This is Monsieur van Damme's guard. There has been a slight incident of illness and I have called our private ambulance service. We must be very discreet, you comprehend? The illness is not serious, the ambulance is merely a precaution, but we think it best—."

"Ah, yes, yes. . . ."

"Exactly. Therefore, let in the ambulance attendant without delay. And say nothing!"

"Ah, yes, yes . . . discretion. . . ."

"Exactly! Tomorrow's financial market could be a calamity if this got out."

Tarp immobilized the guard with adhesive tape but left the dead man where he lay. *No points for neatness with the dead.*

They took van Damme between them and went down to the third floor, where Jenny Barnwell had found a dark alcove on a floor of offices. There they waited in the shadow with the unconscious man.

"He is late," she said. It was her first betrayal of tension.

"No. Almost two more minutes."

Craik arrived thirty seconds early. He brought a folding wheelchair. They bundled van Damme into it and put Craik's medical bag in his lap.

"Go."

Craik wheeled the unconscious industrialist through the empty lobby at a run. Beecham's daughter came behind, her heels tapping like little hammers, her sobs just loud enough to seem convincing.

The concierge had come out of his booth. "The heart? Is it the heart?"

Tarp held up a hand. "Discretion!" he moaned, and swept on past.

A van with ambulance markings was waiting at the curb. Craik set the red light on the roof flashing as they pulled away, but he shut it down as soon as they had turned a corner.

"How far, Eddie?"

"Over behind the Invalides. No sweat, chum."

Sheila was in the back with van Damme.

There was a coffin back there, too.

"You did well, Eddie."

"You pay good, chum. Don't applaud, just send money."

Craik pulled the van in behind the little car in which they had made the trip from the hotel to the theater. He jumped out and stripped the magnetic signs from the doors and sides, yanked the light from the roof, and dumped them all into the little car. Tarp had already moved into the driver's seat.

Craik leaned in the driver's window. "I'll change plates between here and Calais. Car'll be in Dover tomorrow dawn."

"Take care."

"Not to worry. My best to the lady . . . she's a winner."

Craik slapped the side of the van and Tarp pulled away.

He headed for the high-speed road leading northeast. On the open road, he pulled off into the darkness and put a new set of signs on the van's sides. They were discreet, silver and black, and they said that the vehicle belonged to the Brècque Frères Funeral Service. As he drove, Sheila changed into black clothes that Craik had left for her and then joined him in the cab. At Metz, he left the highway and drove through the dark, deserted streets to the railway station.

"Thirty minutes to spare," he said. "Let's get him into that coffin." When van Damme was in the box and the lid was screwed on and the forged seals had been put in place, Tarp got out and took a sheaf of forged papers. He found the station master's office on a level above the tracks, its lights a little island of brightness in the cool night; Tarp climbed toward them with relief.

"Ah, ah . . . you are the man with the corpse heading for Germany. Correct?"

"Poland, monsieur."

"Poland, Poland . . . why do I think Germany?"

"We go through Germany to get to Poland."

"Ah, ah . . . exactly." He was only an acting station master. He looked at the papers, at their endorsements, at their stamps. Some of them were even genuine: Craik and Jenny Barnwell had good connections. "Everything is in order," he said.

"Thank you."

"There is a lady going on with the dead one?"

"His daughter, yes."

"In a sleeping compartment."

"Yes."

"And you also are going?"

"One would not want to trust a deceased Frenchman to a Polish mortician."

"Ah, ah. Indeed. Ah, ah. Yes."

The late-night special arrived with rigorous punctuality, and Tarp saw the coffin loaded into a baggage car by two porters. He tipped them both generously and went forward to the sleeping cars. Sheila Beecham was waiting. He simply left the van in the parking lot, its signs again removed.

Tarp had been ready for many things from her: depression, guilt, a return to her angry accusations of earlier days . . . but not for the pleased excitement that she now radiated. For the moment, that excitement expressed itself as delight with the train and everything around it: the lights of the station, the darkness of the countryside as they headed toward Germany.

"It's all so wonderful, Tarp! It's wonderful!"

"I'd forgotten. I suppose you've never been on a train before."

"Oh, yes I have!" she said proudly. "I was sent to prison with my mother on a train. But nothing so grand as this! Look! When you turn the handle in the sink . . . *the water runs*!"

"I ought to go to my own compartment," he said. "They'll put us through a border check in an hour."

"Not yet!"

"It's late."

"But I'm wide, wide awake! I *don't* want to sleep. I want to eat, to, to. . . ." Her eyes, still peering at him through Vitry's lavish makeup, widened. "I am astonished at myself, but I know what I want to do."

Tarp knew that reaction. He felt it himself.

He put his hands on her hips, and she wrapped her arms around his shoulders.

chapter twenty

They drove in a small black car through a scruffy industrial district, led by a huge black hearse that must have been in service for twenty years. But then, hearses do not put in long mileage, as a rule; unlike their contents, they are made to last. The little city was not in Poland, after all, but in East Germany; Repin had arranged their movement over the border under another set of papers in case the German police were already on the track of the terrorists who had kidnapped the highly respected industrialist, Adrien van Damme. It was only seven hours since they had left Paris, however; if van Damme's absence was known, it was a secret to the Frankfurt newspapers, which Tarp had bought when they changed trains there.

The two East Germans who drove the vehicles preserved a gravity that seemed to be a simulation of mourning, and even when they had reached the garage that was their destination, they addressed Tarp and Sheila as "Monsieur" and "Madame" in hushed voices. There, with as much care as if they really were handling somebody's father's remains, they slid the casket out of the hearse to a dolly and rolled it some feet away, as if to give it privacy. They touched the brims of their too-wide hats and disappeared through a door that had once been marked VERBOTEN and that now merely said RBOTE.

The garage had once held buses; there were at least twenty stalls for them, all empty now. From the ceiling hung sad, neglected hoses for pneumatic tools and water. Perhaps because of the casket and the dolly, it seemed somehow like those terrible rooms where morticians use the trocar and practice their primitive trade. He would not have been at all surprised to see figures in surgical green or white, perhaps the two who had just left, cutting somebody's father up.

Sheila said nothing. Sex had brought intimacy between them, not the temporary intimacy of the act, but the real thing: relaxation in each other's presence. Until the two men had appeared at the station, they had touched often, as people who have just begun to make love will do.

"Are you tired?" he said very low.

"Oh, no." He looked at her broad face now, which she had scrubbed clean of the makeup, and wondered how he could ever have thought her ugly. He saw strength and intelligence now, and delight.

He heard a door open behind them, and he turned and saw Repin just closing a metal door so heavy he was having trouble with it. He was wearing his black homburg and a black vicuña coat. As he crossed the oily floor toward them he removed one gray glove and held out his hand, the left hand, in that European fashion that Americans find slightly insulting.

"You work very quickly, my friend."

"I was in a hurry."

Repin was still wearing the flesh-colored eye cup under his glasses. He turned his head to look at the coffin. "You are sure it is he?"

"No. But I believe it is."

"We will find out."

Repin banged on the door that had once said VERBOTEN, and the two Germans came bustling out of it like two dice poured from a cup; within seconds, they were breaking the seals of the coffin and unscrewing the lid. They worked fast and so quietly that their breathing was quite audible. When they lifted the lid, Sheila looked in and then withdrew to the hearse, as if what followed was not her business.

"You haven't killed him in that box, I hope," Repin said.

Tarp put his hand on the clammy skin. There was a pulse in the throat. "He's very heavily sedated. A real dose."

Repin put his head into the coffin. He gave a laugh like an actor who wants the audience to understand that he has made a discovery. He snapped orders in a rapid, accented German that Tarp found hard to follow; one of the Germans began to take van Damme's fingerprints while the other pricked an earlobe for a blood sample. Then, together, they looked into van Damme's mouth with a flashlight, one calling numbers of teeth and descriptions of dental repairs while the other made marks on a chart. "Number four, double medial, silver amalgam, crumbling; facial, small silver amalgam upper right quadrant. Number five, missing, bridge replacement, recent; number six. . . ."

When they were done, they vanished through the VERBOTEN door. Tarp, feeling like a salesman whose buyer might decide that he had picked the wrong car, hung by the coffin. Repin took a turn halfway up the garage, kicking at bits of refuse with the toe of a shiny shoe and then coming back. He avoided the coffin now as if he might contaminate it—or it him. He and Tarp stood almost side by side, in the position of mourners who do not know each other. "Who is the woman?" he said at last.

"A colleague."

"Professional?"

Tarp had not thought of her that way. He considered Sheila Beecham's performance at van Damme's flat, her earlier work with the knife. "Yes." He reflected almost idly on how important it was to keep her identity from Repin.

"Have you had her?"

Tarp remembered Repin's reputation for womanizing. It may have been merely self-aggrandizement. Sex for Repin, however, was certainly a very important experience. Without meaning to, Tarp expressed his dislike of the question with an exhalation of air.

Repin laughed. "That means you *have* had her." He laughed again, not at all unpleasantly, but as an indulgent father might have laughed. "It always changes things. Putting two bodies together. Skin to skin changes the world." He put the palms of his hands together, one gloved, one bare, and wagged the long third finger of the bare one through the gloved fingers. "It is not supposed to make a difference. We are only animals. But it makes a difference!" He sighed. "One gets involved." He looked at Tarp and at Sheila, who probably could not hear him. "Professionals would maybe be best if they had no sex. No male, no female. No chance of that intimacy. The Turks castrated their best soldiers. Myself, I would not have liked that."

Tarp thought of Sun, who had been castrated in prison. "I don't think it makes a man better or worse."

Repin made a face. They were talking now merely to fill the time. "The Italians castrated boys for their voices. Female voice, male strength."

"They got fat."

Repin, who was hardly thin, said nothing about that. "Is she a Slav? She looks like a Slav."

Tarp did not answer. Repin said again, mostly to himself, "She looks like a Slav. Terrific thighs on her, I'll bet. I know the type. Ah!" The exclamation had nothing to do with Sheila but was a response to the opening of the door. The time for small talk was over; Repin almost bounded across the garage. One of the Germans stood there, still wearing his suit and his wide-brimmed hat like a movie gangster, but he had on elbow-high plastic gloves, and he was holding up a metal frame with sets of fingerprints clipped into it.

My God, they must have a whole laboratory back there. Knowing Repin, KGB Central is probably on the other side of that door. No wonder it's verboten.

Repin held the frame up toward a window. He looked at the dental chart and at a file that the man handed him, and then he studied another paper.

Blood test. They're thorough. East or West, they're Germans.

Repin came back to Tarp. His excitement had vanished. He, too, now seemed funereal. "You did damned well," he said.

"It's Balkan?"

"It is."

"And my payment?"

"*Poste restante.* What city you want it sent to?"

"Amsterdam." He had to trust Repin now. He had no choice; even getting out of the garage, much less out of East Germany, much less getting the information that he wanted, was up to Repin. "My part is done, then. Viktor Balkan is yours."

Repin made a little sound, a sound like retching. He took a small Beretta from his overcoat pocket, walked to the coffin, and almost casually reached inside with the gun. There was a small report, and Tarp knew that Repin had pressed the muzzle tight against the chest, probably right over the heart. One of the East Germans felt for a pulse, waited, waited—and then nodded at Repin.

"Get rid of it," Repin said. He did not look in the coffin again, but came to Tarp. "I like doing business with you. Are you a sentimentalist?"

"Meaning?"

"Meaning, must your heart always be with your work?"

"I think my heart is like yours, Repin."

"Maybe we will do business again."

Seconds later, Repin was gone.

Tarp took Sheila's arm and walked her out of the garage. They made their way back toward the city center, at last finding a taxi to take them to the railroad station. They were both quiet in the coach that took them west, stopping every twenty miles at another town. She linked her fingers through his.

"Why did he do that?" she said. "Why did he shoot that man?"

"It was a statement. It was a way of saying that he is an old man but he's still dangerous."

"Whom was he warning?"

"Young men."

Repin's papers got them over the border again, this time without the burden of the coffin. At Frankfurt, they caught a flight to Brussels. There, he rented a car and drove north through the fading light of that long, difficult day to break the trip at Delft. He found a little hotel; they ate in its almost empty dining room, served by two women who were far more pleased to have them than seemed justified. Their room was small and old and chilly; they got into the high old bed and made love, and later they leaned by their window and looked out over the dark canal. She was drowsy. He held her, feeling the tension running out of her like grain from a sack.

"I am glad," she said sleepily. "I am glad about it all."

"So am I."

Next morning, the story of van Damme's abduction was in the newspapers. The description of Tarp was not a very good one. That was Laforet's work; he was to get a copy of Repin's information in return. Had Tarp kidnapped the wrong man—or if there was no information—

the description would suddenly become much more accurate.

They took a picnic to the country and Tarp burned the papers that had been used. He was traveling now on the passport that Steinberg had first given him, the Canadian one. It was all he had left, and using it was a lapse on his part, because he had used it before and Hacker and his people had seen it. It worried him, but there was nothing he could do about it.

He spent the day showing her places he knew in Holland. They spent the night in Leyden and then went next to Amsterdam. He stood in the poste-restante line waiting for a bullet or a hand on his shoulder that would mean discovery, but none came; the clerk handed him a business-sized envelope, and that was that.

At the door, then, he thought. When no one came for him there, he thought, *At the corner. By the taxi stand. By that bus stop.* Nobody stopped him, however, and he knew that one of two things had happened: either he was unrecognized, or somebody wanted him to take his operation to the next step. In either case, there was nothing he could do.

Tarp sat on a bench in the sun and tore open the short end of the envelope. Inside was a single tear sheet from a computer printout.

Truth at last. If there is truth.

chapter twenty-one

Craik's taxi moved through Bloomsbury's silent streets. Two couples walking together were the only other signs of habitation; the row houses were dark, the shops below the University of London empty. In the passenger compartment, Tarp stared moodily out the window and said nothing. He had left Sheila in an obscure little bed-and-breakfast hotel above Russell Square, and in the hour before Craik had picked him up, not even she had been able to penetrate this concentration.

Two squares from Hamish Penhurst's house, Craik pulled to the curb. Tarp sat so long that Craik said, "Something wrong, chum?"

Tarp moved reluctantly. "Thinking."

"Better to get on with it, sometimes."

"Indeed." Tarp handed a key forward. "That'll get you into the garage. Park the car in the next street. The same key will get you into a passage that leads into the rear of the house—kitchen. Wait at the end of the passage; nobody goes out. Got a gun?"

"Two. Need one?"

"I'm going in the front door. When I was there before, there was a metal detector. I'll do without."

"Ain't we brave, though."

"I hope it won't come to guns." Tarp leaned a little forward. "Metropolitan Police car makes its run in three minutes; down the street behind the house, along the cross street, back up along the front. Once it's gone, I'll go in the front door with my key; give me five minutes and then go in the back. When I'm done I'll come down and get you." He thought about that. "Don't shoot me."

Tarp got out and began to walk slowly toward Penhurst's. The police car was a minute early that night, and he watched it turn into the cross street and then turn again and disappear toward the Penhurst house. Such patrols were supposed to discourage IRA bombers.

He followed the police car's route. The houses that he had seen only weeks before as the bright setting for a debutante party were dark now, their occupants hidden away in rear bedrooms or cloistered somewhere with insomnia and television. It was an hour after midnight.

Tarp went up the front steps quite boldly. The front-door key, made weeks earlier from one of Gillian's, was in his hand. Yet with the key touching the lock, he waited. It was the last chance to turn back, the last window through which that seductive hand—which he took to be the hand of Forgiveness, but which might be Cowardice—could beckon.

He thrust the key in and turned it.

A single light burned in the large two-story foyer. He had first seen Gillian here, and here, from the top of the stairs that curved so handsomely to right and left, he had watched her meet Johnnie Carrington. The space, which had been so crowded that first night, was empty now and insubstantial. He crossed it, his lightsoled shoes tapping softly on the marble. If anyone in the house heard those quiet footsteps, they did not respond.

On the second floor were a suite of large public rooms; on the third were Gillian's room and the room he had been given, and Penhurst's study and his bedroom and sitting room, and farther back, a library and an almost miniscule private dining room. On the floor above were Mrs. Duffus's domain and the servants' rooms. At least one light was burning on each floor, and he had no need of the small flashlight that he had brought. He continued quietly up to the third floor and went to the room where he had stayed. It was empty except for his own few belongings.

He went to Gillian's door. He meant to warn her that he was in the house. *Like a thief.*

Her bed was empty. She had been there; although a maid had picked up after her, the signs of her were clear in the open cosmetics on the dressing table, in the stacks of rumpled towels in the bath. Tarp stood for almost a minute in the middle of her bedroom, a man undecided. *Did I count on finding her? Did I need her permission?* He silently opened drawer after drawer in her dressing room, finding her lingerie and then, buried in it, his pistol. *Where she said it was.* He chambered a round and put the holster where he was used to carrying it, against his back.

He closed her door with care and went along the corridor. There was a turn, then a step up and another door, which he found open; to pass through it was to enter Hamish's part of the house. And there, up the corridor to his left, was the door of the study with a light showing under it, picking out the carpet's texture but not its colors. A sliver, a knife edge of amber brightness.

Tarp put his hand on the doorknob, which was a large ball of brass with a shield and a coat of arms cast into it. He had never bothered to ask himself if that coat of arms was the Penhursts'; now, feeling its slightly worn surface with his thumb, he was reminded of that first evening with Penhurst back in Maine. *The sunset gun. England and Empire. And good-bye, Mr. Chips.*

He opened the door, stepped through, and closed it, to stand with his back against the door. At the desk, Hamish Penhurst looked up, caught in the spill of light from a brass desk lamp like some nineteenth-century clerk working late at his master's books. Glasses that had been perched on his nose were moved a fraction of an inch lower so that he could peer over them to find who had come in. Recognition came a little slowly: Tarp, in evening clothes, was hardly visible in that darkness.

"My boy," he said confusedly.

"Keep your hands above the desk, Hamish. Please."

Penhurst's face seemed to crumple, like a sheet of paper held against a fire. Too late, Tarp realized how much those words had hurt. He had not come there to hurt. "Oh, my boy!" Penhurst said in an agonized voice. As if to emphazise the cruelty of Tarp's words, he raised his hands several inches above the desk, where they floated in the yellow light like disembodied spirits.

Tarp reached behind with his left hand and locked the door.

"I've come for a talk, Hamish," he said, coming a few steps into the room.

"You've taken a very long time."

"There was more to be done than I expected."

"Yes . . . yes. You've been so long, I had almost given you up."

Their words seemed to come from other mouths. They were looking intently at each other, and the rather polite, almost perfunctory words might have been read by a voice from the shadows.

"I know the truth, Hamish."

Penhurst played with a long, very slender silver pencil. *Would you like something with more finesse? A fountain-pen gun?* But this pen seemed too slender to fire a bullet. *You're a Romantic, Hamish.*

"Just what is it you think you know?"

"Oh—lots of things. About Yugoslavia. You and Tommie Carrington and the KGB man who became Adrien van Damme. Who became Viktor Balkan."

"Was it you who abducted van Damme?" Penhurst asked. He sounded shocked.

"Yes."

"Why? In the name of God, *why?*"

"To find the truth."

"From him? The man doesn't know what truth is."

"From somebody else. He was just a bargaining chip."

Penhurst closed his eyes as if he were being asked to look at something horrible: to identify a corpse too long dead. When he opened them again, his face was bleak. "What is it that you think you know?" he asked again.

The repetition of the question suggested that Tarp was to think very carefully of his answer, that he had been given this second opportunity in order to save himself. Very deliberately, then, he said, "I know you're a traitor."

"How *dare* you!" It was the most passion he had ever seen in Penhurst, almost an animal snarl. "Don't presume!" He straightened his back proudly. "I have served England well."

"And Moscow."

A fractional hesitation, and then, "I have served well."

"Can a man serve two masters, Hamish?"

"They were not my masters!" Penhurst started to get up, checked himself, looked at Tarp. "May I stand?" he said sarcastically, "or do you mean to shoot me?"

"That's unfair."

"Oh, is it? Nonsense, it's exactly the sort of thing you'd do. It's the quality I've always valued in you. Unsentimentality." Penhurst stood slowly. "I'll keep my hands in sight. Put on another lamp, will you, there's a good fellow." He allowed himself a grisly smile. "None of them's booby-trapped." When Tarp had found a switch and the room was brighter, Penhurst began to move about it, looking at its contents like a stranger who has been forced to wait in a strange place, passing his time by looking at the spines of books and at pictures and at pieces of furniture. It was a very rich old room, with family portraits on two walls, and ceiling-high bookcases on another, and in a corner, framed photographs from other days: Penhurst with Churchill, with Prince Philip, with Dulles.

Gently now, Penhurst murmured, "I had no master, my boy. I have always had colleagues—friends—men with whom I shared certain beliefs about, let us call it history." He sighed. "You will not understand me. I don't say that to belittle you, for it's only a fact. You're not English and you're not of my class. Or of my age. You'll not understand what it was like before the war, and then again afterward, when a few of us knew that England, the England that we loved, was dying. Winston believed that the answer was to turn the clock back and to make a big noise. Winston loved war, and for a while the war was a good mistress to him; she proved him right, or so it looked, but it was all sham. Postponement of the inevitable. The war hadn't been over for five years before India was lost; the economy was a hideous mess, just as it had been before . . . and what did Winston do? He made speeches about an 'iron curtain': he wanted another war! Madness!"

Penhurst sighed and sat in a deep leather chair. "I had known it was madness in 1938. There was no saving England even in the old ways. The base was gone; those good old days of buying raw materials cheap in one's colonies and flogging them in Europe at high prices were done. And the answer didn't lie in touting the upper-class pieties, either, the sort of thing that Winston did with such rhetorical flair. The answer lay, I became confident, in total social change. The answer lay in the English people, always our strength and our glory, ever since Agincourt. And every English government in my time has turned its back on the people and tried to preserve a social order that would guarantee business as usual. Madness!" The chair he sat in had a pivoted arm of polished oak that could be pulled across to make a lap desk; he pulled it across him now and opened the book that lay on it. After studying this for some seconds as if he had never seen it before, he closed it and peered at Tarp over his eyeglasses as he had earlier. "I was right, you know. Look at the mess we're in: race riots, strikes, the Irish ghastliness!"

"Where were you recruited?" Tarp asked. The question was brutally plain, like a staring white light put on in that room of golds and browns; Penhurst, however, did not flinch from it. He seemed to have accepted Tarp's knowledge as proven, and he made no attempt to deny his past.

"There were overtures at Oxford. I wasn't part of that group one always hears about, however; they were rather dilettantish, I thought."

"Who ran you?"

"No, I didn't mix with that bunch much," Penhurst said as if the question had not been asked. "I didn't care for them, you know, as *people*."

"Who ran you?"

Penhurst pushed the pivoted arm away, stood up. There was a wall of books behind him. He looked up at it. "There's a 1676 Walton and Cotton up there someplace. I saw it a year or two ago and haven't been able to locate it since. I believe it came into the collection in early Victoria."

"Who ran you?"

Hamish Penhurst turned to look at him. He was still wearing the glasses far down on his long nose. He stood with his hands joined in front of him, his weight up and forward on the balls of his feet. He looked like a tutor examining a not very bright student, and Tarp had the feeling that they had reversed roles. Penhurst had recovered from his earlier wound and was now the aggressor; if Tarp gave stupid answers, the tutor would become caustic and ironical. Penhurst bounced a little on the balls of his feet as if to emphasize that impression and asked, "Where *have* you been all this time?"

"Getting out of China was harder than I expected."

"That was not my fault, my boy, not my fault at all. . . ."

"The plane you sent in was a bogey."

"Ye-e-e-e-s." Penhurst beamed. "I was sure you'd find them out and get round them. As you did."

"That plane would have taken me to Moscow, Hamish."

"But it didn't! Did it? No. So I was quite right to count on you. I knew you'd get round them. But it's taken you the devil's own time to get back here, I must say. I expected you two weeks ago. Did you make a detour to find out the 'truth,' as you call it?"

"Not 'as I call it,' Hamish. *The truth.*"

Hamish eyed him, very much the tutor again. Very much the master who may have a trick question on the quiz. "How do you know? How do you know that your 'truth' is really truth, and not a trick that somebody's playing on you?"

It was a well-aimed shot. It was the question that Tarp had asked himself again and again. *Suppose Repin is playing me? Suppose I'm being run without knowing it?* He gave Penhurst the same answer that he had given himself. "It's the only truth that fits. Nothing else 'scans,' as you used to say."

"Ah. And what scans is my being a traitor."

"No. What scans is my being set up to bring Arthur Beecham out of China so that nobody's hands would be dirty but mine, so that then he could be turned over to Moscow."

Penhurst looked down. "I didn't lie to you, my boy."

"But you didn't tell me everything you knew."

"Ah, no. Not everything."

"That's sophistry, Hamish. 'What is not given becomes a lie.' I believe I learned that when I was taught how to do a briefing."

Penhurst moved away toward the desk, starting to talk more quickly. "You didn't *need* to know everything; there was no point—."

"Keep your hands where I can see them, Hamish!"

Penhurst turned a stricken face to him. "How could you?" he whispered. They were no longer don and student or father and son; now they were prisoner and interrogator. Penhurst even entered into the new role with some willingness, perhaps because he thought it would make Tarp guilty.

"You were going to turn Beecham over to Moscow, weren't you, Hamish?"

"No! No, I was not. No, no . . . you must believe that. This time, I was not." Clearly, there had been other times when he had turned people or things over. "I told you that I had served England well and I meant to serve her well in this. I meant for England to have Arthur and his discovery."

"I don't believe you."

"Arthur is . . . a piece of unfinished business. I kept an eye on him in the first days after the war; if he'd made a breakthrough then, I'd have taken action. But he disappeared; now he turns up again. And I wanted to finish it. It seemed like . . . an opportunity."

Tarp supposed that Penhurst was being deliberately unclear. He waited for an explanation. "An opportunity for what?" he said finally in a flat, awful voice like an actor who hates his lines.

"An opportunity to prove that I was not a traitor to England. To prove that I was not part of this comic parade of MI-5 men who flit off to Moscow when their perks are threatened. To prove that Viktor Balkan was a slimy, cheap journalist."

"But Hamish . . ." Tarp almost laughed. "You *were* a Moscow double agent!"

"But I served England well!"

"But. . . ." Tarp gave it up. He wondered if Penhurst was quite sane. "If you were going to deliver Beecham to England, how come I was almost picked up by a Soviet aircraft made to look like an English one?"

"I couldn't help that. It wasn't my doing."

"I don't get it."

"There was a plan that I had to work around, you see; there was somebody looking over my shoulder—."

"Who?"

"I knew there were dangers for you, but I hoped you'd overcome them."

"You were being run from Moscow and you were going to betray them?"

"I don't like the word 'betray.' And I don't like the suggestion that I was being run. Nobody ran me."

"But there was oversight."

"Verification, let's say."

"Who? Hamish—who is looking over your shoulder?"

But Penhurst moved away again, this time to a portrait, a Lely of a female Penhurst of a pale and plump voluptuousness. Penhurst seemed to be studying the brushwork in the dim light. "What made you suspicious of me?" he said without taking his attention from the painting.

"Something you said in Maine. Just before we jumped the two agency men."

Penhurst turned. "The tale about Yugoslavia."

"Yes."

"Good God, why?"

"Because it was a story about an operation and a betrayal. Some connection, I thought, between what you wanted from me and what you'd done then. The story popped into your head, I suppose, simply as something to say while you were walking along that path pretending to talk to me. But why *that* story at *that* moment? You may not like the word 'betray,' Hamish, but you were planning to betray me just as you had betrayed that poor bastard in Yugoslavia."

"My dear boy, I was planning nothing of the kind! I was planning to use you a bit, true. But if you were suspicious . . . why on earth did you go through with it?"

"It was only a suspicion. And I wanted to prove it wrong."

Penhurst seemed to sag away from the painting, whose study he abandoned. He made his way slowly to the desk, where he again sat into the glow of the brass lamp. After staring at his hands for some seconds—they were spread on the leather of the desktop, as if he had reminded himself of Tarp's caution—he said quietly, "It is very, very important to me that Arthur be brought back. It is important to me personally. Not as some kind of apology, but so that—. A generation or two from now, when the world is utterly changed and the kinds of reforms I know must be made *have* been made, I want other Penhursts to be able to say, 'Yes, he did serve well.' "

Tarp was unmoved. "You said I couldn't understand it. You were right. I don't understand it."

Penhurst flattened his hands on the desk several times as if testing its solidity. "What made you suspicious after the Yugoslavia story?"

"The Dammeco airplane."

"Oh, yes, yes! I was so afraid about that! But I had no time, you see; everything moved so quickly and I had to get to you at once. That aircraft was always available to me and I had to take the risk. Not a very large risk, I thought. But large enough." He smiled ruefully at his fingers.

"I had no idea that van Damme was Viktor Balkan," Tarp said. "Balkan meant nothing; simply the name of a journalist who'd written something about you. I found out that van Damme had been an MI-5 contractor; that seemed rather English: doing business with one's friends, the old school tie. But I learned as well that Tommie Carrington had been with you in Yugoslavia and then that he had been murdered about the time you took over MI-5. I didn't really connect his murder with you, Hamish—you're hardly the kind of man to murder a rival, especially in that ugly way—but it could have been the sort of thing somebody else had done to assure your promotion, or maybe to shut Carrington up if he knew something about you. There were only two things I could think of that he might have known about: first, the Moscow thing; and second, the drug traffic out of Malaysia back when van Damme first contracted with MI-5. So I had van Damme backgrounded, and I found out that he was a fake."

"Ah, did you!"

"With all the marks of an MI-5 identity cover. That meant he was a defector. So I thought maybe you'd turned over some minor Moscow type and given him the identity after he'd been washed. And maybe he became a perfectly legitimate businessman who started a perfectly legitimate business and made a large amount of perfectly legitimate cash. But it bothered me that MI-5 had used him as a contractor, which is a very risky thing to do. The agency wouldn't have done such a thing. And Tommie Carrington's son, who was still looking for his father's murderer, was very interested in van Damme.

"So I thought it was possible that van Damme had something to hold over MI-5 or over somebody in a position of power in MI-5. Maybe he used something that he knew to get those contracts, which in turn made him awfully rich because he used them to bankroll a drug route. Nice fellow.

"And as for Tommie Carrington's son, the likeliest reason for him to take an interest in van Damme was that he had access to the MI-5 files, and they showed a common link among his father, van Damme, and his father's work in MI-5. I thought of Yugoslavia again. You'd said there was a 'third man.' "

"Yes. There were three of us."

"You, Tommie Carrington and—van Damme? Another source told me that the journalist now called Viktor Balkan had been a Russian defector who'd been turned over about the same time that van Damme was. In Yugoslavia. That made a picture that was not very handsome, Hamish, but at least it fit together: the end of the war, you and Tommie Carrington and a Russian in Yugoslavia. The agent is your Moscow contact, but Carrington doesn't know that; he thinks it's all part of being allies. Still, he's ambitious and he's suspicious: 'straight as a seam and mean as sin, and he never let go,' was the way he was described to me. The three of you make your deal with the Nazis to blow up your Yugoslav friend, and then you and Carrington go back to London. A year or two later, you bring your Russian over. Maybe he was a real defector; maybe he was a setup. Anyway, I believe he stayed clean, because he'd be able to blackmail you later about the Moscow connection without risking anything himself. And MI-5 went through their ID files and came up with the name of a dead South African for whom lots of papers and real background existed, and the Russian became Adrien van Damme. And Tommie Carrington got suspicious. And in the sixties, when van Damme began to make a pile out of his MI-5 connection, Carrington knew that something was rotten . . . and he got too suspicious to be tolerated, and he was eliminated."

"I didn't do it. I swear. I swear it, my boy!" At some point, Penhurst had given up the inspection of his hands and had lighted a cigarette. Tarp hated its odor. Penhurst tapped the desktop with the hand that held the cigarette. "Nor did I cause it to be done," he said.

"But you know who did it."

"No, I don't. Not with any certainty."

"You mean you never dared to ask." Penhurst frowned into the cloud of cigarette smoke and said nothing.

"Van Damme was a greedy man," Tarp went on. "A

shark. Why in the world did he create the Viktor Balkan personality?"

"In the beginning, he needed money. We found him some sort of job in a library up north; he hated it. So he began to write little articles: news analyses, that sort of thing. They often had a Russian slant, so he kept himself distant from them by using the assumed name. Dealt with editors only through the mail, and so on. Didn't want to risk his van Damme identity."

"But lately he's been publishing the dirty stuff about you and others. He was a millionaire. Did he want *more* money?"

"He wanted power over us."

"Power to do what?"

"Merely power."

"But he was an old man."

"No matter. It never stops." *It* seemed to refer to the inner urge, to desire, to aspiration. Repin had said the same thing to him.

Penhurst smoked and Tarp watched him. He was aware of some sound in the house, but he did not recognize it and it was not repeated, and he put it aside. Penhurst put out the cigarette and rubbed his hands slowly together. His fingers sought another cigarette and played with it idly, as if wanting something to hold. When he saw that he had picked the cigarette up, he put it down and took up the silver pen and began to play with it. "You did very well," he said. "Perhaps I knew you'd find out. Perhaps I wanted you to, somewhere in my—in some part of me. Maybe that psychiatric mumbo-jumbo has something in it. We *are* our own worst enemies." He rolled the pen between his palms and then stared at it. "Are you going to expose me?"

"I already have."

Penhurst winced. "To whom?"

"Laforet in Paris. It was part of the package that

involved van Damme." In fact, he had put the computer printout about Penhurst in the mail that afternoon.

"To the French! Oh, God." He balanced the pen on his palm, seeming to weigh it. "No turning back?"

"Too late, Hamish."

"And Arthur?" he said pleadingly. "You won't bring Arthur to me so I can make it right?"

"You know I can't." Despite himself, the words came out as an apology.

Hamish Penhurst looked at Tarp, then at the wall of books, then at the Lely portrait. "All gone to smash," he said quietly, and he put his thumb on the end of the silver pen and put its tip against a blue vein in his slender left wrist, and he pushed with his thumb exactly as if he meant to push a penpoint out, and a needle was ejected directly into the vein, where it squirted a jet of chemicals into his bloodstream.

Tarp made a movement forward but stopped himself. It was probably too late even then, but it was not the lateness that made him stop. He simply accepted Penhurst's decision.

"All gone to smash," Penhurst whispered again.

Tarp leaned on the desk. "Hamish, who is your control? Who's looking over your shoulder?" The old man leaned back in his desk chair. Already, his high color was going, and his look of vigor with it; he was growing old as Tarp watched. His eyelids drooped, his mouth opened, the lower lip quivering. "Hamish! You're dying, Hamish! It doesn't matter anymore. Who's looking over your shoulder?"

The old man made a sound like a snore. His right hand twitched. The eyelids opened a little, fluttered. The trembling of the lips seemed like an attempt to form a word or a name, but no sound came.

"Hamish, for God's sake!"

Hamish Penhurst gathered himself and tried to sit up. His right hand stiffened and his right forearm rose so that there was a straight line from elbow to fingertips. The arm fell in a chopping stroke. It rose again, fell, rose as if to repeat the gesture. The stiff hand, however, relaxed and then tensed into a fist, and he fell back into the deep chair with another sound like a snore, and his limbs went into tremors as his head arched back and he died.

Tarp took the pulse at the throat. He closed the eyes and tipped the head a little forward so that the mouth closed.

He thought of that last gesture. It tied somehow with the knife that had killed Tommie Carrington. *Knife. Or ax.* He made the gesture with his own hand and arm. *Chopping. Cutting. Maybe some kind of karate blow.*

Death was ugly on Hamish Penhurst's face, coming to him, not as a last touch of privilege, but as an insult. Probably it was the posion, the oysterish pallor, the waxy skin, the sprawled positions of the limbs as if they had been a little wrenched in their joints. *Hamish is dead.* He had to look at the little, dead old man to remind himself of that. *I failed him. He thought I was going to save him, and I turned him in. I killed him.*

Tarp looked over the room quickly. He had left no marks. Switching off one lamp, he went to the door and then looked it all over again. The silver pen was on the desk where Penhurst had dropped it. The MI-5 people would know what to make of that. They had supplied it, after all.

He listened at the door, more from old habit than from suspicion, turned the lock and opened it. The corridor was empty, the house quiet, except for those sounds that all old houses make. To his left was another turn in the passageway and darkness; to his right were the door and the step down and Gillian's room. He went that way and then down through the sleeping house.

On the first floor, a narrow passage ran next to the reception rooms, connecting with each by a door; another door led from the passage to the kitchen, and at the end of the passage was a door and three steps down to a flagstone-paved room where flowers were sometimes prepared. Craik would be there by the door to the garage.

Tarp walked across the first reception room and opened the door to the passage, after first listening as he had upstairs. The passage was dark; he looked on the wall near him and found a panel of four switches. One put on a chandelier in the room where he stood; the second seemed to do nothing; and the third put on three overhead lights in the passage.

He had an impression of very low vibration. *Maybe something in the street.* He had drawn the pistol. Thinking of Penhurst's last gesture. *Cutting. Chopping. Knife.*

Along the passage now, past the first door, then past the swinging door to the kitchen, in which a pane of glass at head level reflected his own intense and angry face. His face startled him. *I'm spooked. Why?* Perhaps Hamish's death had unsettled him. *Somebody looking over my shoulder.*

Ahead of him was the door to the three steps and the room with the flagstone paving. The door was closed. That was normal enough. And yet it might have been the closing of this door that had caused that low vibration. Craik might have done it, not knowing who was coming. Craik would be nervous by now, after waiting in the dark for an hour.

Tarp rapped lightly on the door. *Don't shoot, Eddie. Nobody else would knock; you've got to figure that out.* When there was no answer, he knocked again.

Tarp looked at the hinges and the doorknob. The door would swing toward him when it opened. If somebody was standing on the other side, they would be at least one step below his level. If somebody was there waiting to jump him, they would have to come up the stairs at him.

Tarp stood close against the wall and opened the door a crack.

"Eddie?"

The silence and the darkness were both absolute.

"Eddie?"

There was a panel with two switches on the wall next to him. He expected one to put on a light in the room below, but nothing happened. The other switch put out the lights in the passage. He left them out. He was now standing in utter darkness, the doorknob in his left hand, the pistol in his right. He let go of the door and took out the pocket flashlight, slowly opening the door with his left toe. He held the light away from his body and as high as he could reach to confuse anyone standing below.

The little light picked out the shiny edges of polished flagstones. It flattened surfaces, deadened colors. Still, it reflected brightly from a shiny surface that covered the stones in a large, irregular pool and showed enough color so that he knew it was blood. Then the light picked up a shoe, perched vertically on its heel, and then the dark pant leg behind it, and then a mound of loathsome gray-green that Tarp had seen before.

"Oh, Eddie."

Eddie Craik had been disemboweled. No need to wonder how it had been done.

Tarp heard the same low vibration behind him that he had heard before, and smothered sounds of scurrying, whispering—cloth rubbing on cloth and suppressed human breathing.

The kitchen door was three long strides away. The vibrating sound, he knew now, was from a thick spring that was meant to pull the swinging door closed: in the darkness, somebody was standing in that doorway. *With a knife. Chopping. Cutting.*

He had doused the flashlight at the first sound and now he ducked low, feeling an infantile urge to roll himself into a ball and hide from the knife that was a few feet away. He pulled his left elbow tight across his belly with the forearm straight above it and the fist knotted in front of his face, and then he crouched beside the open doorway that led down to Eddie Craik's body.

For a full second, they both waited, Tarp and whoever was up the passage, neither sure where the other was in the blackness. Tarp had to fight against a terror of the knife, which had become more than a weapon for him. He had seen its use too much. He shrank from being touched, knowing that the killer had only to find him with a single, testing finger to begin the thrust.

He heard movement. Odor reached him. *Woman. Sweet, salt. Seamarsh and vanilla. Sachet.*

He aimed the light at the sound and pressed the switch.

She had the knife ready in her left hand, ready to plunge it in; no need, this time, to feint with the right and make the switch. It was a chef's blade, thick in the backbone and sharp enough to slice meat paper-thin. The light picked up the broad blade as if drawn to it. Behind the knife, dimly, he saw her dark dress, her face, her mouth twisted in hatred.

She surged forward and he fired, hating the knife; the little gun had no stopping power, and he fired again, childishly, almost hysterically, thinking of Craik and Qiu. He fired as fast as he could pull the trigger; the knife ripped at his rigid left arm and sliced into the outer muscle; he fired again; he heard himself cry out, a whimper of fear, and he pushed the knife away as if it were alive; fired again; the knife caught in his sleeve and was swept away from his abdomen; and she was falling back against the passage wall and her lips were working, snarling at him, and she was dying.

The knife clattered to the floor between them.

Tarp switched on the passage lights. Blood was running down his arm into his armpit because he had raised it, beginning to soak his shirt; when he lowered the arm, blood ran down his fingers and dripped on the linoleum.

Mrs. Duffus lay in the angle of the wall and the floor with the base of her spine just at the junction, as if she had fallen back against the wall, standing, and had slid down into that position. She began to topple slowly to her left. Her left arm tried to hold her up, but it had no strength and she fell over gradually until she was lying on her left side with her head turned back to look at him. Blood welled into her mouth and dribbled down, but her eyes were clear and intelligent. Her dark dress hid the places where she had been shot.

Tarp wriggled his left arm out of the sleeve of his dinner jacket. The white shirtsleeve was soaked with blood from the elbow down now; he tore it off at the shoulder and looked at the long gash on the forearm. She watched him. He made a tourniquet of the sleeve and wrapped it tight above the elbow, bending his arm to press the twisted lump of the ends deep into the crook.

Poor Eddie, he thought. *He never had a chance.* The scene was easy to imagine: Craik waiting below there, the old woman opening the door and turning on the light, probably feigning fear of him and confusion until she was close enough.

Bright red blood from her lungs pooled on the linoleum floor. This is the way that hunters' kills die, their lungs punctured, except that sometimes they run before they fall. The kind hunter puts another bullet into the head. Tarp did not want to be kind; nor did he want to mark the head, for he was thinking already of the MI-5 investigation that had to come.

Her life flickered and went out. She died hating him. She must have lived hating him, too, he thought, ever since he had come to the house. Ever since she had known he was the Enemy. Like Tommie Carrington, who had got too close to Penhurst's truth, too.

Tarp left her where she had fallen, and he left Eddie

Craik, who was beyond any help of his now. Tarp felt suddenly very clearheaded; a little loss of blood is good for the body, or so they thought in the days of bleeding. His mind was focusing down to a point, and at that point was the conclusion of this whole messy business. At that point was a person—a face. He tried to make it out, wondering if it was, in fact, the face of Mrs. Duffus. *Somebody looking over my shoulder*. Recognition might depend upon deciphering Penhurst's dying gesture. *The knife. Cutting. Chopping.*

He heard the front door of the house open softly.

chapter twenty-two

Johnnie Carrington and Gillian were embracing. There was a muffled female giggle and a quick intake of breath, as if one of them was about to dive, and they kissed. Tarp, feeling like a voyeur, let the passage door close again. They had just come in, both dressed for a party.

Tarp holstered his pistol. Releasing the bandage, he let the blood flow again before he bandaged it once more and bent the arm tight within the shelter of the black jacket, which he now wore capelike over his shoulders. He turned up the collar and pulled it tighter to hide the bloodied shirt.

The couple were still kissing when he looked again; Carrington's left hand was under her light cloak, a giveaway of intimacy, of an established trust. He saw it objectively, without rancor.

He tried to make a sound as he came through the doorway. The couple separated, both of them blushing as if it was something they had learned to do together on cue. When Carrington recognized Tarp, he was obsequious. "Oh! Good evening, ah . . . sir . . . ah. Look here. . . ."

With a shake of his head, Tarp dismissed the personal. He stood at the rear of the foyer, the width of the black-and-white-tiled floor between them. "Johnnie, can you do something for me? Something important has happened."

"Oh, of course, sir. But . . . look here. . . ."

"Come here."

Carrington crossed to him at once. Gillian hovered uncertainly near the front door, then sat on a white bench at the side. Tarp put his right hand on the silk lapel of Carrington's jacket and turned him so that he blocked Gillian from their conversation. "I've found your father's killer," Tarp murmured.

"What?"

"She's dead."

"*She?*"

"I want you to listen to me, Johnnie. I want you to go through the door behind me and along the passage. You'll find her at the far end. In the room beyond is . . . the proof. Very ugly proof. Got a strong stomach?"

"I don't know."

"You'll have to find out. I'll explain everything later, but I want you to go back there and look and then come back to me here." He handed Carrington his flashlight. "It's going to be a level three."

Carrington did not look foolish now, nor was he blushing. "You'll have to justify that before I'll have any part of it." A level-three investigation intervened before the Metropolitan Police were allowed to take part. It was a very serious matter, for it inevitably involved high security and some degree of cover-up.

"Yeah, well, you go back and have a look, and I'll justify it to you when you come back. I need to talk to Gillian. Nothing personal."

When Tarp crossed the foyer toward her, she raised her face to smile at him. She had had time to compose herself, to invent a bright line or two if she would need one: something clever about lovers and fidelity. Tarp anticipated her, however, with the cold words, "Your grandfather is dead."

She stood up. Her eyes were a little too bright, as if she had drunk a little too much. Honest tears were there, too.

"I'm sorry, Gillian. It was his heart, I think. I was with him."

"Poor Polly." She had hardly breathed the words. Polly was Penhurst's wife Penelope.

"I need for you to take care of the servants, Gillian. Can you do that? There's got to be an MI-5 survey at once. Much, much better if the servants aren't involved until it's over. Your grandfather's position makes it necessary. You do understand, don't you?"

"Yes. I think so." She turned away and held a very small handkerchief to her face. Her sorrow was conventional and contained—real enough, but limited. "*What* do you want me to do?"

"Go up to the servants' floor. Stay up there. Make sure nobody goes down the back stairs or tries to come into the rest of the house."

"Can't Mrs. Duffus do that?"

"Mrs. Duffus is doing something else."

"Then of course. Yes, I'm happy to help. Poor Grandfather." She was of her class, ready to do those duties that kept her well-organized life in balance. Her voice suggested that she might have been agreeing to visit a hospital for refugee children. "Yes, I'm quite happy to help. Where is he?"

"In his study. Don't go in, please. MI-5 dustmen will want it untouched."

"Oh, no, of course!" She started for the stairs. "Could you or Johnnie sit with me? Or provide a cup of tea?"

"Maybe later. Go on, now."

"Of course." She looked wan and a little forlorn. One moment she had been the center of a drama involving two men, and now she was a lone figure pushed out to the periphery of a much larger drama, a very minor character whose only role was to climb three flights of stairs and sit in the servants' parlor.

Tarp pushed open the passage door, walked to the kitchen, and opened the door with the window in it. The low vibration of the stretched spring sounded. Mrs. Duffus was a mean little heap at the end of the passage, and he ignored her.

Lights had been put on in the kitchen, cruelly chill fluorescents in long banks hung from the high ceiling; when he walked in, Johnnie Carrington was just getting over being sick in one of the double sinks against the farthest wall. His eyes were filled with tears, and he was patting his mouth with a paper towel. "Sorry, sir," he said. "I thought I was beyond th-this sort of thing."

Tarp was looking for a first-aid box. He found it on the wall above a butcher's block that bristled with knives. "You're doing fine." He took out hydrogen peroxide, alcohol, bandages. "Let's talk about what's next. We have to move very fast."

"Yes, sir. How long—?"

"She's only been dead for minutes. The dead man in the far room somewhat longer."

"Shouldn't Sir Hamish—?"

"He's dead. I've sent Gillian up to the servants' rooms. He killed himself, but I told her it was his heart. MI-5 will be very proud; he used one of their poison pens."

"Oh, damn." The young man patted his mouth with the towel. "Poor old Polly, whatever will she do! Shattering. But, see here . . . I mean, this is ghastly. The scandal. . . ."

Tarp had dropped his jacket to the floor and he removed his makeshift tourniquet, letting the arm drip blood into the deep sink. Carrington winced when he saw the gash. "I'd like you to make the contact with MI-5," Tarp said.

"Yes. . . ."

"Call the duty officer, flag a level three. He's going to have to get somebody out of bed—."

"—the minister, yes—"

"—and deal with the mets." Tarp poured alcohol down his arm. "I'll need a doctor for this arm, too. And a photographer. The dustmen will insist; makes their work easier if they can explain self-defense. I believe there's a telephone with a scrambler in Hamish's study." Tarp was following the alcohol with hydrogen peroxide, which bubbled at the edges of the cut and mixed with the blood. When he was done with that, he began to scrub at the blood that had dried on his arm and fingers.

"But those two bodies, sir. It could be a dreadful scandal. . . ."

"There doesn't have to be a scandal if we keep our heads."

"But I can't justify a level three simply to keep this sort of mess out of sight, sir."

"You can justify it because Sir Hamish was a Moscow double." He kept on scrubbing. "As soon as you've talked to the DO, you'll have to raise somebody at the top. Not the minister—a professional. Somebody inside. Somebody who can cope with the news that Penhurst really was a mole."

Carrington took it well, although he was pale and he looked as if he might need a drink in a few minutes. He was like a fighter who is brutally overmatched and knows it, but is determined to stay on his feet as long as he can. "My chief," he said in a breathless voice. "Ramsay Mathiesson."

"Get him, then." Tarp threw the towel away and looked at Carrington. He knew that his own face was terrible; death and fatigue had piled on his usual anger. "I know that I'm right in the middle of the whole business, Johnnie, and I know you don't trust me—you certainly shouldn't—and you can't much like my giving you orders. But I know this drill. All right?"

"Yes, sir."

"Get on that scrambled phone, then."

"One thing."

"Well?"

"Did she really—Mrs. Duffus, I mean—kill my father?"

"I'm certain that she did."

"Why?"

"She was Hamish's *bamsha*. What you people call a 'nurse.' Put in place by Moscow to run errands and clean up after the double agent. To Hamish's credit, I believe that he didn't put her up to it."

The young man jammed his hands deep into his jacket pockets. He was staring at something beyond that room that made his face middle-aged. When he had left the kitchen, Tarp stayed behind, staring at the butcher block and its array of knives and wondering if Mrs. Duffus were indeed the end of it all: the face, the final answer. The one who looked over Penhurst's shoulder. *Chopping*. He wanted her to be, so that it would be over, but he knew that Moscow did not work that way. They had put her there to serve Penhurst, not to oversee him.

He wrapped gauze over the long cut, made another tourniquet, and went up to his old room to find a shirt. It was awkward to deal with because his left arm was stiffening and the fingers felt numb. He shucked off the black trousers and the evening slippers and put on his own old clothes that he had brought from Maine: worn cotton pants and a sweater and ankle-high canvas hiking shoes.

Johnnie Carrington was on the telephone when he walked into the study. He was using the regular telephone, so Tarp knew he had finished his call to MI-5. "The utmost importance, sir, yes. . . ." Johnnie looked at Tarp but showed no recognition. "On *my* authority, sir. Yes, sir, yes . . . no, sir . . . yes. No, sir, I can't explain over an open telephone. No, sir. Yes. If you insist, sir. I can have a scrambler call routed, yes, sir."

Tarp heard a voice making nasty noises at the other

end, like a recording of a political speech played at the wrong speed. Johnnie Carrington looked grim, but he said politely, "Thank you, sir. I quite understand how you feel. I shall speak with you again when I can route a scrambler call, sir." He hung up and looked at Tarp desolately. "It's my career if I get him down here and he doesn't think it was justified."

"It's always your career, if you're any good."

"I've had your file pulled and made ready for him, Mr. Tarp. I couldn't use your name or even Sir Hamish's over that phone, but I couldn't get to him on the scrambler. Got to do that now."

"Did you get to the DO?"

"Yes, yes. Internal Investigation are on the way. Once they're here, there'll be no keeping quiet in the house; the servants will know. And Gillian."

"They'll post guards up there. She'll be up there with the maids until morning. I believe she'll survive it."

"Don't be too hard on Gillian."

"Sorry, I thought I was being kind. You can go sit with her, if that's your idea of the proper thing to do."

"I love Gillian, sir, and I want her to marry me. However. Obviously, I must stay with you. I'm responsible until II get here."

"Good." Tarp led the way out of the study. As the door closed he wedged a small piece of folded paper into the hinge side. "I suggest that we wait down in the kitchen passage. In case somebody wanders in. The butler lives out; God knows what he'd be doing here at this time of night—morning, whatever it is—but we need to be careful."

"And perhaps you can tell me everything, sir."

"That's what I intend to do. Everything." *Well, not quite everything.*

Ramsay Mathiesson was as well put together as if it were teatime in his office. His vested suit was unwrinkled; his glossy boots were without scuff marks. His hair was smoothly brushed and it looked almost black, although he was nearing fifty. Mathiesson had the successful manager's habit of showing his teeth in quick, false smiles that were sometimes highly sarcastic in order to set off the errors of his subordinates. An undercurrent of annoyance ran through everything he did, as if he was aware of a quantity of mistakes that he simply lacked the time to point out. I am, his manner seemed to say, a man beset by fools, but I do my best to rise above them.

"Let's have it through once more, shall we?" His voice was nasal and his accent was faintly middle-class, as if he were a Labourite who had crossed party lines. " 'One more time,' as jazz musicians are reputed to say. And uh-one, and uh-two, and. . . ." He turned at the opening of a door, ready to unleash his sarcasm because his joke had been interrupted. "Ah, Jenkins! What news from town?"

Jenkins was older and would never rise above his present position. Like a good dog, he pretended to bathe in his chief's contempt. "Dug out the report on the Carrington killing, sir. Matches to a T. Medical men say they'd go to court it's the same tactic."

"But we *knew* that, Jenkins." Mathiesson showed his teeth. "Is that *it*, Jenkins?"

"Yes, sir, that's it."

"*Thank* you, Jenkins. Thank you for this needless interruption."

"Yes, sir." Jenkins went out backward, like a dog who knows he has been a bad dog.

"Where was I? Aha! Our cover story. Yes, our little romance!" He seemed to consider going back to his joke about being a musician, but he wisely gave that up. "Brandy, Mr. Tarp?"

"No, thank you." Tarp was sitting in the shadows on a sofa. More than anything, he was tired. He had decided that he did not like Mathiesson, who seemed to him to be like a dozen senior officers he had known who cared about their own images more than about their work. Mathiesson had to be endured, however, for he was the one who would take all this to the minister. Tarp lay back, trying to find a comfortable position for his left arm, which had been anesthetized, sewn up, and put into a nylon-web sling.

"*No* brandy?" Mathiesson seemed unable to accept that. He flashed his grin again, as if he knew something about Tarp's real drinking habits. "I, on the other hand, will have one. Carrington?"

"Thank you, sir. No, sir."

Mathiesson poured. Tarp supposed that he drank too much.

"Here's the tale, then." Mathiesson stood in front of a tall double window, beyond which the sky was brightening with the dawn. They were in the library of Penhurst's house; in the next room, the dustmen of MI-5 were making their third and final check. Mathiesson pretended to be intoning a printed statement, as if he were a public-relations officer. "Sir Hamish Penhurst, much-respected former head of MI-5, died last night of natural causes in his town house in London. Although a subject of speculation in the sensational press in recent months, Sir Hamish was judged entirely innocent of allegations and suspicions concerning any connection with etcetera, etcetera, etcetera." Mathiesson's voice became his own again. "No mention of poison or any of that." He returned to his story-telling voice. "Sir Hamish was alone at the time of death and was believed to be working on his memoirs. The house was empty except for servants. Lady Penelope was at the Hamish country estate, etcetera, etcetera, etcetera." He cocked an eyebrow at Tarp. "*No* American visitor, *no* Arthur Beecham. We can count on you, Mr. Tarp?"

"Oh, absolutely. It's my ass if I don't, right?"

Mathiesson showed his teeth. "What a colorful way of putting it." He drank. "Now, about your French *friend*." Mathiesson made the word sound like an insult. "You got in touch with your *ami francais*?" Like many Englishmen of his class, he affected an abominable French accent.

"Yeah."

"He'll keep his counsel about Penhurst, will he?"

"For the favor I mentioned."

"I don't consider my handing over the name of two Polish cutouts a 'favor,' Mr. Tarp. I consider it a damned high price."

"You're lucky they don't go public just because they're French and you're English."

"I know. Our beloved allies." Mathiesson drank again, straightened, put one hand in the small of his back, and pushed his pelvis forward. "So that part's all right. I shall have to call on the PM first thing in the morning. Good God, it's morning already, *isn't* it?" He looked at his glass. "I believe, however, I shall go on thinking of this as a nightcap rather than as an eye opener." He snickered. "Now, as for the terrible little lady in the very dark dress. The demon barberess of Fleet Street."

"The murderer of Carrington's father," Tarp said pointedly.

"How's that?" Mathiesson, sensing that he had been corrected, looked at Tarp as if he dearly wished Tarp were one of his subordinates. Getting no satisfaction there, however, he turned on Johnnie Carrington. "No offense, I prithee," he said. His tone made it a joke, and the joke, of course, made it offensive.

Johnnie Carrington did not smile, but said stiffly, "You were saying, sir. Mrs. Duffus."

Mathiesson eyed him. Mathiesson was not pleased to have even an offensive apology rejected. "Ye-e-e-s, the notorious Mrs. Duffus. *Here* our tale gets a bit—just a bit, just a sliver, just a morsel—*thin*. Thin as a knife edge, ha-ha. The story goes thusly: hearing of her beloved employer's death, Mrs. Duffus retired to a nearby room to compose herself. Investigating officers, aware sometime later that she had not reappeared, went to the room and found her the unfortunate victim of an arrest of the heart. Etcetera, etcetera, etcetera. Will it go down? Can't say, can't say for the life of me! *However,* Her Majesty's government naturally required a full autopsy: delicate nature of the circumstances, desire to dot every I—etcetera, etcetera—which will show cardiac arrhythmia or some such finding. It also allows us to ship her off to the relatives already gutted and trussed up again with the bullet holes prettily minimized by our specialists. She does have relatives, does she?"

"A sister and an aged aunt, sir."

"No *Mister* Duffus?"

"No, sir. Widowed. I put out her file for you."

Mathiesson's eyes glittered. "And I *read* it, Carrington! Heaven forfend that you should find your chief remiss in these little tasks you plan for him." He smiled. He joined his hands in front of him and beamed. His eyes fell suddenly on Tarp as if to trick him. "Convinced she was an agent, are you?"

"Attached to Penhurst by Moscow. Mail clerk, errand girl. Nurse."

Mathiesson pretended to marvel. "And she a sweet little thing from Brig o' Dee! How, do you suppose, did this pass our security check?"

"I suppose Hamish faked her dossier."

"Dear, dear." Mathiesson put his right elbow into his left palm, like a certain kind of sexually ambiguous British comedian, and tapped his cheek. "What a nasty, nasty business ours is! Ah, well, if you haven't pricked the poor old thing so full of holes she can't be patched up, Mr. Tarp, we shall hope to send her home for burial with nobody questioning the mode of death. But six bullets . . . *really.*"

"Ever been up against somebody with a knife in the dark?"

"We normally issue something rather heavier for close work. A nine millimeter would have knocked her heels over tup."

"And been heard on the servants' floor."

"Dear, *dear*. I do believe I'm being instructed in weaponry."

"Dear, dear. If you'd get on with it and stop stunting, we'd be out of here."

A lesser man than Mathiesson might have blushed or stammered or even fallen silent. To Mathiesson, however, the insult was like a fresh supply of logs on a dying fire; he positively glowed. "*Stunting!* What a lovely, what an absolutely *lovely* word. Do you hear him, Carrington? I do hope that somebody will ask me what I was doing at break of day so that I may say I was 'stunting.' "

Tarp sighed. "Get on with it."

Mathiesson took quite a deep breath and held it. Perhaps he was thinking of something terrifying to say. Perhaps, then, he could think of nothing, for he became quite businesslike. "Our third problem involves the man whose body was found in the flower room. Mr. . . . ?"

"Craik, sir."

"Yes, yes, thank you, Carrington, it was on the tip of my tongue, *Edmund* Craik. One of ours at one time, I note. Mr. Craik's body has already been removed to the mortuary and the Metropolitan Police have cooperated by setting up a barricade and other paraphernalia on Hampstead Heath, where, they will say, he was discovered at daybreak by an aged pensioner crossing the heath with his dog . . . actually one of ours. His taxi is parked nearby. It will be treated as a routine robbery and killing, death result of a blow to the head." Mathiesson looked around. "Questions? No? Then I believe that that is that." He drained a drop from his glass and poured himself more.

Carrington cleared his throat. "Miss Gillian Penhurst, sir."

"The granddaughter." Mathiesson glanced at a notebook, holding it far away in order to read his notes. He seemed to have lost some of his buoyancy as daylight had come; perhaps, Tarp thought, the alcohol was hitting him harder than he had expected. "I see," Mathiesson said delightedly, "that *you*, Carrington, came in with the young lady at two-something. A *personal* involvement, Carrington?"

"Ah. . . ." Johnnie looked at Tarp. "Yes, sir. I hope so, sir."

"Then *you* try out the tale of Mrs. Duffus's heart attack on her. Bring her down here when you're done and we'll have our man give her a shot of something . . . exhausted young woman, stricken by loss of her grandfather, etcetera, etcetera. Keep the reporters off her for twenty-four hours."

"I believe she can be trusted without that sort of treatment, sir."

"*Do* you, by God! And of course, you're in a position to make an objective judgment, I suppose!" A little color had come into Mathiesson's gray cheeks. "Go away, Carrington. Go talk to your young lady. Go, go."

Johnnie Carrington left the room, his face proud and miserable at the same time. He was about ready to resign, Tarp thought. It would serve this urbane little court jester right to lose him.

"*Now!*" Mathiesson perched on the edge of a Georgian table. "About Arthur Beecham, Mr. Tarp." His voice was painfully nasal. "I want him, Mr. Tarp."

"Yeah. You and everybody else."

"I sent Young England away because I want to discuss it, just the two of us. Arthur Beecham came as a considerable *shock* to me, I may say, and these old bones have become inured to shocks. A *revelation*! I'd no idea he was still active as a scientist, or even still alive. Certainly hadn't a hint that Hamish was after him. Now, I *want* him."

"Yes?"

"Where is he?"

"Safe."

"Mr. Tarp, I spoke with the minister. I told him how completely cooperative you'd been, how very generous you were with information about poor Penhurst and your involvement with him. I also told him what you'd told me about the Beecham matter. We are prepared—dependent, of course, upon certain tests and investigations—to pay you very handsomely for Arthur Beecham. *Very* handsomely."

Tarp felt his anger building. "Naturally I'd want to be paid handsomely."

"Mr. Tarp, why don't you just tell me where we can gather him in? I daresay we can have him safely on a British ship or aircraft in a matter of hours. See here . . . you're very tired; you're wounded; you've done yeoman's work through all of this . . . and now it's time to reap your reward. Time to savor your victory and return Arthur Beecham to England. Her Majesty's government would be *most* generous."

Tarp shifted the position of his left arm. He looked at Mathiesson's puffy eyes. "Who the hell are you?" he said rudely.

Mathiesson put his hand over his necktie, probably meaning to indicate something about his heart. "I am the number three of MI-5."

"How do I know that? And what does it mean, anyway?"

"What a delightful question!" Mathiesson tried to laugh to show his delight. "Do you think all of these people would do as I tell them—especially when I do it *so* offensively—if I *weren't* the number three?"

"It still doesn't mean I can trust you."

"Mr. Tarp! I speak for Her Majesty's government in this!"

Tarp scrambled to his feet. "Hamish Penhurst said that he spoke for Her Majesty's government! Now you come along, and after three hours of your little performance here you expect me to turn Arthur Beecham over—just like that? I don't even like you, Mathiesson, and I don't know you . . . and I won't turn Beecham over because *I don't see any reason to trust you*."

"But you've got to trust somebody."

"Why?"

"Because—because, not trusting anybody is a form of madness."

"Not in the world we live in."

"You're a paranoiac!"

"And you're a pain in the ass. I'm going to get some sleep."

Mathiesson pursued him to the door, glass in hand. "We can make things very, very difficult for you! It would be very easy to charge you with murder, Mr. Tarp. Violation of the Official Secrets Act, too, I daresay . . . the gun laws. . . . *Think*, man. The government will be *very generous* if you cooperate."

"You go to hell."

He felt as if his legs were being flung along the street by a wind, flapping and rattling like jointed sticks. Fatigue had destroyed his coordination. There were other people out now who were cheerful and quick in the morning light as they hurried for their buses. *Normal people. People who trust other people.* Six hours earlier, Eddie Craik and Mrs. Duffus had been like normal people. Hamish Penhurst had seemed like the normal people.

A dark little car followed him ten yards behind. There were two MI-5 men in the car and another on the sidewalk behind him; up ahead somewhere would be another, ready to pick him up when this one veered off. Tarp did not care about them. They would be Mathiesson's people, a little frightened of their chief, a little frightened of Tarp because he was "uncontrollable."

Tarp made the difficult crossing to Russell Square and started on the diagonal walk across the park. He put Mathiesson out of his head and concentrated on Penhurst's last gesture. *If it was a gesture. A signal.*

Maybe it was simply a reflex action. Death. Seizure. The arm had risen, fingers stiff. They had fallen. *The knife.* He thought of Eddie Craik. *Chopping. Cutting. Maybe hammering. . . .*

"Hey, ol' buddy!"

Chopping. . . .

Tarp turned, hugging the injured arm close to his body. He knew that voice and its accent.

"Hey, hold up there, Tarp. . . ."

Chopping. Hacking. . . .

Hacker!

"Hey, man, you really make time on those long legs o' yours. Man, I had some kinda problem catching up with you."

"Hacker."

"Thass right, buddy. Hey, man, you been playin' fast and loose with me, you know that? I thought you were gonna keep me informed, man, and now what's this I hear about you and some old-time English scientist and some kinda ray machine? You ain't done me right, Tarp."

"Stay away from me, Hacker."

"I think we gotta have ourselves a little talk, Buddy. The thing is, see—."

"Stay away from me or I'll break something, Hacker."

"—the thing is, I had breakfast with your lady friend there, Miss Beecham, and you and I need to talk. I mean it, man, I really do." The low forehead wrinkled with concern, evidently for Tarp's and Sheila's situation, and the little eyes looked out at him through early-morning lids still swollen from sleep, like a child's. For the first time, however, Tarp understood how dangerous those eyes were. And how good Hacker really was. Now he was saying, "I mean, I got Miss Beecham there in what you might call protective custody. You understand me, buddy?"

The two MI-5 men were trying to maintain their place across the end of the walk at the park's entrance, but other drivers were veering around them with blowing horns and a considerable lack of British restraint in their language. Closer in, the walking MI-5 man was pretending to interest himself in a small bird, while nearest of all, a man in American clothes was watching them.

"We've drawn a crowd," Tarp said.

Hacker waved a pudgy hand. "No problem. Us and the English are real close. Real close."

"Us?" Tarp felt depression settling over him like a suit of heavy clothes. The morning seemed darker and his fatigue made him want to sink to the ground. Because this was all that it had come down to: a tawdry string of second-raters from two countries, badgering him in a park. Because Sheila Beecham, who had discovered the delight of freedom only days before, was a prisoner again. "*Us?*"

"Yeah, us at the agency. Now, look here, buddy. . . ." And, as if he believed that Tarp must be chastened, he put his hand on Tarp's left arm.

The touch was like a flare of light. It came directly on the cut, which had begun to hurt as the anesthetic wore off. With this new pain, Tarp's frustration erupted. He had been unaware of how much effort he had been devoting to keeping himself under control all night; now the controls vanished and his rawest emotions escaped. His right hand fastened on Hacker's face like a claw, the fingers just below the eyes and the thumb under the chin. His right knee came hard into Hacker's groin, and then he pushed away with the right hand and the American went backward, doubled over, gasping; his foot struck one of a row of low green hoops that fenced a flower bed, and he went over backward into a bed of daffodils. The second American—Tarp doubted that he was American, in fact—was coming to Hacker's aid, but he was too tentative, and Tarp dropped him next to his boss.

He sprinted across the park. Behind him, the MI-5

man was coming as fast as he could, but Tarp was going the shortest route over flower beds and benches, hurdling hedges and bursting from a clump of shrubbery at the park entrance on Great Russell Street, where people queuing for a bus were astonished by his sudden appearance. He slowed at the corner only enough to look into the oncoming traffic and dare it with a snarl as he hurled himself at the crossing like a runner seeing the finish line just on the other side. The MI-5 car had circled the park and was zipping toward the same intersection on the cross street with the same intention of getting across before the bus and the other traffic did. Its horn honked and honked. The little car just cleared the front of the bus, and there was a wrenching thud as it was hit broadside by a Citroen.

Tarp made it to the opposite curb with curses and the squeal of brakes to spur him on, sprinted past a huge Victorian hotel, and cut down the side street. He heard more shouts and horns as, somewhere behind him, the three MI-5 men were trying to disentangle themselves from a rapidly growing crowd.

He ran to the hotel where he had hidden Sheila and pounded up the stairs to the third floor. A startled woman in a robe looked at him and then darted back into her room instead of going to the bath. Two early-rising Germans flattened themselves against the wall as he charged up the stairs, according him the respect that the Germans have always shown to violence.

Their room was empty. The bed had not been made. The suitcase that they had shared was still standing next to the ugly dressing table.

"Sheila!"

She could be in the bath, in the WC, in the breakfast room; she could have gone out for a paper. . . .

A knock on the door barely preceded the appearance of the hotel owner's face in the door opening. "Telephone for you."

"What?"

"Call downstairs, Mr. Simons."

Simons. Simons. Yes, that was the name I used.

"Thank you."

There was a wall telephone in the cubicle by the hotel reception desk, which was only a closed-off passage between what had been the front and back parlors when this had been a house and not a hotel.

"Yes?"

"Go to the coin box at the corner of Great Russell and Tavistock."

"Who is this?" A stupid question. He knew who—or what—it was.

"Great Russell and Tavistock. Be there in fifteen minutes."

Tarp hung the receiver on its little hook and stared at the wall next to the telephone, where a garish flyer asked him to book a tour of London. He could make no sense of it.

"Not bad news, I hope, Mr. Simon?"

The hotel owner "liked people." Or so he said. He wore a baggy sweater and a regimental tie and he looked as if he would be comfortable behind a bar.

"No. Not bad news."

"That's good! Never nice to start the day with bad news!"

Tarp had located a rear door in the basement floor when he had first arrived; he went down to it now despite a feeble warning from the owner that guests were not supposed to go down there. He passed the kitchen, where the owner's wife was making guests' breakfasts, and let himself out into a place of ash cans below street level. He reached the telephone booth well before the phone rang.

"Yes?"

"Hey, buddy."

The incident in the park might never have happened.

"Talk, Hacker. What's the deal?"

"Well, I got this young lady, and you got the old

man. I think they ought to get together." Hacker decided to make a joke. "I'd like to have the set."

"What if I say no?"

"Aw, you wouldn't do that!"

"I might."

"Well, now, buddy, you gotta realize this is a high-stakes game. I got to think of the big picture. I b'lieve you see the desirability of not puttin' me in a position to take measures against a woman."

It would take Hacker, he supposed, two to three days to find out her father's location from her. She could give him only vague directions, but once she said Sri Lanka he would know enough. And she would say it. *She's tough, but she'd tell him.*

"All right. Talk."

"An exchange, buddy. You bring me the old man and the machine—I got this report from Afghanistan yesterday, gave me a pretty good idea what you been up to and what to look for, so no funny business—and naturally, man, this an exclusive deal. I mean, nobody else talks to the old man in the meantime. If you folla."

"Yeah, I *folla*." Tarp looked out the mullioned window of the booth at a Pakistani who was leaning against a blue car. He would be one of Hacker's people; there would be at least one other, probably two. They meant to keep track of him once they had him on the run.

"You there, ol' buddy?"

"I'm thinking."

There was a car rental about six blocks away, up in the less picturesque area of London beyond St. Pancras Station. He would need to shake his trackers before he went there. He made a mental inventory of his belongings. *Canadian passport. Obviously it's been busted, but it has a limited use. Credit card to match. About three thousand dollars.* He had left the .22 with Johnnie Carrington.

"You about through thinkin', buddy?" Hacker's voice had an edge now. Hacker disliked him, no doubt of that; keeping up that pretense of geniality must have been very wearing.

"I may decide not to do it, Hacker."

"Like hell!"

"No, not at all. Think back, Hacker. Remember when I was with the agency?" What he was saying was quite true: he had been harsh when individuals had to be balanced against larger gains. Looked at that way, Sheila Beecham could not be made to outweigh the value of her father. *No contest.* "But I'm willing to think about it."

"I need an answer *now.*"

"No, you don't."

"Like hell I don't! What d'you know, anyway?"

"I know you'll wait a while. You want to do this one right, I'm sure. Moscow would be really unhappy if you blew it."

Hacker cleared his throat. "This is an American operation. I don't know what that Moscow shit means."

"Yeah, sure. And you look in the mirror every morning and thank God for making you beautiful, too. Where do I call you next time?"

"There can't be a next time! Goddammit, I want to set up an exchange!"

"*If* there's an exchange, it'll be when I say and where I say. Tell me where to call you."

He could hear Hacker breathing, like a seal coming up from a long swim. Apparently Hacker used that heavy breathing as a means of recovering his jollity, for he said in his old, warm voice, "We really gotta set this thing up by this time tomorra, man. I mean, we *gotta.*"

"Tell me where to call you."

Hacker gave him a number in suburban London. They might have been arranging to go bowling.

Tarp left the coin box and went into the underground stop at the end of Bedford Street, where he slipped two of his pursuers by lunging out of the elevator just as the doors closed. A third man had been posted by the ticket box in case he did something like that; Tarp identified him as he passed, and when the man came out of the entrance five seconds behind him, he was met by a fist that knocked him back into a fruit stall. Tarp left running, feeling good about himself again. Twenty minutes later, he was in the Godfrey Davis rental office.

He drove across the Thames and parked near Elephant and Castle and dialed Gillian Penhurst's private telephone. She sounded sleepy when she answered, and she was embarrassed but she told him that, yes, Johnnie Carrington was there. Tarp asked her to send Johnnie out to a coin box and gave him a number. Several minutes later he was saying, "Johnnie, I've got an offer for you."

chapter twenty-three

The sun slanted across the treetops and sparkled on the widening rings where a trout had risen in the pond. The near side of the mountain behind it was black, and it reflected in the pond's surface as an inky background for the leaves that were already in sunlight. Tarp watched another rise and then slipped back into the cabin and poured himself more coffee. In the narrow bed, Arthur Beecham snored quietly and steadily.

Tarp pressed a button. "Six A.M. report. Check in."

An American voice said, "Okay here. Check one."

A British voice said, "Okay here. Check two."

Tarp changed frequencies and said cheerfully, "You out there someplace, Dickie?"

After a crackle of sound, a voice said, "Yessir, sure am. We're out by Merritt's Pond." He pronounced it *pawnd* in the Maine way.

"You got some help, Dickie?"

"Oh, sure. Tom and Bob and the two Coffin brothers."

"Be careful, Dickie. These people will be armed."

"Well, if they are, they're goin' in for a violation of Section 71."

It pays to stay on the good side of the game warden. And the state cops and the deputy sheriff.

Tarp put an egg in the pan and then waked Arthur Beecham. The old man's mouth closed and his eyes opened. He stared at the ceiling for several seconds. Tarp was sure that he woke up each morning thinking that he was still in prison, and then, each day when he remembered that he was not, he had to figure out where he was.

"You're in my cabin in Maine, Mr. Beecham."

"Oh, yes."

"We're going to make the exchange this morning."

"Oh—oh, yes. Thank you." Still he lay there, looking at the ceiling.

"Want to sit up, sir? I've made some tea."

"All in good time. At my age, sitting up too quickly is a threat to life itself . . . surprises the heart. *The Surprised Heart*—is that the title of something? If not, it ought to be." He propped himself on an elbow. "*Will* it work, do you think?"

"I think it has a good chance, sir."

"Yes. Exactly." Arthur Beecham sat up carefully. "Isn't this a lovely little place, though! Now, one thing must be made absolutely clear, and I have to insist on it."

"Sir?"

"If it doesn't work—or if at any time it appears that there's no hope—you are to shoot me. That *is* clear, is it?"

"Yes, sir."

"A clean kill, if you can." Beecham plucked at the red L. L. Bean blanket. "I've such a fear of pain. I'm such a coward."

"I'll be behind you. One shot—I promise."

"Good." Arthur Beecham unfolded himself from the bed. He had skinny old legs and feet that looked like roots. "Because," he said as he stretched, "they must not get me in order to use my invention. If they have hurt Sheila, then I shall take my revenge on them, and so must you. Without pity. I shall be merciless if they've hurt Sheila. Well, enough of that. Is there breakfast?"

"Absolutely. Egg?"

"Oh, yes, please. And toast . . . I can smell toast, oh, isn't it nice after years of rice and fish. *What* a delightful place!" He straightened up from reaching for his trousers. "I'm terribly frightened, you know. I'm just nattering along because I'm frightened."

"You're simply getting ready for action, sir. Come eat your egg."

At seven, a little Bell helicopter from the customs and immigration patrol passed along the river and went southeast. Tarp checked the computer screen and turned on an audio amplifier for the warning system.

"Almost time, Mr. Beecham."

"Thank you, my boy."

Tarp pulled the cabin's only table over to the large window and laid the Chinese rifle on it. He opened the windows as wide as they would go and removed the screens. The black drop bag, which had come from China after its stopover in Sri Lanka, went under the table. Tarp took the PPK that had once belonged to Comrade Qiu, checked it, and put it back; he did the same with the Chinese Browning.

"Are our friends ready?"

"So they say. They're out of radio contact now."

Tarp put a thirty-round clip in the rifle and ~~put~~ the other one on the table.

"Here it comes."

He could hear the faraway flailing of a helicopter's rotors.

"Oh, dear," Arthur Beecham said. "Oh, dear, oh, dear." He rubbed his hands together. "*Oh*, dear."

"You're to be sitting on the porch step where they can see you."

"Oh, yes. I remember. Yes." Beecham went out and

Tarp heard him say "Oh, dear" once more before he grasped the peeled spruce post next to the steps and slowly let himself down until his lean old buttocks rested on the top step. Arthur Beecham was wearing a blue work shirt of Tarp's with a very old tie and his suit from China. He looked almost as if he might be the Irish journalist that his forged passport said.

The helicopter was a big six-place civilian job with private markings, painted a garish metallic blue below and silver above. It came from the northwest, passing over the pond and then making a circle around the edge of the clearing before hovering two hundred feet from the cabin.

"Wave at them," Tarp called. The old man waved. He went on waving as people will when they feel silly and have no reason to have waved in the first place.

A voice boomed from a speaker on the helicopter. "Sending a man down." It sounded like Hacker's voice.

Nothing happened for over a minute. Then a figure appeared in the hatch and, after another wait, began a slow descent on a winch-operated line. He touched the ground, unsnapped himself, and waved; the helicopter, as if disowning him, sped away southwest. Tarp aimed a bullhorn at the man. "You're covered with an automatic rifle. Come up slowly. If you're armed, drop them out there, because you'll be searched when you get to the cabin."

He came up slowly, one shoulder lower with the weight of an aluminum suitcase of the kind that photographers use. He was in his thirties, a little overweight. His red hair had thinned to a scalp lock on top of his knobby head.

"Far enough." The bullhorn's magnified voice rebounded from the mountain as an unrecognizable growl. "Strip."

"What the hell!" The man's voice was puny after the bullhorn.

"Strip!"

"That isn't in the agreement."

"Strip!"

He stripped until he stood naked in the clearing, and then he was made to turn all the way around slowly. "Turn around again. Spread your cheeks. Okay, you can dress."

"Christ, thanks! What are you, a fairy?" When the man was dressed, he started for the suitcase and then looked at the window and the rifle. "Okay?" Tarp put the bullhorn aside, shouted "okay," and the man knelt down, careful to keep clear of Arthur Beecham and to let Tarp see everything that he did. Tarp heard the helicopter make a north-south pass a quarter of a mile away. *Scanning,* Tarp thought. *Looking for my army.*

The red-haired man held up a box. "I'm going to fingerprint him—okay?"

"Empty the suitcase and hold it up."

The man laid out pieces of equipment in the grass and held up the suitcase, which was lined with heavy gray foam rubber. Tarp made him rip out the foam until only the aluminum shell was left. "Okay, fingerprint him."

"You bastard, that box cost a lot of money."

He held the inkpad at arm's length and Arthur Beecham daintily inked his fingers and pressed them where he was told, and then he took the tissue that the red-haired man had brought and wiped his fingers. "Photo—okay?" The man held up an instant camera. He took three pictures of Arthur Beecham. The helicopter passed behind the cabin and came back toward the river. *Scanning.*

"I'm supposed to look inside," the man said.

"Thirty seconds, no pictures."

Tarp had been glancing at the computer screen every few seconds. In one mode, it registered the passage of the helicopter; another showed the ground-level surveillance grid and revealed no penetration. Tarp switched it briefly to show more distant sensors from the very edge of his property, and there he saw three signals. *My friend the game warden and some questionables. Go to it, warden.*

The red-haired man made a quick circuit of the cabin's interior. He looked in every place big enough to hide a man, even under the bed, and made a quick sweep with a sensing device.

"That's thirty seconds. Get out."

In the clearing, the man took an infrared scope from the ground and searched the fringe of the clearing. He made a complete sweep and came back.

Tarp called him up on the porch. The man came to the top step and hesitated. "Closer." He took two steps. "Closer." He came so close that the flash suppressor on the rifle was almost touching his chest. "Tell Hacker," Tarp said quietly, "that if he tries to screw me, the *first* one I shoot will be the old man. The second one will be Hacker. Now get out of here."

He put things back into the suitcase, trying to pack the torn pieces of foam so as to protect them, as silent and angry as a husband packing under the eye of the wife he is leaving. He talked into a small radio; within minutes, the helicopter was hovering again and the line was being winched down.

"Why did they take my fingerprints?" Arthur Beecham said when the man and the helicopter were gone.

"They want to make sure it's you. The cheapest way out would be to trade Sheila for a stand-in."

He carried the wooden box out into the clearing and put it down in a fairly flat place, rolling away a rock to make room for it. He put one of the SM-11s that he had taken from the agency men into the grassless depression where the rock had lain and put the box over it.

He handed the PPK to Beecham. "As soon as Sheila reaches you, give her the pistol."

"Yes, I remember."

"But don't use the guns unless you have to. He'll

have people out beyond my sensors, even though he's not supposed to. If they hear gunfire, they'll come in."

Tarp checked the sensors again. Two of the signals out there had merged. *Checking them out. No guns in the woods out of season. My friend the game warden and my friend the deputy sheriff and my friends the Coffin brothers, who are the best poachers between Jackman and Fort Kent.* Tarp switched to the more sensitive inner perimeter and found it still undisturbed.

He hauled a heavy cable from under the cabin and dropped the end next to the box. "Hook it up and we're ready."

He waited inside the cabin, dividing his attention between the computer screen and Beecham. On the table now were the rifle and the two Brownings and the silenced submachine he had got from Sun; at the other end of the table were a spotting scope and a directional microphone. Tarp chambered a round into each weapon and sat back to wait.

"Mr. Beecham! Remember—you have to identify Sheila before she reaches you!"

"I remember." His voice came very weakly from his place down in the middle of the clearing.

"If it isn't Sheila, you've got to warn me!"

He had to shout because the helicopter was coming back. They had been over all of it the night before.

The chopper came in from behind the cabin and hovered at the far end of the clearing, not far from the short, dark path down to the pond. "Coming down!" the hollow voice of the loudspeaker bellowed. Tarp had insisted that the helicopter never land. He had piled condition on condition, irritating Hacker, then maddening him, winning concessions because Hacker knew that Tarp could take Beecham and his device away forever. Tarp studied the two men who came down the cable. One was Hacker. The other was an oversized man with big ears and big bones. Both of them were armed with M-16s.

"Stay right there, Hacker!" Tarp shouted over the bullhorn. Hacker nodded. He gave the rawboned man a push with his right hand and then he pointed at a rock partway around the clearing. He said something that Tarp supposed was insulting, because the rawboned man shambled off with a hurt look on his face. Tarp switched on the directional microphone and focused it on Hacker.

"Say something, Hacker."

Hacker said something, and the microphone did not pick it up; he had to say it twice more and then Tarp got the words clearly: "This is goddam ridiculous."

"It's your idea."

Hacker and Tarp now faced each other across the clearing with Arthur Beecham between them and slightly to Tarp's right. The rawboned man was to Tarp's left. Thus, Arthur Beecham was at the center of a clock face whose outer circle was the clearing itself, with Hacker at twelve o'clock and Tarp at seven and the other man at nine. Behind Hacker were the pond and the mountain; behind the rawboned man was deep woods.

Tarp checked his sensors. Nothing.

"Back the chopper off."

Hacker talked into a radio and the helicopter veered away.

"Your move, Hacker."

Hacker cleared his throat and the microphone picked the sound up clearly. Tarp watched him through the spotting scope. The man was excited, like a hunter with buck fever. *The big kill. Going after a trophy rack.* He remembered Penhurst's dying gesture and wondered for the hundredth time if he had really meant that it was Hacker who had looked over his shoulder, and for the hundredth time he told himself that yes, Hacker was exactly the right type: Hacker the functionary, Hacker the politician, Hacker the wielder of power. Penhurst had become questionable in Moscow after the Viktor Balkan article, and somebody had been put on him to keep watch. There had been a tipping of some balance. Now Penhurst was dead and Hacker was ready to make his first big kill after years in place.

"I wanta see a demonstration of this here device."

"Show him, Mr. Beecham."

Arthur made some small adjustment to the long wooden box. Without flourish or warning, he threw the switch. The blue light glimmered between the metal tube and a dead tree across the clearing, and the tree exploded and limbs crashed down into the small pines. Two crows flew up, scolding, and Tarp wondered if the noise would bring in Hacker's troops. "Satisfied, Hacker?"

He watched Hacker lick his lips and sweat. What he had just seen had excited him more than any other part of the hunt. He must be thinking of what they would say in Moscow when this machine was demonstrated; he must be thinking of the fact that when the machine was his, it would not matter so much whether he got the old scientist or not. The machine was the cake now, Beecham the frosting; Moscow scientists could reconstruct it from the prototype.

"I wanta see it again."

"Come on, Hacker; a demonstration's a demonstration!"

"I wanta see it again!"

Tarp studied him through the scope: sweat glistening on his forehead and throat, his hands gripped around the M-16 like talons. "Once more, please, Mr. Beecham."

The old man knelt over the box and adjusted its aim. The blue light crackled and a bank of earth erupted.

"End of demonstration, Hacker. Let's see Miss Beecham!"

Hacker licked his lips. "After the machine's in the chopper."

"I want to see her. I want her *on the ground* next to you before we send that gooddam box up."

Hacker said something into his radio; there was muted conversation back and forth. Tarp looked at his screen, close and distant; the signals on the distant monitors had separated again into three and were poised about a half mile away from the clearing. *Just keep them there, Warden. Just give me time.*

"What's happening, Hacker?"

Perhaps Hacker was wondering if he and the rawboned man could get across the clearing to Arthur Beecham and eliminate the need for the exchange altogether. Perhaps Hacker was balancing a run across the open space—slightly uphill, in his case—against Tarp's ability with a rifle. He had to know that Tarp planned to keep the old man; that was the nature of such an exchange, that there was always hope. He would have to reason that Tarp's hope was to give away the weapon and keep the scientist, thus getting half a loaf. And so Hacker had to be plotting how he could prevent that. And he had to be thinking that giving up Sheila Beecham now cost him nothing.

"She's on her way. Hold your goddam water."

The helicopter hovered again. This time, they lowered a wire basket over the side as if they were going to pick up wounded, and Tarp felt cold rage when he thought that they had hurt her. But he saw her step into the basket while two men held on to her and then lie down so she could be winched to earth. When the basket had settled in the grass and she had clambered out of it, awkward in a skirt and—oddly—bare feet (*So she can't run; not bad, Hacker*), she stood near Hacker, who kept the M-16 pointed at her. The rawboned man's weapon was pointed at Beecham.

Tarp examined her through the spotting scope. There was no mistaking the broad face, the monkey cheeks, and the wide eyes or that frizzy discharge of long hair.

"They can pick up the box."

The basket went up into the air and the helicopter moved up above Beecham and lowered it again. The wooden box was heavy for him, and the basket was poorly adapted to its shape. He wrestled with it quite patiently, however, backing off when a corner wedged in the mesh, getting one end up on the metal frame, pushing it in, and then swinging the other end around. Tarp watched Hacker, whose shoulders were actually moving in little empathetic movements as he tried to help the old man move it faster. Beecham backed off and waved. He squatted on the ground, as he had learned to do in China. The SM-11 would be right in front of him now.

"Take it away, Hacker."

Hacker shouted eagerly into his radio and the basket rose. Tarp told him to make the helicopter stand off as it had before and again it veered southwest.

"When I give the signal, I want Miss Beecham to walk *slowly* toward her father. When I tell her to stop, she must stop. At no time is she to get between me and Hacker. If anything goes wrong, I start shooting."

She came across the still-damp grass with the slow precision of a child or a lunatic, for whom the exact placing of the feet is a matter of keeping the world in order. Her bare feet glistened with the dew that still clung to the stems, and the hem of her skirt was wet with it. She carried her hands one over the other against her body just below her breasts, like a madonna. She looked like a child or a madwoman or a saint—not like a victim who might die at any second. Tarp saw the shadow of a nipple where it pressed against fabric (*She wears no underclothing, monsieur*), the strong rhythm of her legs (*Terrific thighs on her*), and ached to touch her.

He glanced at the computer screen, at the rawboned man, at Hacker.

"Stop."

She was ten feet from Arthur Beecham. She had stopped as if she were, indeed, a child playing a game in which it is required to stop in exactly the position that the body finds itself when the command is given. She had stopped in mid-step, her head on one side, her eyes searching the ground in front of her. Beecham said something to her in Chinese, just as he and Tarp had planned; she replied, hardly raising her eyes.

"Is it Sheila, Mr. Beecham?"

Now she looked up at him. Wounded. Furious.

"Oh, yes—it's she! It's she!" His voice was thin because of the distance, but he was triumphant.

"Come ahead, Sheila."

Tarp sighted in on Hacker's face. If there was to be any black work, it would begin here: Hacker would kill them and the rawboned man would try to kill Tarp. That way, there could be no risk of somebody else getting the old man if the rest of the exchange didn't work. Tarp counted to ten and reached for the small communicator without taking his eyes from Hacker's face.

"Checking," he said softly. "Ready?"

"Ready one," the American voice said.

"Ready two," the English voice said.

"Go."

He picked up the bullhorn. Arthur Beecham and Sheila were embracing, but Arthur had his hand in his coat and was reaching for the PPK.

"What next, Hacker?"

"I take the old man."

"What about his daughter?"

"I made the deal for the old man."

"She may want to go wherever he does."

"Well, what'd we waste all this time on diddle-shit for, then?"

"I had to make sure she was safe, Hacker."

Tarp had put down the rifle and picked up the silenced submachine gun. He looked at Hacker through the spotting scope. He was really sweating now; there were patches under the arms of his golf jacket; where he had moved one hand, there was a blacker patch of sweat on the M-16.

Tarp saw faint movement in the branches behind Hacker. He shifted his attention to the rawboned man.

"I'll tell you what I'll do, Hacker."

"What's that?"

He checked the computer screen.

"Send your helicopter away."

"Like hell."

"You get the particle beam; I keep Mr. Beecham."

"He leaves here with me or he don't leave here alive!"

"That would give Moscow a monopoly, Hacker. I'm offering a balance of power; Moscow gets the machine, London gets the inventor."

"No deal."

He stepped back from the window where he could not be seen and sighted the submachine gun on the rawboned man.

"They won't like you in Derzhinsky Square if you screw it up."

"No deal!"

"Send the chopper away, Hacker. Take the machine and run."

"If I don't get that old man in thirty seconds, I'm calling that chopper in here to burn this clearing from one side to the other. You hear me, Tarp?"

A figure detached itself from the branches behind Hacker, and at the same moment Arthur Beecham pulled Sheila to the ground and the rawboned man's attention shifted to Hacker; in that fraction of a second, Tarp loosed a three-round burst of silenced fire that caught the rawboned man in the neck and head and knocked him flailing into the tall ferns that waved by the deep green woods.

Tarp could hear Johnnie Carrington's voice on the directional microphone: ". . . and *please* don't do anything silly or I shall blow your lights out with this gun. It's a very large gun; one of yours, I understand, an Ingram machine pistol."

"It won't work, it won't work!" Hacker was shouting, forgetting the microphone. "They'll come in for me, you stupid shit. You hear me, Tarp?" He shouted louder. "That chopper will blow you all away if I don't call them soon!"

"They'll never get here, Hacker. I'll blow them up first." He put the sights of the silenced submachine gun on Hacker's chest. "The wooden box is mined."

"Like hell!"

"I blow up the chopper, and Moscow gets nothing. The chopper goes away, and Moscow gets the box and I keep Arthur Beecham."

"That isn't the deal!" Hacker was hoarse from shouting.

"It is now. It used to be a trade, Miss Beecham for the box and Mr. Beecham. Now it's the box for you. Send the chopper away, Hacker. You've got thirty seconds."

Johnnie Carrington, dressed in a diver's wet suit, was standing behind Hacker with the SM-11 pushed hard into his spine. Hacker kept his feverish grip on the M-16, but he had to be wondering what good it would do him now to try to kill Arthur Beecham, who was out of sight in the grass, anyway. And he had to be trying to untangle the implications of Tarp's new offer. If the box got to Moscow, he would make his kill; but if Beecham stayed in the West, the kill merely balanced another by Moscow's enemies. If Tarp and Carrington kept Hacker, would they reveal him? And what would they use as hard evidence? And if he tried to kill Beecham now, Carrington would kill him and the box would be blown up. Or perhaps Tarp was lying and the box was not mined; or perhaps the box *was* mined and Tarp would blow it up no matter what happened—in which case, the sooner the helicopter got out of radio range behind the mountain, the better off he'd be; but even if the box got away, he ought to kill Arthur Beecham. . . .

Tarp heard the sound of another, smaller helicopter.

"That's a customs and immigration chopper, Hacker. They'll pass right over. You don't want anything funny going on when they go over."

Hacker took his left hand from the foregrip of the M-16. One danger was past: no matter what he said on the radio, Hacker could not shoot accurately with one hand. Tarp watched the radio and the left hand come up into his sights again. The directional microphone carried Hacker's dispirited voice.

"This is Alpha. This is Alpha. Return to base and follow Plan Three. Return to base and follow Plan Three." Hacker cleared his throat. "Over."

Tarp watched the blip cross the computer screen as the larger helicopter cut northwest again. It went straight and low and fast, as if the men inside were glad to go.

Tarp checked the sensors. Nothing.

He climbed over the windowsill and came down the gentle slope to Arthur Beecham, who was still lying on the ground with Sheila. They looked like sunbathers.

"Ready to go, sir?"

"Oh, yes!" Arthur Beecham shaded his eyes. "Will it *really* be England this time?"

"They'll have you there in a matter of hours. Stay on the ground, please."

Tarp walked down toward Hacker and Carrington. Perhaps, he thought, Hacker would try to shoot him now. But Hacker was probably thinking of ways out, and the way out of this was not to commit murder now. It was too late for that, and Hacker must know it.

"Put your weapon on the ground, please."

"Huh? Oh, yeah." Hacker lowered the M-16 into the grass as if it was something he had been meaning to do for some time.

"Enright, you there?"

Enright—the agency man whom Tarp had sent downriver in the canoe, the man who had beaten him in the airport room, the man with whom he had declared himself "even"—came out of the shadows under the pines. Like Carrington, he wore a diver's wetsuit; the two of them had been in the pond, under the dock and invisible to scanning.

"Well, Enright?" Tarp said softly. He turned to Hacker. "Enright's here as an observer; strictly as an observer, that was the deal."

Hacker reverted to his role as blusterer and bully. "Enright, what the hell!"

"I'm on three days' vacation, sir."

"I'll bust your ass for this!"

"Yes, sir." Enright snapped open his black hood. "Unless this guy is right. About Moscow."

"Moscow! You believe this diddle-shit about *Moscow*? What the hell single goddamn shred of evidence does anybody have about fucking Moscow?"

"I guess we'll know that better, sir, when we find where that box ends up. The one in the helicopter, sir."

Ideas passed over Hacker's face like the shadows of fast-moving clouds. His defense would have to be, of course, that he was in Maine to get a valuable scientist out of the hands of an unreliable, uncontrollable, dangerous, and probably treasonable man with known internationalist tendencies, forged passports, and more weapons than were good for him or the country. On the other hand, if the wooden box never showed up in Washington—and if, at some time in the future, a defector's report showed that it had appeared in Moscow—matters would be decidedly sticky.

"Goddamn you, Enright!"

"Sir?"

"I'll have your ass tacked to the woodshed wall, Enright!"

"Yes, sir. And I'll deserve it, sir. If that box reaches Washington safely. But I got an official request from MI-5 to participate here as an observer, sir, and it seemed to me, sir, that given the very delicate nature of this situation, you'd probably welcome a witness in case of an oversight review."

Tarp picked up the M-16. "Check Mr. Hacker for other weapons, please, Johnnie. I'd like to see Beecham get on the way. He's been a long time getting home."

Carrington nodded. "Quite right. Call in your friends, will you, Nickie?"

Nickie? Good God, that must be Enright. Tarp, who had never made friends easily, marveled at the two young men. They seemed to have known each other for years, although their first contact had been an overseas telephone call thirty-six hours before.

Enright flipped open a box the size of a can of spice. "Bring in the chopper. This is Enright."

The customs and immigration helicopter came over the trees behind the cabin. Carrington felt a need to explain it all to Hacker. "We're being deported across the river to Canada, Mr. Beecham and I. We're illegal aliens." He was very happy about it.

Tarp watched him take a pistol and an agency death kit from Hacker's clothes. "If you don't do anything silly, Hacker, you'll lead a long and very useful life. I think the agency could have big plans for you. I suspect they'll want to turn you around one more time. A turned double agent has a certain status, Hacker—gets a certain fame in time, as you must know. I've heard of one who even got a medal. That may be legend, but it's an awfully good story. Your life wouldn't change much. They might even make you director of Clandestine Ops . . . think how pleased Moscow would be!"

"*I'm not a double agent!*" Hacker muttered.

"You'll get lots of opportunity to say that. I believe Uncle's people want to spend the weekend with you."

The skin over Hacker's temples tightened. A weekend in an agency safe house with a team of interrogators could become a week or a month. They would not let go until everything added up.

Tarp walked to the small helicopter, which had put down in the middle of the clearing. Carrington got in. "I owe you an apology," he said. "About Gillian, I mean."

"You're a good man, Johnnie."

"Now you've embarrassed me."

"I'd like to work with you again sometime. Maybe we will."

"*Could* we?"

Tarp reached down for Arthur Beecham's hand. "Time to go, sir." He tried to smile at Sheila and found that he could not. His voice was rough when he spoke to her. "There isn't room for you, this trip."

She looked at him with all her old suspicion.

"What is to become of me?" she said.

"You're to go to England with me. Today."

"Did you really think it was somebody else when I crossed the grass down there?" She was angry and hurt.

"I knew it was you. I knew your hips." He tried to smile again, to make her smile, but he failed. "I had to bring Hacker along step by step. If I'd skipped that step, I might have ruined everything. I had to get him to the point where he sent the helicopter back."

She came to him slowly and merely walked up against him and leaned her head on his shoulder. "I hate you sometimes," she muttered.

He gripped her arm. "Yes. But it has to be that way." He kissed her hair.

Arthur Beecham looked just a little surprised by all this, and he went by them shaking his head and muttering "Oh, dear." Still, he had cheered up by the time he buckled himself into the helicopter, taking the place of a tall young man who got out. "I shall be in England tonight!" he crowed. "Oh, Sheila, you'll be there, too! Oh, my dear—England. England!" And he bent to kiss his daughter. "Good-bye, my darling. It's only a few hours now. Good-bye, good-bye, yes, good-bye. . . ."

Tarp pulled her away, ducking low as the rotors began to turn, and the machine rose slowly, turned toward the mountain, and sailed toward the river and Canada.

The young man who had just joined them was showing Hacker his credentials. He was from the agency's internal security force, and he was saying quietly, ". . . purely voluntary, Mr. Hacker, and of course you can refuse. We simply feel that under the circumstances, under these particular circumstances, I mean, a check of certain aspects of certain things is in order."

"Like what?"

"I'm not at liberty to say, sir."

"I can goddamn well clear myself right here and now."

"I wouldn't be in a position to judge if you could, sir."

"You're going to take the word of a man who was fired because he was irresponsible and uncontrollable over mine?"

"No, sir. We only want to check some things, sir."

"You're accusin' me of treason!"

"No, sir. We just want to check some things, sir."

"I'm damned if I'll do it!"

"Are you refusing, then, sir? That's certainly your right. I'll report your refusal to my boss and he can report it to the director. Are you refusing, sir?"

Hacker seemed to withdraw behind the puffiness of his eyelids. When he came out again, he growled, "Hell, no. I got nothing to hide." Difficult weeks lay ahead of him. And difficult years, for the life of a double agent who has been turned back is even more difficult than the life of a double agent.

"No questions for me, Hacker?" Tarp said.

"Like what?"

"Oh, I thought you might wonder why I let the machine go. That gives Moscow the machine and London the inventor—not a very happy standoff. I thought that might bother you. So I was going to answer you that Moscow isn't getting the machine. The machine is already in London."

Hacker glared at him from his puffy eyelids.

"You saw a demonstration of a Japanese-made light-show laser. The explosions were two Chinese hand grenades. I wouldn't have let you have either Arthur Beecham or the real box in a million years. But not to worry, as the British say—there's enough electronic junk in that box to entertain Moscow for a while. By the time they know they've been hoaxed, you can start feeding them false data, and they'll buy some of it because it will sound awfully good, and they'll accept your story that you were hoaxed, too. That ought to be good for about three years. If you do it right, they'll never catch on that you're diddling them—and you really do want to do it right, because they're very vindictive in Derzhinsky Square."

Tarp talked to his friend the game warden, who said the groups of people out around his property had decided to go home, and he thanked the warden and asked him what he'd like from England. He put some of the weapons away, including the two M-16s that Hacker had brought in, and by that time, three cars had driven into the clearing, their shiny government finishes spattered with good Maine mud. Enright got into one car, and the security man and Hacker got into another, and two dour men loaded the body of the rawboned man into the third, and the caravan disappeared down the rutted, barely visible forest track toward the highway.

"I've got to clean up a little more," Tarp said. "Then we'll be on our way. Tired?"

"No. I'm very strong, remember?"

"I do, indeed." He kissed her. "Any questions?"

"One."

"Shoot."

"Who is Gillian? I heard that young man talk about Gillian to you."

Tarp sighed. "That's a *good* question." He got very busy with cleaning up.

A few minutes later, he carried the canoe down to the river and went back to lock the cabin. She waited for him at the edge of the clearing. He had brought the breakfast crumbs out and put them on the porch railing for the birds, and when he turned from fastening the locks on the big window, he heard a familiar thump and there was the badger.

"Thought you'd forgotten me, this time." He tossed it a piece of crust. "Going away, old friend. Back in a while. I always come back, after a while."

The badger snarled. Tarp smiled.